AFTER *the* FALL

LISA BINGHAM

DIVERSIONBOOKS

Also by Lisa Bingham

Into the Storm
The Bengal Rubies
Distant Thunder
Eden Creek
Silken Dreams
Silken Promises
Temptation's Kiss

Diversion Books
A Division of Diversion Publishing Corp.
443 Park Avenue South, Suite 1008
New York, New York 10016
www.DiversionBooks.com

For more information, email info@diversionbooks.com

First Diversion Books edition August 2015.
Print ISBN: 978-1-62681-711-1
eBook ISBN: 978-1-62681-710-4

To my father, who fought in the Pacific.
And to all who served, past and present.
Thank you.

Author's Note

Some novels write themselves, and some are an exercise in frustration. *After the Fall* was a bit of both.

Originally, I'd planned a book that would focus on the surrender of the American military personnel and their subsequent imprisonment. Although I understood the basics about the Bataan Death March, I knew very little about the events which led to this horrible event. So, I began to read voraciously on the subject. Some of the works I found particularly helpful and compelling were Elizabeth M. Norman's *We Band of Angels: The Untold Story of the American Women Trapped on Bataan*; John D. Lukacs' *Escape from Davao: The Forgotten Story of the Most Daring Prison Break of the Pacific War*; Michael Norman's and Elizabeth M. Norman's *Tears in the Darkness: The Story of the Bataan Death March and Its Aftermath.*

The more I learned, the more I came to admire and respect those who were part of this dark chapter of American history. But try as I might, I couldn't force the characters I'd created to bend to my will. So I went back to my research again, trying to pin down where my problem lay.

I soon realized that I was trying to do too much. For an author who habitually "writes long", compressing years of Japanese occupation into 100,000 words would come at the expense of my characters. The lives of the men and women who served in the

Philippines during this period deserved more care with their stories.

It was then that I realized that the overriding theme, one which broke my heart with each account I read, was the way these men and women fought with every fiber of their being because they knew—they *knew*—that reinforcements were on their way. If they could only hold on for another day. And another.

Little did they know that those reinforcements would never be sent.

And any help the U.S. Government might offer was years away.

This heartbreaking truth became the crux and the driving force for *After the Fall*. Once I allowed myself to truly ponder the ramifications of a doomed defense—not in connection with political policy or warfare strategy, but on a personal level to those involved—the book literally wrote itself.

L.B.

Darkness pressed in upon him with a tangible weight. The blackness was heavy. Moist. Filled with menace. Consciousness returned to him in a symphony of pain—the low, throbbing undercurrent of bruised muscles…the sharper, high-pitched sear of open wounds. And through it all, jabs to his chest every time he tried to breathe.

He couldn't remember the last time he'd been able to take a gulp of air without moaning. Instead, he tried to sneak the oxygen into his system, praying he could baby his broken ribs and remain as small and imperceptible as possible.

How many days had it been? Nine…ten?

Fewer than that?

More?

He couldn't remember. The days had begun to blur together as he had slipped in and out of consciousness. His stomach gnawed at the emptiness in his belly until he curled into a ball to ease the ache.

And he was thirsty. So thirsty.

It would be so easy to give in. Give in and give up. But settling deep within the pit of his ravenous stomach was a knot of anger that twisted as powerfully as his hunger. His body might succumb to the hell that surrounded him, but his mind would never surrender.

Not now.

Not ever.

Not until he'd seen her one last time.

Chapter One

December 6, 1941
Luzon, Philippines

Even at birth, Glory Bee O'Halloran had made a flamboyant entrance. At barely five pounds, five ounces, with more bright red hair than a two-year-old, she hadn't bothered to cry. Instead, she'd stretched her arms wide as if delighted to be free from the confines of the womb, opened her pansy blue eyes, and smiled. Startled, the doctor had blurted, "Glory be!" And the name had stuck—especially when her mother, mere hours after the birth, was back to drinking herself into a stupor.

Not much had changed since then. Glory Bee's mother was still a drunk, and Glory Bee had honed making an entrance to an art form. Which was why, the moment the military band on the dock struck up a rousing rendition of *Stars and Stripes*, she paused dramatically at the top of the gangplank, lifted her arms wide, posed to highlight her voluptuous figure, and called out, "Howdy, boys!"

The resulting cheers from the men on shore were gratifying, cutting through her nausea and giving her the strength to hold her "Happy!" face for a few more minutes, even though there was nothing she wanted more than to run down the gangplank, drop on the ground, and kiss the earth beneath her. Heaven's sake, she'd kiss the most loathsome creature the Filipino forests could offer if she could just get off this damned boat.

The rise and fall of the ship caused the gangplank to tilt and sway, and her stomach lurched again. She had to move, now, or risk embarrassing herself by doubling over the railing and losing what little food she'd managed to eat that morning. And wouldn't that be a sight for the welcoming committee gathered below?

Surreptitiously gripping the handrail, she made her way down the steep ramp until she touched dry land. But her relief was short-lived when she realized that while her mind may have acknowledged that her feet were on solid ground, her body felt as if she were still dipping and swaying.

"Miss O'Halloran!"

An officer dressed in a stiffly pressed uniform marched forward, extending a huge bouquet of flowers. "Welcome to the Philippines."

"Thank you…" she quickly checked the brass eagles pinned to his shoulder boards, "Colonel."

"Ross."

"Colonel Ross. It's wonderful to be here." After three weeks at sea and most of them spent lying sick on her bunk, she had never been so sincere.

"We're looking forward to your performance tomorrow night. Your ship arrived in the nick of time, I'd say."

Glory Bee opened her mouth to make a pithy remark, but checked herself just in time. *Be on your best behavior*, Michael had warned her when she'd boarded the damn boat. And there'd been just enough doubt tingeing his tone to imply he didn't think she could do it.

So she altered her initial response to drawl, "Truer words have never been spoken, Colonel." No one else needed to know that if she'd been forced to endure another day or two on the high seas, the crew would have been forced to scrape her off the deck.

"My aide, Sergeant Wilcox, has been assigned to see to your every need."

Wilcox snapped to attention, a blush spreading over his cheeks. He was little more than a kid, really. He reminded Glory Bee of the pest-next-door type with hair so blond it was nearly white, and blunt features that would give him a boyish air even in his dotage.

"Ma'am!" he said a little too loudly, offering her a slight bow.

One of Glory Bee's brows rose at his effusive gallantry, but she awarded him with a slow smile. “I’m sure Sergeant Wilcox and I will get along famously, Colonel.”

If possible, the sergeant’s skin took on an even redder tone. So much so, she feared his hair might burst into flames.

The colonel discreetly cleared his throat, “Sergeant Wilcox has already notified the rest of the cast of your arrival as well as the band that will accompany you during your…er…act.”

Glory Bee remained serene, even as she inwardly laughed at the man. Colonel or no, Ross’s eyes were rife with a combination of puritanical dismay and prurient curiosity.

“I promise to make all your hard work worthwhile, Colonel Ross. I’ll entertain your men as grandly as if it were my final performance.”

This time, it was the colonel’s skin that grew ruddy.

But the joke was on him. Tomorrow’s show *would* be her last. Then she would slip into obscurity for a while. In the meantime, it was fitting that her last strip tease would be for the troops since the biggest share of her audience while in Washington, D.C. had been the military.

Glory Bee felt only a twinge of regret for the forced hiatus. The past few months had worn her out, body and soul. She craved the seclusion she’d come to the Philippines to find. She only wished she could begin it sooner.

But she couldn’t tell the colonel that. So she smiled instead—a smile artfully reflecting pleasure mixed with a touch of come-hither.

“I’m sure that you could do no wrong in the men’s eyes, Miss…”

“Call me Glory Bee.”

“Yes, well…er…”

The man had to be thirty years her senior, but he stammered and shifted in front of her as if he were a teenager—an effect that was not unfamiliar to Glory Bee. So she took pity on him, interrupting with, “I’m honored I can be of service to you and the men stationed at Fort Stotsenberg.”

See, Michael. I can be as sweet as sugar if I have to be.

Colonel Ross turned, sweeping an arm toward the official military car waiting behind him.

"If you'll come this way, Sergeant Wilcox will escort you to the camp. It's a bit of a drive, but he'll show you to your quarters where you'll be able to rest and get your land legs. Then he'll return with the car around three in the afternoon to take you to the dress rehearsal."

And wasn't that just the slice of heaven she was longing for? Several hours alone on dry land.

"You're too kind, Colonel." She looped her arm through his, attempting to look blissfully enchanted while inwardly, she counted the steps she would have to take before she could sink onto the padded seat. Moving with the same exaggerated sway to her hips that had become her trademark, she paused only once—just in front of the open door. Bracing herself against the hot metal of the hood, she lifted her arm in a broad wave, and called out to the other military personnel on the quay.

"I'll see you all at the show!"

The resultant roar punctuated by wolf whistles bolstered her flagging spirits, and briefly, she forgot about the lurching of her stomach and the pounding ache at her temples. Laughing, she gazed out at the boys who surrounded her—lanky sailors in their whites, infantry in their tans, dockside workers and curious Filipinos. She waved to them all, absorbing their energy and their youthful exuberance like an addict might inhale opium smoke. Then she blew them a kiss and settled into the car amid the resulting cheers.

* * *

Riley Patrick Gilhouley slid a pair of sunglasses over his eyes to cut the glare of the hot tropical sun. Like the other men present, he'd been held momentarily transfixed by the arrival of the statuesque redhead. Sweet baby Jesus, Mary and Joseph, he didn't think there was a male alive who could have looked away. Women here were scarce, and women like that…

Well, there were no women like that, thank God, or nothing would ever get done.

Weaving his way through the crowd, he passed the commotion

near the ship and headed further down to the docks where a battered civilian seaplane was pulling into position. He waited patiently as it was tied to the pier, then drew closer as the pilot emerged and jumped onto the weathered boards.

The moment the grizzled older man lifted his head and caught sight of Gilhouley, he grinned.

"Well, I'll be goddamned! As I live and breathe, if it ain't the Great Gilhouley in the flesh!" His weather-beaten face split into a grin. "How the hell have you been?"

Gilhouley held his hand out, but Napoli ignored it and pulled him into a crushing hug. "I couldn't believe my ears when I got your message. What brings you to purgatory, my friend?"

"I was reassigned here about six months ago."

"The hell, you say. And who'd you fuck with to end up here—or should I say whose wife did you fuck to end up here?"

Gilhouley laughed, a betraying heat seeping up into his cheeks. Napoli knew him well. In his first few years in the army, Gilhouley had been in trouble on more occasions than he could count. He'd had a hard time keeping his mouth shut—and an even harder time keeping his fly zipped. But after being caught in the bedroom of a brigadier general's wife, and enduring a stint in the Aleutians, he'd vowed that if the Almighty could arrange to transfer Gilhouley someplace warm, Gilhouley would do his best to mend his ways.

So far, he hadn't completely kept his bargain with God, but at least he wasn't freezing his balls off in Alaska.

"Were you able to get what I needed?"

Napoli motioned for Gilhouley to walk toward the plane where cases of tinned food and alcohol were being unloaded by a pair of bare-chested Filipinos.

Gilhouley quickly scanned the labels and nodded in approval. "I've got a Jeep parked at the end of the pier. Have your boys load it into the back."

Napoli motioned to the men, shouting to them in a broken mixture of Spanish and Tagalog, waving his arms as added punctuation. Then he reached into the plane and withdrew a small cardboard box.

"Here's the other item you asked me to get."

Gilhouley sobered, taking the box and tucking it under his arm. After a quick glance around the pier, he removed a roll of bills from his pocket and handed it to Napoli.

"For your troubles."

Napoli offered him a half salute. "Tell your poker buddies in the press corps that I appreciate their business."

"I'll be sure to do that."

Gilhouley was striding away, when Napoli called to him.

"Gilhouley!"

Turning, Gilhouley squinted against the sparkle of sunlight off the waves. It was barely nine in the morning, yet he could already feel the sweat pooling between his shoulder blades and beneath his arms.

"If I don't see you for a while, take care of yourself, y'hear?"

Gilhouley frowned. "Are you planning a trip, Napoli?"

The grizzled pilot took a stubby cigar from his shirt pocket and clamped onto it with his teeth. Removing a lighter from a baggy pair of pants, he shielded the flame from the wind and drew deep until the tip flared. Then, he stood staring up at the brilliant blue sky as if the clouds were tea leaves that held his fortune.

"I don't like what's happening with the Nips in Indo-China." He chewed on the end of his cigar, then grabbed it in two stained fingers and blew a cloud of smoke into the air. "I gotta a bad feeling, buddy."

"You think trouble is headed this way?"

Napoli made a sound of disgust. "Hell, trouble follows me more closely than my own shadow. You're safe enough with American might at your back, but me? Let's just say I don't want a Jap Zero tailing me anytime too soon. I'm thinking I'll make a few more runs, then head south, probably by the end of the month. I doubt it'll be much longer before the Japs show up. Maybe I'll bide my time in Australia until I know which way the wind is blowing. So if you need something, let me know as soon as you can. I still owe you big for backing me in that bar fight in Dago."

"Take care of yourself Napoli."

"Same to you, buddy!"

Gilhouley nodded, walking backwards so that he could study Napoli for as long as he could before the older man unhooked from the pier, climbed back into his plane and latched his door. With a sputtering rumble, the engine caught and the propellers spun. Minutes later, Napoli was edging back into the bay, picking up speed, seawater spraying behind him until, with a bounce, two, three, the plane lifted into the sky like an ungainly pelican.

Gilhouley couldn't prevent the involuntary chill that skittered up his spine. Word had it that MacArthur was sure the Japs wouldn't attack before spring. But if Napoli figured the Philippines would become a prime target within a few weeks…

How long would it be before the Japanese came to the same conclusion?

* * *

"I thought you'd be in Manila meeting the new nurses this morning. Did you decide not to go?"

Major Rosemary Dodd looked up from her reports to find Alice Strickland peering at her from the doorway to her office. Alice was a tall, slender woman with who normally wore a stoic mask, but today there was no disguising her amusement.

"Can you blame me?" Rosemary asked, leaning back.

Alice laughed and took a seat on the chair opposite Rosemary's desk. "What's not to love—brass bands, a stirring dockside speech…?"

"You obviously haven't heard."

"What?"

"Our nurses aren't the only passengers on this particular transport. The boat also brings the guest performer for the troops' annual Holiday Revue."

Alice's brows rose. "The Andrews Sisters?" she asked hopefully.

"Even better. A stripper."

Alice's carefully plucked brows nearly disappeared into her hairline. "You're kidding, right?"

Rosemary shook her head. "I have it from a pretty good source. She's coming all the way from Washington, D.C. to entertain our boys."

"Good lord, that means the men who invariably gather as an impromptu welcoming committee will be especially out of control."

"Now you see why I skipped the adventure. I've arranged to introduce myself to the new women at orientation tomorrow morning, then I'll invite them for drinks at the officers' club before the party later in the evening."

"So who's meeting the new staff at the docks?"

Rosemary grinned. "Lieutenant Wakely."

Rosemary saw the moment that Alice absorbed the fact that straight-laced, old-fashioned Lt. Wakely had been thrown into the middle of what would probably become a testosterone-laden melee. Laughing, Alice gathered her things. "I hope you gave her hazard pay."

"No, but I should."

As she straightened, Alice eyed Rosemary in concern. "Don't stay too much longer. You've got the evening shift again tonight, and you haven't even been home yet from last night. You've been pulling sixteen-hour days for weeks now. If you keep this up, you'll be in a hospital bed yourself."

Rosemary grimaced, but didn't respond. Her head throbbed and her shoulders were taut with weariness. But there was still so much to do.

"I'll leave in the next few minutes."

"You'd better," Alice said as she turned into the hall. The sound of her footfalls had nearly disappeared when she called out, "Oh, and if I don't see you tomorrow…happy birthday!"

The slam of the outside door added a note of punctuation to the resulting silence. Rosemary sat motionless. She didn't even want to think about it—certainly didn't want anyone else to know or make a fuss. But it didn't surprise her that Alice knew. The two of them had become good friends since Alice's arrival more than a year ago. But Rosemary had taken great pains to keep the knowledge away from everyone else.

She shoved her reports into a folder and the folder into the filing cabinet. After carefully locking everything away, she decided Alice was right. She'd been at the hospital since early the previous evening. She needed a cool bath and several hours of sleep before checking on the arrangements for the welcoming party being thrown in honor of the new nurses tomorrow night. It was a tradition here in the Philippines—a grand welcoming dockside with a brass band and speeches, a quick tour of the area, martinis at their new quarters and plenty of time to absorb their surroundings, then orientation and a party and dance at the officers' club the following night. After that, the new girls would be given a week off to acclimate themselves to the heat before beginning their duties at the hospital.

Not a bad assignment. In fact, it was considered one of the plum spots here in the Pacific. Duties were usually routine—appendectomies, a few tonsillectomies, broken bones, and sunburn.

So why did Rosemary suddenly feel restless? She'd loved her time in Luzon—proving herself so capable that she'd been given command of the nurses at Fort Stotsenberg.

Grabbing her purse, she locked her office door and made her way into the hot tropical sunshine. There was a cool breeze today and it rustled the palm leaves overhead so they left dancing fingers of shadow on the walkway under her feet.

Was it time for a transfer? Rosemary wondered as she traversed the few blocks to the private bungalow assigned to the head of the nursing staff. She'd been in the Pacific for more than a dozen years and in the Philippines for ten. Maybe she needed a change of scenery. Someplace with snow. It was one of the few things she missed about the farm in Nebraska—snow in December.

But as her brisk pace blew away the cobwebs, she realized it wasn't her locale that filled her with discontent. Perhaps things had grown too easy and she needed a challenge. Or maybe, just maybe, she needed a vacation. It had been a long time since she'd been home. Mom and Pop would appreciate a visit.

She turned onto the walkway that led to her front stoop, then halted, arrested by the small white box left on her doorstep. She glanced over her shoulder as if the person who'd left it there loitered in the bushes. But there was no one there. She picked it up, recognizing the label from an expensive dress shop in Hawaii.

Hawaii?

Tugging at the ribbon, she lifted the lid, trying to remain blasé about the whole affair, but her heart secretly knocked at her ribs as if she were a child opening the first gift on Christmas Day.

Alice must have sent it. Who else even knew that it was her birthday?

She gasped when the contents were finally exposed. A perfectly formed corsage of milliner's violets lay nestled in a bed of green tissue, their faces so life-like that she reached out to touch them to ensure that they'd been made of silk and velvet.

Violets.

Her favorite flower.

A card had been tucked into the delicate blooms and, as she tugged it free, a tiny sachet dropped from the envelope. Almost immediately, she caught the ethereal, wafting scent of *Violettes D'Avril*, her favorite perfume.

Lifting the card, she noted that the hard-edged, angular penmanship was obviously male and the sentiment was brief.

Sweets for the sweet.

Turning, she searched the surrounding area more diligently for the unknown sender. Plenty of personnel made their way over the carefully groomed grounds. Jeeps and transports carried on with the business of the base. Some of the mounted cavalry officers were heading their horses to the green expanse of lawn for polo practice. But no one gave her any real attention.

Nevertheless, someone knew her birthday. Her birthday, her favorite flower, her favorite perfume...and her favorite play. Even Alice couldn't have done that.

* * *

Sgt. Wilcox drove through a pair of tall pillars announcing their arrival to Fort Stotsenberg. As they followed a lane that wound around a verdant expanse of lawn, Glory Bee leaned forward to catch a closer look.

Although the area was bristling with men and women in various uniforms, there was a Country Club air to the compound. The lawns were brilliantly green and lush flowerbeds overflowed with frangipani, birds of paradise, and bougainvillea. Even the palm trees with their whispering fronds were bedecked in orchids.

The layout of the base took her by surprise. In her mind, she'd pictured Fort Stotsenberg as a classical fortress surrounded on all sides with huge brick walls and razor wire. But from what she'd seen so far, Stotsenberg looked more like a holiday resort than a military installation. Walkways were shaded by trees and bordered with clumps of flowering bushes. In the distance, she could see the brilliant green of the parade ground and what looked like a golf course.

Sgt. Wilcox turned down a tree-lined lane bordered on either side with whitewashed cottages built high on stilts. Each one was identical, with lattice around the high foundations and broad wooden steps leading up to the front door. But Sgt. Wilcox could tell them apart because he brought the car to a halt in front of the last of the bungalows. A discreet sign read "Visitors Quarters."

"This way, Miss O'Halloran."

"Call me Glory Bee. Everyone else does."

Glory Bee allowed Sgt. Wilcox to usher her up the cement sidewalk to the freshly painted steps. Balancing her bags under his arms, he turned the knob and threw open the door.

Stepping inside, Glory Bee found the air blessedly cool and dim; the curtains had been kept closed against the morning sun. Rattan furniture had been scattered around the room along with a huge free-standing radio and what looked like a wet bar. If it weren't for the predominant use of stars and stripes in the decor, she might have thought she was at a fancy seaside hotel.

Sgt. Wilcox set Glory Bee's suitcases on the floor near a door that she presumed led to the bedroom. "Would you like me to take these…?" He flushed and gestured to the room in front of him. "I mean…if you want, I could…"

Glory Bee took pity on him. "No. Thanks. I'll only need a couple of things tonight. Once the performance is over tomorrow, someone will be picking me up."

"Oh?" His brows rose. "You have another show scheduled?"

She nearly laughed at his eagerness. "No. A vacation."

"Ah." He appeared confused that she'd come all the way to the Philippines for a holiday. "Well, then…" He stood awkwardly.

"You'll be fetching me later for rehearsal?" she prompted.

"Yes! Yes, I'll be back at three." Sgt. Wilcox began backing toward the exit. "Um. Well." He waved toward a kitchenette that was separated from the sitting area by a low counter. "There's an electric ice box with drinks and juice as well as a basket with a bottle of champagne and snacks compliments of the Base Commander. If you need anything else, let me know."

He had opened the door and was stepping onto the stoop when Glory Bee spoke. "Actually, Sergeant, there is something."

He eagerly turned. "Yes, ma'am?"

Ma'am. *That* wasn't an address she was used to hearing.

"I need to send some…personal telegrams. Is there a place off base where I could go?"

If he thought it odd that she wished to circumvent the facilities available at Fort Stotsenberg, he didn't let on.

"I'd be happy to take you into town after the rehearsal if you'd like. There's a post office in one of the stores not too far away. They do telegrams as well."

Glory Bee flashed him a wide smile. "Swell! I'd appreciate that. Thanks."

"Not at all, ma'am. Not at all." He lifted his arm as if he were about to salute, caught himself, then hurried from the bungalow, shutting the door behind him.

As soon as he'd disappeared, she felt the tension drain from her body. Exhaling, she kicked off her shoes and padded barefoot to the bedroom.

Someone had decorated with visiting brass in mind because a carved wooden eagle with American flags grasped in its talons adorned the wall over a large iron bed. A red chenille spread and fringe-edged silk souvenir pillows in garish yellows, pinks, and blues completed the effect.

Grimacing at the tackiness of it all, she padded to the bathroom beyond. Much, much better. An immense claw foot tub took up one whole wall. The commode and sink were utilitarian white porcelain. But the towel bars were adorned with thick fluffy linens, which had obviously not been furnished by the government.

Retrieving her makeup and overnight cases from the other room, Glory Bee settled the stopper in the drain and began to fill the tub. She would take a long bath, cool herself off, and wash the stickiness of her journey away. Then she'd have time for a nap before Sgt. Wilcox returned.

With a snap, she released the locks to her makeup case and withdrew a bottle of rose-scented bath oil. Unscrewing the lid, she dribbled a capful into the pool forming in the tub. As the heady scent filled the room, she kicked the door shut with her foot, exposing a long mirror.

The sight of her reflection caused the forced energy to drain from her body like air leaking from a pricked balloon. Unbuttoning her suit, she watched as the features of her face melted from her pasted-on smile to an expression so serious, so...melancholy that she felt as if she gazed into the eyes of a stranger.

The lavender jacket fell to the floor, then her skirt. Lifting the slip over her head, she stared at the unfamiliar figure dressed in silk tap pants, a heavily boned girdle, and a silk brassiere that strained to contain her breasts. Her chin quivered and tears formed behind the dam of her lashes as she unhooked the fasteners of the girdle one by one.

The relief was instantaneous. As the hated foundation garment fell to the floor in a heap, her belly expanded, becoming rounded and oh, so alien to her. Palming the unfamiliar swell she prayed that no one on the voyage had guessed her secret. She'd tried to keep to herself as much as possible—and the fact that she'd been sick throughout most of the journey had helped. She was able to blame her nausea on being a poor sailor. But with a ship full of nurses being transferred to the Philippines, she'd been so afraid one of them would guess the real reason behind her illness.

Swiping at the tears that suddenly broke free from her lashes and spilled down her cheeks, she turned her back on the sight of her body and stripped the rest of her underthings away. Then, settling into the tub, she sank below the level of the water and closed her eyes.

There was no use crying. It had happened. She was pregnant. And no amount of blubbering would change that fact. She'd already sobbed most of her way across the Pacific Ocean and it hadn't solved a thing. She was here now, away from prying eyes until the baby was born. After that, Michael would take care of things. As soon as the infant was old enough to travel, she would return to Hawaii where he'd made arrangements for the baby to be given away.

The thought brought no regret, merely a surge of relief. She couldn't be a mother. She didn't know the first thing about raising a kid. As it was, she wasn't sure how she was going to cope until she was able to take the baby to Hawaii.

Maybe she could hire someone. A nanny or nursemaid, or whatever the hell they called a person who took care of babies. She had to stick things out for a few more months. Then she could return to her life, her career.

And Michael.

With a pang, Glory Bee wondered what he was doing now. Was he hard at work on Capitol Hill? Or home having cocktails with his wife? Glory Bee wasn't sure of the time change. It was yesterday in Washington, wasn't it? The other passengers had made a big fuss on the ship when they'd crossed the International Date Line, so it had been drummed into Glory Bee's head that the Philippines was a day ahead of the states.

So she wasn't just thousands of miles away from Michael.

She was thousands of miles and a day.

Using her toes, she shut off the taps and sank deeper into the water, until only her face bobbed free. Biting her lip, she tried to focus on the silken caress of the bath, the sweet, musky scent of roses, the upcoming rehearsal, and the beauty of the Philippines. Anything that would push away her tears.

She couldn't cry anymore. She wouldn't. After all, she had everything in the world for which to be grateful. She was in paradise, just like Michael had promised. Months of sun and sand would do her good. And she'd have time to explore before she got too big. As the ship had made its way into the harbor, she'd seen a lovely little island in the distance. The purser had told her it was Corregidor. It had looked so peaceful. So green. She'd even heard some of the nurses saying that they planned to arrange for a transfer there after a few months. Maybe Glory Bee could go there for an outing. If not, there would be the hills surrounding the plantation to explore. Manila itself.

She'd have more than enough to keep her busy.

More than enough to push away the hollow loneliness that threatened to consume her whole.

* * *

Darkness had long ago fallen on the Philippines when John Macklin shouldered open the door to the small foreman's cottage and stepped inside, his boots scraping against the lintel. Behind him, the screen snapped shut with a bang, allowing a cool breeze to waft through the metal mesh. The silken air twined sinuously around his aching body, cooling the sweat earned from laboring in the fields and causing an infinitesimal lessening to the tension gripping his chest.

He was tired. Dead tired.

It only remained to be seen if he was tired enough.

Restlessly rolling his shoulders, he dragged the hat from his head, hung it on the hook next to the door and stood for a moment, absorbing the stillness. The utter silence. Even after all these years, he couldn't quite adapt to the solitude of his living quarters. He was a man accustomed to action, bustle, and noise. But here…

Here there was only a stark, hollow emptiness that reminded him that he still hadn't reconciled himself to this new life.

An even stronger gust wove its way through the screen, plastering the fabric of his shirt against the moisture pooled between his shoulder blades. The gentle nudge of air was enough to put him into motion again, his footfalls heavy. Noisy.

The stale heat of the house pressed in upon him, thick and humid. Although the sky outside was clear, there'd be a storm tonight, he'd wager. One of those brief, roaring downpours that would hit like a raging waterfall, then be over again in a matter of seconds. Rather than clearing the stickiness away, it would make things worse.

Frowning, John moved to the window next to his battered chair and lifted the sash, bracing it with a broken broom handle so it wouldn't slam down on his fingers. Then he stood absolutely still, closed his eyes, and breathed deeply.

The cooler air rushed in, redolent with the rich scents of bougainvillea, plumeria—and, oddly enough, the musky perfume of English tea roses from the garden surrounding the Wilmington's plantation house. His ears picked up the familiar sound of soughing palm fronds, the yap of a dog, the distant murmur of voices from the workmen's cottages down the hill.

As always, John waited…waited…until he heard the faint noises of the children—high-pitched laughter, a plaintive call. Then, he pushed himself upright and strode into the kitchen.

Normally, John would have been careful to close the main door, since his front stoop could be seen from the rear bedrooms of the Big House. But tonight there was no need for such precautions. The staff would have gone home, and the Wilmington family had decided to skip the yearly visit to their plantation holdings. Due to the unrest in French Indo-China and the dangers of traveling across the Atlantic, Milton Wilmington would be conducting his business by post from England—a fact that didn't bother John one way or the other. Whether or not the owner was present, the work of harvesting sugar cane was the same, and John would see to it that the farm was run as efficiently and as profitably as possible.

Unbuckling the sheath around his hips, he set his machete on the broad, scarred table, then switched on the radio—more to drown out the silence of the cottage than for any other reason. Silence brought introspection. Introspection brought a sense of inadequacy and loss—something he'd learned to avoid at all costs.

A bird screeched outside, quickly answered by its mate. The noise grated against nerves already frayed from equipment failures and supply shortages. John had spent the day dealing with one crisis after another—and if he'd had his way, he would have continued working for another hour or two. But the workers would have protested, despite the desperate need for more cleared land in the southern field. The men under his command didn't share John's insatiable need to fill another hour with meaningful toil.

Moving to the sink, he ducked his head beneath the tepid stream, wishing that he could sweep his melancholy thoughts away as easily as the dust and sweat. Reaching blindly for the soap, he scrubbed his face and hair, wincing when the lather seeped into the broken skin of his palms. He wasn't used to machete work. Not yet anyhow. Give it time. If he pushed himself harder, longer, his hands would toughen. As would the rest of him.

Turning, he rested his hips against the counter, wiping his face and neck dry as Benny Goodman's band faded beneath the bell-like tones that heralded the news.

"In Europe, fighting continues as the German Luftwaffe wages nightly bombardment raids on London... While in America, a Japanese delegation has arrived for talks aimed at negotiating a possible lifting of the fuel embargo in exchange for a retreat from the French-held colonies of Indo-China..."

John lifted his head, cocking an ear toward the radio.

Retreat? The Japanese had sent a delegation to discuss retreat?

He shook his head, his mind suddenly crowded with noise

and chaos. His eyes squeezed shut, and he fought to block out the memories. Of Nanking. The Japanese invasion.

The slaughter.

"No!"

He didn't realize that he'd shouted the word until the echo reverberated through the room.

He stood at attention, straining to hear more of the newscast. But the reporter had already moved on to local news. Then the soothing strains of a Bing Crosby ballad.

But John felt suddenly chilled, the hairs at the back of his neck prickling with a warning that he couldn't quite understand.

Rushing to the small alcove that held his bed, he reached beneath the mattress and took out a rucksack. Not really conscious of his actions or even comprehending what he meant to do, he filled it with a change of clothing, several pairs of socks and underwear. Then, back in the main room, he added canned goods, a tin of matches, an electric torch, a fresh set of batteries, and his pocket knife.

Flinging the door open, he ran to the battered plantation truck parked beneath a stand of stately palm trees, threw the rucksack inside, and quickly slid onto the seat, twisting the key. As the truck rumbled to life, he froze.

Where was he going?

Why?

Just as quickly, the terrifying memories fluttered away like bats into the darkness. Leaving him empty. Cold.

He wasn't in Manchuria anymore.

The threat of the Japanese was far away.

Resting his forehead against his white-knuckle grip on the steering wheel, he forced himself to take deep, gulping breaths until the horrors disappeared and with them the inner images of bloated bodies, ravaged women, and his students…

Dear God, his students...

Killing the engine, he slid out into the darkness again, praying that no one had seen him. Damning himself for being skittish tonight of all nights, when the sky was clear and the stars were bright chips of ice in a sea of black ink, he reached for the rucksack, intent on returning it to the house.

But at the last minute, not really knowing why, he turned back to the truck and tucked the bag into the corner of the bed near his toolbox, covering it with an old, dusty tarpaulin.

Then, returning to the kitchen, he snatched up the machete. If he couldn't clear the fields, he would work on the vines encroaching on the boss-man's house. He could pull the truck up close and use the headlights for illumination. There was a visitor due to arrive in the next day or two. From what Milton Wilmington had explained in his wire, she was a friend of a friend and she'd be staying indefinitely. John may as well see to the task of clearing away the ever-encroaching greenery himself rather than assign one of the gardeners to do it.

Then maybe, just maybe, he'd be able to fall into a dreamless sleep.

It was the light that pierced his consciousness at first, and for one shattering moment, he thought that he'd died. Died and gone to heaven. But then, a familiar face swam into view. A cocky, worried grin.

"He's alive."

A hand reached down into the darkness.

"Grab hold and I'll lift you up."

For several long moments, he couldn't process the command. The pain had begun to swell within him. And he was cold. Cold and hot and shivering so badly that he feared his teeth would shatter.

"Come on, take my hand, y'hear me?"

He lifted his arm, but was too weak to grasp hold, so, with a sigh, the figure jumped down into the hole beside him.

"Y'gotta help me. I can't lift you all by myself."

His arm was wrapped around the figure's shoulder, and as he looked, hard, the face that swam into view was familiar. His comrade. His friend. And it was that familiarity that helped to bring reality rushing back—and with it, his need to fight the pain that held him in its grip.

He struggled to brace his legs beneath him, and with his friend's help, he made it to his feet. Then, there were more hands in the opening to the pit, reaching, pulling him up and into the searing heat of the sun.

Just as quickly, his strength was spent. He collapsed into the dust, shivering. But this time, when he feared he wouldn't be able to get up, there were men who could lift and carry him away.

Chapter Two

December 7, 1941

Rosemary Dodd cast a quick glance over her roster, then gazed at the women gathered around her.

"Thank you, ladies. I appreciate your willingness to spend your first morning learning the scope of your duties. You'll find that one of our key mottos here is efficiency, so to that end, I'd like to finish off your orientation meeting with a quick tour of our hospital." She allowed her features to relax into a slight smile. "After all, that's why you've joined us here in the Philippines, isn't it?"

Handing the clipboard to Lt. Wakely, she motioned for the new girls to follow her.

"The facilities here at Fort Stotsenberg were built just before the First World War. But as you can see, we've been updated regularly. This year we've received new paint and furnishings as well as a revamped surgical suite."

Rosemary led them into one of the wards. Beds lined both sides of the spacious room. Floor-to-ceiling windows on one wall provided sunlight. Fans overhead kept the air moving.

"We're smaller than the main hospital in Manila." She gestured to the room in front of her. "We have two wards, twenty-four beds in this one, ten in the other. It might sound a bit primitive compared to hospitals stateside, but our needs here are simpler as well. Surgeries are usually routine—appendectomies, gall bladder removal, tonsillectomies. Other than that, most of our care revolves around broken bones, stitches, and sunburn." She lifted her voice and called out, "Isn't that right, Private Diamante?"

"Yes, ma'am," came the woeful reply.

She grinned. "Private Diamante was part of the construction crew building the stage on the PT field. He fell from the ladder and broke his leg and collarbone. Something that might not have happened had he waited until his partner was there to steady the ladder." She lifted her voice again, "Isn't that right, Private Diamante?"

"Yes, ma'am."

The girls giggled. "Due to the heat, we have four shifts, six hours each, plus a rotating clinic duty. You're expected to be at your shift at least fifteen minutes early." She fixed them all with a stern gaze. "No exceptions."

She paused at the door to their only operating theater. "At the party tomorrow, I'll introduce you to the surgeons, Dr. Packard and Dr. Rowley."

Continuing her march down the corridor, she ended in the smaller ward. In this room, there were three patients, all of them much paler and weaker than the unfortunate Pvt. Diamante. "For today, you'll have to content yourself with meeting Dr. Grimm."

A silver-haired doctor glanced up from his examination of a patient's abdomen. After checking the stitches of a recent appendectomy incision, he offered them a warm smile. "Are these the new recruits?"

"Fresh off the boat."

He carefully replaced the covers over the soldier's chest, then stood, reaching to shake each woman's hand in turn. "Welcome aboard," he said, his eyes twinkling beneath bushy eyebrows. "Let's hope you don't live to regret volunteering for the assignment." His brows waggled up and down. "Work here can be murder. I come by my name rightfully, you know."

Rosemary shot him an indulgent smile. Of all the physicians she'd worked with over the years, she'd never met a kinder man. Kind to a fault, some might say. He tended to treat the nurses on his staff as equals—a practice that many in the medical profession frowned upon. But he'd told Rosemary on more than one occasion that he'd never met a nurse who worked as well through fear and intimidation as she did through encouragement. And if the loyalty of his staff was anything to go by, he was right.

"Dr. Grimm has been here at Fort Stotsenberg for almost twenty years."

"So you see, I've been at it nearly as long as the building itself." With a nod, he backed toward the beds again. "Enjoy your day, ladies."

Rosemary led the women from the ward back into the hall. "Lieutenant Wakely will be taking you on the rest of the tour," she said as she made her way to the rear door. "As for me, I've got work to do," she said with a wry smile. "Enjoy your walk around the base and your time off. I'll see you tonight at the party."

She waited in the vestibule until the last of them had disappeared, trotting behind Lt. Wakely like baby geese. It wasn't really that long ago when she'd been one of those women, eagerly trailing after her guide, trying to get her bearings. She'd been so afraid then. Afraid of getting lost, of being late to her shifts, of failing to make a good impression.

"Remembering the good old days?" a low voice said from behind her left shoulder.

She turned, fighting a smile when she found Lt. Gilhouley—or The Great Gilhouley as he'd been affectionately dubbed by her staff. Tall and lanky, with a shock of strawberry blond hair, he cut a striking figure in his army tans. But the crispness of his uniform was belied by his cocky grin and the barely harnessed energy that radiated from him in waves. Not for the first time, Rosemary was struck by the way the man seemed like a rambunctious puppy straining against the leash.

No. Not a puppy.

More like a greyhound or another thoroughbred that had consented to some control, but only for the time being.

"And what is the Great Gilhouley doing in this neck of the woods? Surely the arrival of a few nurses is beneath the attention of the press corps," she said, stepping away from the door and making her way back to her office. As expected, Gil fell into step beside her.

"Apparently, I'm watching you get all misty eyed at the sight of the new help."

She rolled her eyes in his direction. "Hardly."

Pushing through her office door, she crossed to her desk and began sorting the reports from the night shift. With the arrival of a new set of nurses looming on the horizon, she'd spent sixteen hours a day at the hospital or in staff meetings for the past few weeks. And the marathon work sessions were beginning to settle in as a throbbing ache between her temples. But she wasn't done for the day. She still had the welcoming party this evening and drinks beforehand in the officers' club. If she could finish the reports, she might be able to catch an hour or two of sleep before—

It took a moment for her to realize that the reports she'd intended to scoop toward her were held firmly beneath a broad male hand. One with long, slender fingers and carefully kept nails. She stared at that hand for a beat, two, before her exhausted mind realized those fingers, those slender artistic digits, belonged to Gilhouley.

She lifted her eyes and her gaze locked with his own amused stare.

"What do you want, Gilhouley?" she demanded curtly.

"I want a lot in this world, but I've been told I can't have most of it."

She pursed her lips in annoyance, biting back the pithy retort she longed to make.

Sensing her short temper, he said, "I was told to bring you to the parade grounds." He used the same silken, soothing tones one might use to gentle a startled mount.

"Told by whom."

"The Powers-That-Be."

She huffed in irritation.

"Why?"

"If I knew that, then *I* would be one of the Powers-That-Be."

She opened her mouth to inform him she had better things to do than to meet with the Morale Committee, but decided there wasn't much point in shooting the messenger.

"Fine." Grabbing her purse from the desk drawer, she marched out of the office.

"I've got a Jeep at the curb," Gilhouley said as he fell into step beside her.

They strode out of the hospital and into the blazing sunshine. Rosemary took her place in the passenger seat without any help from Gilhouley. After gunning the engine, he burst away from the curb with a jolt of speed and a spray of gravel, winding his way around the hospital. But when he should have turned toward the parade grounds, he kept on going.

Rosemary twisted in her seat, watching as their destination began to disappear. "What are you doing? The field is that way."

"We aren't going to the field."

"But you said—"

"I was told to say anything I had to in order to get you away from the hospital."

"By whom?"

"Lieutenant Strickland."

"Alice? But why?"

"To paraphrase: you've been working too hard and they think you need a break."

Her eyes narrowed. "And if you didn't paraphrase?"

"Major Dodd is a goddamn fuse ready to blow—and if you don't get her the hell out of here for a little R and R, we're all going to be the goddamn casualties!"

Rosemary's mouth gaped. "She did *not* say that!"

Gil shrugged. "Again, I'm paraphrasing. I don't remember her exact words. They were something like, 'Take Major Dodd to lunch. She's been working too hard.'" His words gentled toward the end, causing her to sit back in her seat, speechless. Unsettled.

"So where are we going?"

"Lunch," he said succinctly. "I learned a long time ago not to argue with a woman."

He slowed as he reached the front gates, then turned left, picking up speed until the rush of air cooled her hot cheeks.

"My hair's going to be a wreck after this."

"I won't tell anyone."

"That won't do me much good at whatever restaurant you've chosen."

His smile was slow and wide. She watched enthralled as his face changed completely, his eyes crinkling, the angular shape of his face softening.

Embarrassed, she tore her gaze away when she realized she'd been caught staring. "So where are we going?"

"You'll see."

Sensing that she would get no information out of him that he wasn't willing to give, she stopped trying. She probably should insist that he return them both to the base. But she was suddenly swamped by a heady exhilaration, like a kid who'd managed to slip away from school without getting caught. For the next few hours, no one would know where she was, whom she was with, or how to contact her. If any emergencies arose, her staff would have to take care of them without her assistance.

The sun beat down on her muscles, loosening them from their tense grip, and the wind blew the cobwebs from her brain. And suddenly, she couldn't think of anywhere she would rather be.

"So tell me, Gilhouley, why you?"

He lifted a brow.

"Why were *you* chosen as my abductor?"

"I should think that was obvious, being the most charming, biddable man on base."

She snorted in disbelief. "More likely, it's because Alice knew you have a bit of larceny in you."

"Are you suggesting that your nurses might have bribed me?"

"It's possible."

He shook his head. "No bribe was necessary in this instance, I can assure you."

She opened her mouth to offer a quick comeback, but soon found she didn't have one. His remark had held no amusement, merely a velvety hint of sincerity.

Not for the first time, she wondered what made The Great Gilhouley tick. He'd always struck her as a walking, breathing anachronism on the base—the last sort of person you'd think would have chosen the Army for a career. He had a wild streak to him and a flair for disobedience. Rumor had it that scandal had followed him to the Philippines and he'd been demoted at least once, but she'd never been able to discover the details—not that she'd tried that hard. She had her own skeletons to protect; she didn't need to be unearthing anyone else's.

"I can't be gone for very long," she said finally, more to reassert some control over the situation rather than a longing to return.

"I'll have you back in time for the festivities tonight."

Since she saw no reason to protest any further, she took a scarf from her bag and tied it around her hair to minimize the damage, then unearthed a pair of sunglasses and slid them up her nose. Closing her eyes, she tipped her head back to enjoy the heat of the afternoon.

Gilhouley didn't speak, for which she was grateful. Instead, she allowed herself to surrender to the sunshine, her drowsiness, and the growl of the Jeep. She couldn't have said how much time had elapsed when the Jeep drew to a sudden stop. She opened her eyes, blinking in confusion. She'd assumed that Gilhouley would be taking her to Manila proper, but instead, he'd brought her to the docks.

"Why are we here?" The area was teeming with life—soldiers, sailors, Filipinos. Vehicles crowded the dusty streets and birds looped lazily overhead looking for scraps of food.

"Lunch."

Gilhouley slid out of his seat, rounding the hood and holding out a hand to help her from the Jeep. This time, rather than offering a show of independence, she accepted his assistance, noticing for the first time that Gilhouley's palms were calloused and strong. Clearly he wasn't a stranger to hard work, despite his reputation for finagling.

As soon as she'd planted her feet on the pavement, he reached behind the seat, taking out two paper sacks and two bottles of soda.

"As promised," he said handing her a cola and a sack.

Her laughter was wry. "This is lunch?"

"Yup." He popped the "p" between pursed lips.

"Where'd you get it?"

"From the mess hall."

She squinted up at him. "So you brought me all this way so that I could eat the same meal out of a sack that I would have eaten had I stayed on base?"

"Not quite."

He snagged her arm, pulling her toward a rough jetty that jutted out into the sparkling water. They were at the far end of a series of docks where palm trees hung low over the sea wall. The wood under her feet was rougher than those used by the military transports, so she supposed this must be an area used for local ferries and pleasure craft.

As they hurried toward the far end, she failed to see the need for rushing. The pier was empty and there wasn't a boat in sight. But then, just when she was about to demand an explanation or a return trip to the base, a seaplane flew in low over their heads, banked, then landed a few hundred yards out in the bay. When it turned toward them, she stutter-stepped to a halt.

"We're going up in that?" she asked.

"Is there a problem?"

She couldn't prevent her slow grin. "No, not at all."

They'd reached the end of the pier, and Gilhouley lifted his arm in a wide wave. Within seconds, the plane was sputtering toward them, the perfumed air of Manila becoming tainted with the scents of diesel and exhaust.

As soon as it sidled up to the docks, Gilhouley reached out and grabbed the handle to the passenger door.

"After you," he said.

Gingerly, Rosemary stepped into the plane, bending low until she could perch on one of the seats. Within seconds, Gilhouley followed, fastening the latch firmly behind him.

"Once 'round the park and don't spare the horses, Napoli."

A weathered leprechaun of a man with a shock of curly gray hair turned to grin in Rosemary's direction.

"And who's the stunner?"

"Rosemary, this is Gregor Napoli. Gregor, Major Rosemary Dodd."

Napoli shoved an unlit cigar between his teeth. "Aren't you only a lieutenant?"

"Don't remind her, Napoli. Major Dodd is a 'by-the-book' kind of woman. If you say anything about the official nature of her position, she'll remember she has reports or inventory to do and insist I take her back to base. And I've been charged with entertaining her for a few hours. So give us your best tour, will you?"

Napoli laughed, a deep belly laugh that caused Rosemary to grin even wider.

"Ever been in a seaplane, Major?" he asked.

"I've never been in a plane at all," she admitted, shoving her sack and drink to the floor. She'd always wanted to ride in a plane. How could she not, stationed so close to Clark Field?

"Then hold on to your hat," he instructed, pulling back on the throttle enough for the plane to rock and shimmy away from the pier, then turn so that its nose pointed to open water.

Unconsciously, Rosemary gripped Gil's hand as Napoli increased their speed, racing over the water, the plane bucking beneath her like a mount at full trot. Then, like a show horse taking fences, it shivered one last time before suddenly lifting into the air.

She sucked in her breath as she was pushed deep into her seat. But, wondrously, the plane went up, up, up and the docks disappeared beneath them, making her feel light as a feather.

Leaning forward, she peered out of the window, stunned at the sight that lay below her—a sea so blue it hurt to look at it and the green, green of the islands.

"It's amazing," she breathed.

"It is, isn't it?"

She turned, her nose nearly bumping Gil's as he leaned over her shoulder to see the view. And for the first time, she realized that she held his hand. Even more troubling was the fact that he didn't seem inclined to give it back.

Rosemary blinked, acutely conscious of the close confines, of Gilhouley's shoulder pressing into hers, the length of his thigh pressed up against her own. Casting a nervous glance at Napoli, she wondered what he must be thinking—that she was one of Gilhouley's girls out for a good time?

But nothing could be further from the truth. Gilhouley was at least ten years her junior and a lieutenant, for heaven's sake. Napoli couldn't possibly think that she and Gil…that they…that he…

For several long minutes, the stunning view of the harbor was forgotten as she stared at Gilhouley instead, wondering why she'd never really noticed how…well put-together he was. The younger nurses whispered about him as if he were Errol Flynn, but Rosemary had never really taken that tack. Gilhouley was simply…Gilhouley. Good-natured, wily, a bit of a goofball. With his snapping cornflower blue eyes and yellow-gold hair, he was the epitome of youth. An all-American male in the tropics. A scrapping young officer with an Irish name and a New England accent. Boston, she'd bet.

Oddly, she felt a wave of regret. If she were ten years younger… she might have given her nurses a run for their money. As it was…

Turning blindly toward the window again, she made a show of looking down at the scattered archipelago scattered like a toddler's toys among its blanket of blue. But it was the warmth of Gilhouley's body seeping into her own that took up most of her attention.

* * *

Gilhouley knew the moment Rosemary acknowledged him as something other than a junior officer. He watched her eyes widen, her pupils dilate. For a split second, her breath hitched in her throat, then she turned away to gaze out the window—even though he doubted she saw much of what lay below. Her body became so still that the stillness became electric, thrumming between them like a charge of static threatening to snap them both.

He felt the slightest of tugs at his hand, but he refused to let her go. Not now. Not after he'd done everything he possibly could to slowly slip himself into her world.

Dear God, couldn't she feel it? Couldn't she feel the want that pounded through his veins, settling in regions of his body that he could not control. He shifted in his seat, hoping to ease his discomfort, yet still managing to brush his shoulder against hers.

"That's Corregidor," he said, using his free hand to point out the window, hoping to distract himself from the caramel-colored wisps of hair that the wind had teased around her face. A faint scent of violets enveloped her, and he wondered if she'd taken the sachet he'd sent for her birthday and tucked it somewhere next to her skin. The thought was enough to send a new jolt of heat through his veins. He pointed to some specks in the distance that at first glance looked like a flock of birds.

"There're some of our boys putting their planes through their paces."

"You can see so far from up here."

He nodded. "When the air is right, you can see the earth curve a little toward the horizon and the sun will be white-hot, like a pat of farmer's butter."

Her lips twitched at that. "It's been a long time since I've seen home-churned butter." Her brow lifted. "I wouldn't have taken you for a farm boy, Gilhouley."

"I've led a checkered past."

"Of that, I have no doubt."

He pointed to the water below. "There's one of our ships."

"The ocean looks so vast from up here and the islands so small," she breathed.

"Take her in toward shore so she can see more of Luzon, Napoli."

The plane banked, and Rosemary was unprepared for the move because she fell against Gilhouley, her hand reaching out to brace herself in his lap—and, dear God, if she didn't land right on the bulge pressing against his zipper. And in that instant, all pretense was stripped away, all artifice, and Gilhouley was suddenly laid bare before her.

He didn't speak. He couldn't. For the life of him, he had lost the ability to communicate at all as her dark eyes grew darker, the pupils expanding with an awareness that he could not ignore.

Gilhouley feared she would slap him, hit him, chide him, or that her spine would become ramrod stiff, her tone prickly. But Rosemary adjusted her hand to his knee, then returned her attention to the window, her body curiously still and thoughtful. And Gilhouley had to resist the urge not to shout "hooray!" because he'd thought with that innocent contact, he'd blown things entirely.

Nevertheless, he knew it was too soon to admit anything—that he'd been attracted to her the moment he'd come to Luzon, that he'd been slowly endearing himself to her, that he'd been watching her from afar for far too long. She'd think he was a wolf, a nickname that he'd often proudly earned. But with Rosemary, he didn't want her to think of him that way. For some reason, it was important that she know he wasn't dangling her along for a little fun. No, even though he didn't entirely understand his own attraction to this woman, he did know that somehow, this time, things would be different. *He* would be different.

And shit almighty, he'd better not screw things up.

* * *

A tinge of red was beginning to bleed into the evening sky when Glory Bee took one last look at her reflection in the mirror, then made her way out of the tent. As far as changing areas went, the tent was primitive, but certainly not the worst she'd ever used. No, it was a bit of adventure performing in the open rather than a smoky, airless theater that reeked of sweat, booze, and stale cigarettes. Here, the breeze was thick with the scents of hot earth, flowers and newly mown grass.

Ducking through the flap, Glory Bee made her way toward the stage at one end of the parade grounds. She had to hand it to the boys in brown. They'd done themselves proud in erecting the structure. It was a near-professional facility complete with colored lights bolted to overhead pipes and a makeshift curtain that looked as if it had been stitched from parachute silk.

Ignoring the curious eyes that followed her every move, Glory Bee tugged on elbow-length gloves, then ran a hand over her waist, smoothing the infinitesimal wrinkles.

The costume was new, a clever concoction made by one of her favorite seamstresses. She was dressed in gold from head to foot—an opera coat made completely of ostrich feathers, a body-hugging skirt and tunic covered in rhinestones and bugle beads. Even her shoes were fashioned of gold satin liberally dusted with beads and rhinestones. From experience, she knew that the minute the lights came up, the effect would be dazzling.

She'd required only a few changes to her usual costume. A seam taken out here, a gusset put in there. Although she was aware of the thickening of her waist, she doubted anyone else would know the difference. Thank god the Base Commander—an old school buddy of Michael's—had insisted she was not to "completely disrobe." As if she would. She'd passed that point weeks ago. No, she was aiming for a "classy" routine, one that was more tease than strip. That way, she could cinch in her waist with lacy corselets and corral the fullness of her bosom with silken brassieres and teddies.

Making her way to the wings, she peeked out at the audience. Folding chairs and benches had been set up in the grass, but there were at least as many soldiers sitting on the ground and standing in the aisles. A "sold out" crowd, of sorts.

Not that she'd expected anything else. Despite an influx of females on the base due to the Nursing Corps, white women were scarce in these out-of-the-way Army bases. And the promise of an American girl taking her clothes off was bound to draw an audience. She just hoped there were enough men left manning the fort should that prove necessary. According to Sgt. Wilcox, rumors of Japanese aggression had been running rampant on the base since the evacuation of wives and children had begun last spring—something Michael had failed to tell her when he'd insisted this was the perfect place for her to come and have the baby. But then, he couldn't have known. He wouldn't have sent her to the Philippines if he'd thought there was any real danger.

A male quartet in dress uniforms was finishing their rendition of *Green Eyes.* That meant Glory Bee would be next. She'd rehearsed three separate numbers, two of which involved singing. But this first routine was little more than strutting to music. Enough to whet their appetite for what was to come. Then she'd add to their interest with her trademark, *Flying Down to Rio,* and finish with a military finale in honor of the locale.

As the quartet crescendoed with their final chord, her heart began to pound in her chest and her throat grew dry. It didn't matter how many times she'd performed her routines or the number of years she'd been on the stage, she felt the same fluttering nervousness. Even now, as the four men took their bows, her hands shook.

Taking a deep breath, she held the air in her lungs as the lights extinguished. Then, hurrying center stage behind the curtain, she turned her back to the audience and struck her pose—arms up, one knee bent.

For a moment, she felt a brief burst of panic as her nervousness threatened to become full-blown nausea. But then the familiar cadence of the drums filled the air, the curtain whooshed open, and the lights burst on.

Momentarily blinded, she held her pose as a swell of applause and catcalls threatened to drown out her music. But when she felt the familiar pulse of the bass drum shuddering through the soles of her feet, she turned and called out, "Hello, boys!"

A roar rose from the parade grounds. Although she couldn't see most of the crowd through the glare of the stage lights, she felt each and every one of them. And in that instant as she moved downstage left, her hips swaying, her arms lowering, she felt a rush of joy.

They loved her.

They wanted her.

"Is it hot here in the Philippines?" She called out to the sea of men as they surged to their feet. She paraded downstage right, the hem of her beaded train twitching behind her. Dropping her voice to a growling purr, she added, "Or is it just me?"

The roar from the servicemen hit her system like a shot of pure adrenaline and she turned her back and gazed over her shoulder. The feathers from her opera coat framed her face, fluttering in front of her so that she saw the men on the first few rows through a golden haze.

She pouted playfully. "They warned me that a girl could suffer from heatstroke if she isn't careful." More whistles, then a swell of drums. "So I came prepared!"

With exaggerated movements, she unhooked the first fastener to the coat. Then the second. She paused, waiting a beat, two, then dropped the feathery concoction to the stage, exposing a gown that hugged every curve in her exotic arsenal.

The noise from the audience grew so loud, she feared she wouldn't be able to hear her music, but just in time, the *wah, wah* of the trumpet cut through the din.

Lifting her arms over her head again, she made a wide circle, waiting for her audience to calm slightly. Once she'd crossed to center stage, she paused for the swell of her music, then began tugging the gloves from her fingers, inch by painful inch, all the while bumping her hips and rolling her shoulders.

"How do you boys stand this weather?"

She'd learned long ago that the way to hold a man's attention was to give all of her movements an air of reluctance—as if she weren't really sure if she should take her clothes off. Not here. Not now. So she made a prolonged effort of her glove, held on to it, turned, seemed to reconsider, turned, then finally gave in and tossed it out into the crowd.

There was a frenzy of uniforms as the servicemen dove after her glove as if she'd thrown chum to a school of sharks. Then, with a throaty laugh, she repeated the process again, this time, tossing the glove further out. She made a show of regret at having lost both of her gloves—never letting on that she bought them by the gross and couldn't care less if they were returned to her or not.

"It must be horrible during the day. All that marching. And drilling." She offered them one last lop-sided smile. Then, turning her back to the audience, she reached behind her to pull down her zipper, inch by agonizing inch. "I'd rather spend my time at the beach."

With that, she tossed her bodice—into the wings of the stage this time. Gloves she could afford to replace. Hand-beaded costumes, she could not.

Leaving her back to the audience, she made them wait, made them wonder, just how much she was exposing in the front. They could see the delicate lace of her corset, but were her breasts bare …covered…?

She tipped her shoulder up and peered behind her, offering them a well-rehearsed pout.

"I never could stand the heat," she playfully complained, then reached behind her for the button to her skirt. Then, as the drums suddenly pounded and the trumpets screamed, she allowed her skirt to drop to the floor in a puddle of sequins. She whirled, facing the men wearing little more than a silken teddy, a Merry Widow corselet, and net stockings held up by a pair of satin garters.

She strode the width of the stage, first one way, then the other. Then, perching on a chair that had been positioned on the apron of the stage, she removed one high-heeled shoe, tossing it behind her, then the other.

Several eager men surged toward the edge of the stage, and she toyed with them, remaining just out of reach as she slowly rolled a stocking down over her thighs, her knees, her calves. Pointing her toes until her muscles ached, she made her legs appear as long and a shapely as possible as she removed the first sock, ran it through her fingers as if she were a conjuror handling a magic scarf, then tossed it out to the men. As they tumbled toward their trophy like puppies eager for table scraps, she removed the second stocking and tossed it as well.

The music and drums soon rose to a fever pitch, and she began working the hooks at the busk of her corset, taunting, teasing. Then, as it fell free, she snatched the curtain in front of her as if it were a large towel and she'd just emerged from her bath.

Normally, the corset would have gone the way of her dress—toward the wings where she could retrieve it later. But tonight, inwardly thinking "What the hell?" she tossed it into the roiling, shouting men. She was tired of wearing the blasted things. In the past few weeks, the restrictive garments she'd adopted to hide her burgeoning figure had become increasingly uncomfortable. She had other tight-fitting foundations ready for her later performances and she didn't need that one anymore, so why not let some poor schmuck thousands of miles away from home have it?

Holding the curtain tightly against her breasts, she posed in a way that made it appear that she was only scantily clad in the sheerest of teddies. In actuality, the costume had been cleverly made with a lining of nude-colored fabric beneath the black chiffon, each seam boned and tailored to support the thickening of her waist and the added fullness to her breasts.

But she didn't think about that now. Lifting her face to the lights, she yelled out, "God bless America and all those who fight in her defense!"

The roar was instantaneous, thundering toward her with such intensity that the boards beneath her feet trembled from the noise. At the last minute, she raised her arms high. The curtain dropped, the men surged to their feet as they were sure they caught a hint of nipple through her costume. Then in an instant, the lights went dark and she was nothing but a silhouette against the last ruby-glow of the sunset.

As soon as the curtain fell into place, Glory Bee dropped her pose. Quickly, she gathered up her discarded clothing, the slack-jawed stage crew watching every move as she padded toward her tent to change for the next number.

He slowly became aware of the noises that surrounded him. A whispering, buzzing rise and fall. The drone of insects.

Or voices.

He struggled to remain in the blackness, but he couldn't fight hard enough against the current, and soon the pain returned.

But it was different this time.

Better.

"He needs quinine."

"Bet the Nips've got gallons of it in that storage shed on the other side of the camp. That and our Red Cross packages."

"Hey, you think they got our letters from home there too? Somebody has to have told our folks where we are by now."

"You're an idiot if you think the Japs have told anyone about us."

"It could happen. They made us fill out those postcards to send to our folks."

"Yeah, and they probably ended up at the bottom of the sea somewhere."

"That's too bad. Ol' Tanaka made me rewrite it three times. I finally put: 'Ma and Pa, I'm alive and well and enjoying my time with the yellow-bellied bees."

"What the hell?"

"You know…yellow-bellied bastards…but instead of bastards, I put bees. I knew my Pa would figure it out eventually."

"You're an idiot, do you know that?"

"Am not. It got past Tanaka—which is more than I can say for…Hey,

he's awake."

He blinked, once twice, then shivered, staring up at the faces that leaned over him.

"Welcome back!" one of the figures said, grinning.

He frowned, the pieces slowly filtering back into place. He counted heads quickly, then sagged when he realized everyone was present.

"We got tenko *in about twenty minutes. Think you can make it?"*

Tenko. *Roll call.*

He nodded, bracing his elbows beneath him in an effort to sit up.

"Not yet, not yet. Save your strength until it's time." A hand pushed him down. "I saved you some rice, but you'd better drink first."

A canteen was held to his lips and he greedily gulped the water, then lay back again, panting. Someone had wrapped his ribs, which helped, but his chest still stung each time he tried to breathe.

He lifted a hand to touch the bandage, then panicked when he realized that he didn't have his shirt.

Damn it! Someone had stolen his shirt…he needed…he had *to have…*

"Easy, easy! We got it here. Everything's safe and sound."

The tattered remains of the garment were thrust into his hands, and as he shivered against the racking chills, his fingers tunneled into his pocket. Only when he felt the fuzzy scrap of fabric, did he relax again.

Turning onto his side, he clutched his shirt against his chest, once again digging deep for the will to go on.

This couldn't be the end.

He wouldn't let it be the end.

Chapter Three

Rosemary Dodd surveyed the crowded dance floor and forced a smile to her lips. Five more minutes. Then her social obligations would be finished for the evening and she could gracefully bow out of the party and leave her new nurses to enjoy themselves.

And she had no doubts that they would "let their hair down" the minute she left. She well remembered her own welcoming party to the Philippines more than ten years ago. She'd been nervous and itching to make a good impression, yet eager to avail herself of the food and cocktails and the handsome servicemen who wanted nothing more than to draw her onto the dance floor.

Had she ever really been that young and carefree? It felt like a lifetime since then.

Grimacing, Rosemary took a sip of her martini—the same drink she'd been nursing for over an hour. She probably wasn't much older than most of the women who'd been placed in her command. But she felt eons ahead of them in experience. Worse yet, today marked a long-dreaded milestone.

December seventh. Her birthday.

At two o'clock in the afternoon, she'd turned forty—which, according to her mother, was the official death-knell of all things youthful. No man would want to marry her now. The chance for children was officially over. She was swiftly on her way to becoming withered and bitter. One of those women that other mothers would point to and whisper, "That's what will happen if you pursue a career rather than marriage."

Rosemary's father had been far more pragmatic in his views.

"Time to come home and stop gallivanting around, Rosie. Your mother and I aren't getting any younger, and we could use your help on the farm," he'd grumped.

Happy, happy birthday to me.

"Swell party."

Starting, Rosemary glanced up to find Lt. Gilhouley standing behind her.

"You think so?" she countered.

"Sure." His expression became wry. "But by the looks of that scowl, you aren't having a very good time."

She took another sip of her tepid martini before abandoning it on a nearby table. It was time to go home. Not to Nebraska, as her father wished, but to her officer's digs here in the Philippines. Turning forty might have been the official end to her parents' hopes of marriage and family in her future, but Rosemary couldn't imagine trading in her career for the limiting prospects of marital bliss.

"I'm not much in the mood for a party, I'm afraid."

His eyes—clear and blue as a Midwest summer sky—skimmed over her. "That's a shame. A person should always be in the mood for a party."

His expression was warm but unfathomable. Not for the first time, she wondered why he was seeking her company. And after this afternoon's outing, he was even more of an enigma. Young, tall, and lean, he looked like the perfect candidate for a recruitment poster. But if the rumors were true, he knew how to make the most of being sent to this backwater post. He had connections upon connections. If there was something you wanted, Gilhouley could probably get it for you.

So why had he volunteered to spend the afternoon with her? He'd led her to believe that he'd escorted her off-base at Alice's insistence, but when Rosemary had questioned her about it, Alice hadn't known anything about Gilhouley's invitation. Gilhouley had been acting on his own initiative, and for the life of her, Rosemary couldn't figure out why. Even if he thought to cultivate her as one of his connections, he knew she would never break the rules. Try as he might, he couldn't get so much as a tongue depressor from her dispensary unless he had all of the proper forms. In triplicate. Add to that, the unbelievable fact that her company had aroused him…

Her cheeks began to heat and she quickly turned away.

"I suppose we have you to thank for the grade-A champagne?" she said, studying the dance floor again in an effort to avoid his regard.

"I had no hand in furnishing the champagne," he said, affecting a wounded expression. "That came from Major Briggs in the quartermaster's office—something about trading it with the squibs for several pallets of toilet paper." Gilhouley grinned. "But I will take credit for the scotch."

Rosemary snorted. "Purchased through the proper channels, I'm sure."

"What would be the fun in that?"

A passing waiter arrived with a tray of new drinks. Gilhouley eyed her questioningly, but she shook her head.

"Ahh. I take it you're about to make your clandestine getaway," Gilhouley said, bending close to whisper next to her ear. At five-eleven, it wasn't often that Rosemary encountered a man who had to stoop to talk to her. "But surely you aren't planning to leave without dancing first."

Before she could muster a response, his hand settled low upon her waist, leading to the space in front of the military orchestra where eager-eyed nurses swayed in the arms of even more eager officers.

The last thing Rosemary wanted was to be seen waltzing with The Great Gilhouley. He had enough of a reputation as a ladies' man that tongues would probably wag if she were caught talking to him, let alone dancing. But as the music of a slow ballad twined around the room and Gilhouley drew her close with a broad hand, she found she didn't want to object. She couldn't remember the last time she'd been asked to dance with a partner who met her at eye level, let alone one who was taller than she was. So many times in the past, she'd been paired up with officers who were a few inches shorter and spent most of the time looking at her cleavage. But Gilhouley was showing admirable restraint, meeting her gaze with his own. His palm was firm at her back but not too familiar, the distance between them was friendly and not too intimate. If she'd wanted, she could have closed the space between them and tucked her head beneath his chin. But she pushed the thought away as soon as it came.

The music flowed around them. Ida Compton—a nurse who'd been in the Philippines since last spring—had volunteered to sing for the evening. The swing band—formed from soldiers on base—was as good as any Rosemary had ever heard on the radio.

In the past, Rosemary had always felt out of place at these soirees. Overtly aware of the invisible divide between her and the girls she'd led, she'd been afraid to truly enjoy herself. But tonight, she melted into Gilhouley's embrace. He cut a fine figure in his Army dress uniform. The heat of his body seeped into her palm and the spot on the waist where he held her. He smelled intriguingly male—aftershave and hair cream, tobacco and freshly laundered clothing. And for some reason, those scents, combined with the faint perfume of violets that came from the corsage she'd worn on her evening gown, were oh so enticing.

Closing her eyes, she allowed herself to surrender to the moment and push aside all of the "should's" and "must's". She felt suddenly feminine and girlish. Not the over-the-hill spinster career woman that her mother despaired she'd become.

When the song came to an end, she made a move to retreat, but Gilhouley held her in place, segueing into a quicker step as Benny Goodman gave way to Count Basie. Rosemary wasn't well acquainted with the jitterbug or the Lindy Hop, and she was grateful when he kept their movements reserved and befitting a woman in charge. Then another ballad, even slower than the first she'd danced with Gilhouley. And this time…this time she couldn't keep herself from moving in a little closer, and a little closer still, until, as she suspected, Gilhouley's chin brushed the top of her head.

They didn't speak. There was no need to speak. The music, the swaying of their bodies were all the conversation they needed, revealing more than she ever would have permitted herself to say aloud—and certainly much more than she would have ever let Gilhouley utter.

As the music drew to a close, she looked up, up, into those incredibly clear blue eyes, and saw something that she'd never seen in a man before. Wonder.

She stepped back and he let her go, following her to the table where she'd left her purse and her stole.

"I think it's time for me to call it a night," she said softly, her voice curiously husky.

"Mind if I go with you?"

"Suit yourself." But there was no vinegar to her tone as there might have been only a day earlier. Instead, her words held a hint of invitation.

Rosemary gathered her purse, allowing Gilhouley to settle her silken stole around her shoulders. Then she weaved her way through the tables surrounding the dance floor, Gilhouley following several paces behind, until she stepped out of the officers' club into the balmy evening.

She didn't think she could ever grow tired of the tropical nights. The breeze was cool against her skin, the faint scents of the sea and the flowers from the beds lining the walkway were welcome, especially after the heat and cigarette smoke of the dance floor.

She nodded toward the far field where the enlisted men were enjoying their own brand of entertainment. A makeshift amphitheater had been built on the parade grounds, complete with a raised stage at the far end. Even from this distance, she could hear the cheers and whistles.

"I'm surprised you deigned to come to our party, Gilhouley, when you could have been with that lot over there." She paused dramatically. "I hear they have a stripper."

She laughed when Gilhouley actually looked discomfited.

"And who told you that?"

"Oh, please. You know how scuttlebutt travels on base. I probably knew about the arrangements before the stripper did."

Gilhouley's chuckle was low and silken. "I should have realized. You're very well-connected with the disreputable element at Fort Stotsenberg yourself, Major."

"So why aren't you over there?"

He pretended to look shocked. "As if I would!"

"Of course you would. Every man on base was there for her opening act, even Brigadier General Bradmore. I was beginning to believe my girls were going to have to dance with each other. Why do you think I scheduled the party an hour later than usual?"

This time, his bark of laughter came straight from the gut. "You are a sly one, Rosemary."

She didn't chide him for addressing her so personally. She'd long ago realized that The Great Gilhouley did exactly what he wanted. And for some reason, despite being more than ten years her junior and beneath her in rank, he seemed comfortable in her company.

"So was she pretty?"

His brows rose to his hairline.

"Come on, Gilhouley, don't be coy. You were there too."

"And how could you possibly know that?"

"I know everything, remember?"

They reached the curb and he automatically took her elbow, even though she'd worn sensible shoes and was in no danger of catching her heel. But at the opposite side of the street, he maintained his gentle grip.

After a moment of silence, she prodded, "Was she pretty?"

"Built like a brick privy," he murmured.

"Is that good or bad? I've never understood that phrase."

His teeth flashed in the darkness. "Very, very good. She was… shall we say…handsomely endowed with all of womanhood's most desirable gifts."

"How much did she take off?"

"Rosemary!"

She laughed. "I'm curious. Despite what everyone thinks, I'm not a prude."

Rather than laughing with her, he paused, drawing her to a stop yards from her bungalow.

"I've never thought you were a prude, Rosemary." His voice slid through the darkness like the shiver of silk against bare flesh, startling her with its gentleness. "Just...cautious."

A frisson of something akin to fear skittered up her spine. "And what kind of scuttlebutt have you been listening to, Gilhouley?"

"No scuttlebutt. Merely an observation."

Her relief was so tangible she felt weak in the knees. The last thing she needed after all these years was for gossip to have followed her to the Philippines.

Gilhouley reached out to touch her cheek and she frowned at the unaccustomed intimacy of the gesture.

"I suppose with your nurses occupied at the officers' club, you'll be finishing off the last few hours of the night shift—despite the fact that you've already had a full day."

She stepped back, abruptly severing the contact and folding her arms in front of her. "Of course. It's nothing I haven't done before."

He nodded. "Then maybe you should get some rest before you head over."

"I will."

They closed the last few yards to her bungalow, but she hesitated at the end of the path, suddenly loath to leave Gilhouley's company. She wrapped her arms around her waist, staring out at the velvety darkness, the glowing street lamps. Even now, she could hear the faint cheers from the parade grounds.

"You're awfully pensive tonight."

Grimacing, she shot him a glance that was rife with apology. "Sorry. I received some mail from my parents. Three letters and at least a half ton of guilt."

"That's not completely uncommon, is it?"

She shrugged. "I don't know about other people's folks. Mine are loving, well-meaning but..."

Gilhouley waited patiently.

"A bit old-fashioned," she said finally.

"They don't approve of your being here?"

She snorted. "It depends on which one you ask. At first, my mother considered my decision to go into nursing as noble. I think she had lofty visions of her daughter floating through the wards dispensing thermometers for a few months before snagging herself a doctor."

"And that wasn't what happened."

"No," she murmured quietly. Too quietly. Before Gilhouley could pursue that line of questioning, she hurried to add, "My father on the other hand, was furious. As far as he is concerned, the only acceptable occupations for a woman are motherhood, teaching, and tending to one's parents. In his opinion, nursing was little better than prostitution. What well-bred woman would expose herself to so many unclothed men?" She pretended to shudder. "Horrors!"

"I take it that their views haven't changed much since then."

She shook her head. "The theme has been the same for years. In the past, they've taken turns trying to convince me to give it all up and come home. But lately, they've begun a concerted effort. They're getting older and they would like to have me closer to home."

"And what do you want to do?"

She supposed she should offer him a glib answer. She'd never seen him remain serious for more than a few minutes. And yet, here he stood, listening with the intensity of a priest in the confessional.

"I don't know. I..." She hesitated, not willing to admit that it was the milestone of her fortieth birthday which had caused the sudden discontent. "There's a part of me that knows I should probably go home. A good daughter would give up her career and care for her parents."

His mouth lifted in a slow grin. "But you're not a good daughter?"

"Evidently not. I love my career. I'm good at what I do, but..."

Again, he waited patiently, not pushing but letting her decide for herself how much she would confide.

"I don't know. Maybe I need a change of scenery, a new challenge." She gestured out into the darkness. "We all know there's a war coming. We can't stay out of things for much longer. The Japanese will probably cause some problems, but the real action will be in Europe. Maybe now's the time to make sure I get a front row seat."

He didn't move, but she sensed a sudden tension to his frame.

"Is that what you want to do?" he asked slowly.

She looked up, catching the way a muscle flicked in his jaw, and suddenly realized that things had changed. She wasn't sure when or how. But they'd changed.

"I don't know," she whispered.

He took a step toward her and the moonlight played over his angular features—the jut of his cheekbones, the square line of his jaw. He bent over her—and she couldn't deny the thrill of looking up, up, knowing that he was taller, broader in a way that made her feel small and feminine.

He was breathing hard as he lifted a finger, a single, square-tipped finger, and traced the line of her brow, her cheek, her jaw, before tipping her face up.

"Don't go, Rosemary. Don't go."

Then, as if it were the most natural thing in the world to do, he bent toward her, kissing her on one corner of her mouth, then the other, before settling softly, sweetly in the center.

She exhaled against him—a sound that was half sigh, half excitement. Then it was she who took a step forward, her palms resting at his waist, her lips parting to his caress.

And suddenly, as if they'd both been longing for this moment, passion flared between them. What had begun as a tender exploration suddenly exploded into a hunger that neither of them could contain.

Rosemary gripped the lapels of his uniform, holding him close, even as his own arms wrapped around her waist. His lips became hungry, demanding, his tongue sweeping into her mouth.

Drawing abruptly away, she urgently whispered, "Not here. Not where someone can see us."

Before Gilhouley could say something that might change her mind, she took his hand, drawing him toward her bungalow. She fumbled with the lock, finally unlatched it, then hurried inside, bringing Gilhouley with her.

* * *

John slid out of the truck, shutting the door behind him with a rusty squeak and a bang. Standing for a moment, with his fingertips tucked in his pockets, he surveyed the grassy field in front of him.

According to the instructions he'd been given at the gate, this was the area normally reserved for drills and physical training. But for tonight, the area had been transformed into a makeshift amphitheater. Soldiers crowded close on chairs and benches. Some sat, some stood. All of them were shouting and whistling.

Intrigued by what had filled them with such excitement, he edged his way around a cluster of men—boys, really—who tumbled into the aisles and stood whooping.

As soon as the stage loomed into view, John halted in his tracks, his own eyes widening.

A woman stood poised near the microphone—one of the most beautiful women that John had ever seen. She was short and voluptuous, with fiery red hair and pale skin made even more dramatic by the pool of the spotlight. She wore what appeared to be an Army dress tunic, but it had been tailored to mold to her body, enhancing full breasts, a slim waist, and curvaceous hips.

Dear God in heaven.

He felt a prickling of his skin followed by a quick heat. Frowning, he ducked into the shadows as he realized he was blushing. *Blushing.* A grown man who was not completely innocent of the ways of the world.

But the sensation didn't ease. Indeed, it intensified as she began to finger the buttons of her jacket, loosening them one by one. Turning her back to her audience, she offered a come-hither smile over her shoulder, opening one side of her jacket, closing it, opening the other side, closing it.

When she faced the audience again, her jacket was shut, but

barely, leaving the tiniest peek of silken tap pants and a lacy corselet.

She continued to taunt and tease her audience, turning this way and that, baring a shoulder, a creamy expanse of hip. Her routine was overtly sensual, her song bawdy. But her routine left the soldiers wanting more and more, until finally, she clasped the curtain, held it in front of her breasts, and threw the jacket out into the audience.

The soldiers' cheers became a roar. A dozen men in the first few rows fought over her costume, so she laughed—an expression of such joy that John felt a frisson of something akin to wonder skitter down his spine. Then, with a final wave, she called out, "So long, boys! It's been a pleasure!"

Amid the tide of soldiers jumping to their feet, John eased out of the fracas again and made his way toward the grassy expanse were a pair of MP's stood casually smoking.

"Excuse me. I've been sent to pick up—" John dug into his pocket to withdraw a scrap of paper, "—Glory O'Halloran."

The two men exchanged glances.

"Lucky you," one of the men murmured before gesturing to a set of canvas tents located near the rear of the stage. "Second one on the left."

John nodded and strode in that direction. The quicker he picked up his employer's guest, the quicker he could be on his way back to the plantation again.

But even as he assured himself of the validity of his errand, that he had every right to be mingling among the serviceman gathered for the show, he couldn't push away the feeling that he'd somehow encroached on a private exchange between the soldiers and that… that…woman.

Dear God, she'd been stripping in front of thousands. So why did *he* feel like a Peeping Tom?

He pushed his way through the performers milling around the rear of the stage. Again, he wondered whom Milton Wilmington had invited to stay at the Big House. It was the first time John had ever known him to make such arrangements. Even the staff had been mystified. For days, they'd been frantically cooking and cleaning lest someone akin to royalty showed up. They'd known as little as John. A friend of a friend had been invited to stay. How long the visit would last would be determined at a later date. John hadn't even had a name to pin to the guest until this morning when a wire had arrived to let him know when and where to arrange the pickup.

Glory B. O'Halloran.

Whoever she was, she must be damned important for Milton to go to this much fuss and expense.

Distantly, he could hear the throaty, crooning voice of a male quartet singing *You Made Me Love You.* The crowd of men had grown quieter—as if the melancholy tune had brought to mind memories of home.

John approached the tent, then stood indecisively. How was a person supposed to knock?

At a loss, he finally wrapped his knuckles against the flap, then grimaced at the ineffectual rustling noise.

"Excuse me? I'm looking for Glory O'Halloran?" he called out, feeling like an absolute fool. If only there'd been someone else he could have sent to retrieve the woman. "I'm here to pick her up."

"Come on in."

Amid the swell of muted trumpets from the accompanying military band, John ducked into the tent, following the husky tones of the woman's call.

The space was surprisingly neat. With the chaos outside, he'd expected to see costumes and makeup scattered around the small confines. Instead, a trunk and two suitcases were stacked near the flap. A dressing table with its mirror had already been cleared and wiped clean.

Seeing no one, he called out, "Miss O'Halloran?"

"I'll be with you in a minute. Take a seat if you want."

His eyes skipped to a changing screen in the far corner, then to the folding chairs in the center of the tent.

Realizing that the woman he'd come to collect was probably in a state of undress, he debated whether or not to go outside again, but before he could come up with a subtle exit strategy, a figure stepped from behind the screen.

John felt his pulse suddenly slam against his temples, then lower, much lower.

It was the woman.

The person who…

The stripper.

Mother of God.

"Can you hand me my shoes?"

She gestured to a pair of heels resting on top of the luggage, even as she settled into one of the folding chairs. As she bent to smooth her hose, he was afforded a perfect view of the valley between her ample breasts.

He jerked his gaze away, reaching for her footwear. In his haste, one of them tumbled to the ground and he was forced to bend to scoop it up. The red shoe with its sling back and open toe was incredibly small in his hand. Incredibly feminine.

Clearing his throat, he nearly tossed them into her lap, but she didn't appear to notice his awkwardness.

"Thanks." She grinned up at him. "I take it you're my ride?"

Her accent was so patently American, flat vowels, a slight drawl. He shouldn't have been surprised. He was on an American military base, after all. But it had been a long time since he'd heard such tones from a woman.

The image of Sister Mary Francis seeped into his brain, but he quickly pushed it away. Not now. Not here.

"As soon as you're ready…" He gestured to the tent flap, deciding he'd wait outside after all.

"I'm ready now. Could you help me with my luggage?"

"Yes, ma'am."

She shot him a wide grin. "Call me Glory Bee—spelled B-double-E. The only ma'am I've ever known was my grandmother."

She jumped to her feet, grabbing a pocketbook from the table, then the smaller suitcase. When she would have reached for the other pieces of luggage, he pushed her hands aside.

"I'll get those."

She flashed him a quick smile, and it was at that moment that he realized she was young. Very, very young. What was even more disconcerting was that she was completely at odds to the sensual siren who'd abandoned the stage.

John slung the trunk over his back, then grabbed the handle of the smaller suitcase.

"Oh, dear," she said in open dismay. "Are you sure you don't want me to get you some help? I'm notoriously prone to over-packing."

"No, ma'am...Miss O'Halloran. I'm fine. The truck isn't far."

She flashed him a brilliant smile. "Swell!"

Preceding him out of the tent, she held up the flap for him, then fell into step as soon as he'd passed through.

"I hope I haven't inconvenienced you," she said, her heels sinking awkwardly in the grass.

John angled their path toward the walkway.

"Oh, thank you." She exhaled a deep breath. "I should have known better than to wear heels, but I'm expected to maintain appearances, you know."

John didn't have a clue what she was talking about, but he nodded as if he did.

"Is it far?"

"Just a few more yards."

She laughed, the sound girlish and so at odds with her surroundings that John nearly stopped in his tracks.

"No, I meant the plantation. Is the plantation far from here?"

John slowed as they neared the truck. He swung the trunk into the back bed, then quickly followed with the suitcase.

"No, not far. About twenty minutes to a half-hour."

A brief twinge of disappointment crossed her features, but was gone so quickly, he wondered if he'd imagined the flicker of weariness.

He held open her door and she slid inside with what sounded like a sigh. Once she'd been safely stowed in the cab, John quickly tied her cases down with a piece of rope. The roads around the plantation were notoriously bad, and he didn't want to take a midnight scavenger hunt for this woman's luggage if they hit a particularly nasty pothole.

As he worked, he whistled softly to himself in an effort to rid his mind of the image of Glory Bee O'Halloran on stage, her shapely legs bared. The roundness of her shoulder. The jut of her hip. Scrambling, he tried to think of something—anything—to say during their long drive to the plantation.

But as soon as he slid into place behind the wheel, he realized that he needn't have bothered.

Glory Bee O'Halloran was fast asleep.

* * *

As soon as the door closed behind them, Rosemary turned to face Gilhouley. In the velvety darkness, he seemed even taller, leaner than before. From his stance, it was clear that he wasn't sure what to expect. For all he knew, the brief respite might have caused her to change her mind about…

About what? What exactly was happening here? Rosemary couldn't have said. She didn't know the precise moment when they shifted from casual friendship to…to what? Even at that point she was at a loss to explain. She only knew that for the longest time, she'd harbored a loneliness within her that had sapped her of energy and joy. And for the first time, she felt a spark of hope, of vitality, of pure feminine awareness. She acknowledged that she wasn't being entirely rational, and that ideally any sort of relationship with Gilhouley could only lead to trouble. But even that hint of danger was infinitely attractive.

She stepped toward him, closing the distance between them. Without a word, she took off his hat and set it on the side table. With dancing fingers, she touched his hair, its fire a muted glow in the darkness. He kept it military short, especially at the sides and back, and the fine hairs were downy soft, tickling the sensitive pads of her fingertips.

As if she were a blind woman, she traced the jut of his brow, the high cheekbones, the line of his jaw. Then his mouth. His beautiful, expressive mouth.

When he bent to take her lips with his own, there was no resistance. Merely an acceptance. An acknowledgement that—no matter what the future might bring—this moment was right. This kiss was right.

Although barely a hairsbreadth separated them, Gilhouley's arms slid around her waist, drawing her against him, thigh to thigh, hip to hip. And she reveled in the strength of him, the angles and planes that proved the perfect counterpoint to her softness.

Sliding her arms around his neck, she lifted on tiptoe so that their kiss could deepen. And with each kiss, each stroke of his hand across her back, her hip, the need within her increased as powerfully as her wonder. How could this be happening?

Breaking away, she gulped for air. He grew still against her, willing to let her dictate the terms of their time together, whether she stopped things now or allowed them to continue. But she was already past the point of no return. She felt as if she'd been lost in a desert of want and had suddenly been offered an oasis that was beyond anything she could have ever dreamed possible. She couldn't have stepped away for anything.

With trembling fingers, she began to unbutton his tunic, sliding it from his shoulders where it fell into a heap on the floor. Without pausing, she worked at the knot of his tie. By the time she reached for the buttons of his shirt, he was helping her, shrugging free, then lifting his undershirt up and away in one swoop.

He pulled her close again, the warmth of his bare chest seeping through the satin of her evening gown. As a nurse, she'd seen her fair share of unclothed men. She'd even had a lover, once, so long ago. But none of that could have prepared her for the strength of Gilhouley's body, the sculpted beauty of his musculature. Again, he bent for a kiss, and she hungrily answered the slant of his mouth, the thrust of his tongue. But her hands continued their questing path, tracing the arc of his ribs, the ridges of his abdomen. Then lower still, caressing the hard length shielded only by the fabric of his trousers.

Gilhouley gasped against her, and the sound was like a shot of adrenalin to her system. He wanted *her.* Rosemary Dodd.

She fumbled with his belt, then the button at his waist. But this time, Gilhouley answered with his own foray, his fingers finding the tiny hooks and eyes of her evening gown, then the button of the half-slip beneath, dispatching them with alarming skill, until they fell to the floor in a whoosh of satin and taffeta and she stood before him in little more than her merry widow, tap pants, and silk stockings.

Rosemary opened her eyes in time to see his rich satisfaction, and felt a jolt of her own pride. *Not bad for a forty-year-old broad*, she had the wherewithal to think. But only for a moment. Because Gilhouley was already tugging loose the fasteners to her garter, then began working at the busk of her corselet.

Before he could finish, she wriggled free, taking his hand and leading him from the tiny living room to the bedroom beyond. She'd left a lamp on at her dressing table and the soft glow spilled into the corners with a golden glow.

Once at the bed, she sat on the edge, rolling down the first stocking and then throwing it over the end of the footboard. Within seconds, the other followed. Then she finished unfastening her merry widow and draped it on a chair. The silken tap pants were held with a single button, and it was an easy enough matter to free the fastener, dropping the last of her scanties before climbing into the bed and pulling the covers around her waist.

Gilhouley wasted no time in ridding himself of his own shoes and socks, then pushed his pants and underwear to the ground in a single movement. Then with a grin that was pure Gilhouley, he slid into the bed beside her.

No words were needed or exchanged, just sighs of pleasure and ardent murmurs as Gilhouley drew her close, their skin seeing to meld together, their bodies fitting in such a way that could only be divine. And with each stroke, each nudge, each kiss and caress, their passion grew to a fever pitch that could no longer be contained.

When he settled above her, Rosemary moaned at the delicious weight of him, her body opening up, her hips settling into position. And when she felt the first intimate nudge, she wrapped her legs around him, urging him to fill her aching void, knowing that if he didn't, she would expire on the spot.

And then, he was thrusting into her, plunging deep, causing her to grip his shoulders so tightly her nails dug into his skin. A groan of pleasure burst from her lips, once, twice, as he continued to thrust over and over again, stoking the fires within her until she cried out with her release, her body pounding in echo to his own as with one final plunge, he froze, trembling, his body shuddering with his climax.

Later, much later, she lay with her back to his chest, his body spooned against hers. She was drained, but more content than she could ever remember being. For the first time, she felt cherished and protected. Safe.

"I have to go to the hospital sometime soon," she whispered against her sudden weariness.

"Can it wait an hour?" he asked, his lips against her shoulder.

"Mmm," she answered sleepily, nodding against the pillow. She hadn't had a good night's rest in weeks, but she felt as if she could sleep for a month.

"I'll wake you in time." Gilhouley said against her ear, his voice low and deep.

"Mmm."

She was ready to surrender completely when a sudden thought jarred her back into wakefulness. "Gilhouley?"

"Hmm?"

"What's your first name?"

She felt him smile against her temple.

"Riley. Riley Patrick Gilhouley."

"Riley," she whispered, her own mouth tipping in pleasure.

Then she fell fast asleep.

A hand touched his shoulder, and he was instantly awake.

"Take this," a voice whispered.

Squinting, he saw that he was being given a small, white pill.

"What is it?"

"Quinine."

"How...?"

"Kilgore had work detail in the garden all week. One of the kids from the village snuck up beside him and asked about you."

"About me?"

"Yeah. Kilgore said you were down with malaria and the kid ran off. He didn't think any more about it until the kid showed up again today and handed him this." He held up a small bottle. When he shook it, the pills inside barely rattled because it was nearly full.

Dear God, a full bottle of quinine.

"Now take the goddamn pill before somebody sees what we've got."

He quickly slid the pill onto his tongue, then took a swig from the canteen. Settling back on his pallet, he closed his eyes and prayed the medicine would work quickly.

"Oh, there's one more thing."

He blinked, focusing on the darker shape of his friend.

"The kid that gave the quinine to Kilgore said to tell you the medicine's a gift from the padre."

"What?"

"That's word for word what Kilgore told me. The medicine's a gift from

the padre."

For the first time in years, he felt a spark of hope. Just a spark. But as it caught hold in his chest, a low laugh burst from his throat.

"Hey, that means something to you?"

"Yeah. Yeah, that means something. To all of us."

It meant help could be near.

Chapter Four

At first, John had been relieved that the redheaded woman—Glory Bee?—had fallen asleep. As long as she was out, he didn't have to worry about carrying on a conversation. He'd never been much good at small talk. And with darkness pressing in on the windows of the truck, he wouldn't have the usual subjects of the weather or the surroundings to pass the time. That would leave politics or exchanging personal tidbits, and he'd rather have his fingernails pulled out one by one.

So he'd driven as carefully as he could, avoiding the potholes and slowing down for ruts and washed out roads so that the American wouldn't be disturbed. But what he hadn't counted on was the way the swaying of the truck altered her position. She'd started with her head tucked against the window, but as the truck bounced and shuddered and swayed, she'd begun to lean to the left, farther and farther, until she hovered in mid-air. Then suddenly, she sagged sideways, drawing her legs up onto the seat and resting her head on his thigh.

"Hell," he muttered to himself as she rooted around for a bit, then fell back into a deep sleep. What was he supposed to do now?

A heat filled his cheeks and he was grateful for the masking darkness. John hesitated for a few minutes, then tentatively prodded her with a finger.

"Miss?"

The woman offered no response, so he shook her ever

so slightly.

"Miss…Glory Bee?"

This time, she muttered something unintelligible. But rather than moving back to her original position, she moved her head, seeking a more comfortable position, then slid her hand beneath her cheek, thereby gripping his inner thigh.

Startled, John nearly drove off the edge of the road. Swearing, he centered the vehicle in the narrow lane again and took a deep breath. "Bloody, bloody hell," he muttered to himself.

Again, he debated what to do, but since the woman was so exhausted, he feared that if he tried to wake her, she might begin rooting around in his lap again and…

So he tried to keep his mind away from the woman altogether. He counted to one hundred—in English, French, and Mandarin. Then he began to hum tunes, recite poems, and yes, even fell back on the all-too-familiar scriptures. All to no avail. He couldn't avoid the warmth of her skin seeping into his.

Sighing, he let her sleep, fearing that waking her might prove more embarrassing for them both. But when he turned into the washboard road leading to the plantation, he knew that he was going to have to do something.

In the end, the decision was taken from him. As soon as he turned off the motor in the Wilmot's drive, she woke, lifted upright and stretched, apparently unaware of the havoc that she had caused John for the entire journey.

"Wow," she said in awed tones as she peered through the side window. From this vantage point, the house was bathed in moonlight, so much so that the decorative wrought iron railings and scrollwork looked like icing on a wedding cake. "This is some place. Wilmot must be rolling in dough."

Her frankness caught John by surprise and he couldn't help laughing.

Realizing her mistake, she covered her mouth with her hands. "I shouldn't have said that, right?" She sighed. "Sorry. I should be on my best behavior, with Wilmot being your friend and all."

"Not friend. Boss. I'm Wilmot's foreman."

Her brows rose. "Really? Jeepers. Then I've really stuck my foot in it, haven't I?"

She looked so honestly contrite, and that expression, combined with her tousled red hair and pink cheeks, gave her the appearance of being little more than a girl. But the figure outlined by her simple dress was anything but girlish.

"I'm Glory Bee O'Halloran," she said holding out a hand. "Glory B—"

"Double 'E'," he supplied.

She flushed. "That's right. I already introduced myself. Sorry. Between the boat ride here and the scramble of rehearsals, I've grown a bit scatterbrained, but I promise I'm not usually like this." She frowned. "Well, not always."

When she finished speaking, she regarded John with an expectant look. It took a few seconds before he realized that he hadn't supplied his own name.

"I'm John. John Macklin."

He shook her hand, one that was so tiny and slim, he feared he might crush her. But she was stronger than she looked, returning the gesture with a firm grip.

When he spoke, her eyes narrowed thoughtfully. "You're not from around here, are you? You sound…I don't know. British or—"

"New Zealand. I was born in New Zealand."

Her smile lit up her whole face. "Lordy, how I love to listen to you fellows talk. I'm from Virginia, myself, and I swear most folk there sound like they've got a mouthful of marbles. But y'all… well, there's a lilt to your speech like a whippoorwill first thing in the morning."

John's mouth dropped. He wasn't sure how he was supposed to respond to that, but Glory Bee didn't require a comment.

"Have you lived here long? In the Philippines?"

"A couple of years."

"And before that?"

He hesitated before supplying, "China."

She whistled softly, her lips forming a perfect bow that John felt deep in his gut. "You've seen quite a bit of the world, haven't you?"

"I suppose so."

"This is the first time I've been more than fifty miles from my home town. I'm not quite certain if I like all that traveling yet. Heaven only knows I'm not a good sailor."

Before John could think of a suitable reply, she twisted in her seat and opened the truck door, then slid to the ground. John followed more slowly, frowning when the front door remained closed. He'd left specific instructions to Kako and Miyoki to stay up in order to meet their new guest, but they had apparently misunderstood and gone home.

That meant he was going to have to make sure that Miss Glory Bee O'Halloran had been made comfortable for the evening.

Irritated at the change in plans, John quickly untied the ropes holding her luggage in place and hefted the bags free.

"If you can open the front door for me, I'll show you inside."

Glory Bee grabbed her purse and her overnight case and went up the shallow steps to the ornate double doors. Twisting one of the knobs, she stepped into the entry hall, where she paused.

Setting her trunk on the ground, he flipped the switch to the chandelier overhead, immediately flooding the room with twinkling star-like glints of brightness as the crystals shimmered in the breeze blowing in from the doorway.

"Here, on the main floor, there's a formal sitting room—" he gestured to the right where a sunken room had been decorated in sleek, modern lines and art deco furniture. Pointing the opposite direction, he said, "Through there is the dining room and the sun room. He pointed ahead of him. "Straight through there's another set of doors leading out to the pool and the courtyard. To the left is the kitchen, to the right is Wilmot's study. He has a fair collection of books should you need something to read in order to pass the time. I'm sure Mr. Wilmot wouldn't mind, but you'll have to ask Kako for the key. Since the room holds his business files, it's kept locked."

"Will the Wilmots be coming to the Philippines any time soon?"

She was nervous at the prospect, so he quickly reassured her with, "No. They've decided to remain in England. With London being hard-hit and U-boats prowling the Atlantic, they didn't think it would be wise to travel."

Although the house was quiet, John called out, "Hello? Kako? Miyoki?" There was no answer, no sound at all other than the rustling of the palm trees outside. He motioned for Glory Bee to precede him up the stairs. "There's a staff of seven who come and go in the house, including me. There might be a language barrier with some of them. Kako and Miyoki are in charge of the Big House, for the most part. They're Japanese, but they speak passable English. The others—a couple of maids, an errand boy, and the gardener, are Filipino with only limited English. If you have any problems communicating with any of them, feel free to send for me."

"And where do you stay?"

"I've got a little place opposite the house." He gestured in the direction they'd just come. "I spend most of the daylight hours in the fields, but you can send a message or leave a note under the door if you want."

"Thanks."

The staircase swooped up, up, in a semicircle. Once at the top, John nodded to the right. "The Wilmots' rooms are in that direction. You'll be staying in the visitor's wing to the left."

He pointed to the first door. Stepping inside, he set her baggage on the ground and flipped on the light. "Naturally, if the room isn't to your liking, there are plenty of others you can choose from."

Glory Bee stepped inside. As she gazed around the room, her eyes grew huge and her mouth dropped into a perfect "O".

"No, no," she breathed. "This will be fine." Then, as if she couldn't contain herself, she blurted, "Holy, Moses! Would you look at that bed!"

John laughed. He couldn't help himself. The bed was indeed a sight, large enough for a small army and swathed completely in pink—pink bed skirt, pink satin coverlet, mountains of pink ruffled pillows, and yards and yards of pink mosquito netting that draped from the towering canopy.

"Make sure you put the mosquito netting over you at night," John said. He strode to the far end of the room and opened another door. "There are drawers and closet space here for you."

He stepped into the hall again and she obediently followed. "The bathroom is here. Since there are no other guests, you'll have it to yourself. I'm sure Kako and Miyoki have left towels and soap out for you." He continued midway down the hall to another small landing and gestured down a narrow set of stairs. "If you go down here, you'll end up in the kitchen."

As if on cue, the unmistakable sound of a rumbling stomach punctuated the silence.

Glory Bee laughed in embarrassment, pressing a hand to her waist. "Sorry."

John frowned. "How long has it been since you've eaten?"

"Breakfast," she said ruefully. "I didn't have time before the show."

John sighed. Kako and Miyoki were supposed to have remained at the house until Miss O'Halloran had arrived so that they could give her the tour and then offer her something to eat.

Motioning for Miss O'Halloran to follow, he went down the steps, ducking through the low arch, and stepped into the kitchen beyond. He flipped on the lights, and was immediately rewarded with a glare that reflected off the white tile floors, glossy cabinets, and a huge farmer's table surrounded by straight-back chairs.

Miss O'Halloran seemed entranced by the room. Her fingers trailed over the counters as she passed a wall of windows that made the space sunny and bright during the day. Her eyes widened as she noted every modern convenience—a huge gas stove and a refrigerator as big as a closet. There were freestanding mixers, blenders, and a small army of electric toasters. There had been times when as many as thirty guests and family members had been housed at the plantation and the kitchen had supplied meals 'round the clock. But tonight, the range was quiet and the hum of the refrigerator was overly loud.

John had thought that Kako might have set out a plate for their guest, but the table and counters were empty. Yanking open the refrigerator, he found sliced meats and cheeses, glass containers of fresh vegetables, cold roast chicken, eggs, milk, and butter, pies, pastries, and fruit suspended in golden syrup—but no plate left for Miss O'Halloran.

At a loss, John finally motioned to the contents. "Feel free to make yourself at home. There's bread in the breadbox and tinned foods in the cupboard. If you need anything and can't find it, Kako can help you in the morning."

Now that the tour was finished, John found himself suddenly eager to leave. The darkness pressing in on the windows made the room feel smaller than it actually was and the atmosphere much too intimate.

He touched a finger to the brim of his hat, realizing too late that he probably should have removed it altogether upon coming into the house. "I'll leave you to settle in."

He'd taken only a few steps when Glory called out, "John?"

He turned at the door to the hallway, his brows lifting questioningly.

Glory Bee wrung her hands together, indecisive about what she wanted to say, but she finally asked, "Have you eaten? I-I mean I really would welcome your company…at least until I can get the feel for things and…if you'd care to join me…"

John felt something inside him melt. Glory Bee might have traveled thousands of miles to reach her destination, but now that she was here, she wasn't entirely sure of herself.

But he couldn't allow the lines between them to blur. She was an invited guest at the plantation. He was only a hired hand.

"Sorry. I've got some accounts to go over and…"

She flushed, embarrassed. Obviously, she'd interpreted his words for what they were, a hastily contrived excuse.

"Of course. I pulled you away from your work, didn't I?" She held her hands together, fingers entwined in an unconsciously meek pose. "Thank you. For all your help."

Again, he touched a finger to the brim of his hat. "Good night, Miss O'Halloran."

Anxious to put as much space between them as possible, he strode into the hall. He'd taken only a few steps before something pricked at his conscience. Swearing softly under his breath, he returned to the kitchen—and for one split second, he caught Glory Bee O'Halloran with her features naked and unguarded.

Afraid.

And oh, so alone.

Just as quickly, she pasted a quick smile on her face. One that didn't entirely dispel the shadows in her eyes.

"On second thought, Miss O'Halloran. I'd be happy to share a quick bite with you. But, I need to wash up first."

This time, when she smiled at him, her expression contained the pure brightness of the sun. And her eyes…a man could get sucked into the deep pansy-blue depths.

"Thank you, Mr. Macklin. I would deeply appreciate your company."

* * *

Since John had returned to his own house to wash, Glory Bee took the opportunity to change herself. Stripping from her heels and hose, her dress, and the much-hated girdle, she took a quick bath, combed her wet hair, then threw on a loose, flowing nightdress and an embroidered robe.

As she hurried down the staircase, she was suddenly struck with the fact that John might be appalled by her state of undress. But after months of worrying about what she wore, how she talked, and who saw her with whom, she decided she really didn't care. She'd entertained men in her dressing room wearing far less than she had on now. And she would bet money that John had watched her strip at the show, so he'd probably seen her in less as well.

The marble floors felt cool against her feet as she padded into the kitchen. Yanking open the refrigerator, her jaw dropped at the bounty hidden inside. Lordy, she could have fed the army at Stotsenberg and not put a dent in the assortment. But after a hard day and the vagaries of her stomach, she longed for something simple and familiar.

Taking eggs, butter, cheese and vegetables, she began to make the fixings for omelets. If the truth were told, she was a horrible cook—a legacy from a mother who drank her meals from a bottle, no doubt. But she could crack and cook eggs and make a mean Bloody Mary.

She was scooping chopped peppers and onions into a bowl of frothy eggs when she heard the front door open and heavy footfalls on the marble floors.

"I'm in the kitchen!" she shouted, twisting to turn on the closest burner.

There was a moment's hesitation, then John appeared in the doorway.

He stood with his hat in his hand, his hair still damp and combed away from a side part so meticulously, she could still see the little furrows left by the tines of his comb. He filled the doorway. The effect wasn't caused so much by his height or the width of his shoulders. No, there was something about the man, something compelling and frightening at the same time. His manner was quiet and watchful, as if he weren't entirely comfortable or trusting of his situation, as if he were constantly on his guard.

"You're just in time." She motioned to the copper pans hanging from a rack over the kitchen table. "Could you hand me one of those frying pans?" she asked. In her bare feet, it had been almost impossible to reach them herself.

John had no trouble whatsoever. He was a tall man, an inch or two above six feet. As he moved, the light glinted in the flecks of gray visible in his dark hair. His arms were so long, he could extend the pan to her without taking a step.

"How tall are you?" she asked. Then waved aside any answer he made. "Don't answer that. I suppose that falls beneath the *personal* line of questioning, and I have a bad habit of asking too many personal questions. Michael is constantly telling me—"

She broke off suddenly, realizing that part of the bargain for her living arrangements here in the Philippines included ensuring that no one would ever connect her to Michael Griffin, Senator from The Great State of Texas.

She grimaced, dumping the egg mixture into the pan. "Never mind. I hope you like eggs. I'm not much of a cook, but I can make an omelet if I'm hungry enough." She pointed to the refrigerator. "Why don't you look in there and scare up a few things to go along with our meal?"

As John bent to gaze into the refrigerator, she searched through drawers, finally finding a small linen tablecloth and flatware. From the upper cupboards, she took out plates, glasses, cups and saucers. In the breadbox was a beautiful loaf, which she cut into thick slices that made her mouth water. If she had one weakness, it was bread slathered in butter, and since becoming pregnant, she'd craved it more than ever.

Within minutes she'd transferred the fat omelet to a serving plate. She cut it in two and carried it to the table as well where John had also placed a pitcher of orange juice, a bottle of milk, a crock of butter, a jar of jam, and a cheese keeper with a wedge of white cheese.

"We have a veritable feast!" Glory Bee exclaimed as she surveyed the results of their impromptu meal. "Sit, sit."

But John remained standing, one square hand resting on the back of the chair until she'd taken her own seat, then he settled into place.

Through sheer habit, she folded her hands together, cast her eyes skyward and hurriedly offered, "Good God, thank you for the toast and jam, thank you for the eggs and SPAM. Amen."

The prayer was a carry-over from her youth and had become more a mindless tradition than real grace. It wasn't until she caught John's hand moving in a quick genuflection that she realized her actions might be construed as blasphemous by a true churchgoer.

"I'm sorry. Would you like to offer some words yourself?"

"No. Thank you." He seemed embarrassed that she'd caught him.

"You're sure?"

He nodded.

She transferred his portion of the omelet onto his plate, then did the same with her own. "Have you worked here long, Mr. Macklin?"

"John, please." He took a careful bite of his food, then seemed to like it well enough, because he began eating with the enthusiasm of a hungry man. "No. I've only been here a little more than a year."

"What do they grow here on the plantation?"

"Sugar cane."

"I see."

She couldn't think of anything else to ask without becoming personal again, so she followed John's example, centering her attention on her food.

During her journey, she'd had a hard time keeping anything down, and she'd begun to fear that her illness was not due to the rocking of the ship, but her pregnancy. But now that she was finding her "land legs," she was discovering that her appetite was returning with a vengeance. She finished her omelet without so much as a grumble of protest, then moved on to the bread, fruit, and cheese. Then, after a drink of juice and milk, she finished a second slice of bread.

She couldn't remember a time when food had ever tasted so good. The eggs were soothing and savory, the fruit—she'd never known fruit to taste so bright and fresh. And the bread…

If John hadn't settled back in his chair and begun to watch her with amusement, she probably would have polished off the entire loaf.

Catching his regard, she covered her mouth with her hand saying, "You must think I'm a horrible pig. But I spent the entire sea voyage with my head over the rail."

To her amazement, John's lips spread into a slow grin, his eyes losing their turbulent sheen as they sparkled in amusement.

"I'm glad something finally tasted good."

For a moment, silence pooled between them, thick and warm and sticky with her curiosity. But while she'd been forthcoming about herself, he'd remained strictly private.

As if sensing the questions she wanted to ask, John stood and reached for his hat.

"Thank you for the meal. Don't worry about cleaning up. Kako and Miyoki will see to it when they come in."

Then, with a nod in her direction, he left.

But this time, the silence that swirled in his wake wasn't nearly as unsettling as it had an hour before.

* * *

As soon as he'd stepped into the hall, John paused, turning to regard the swinging door to the kitchen as it slapped into place. For several long minutes, he stood still, listening to the muted noises coming from the kitchen—the clink of cutlery, the snap of the refrigerator door. Despite what he'd said, Glory Bee had felt the need to clean up after herself, which he found more endearing than he would have believed possible. Wilmot's guests didn't normally trouble themselves with tidying up.

But then...Glory Bee O'Halloran was clearly not one of Wilmot's normal guests. A friend of a friend, John had been told, and that phrase somehow took on new meaning.

Shrugging away the tendrils of curiosity, John jammed his hat over his head and strode toward the front door. Slowed. Paused.

Something needled its way into his consciousness, pushing aside the warm echoes of Glory Bee's laughter. Turning, he frowned, searching the shadows for the reason for his disquiet. And then he saw it. The door to Wilmot's study—one that was nearly always left locked—was ajar.

Moving as quietly as he could, John crept toward the door. Reaching inside with his hand, he flipped on the light then burst inside.

But the room was empty. The books and ledgers were

undisturbed, the blotter cleared and ready for its owner to return.

Deciding he would have to mention to Kako that she needed to be more careful when she cleaned the room next time, John turned to leave. His hand was on the light switch, his body halfway out the door, when his eyes fell on the radio that Wilmot used to communicate with the other plantation owners in the area.

The hackles rose at his nape.

The radio had been smashed. Broken pieces of metal and vacuum tubes were scattered over the rich wool rug. In the midst of the rubble lay a shiny new ball-peen hammer.

* * *

Rosemary looked so peaceful that Gilhouley warred with his conscience before waking her. In the end, he dipped to kiss her bare shoulder, startling her out of her slumber.

As much as he would have loved to let her sleep—or spend the next hour or two with her in bed—he knew that it was important to her to fulfill her duty as she'd planned.

"It's ten-thirty," he whispered against her ear.

She sighed in regret, but didn't complain.

Turning onto her back, she reached out to pull him close, kissing him with such sweetness that it was hard to remember that if he was going to make a go of things with Rosemary, he couldn't make too many demands. Not yet. Not when things were so new. Instinctively, he sensed that if anything infringed on Rosemary's work at this early stage, he wouldn't be given another chance.

When she rolled away and frowned at the clock, he balled his hands into fists to keep from pulling her back again.

"I've drawn you a bath and set out a fresh uniform on a hanger behind the bathroom door. I don't know if I got everything, but at least the basics are there." Unable to stop himself, he brushed the tousled waves of her hair away from her brow, her cheek. He loved her hair, the baby-fine texture and the way the heat made it curl into ringlets at her nape when the weather grew muggy. And the color.

The color was rich and golden like a field of ripening wheat.

"Are you a mirage?" she asked, stroking his cheek.

He turned and quickly pressed a kiss to her palm. "If so, I'm a piss-poor one at that."

She shook her head. "I wish I could stay," she whispered with patent regret.

Her words were enough to reassure him that she felt no regrets.

"Tonight then?" he whispered. "I've got to go to Clark Field in the morning for an article Brigadier General Bradmore wants me to write for *Stars and Stripes*. I've been asked to sit in on a pilot briefing, then a buddy invited me to spend a few hours in the tower so I can see how they handle the flyboys. But I should be back by six."

She nodded. "I'll be off by eight at the latest, then I've got the next three days free."

He grinned. "Come home and take a nap as soon as you're off. I'll sneak in through the back and wake you. Then we can replay this scene and give it a better ending."

"I'd like that," she whispered.

Again, he was surprised. She had always been so careful with her privacy, that he hadn't thought she would like the idea of his intrusion.

He bent toward her, kissing her lightly on the lips. Once. Twice. Then a deep and lingering caress that held echoes of the passion they'd shared.

"Until tonight."

* * *

John was still unsettled when he let himself into his quarters and shut the door behind him. This time, he didn't turn on the light. Rather, he moved through the familiar confines, taking a shotgun from a nearby closet and loading it with a couple of shells.

In the past, the gun had been used to ward off the pesky rodents who occasionally raided the chicken coops, or to keep drunken field workers in line after payday. But tonight...

He moved to the window, fingering the curtain out of the way. It was too late to call the local constable about the break-in at the house—and he wasn't sure what he would report if he did. Granted, the radio had been ruined beyond repair, but he couldn't see evidence of anything else having been taken. Wilmot's prized collection of art and antiques had not been touched. His desk was still firmly locked and the glass case of guns proudly intact. Even the safe in the corner appeared solid and unscratched. The house had been unlocked—as it usually was if someone was in residence. With so many servants and workers swarming over the property, there had never really been any reason to fear a break-in before.

Most likely, the damage had been done by a disgruntled worker or teenagers from the village looking for a thrill. But it still didn't sit well with John, especially with the house empty except for Wilmot's guest.

Sighing, he decided he'd better keep an eye on things. At least until Kako and Miyoki came early in the morning.

Grasping a box of shells and a couple of bananas from a bowl on the table, he went outside where he set a chair on the stoop. Using an extension cord, he placed his radio on the top step and tuned into a station that would play music all night long. Then, he slouched in the chair with the shotgun draped over his lap.

After the day he'd had, he was tired. Probably tired enough that he could have slept if he'd been given the opportunity. But he didn't entirely mind the guard duty. As always, the darkness and the sounds of the cicadas were soothing, and the radio provided another layer of peaceful enjoyment.

But then, when he least expected it, a light blinked on in one of the upper windows of the Big House.

Too late, John realized that he'd taken a spot in direct view of Glory Bee O'Halloran's bedroom window. Embarrassed, he started to rise, fearing that she would think he was spying on her. But as she opened the window wide to catch the breeze, he realized that she probably couldn't see him sitting in the darkness. If he tried to retreat, he would have to move in front of the glowing dial of the radio and she might sense he was there. If he remained still, silent...

For long moments, Glory stood illuminated in the yellow patch of light gleaming from the upper floor. Then he saw her take a step back, her hands on the tie of her robe. She moved, stepping out of his line of sight, then returned, wearing only a delicate nightdress.

He swallowed hard, his mouth growing dry. Although he'd watched this woman strip in front of thousands of men, he couldn't account for the way that her thin, girlish nightgown caused his body to thrum in anticipation.

She moved out of his sight again, this time, returning to fuss with her bed and the mosquito netting. But she might as well have been naked for the way the light pierced through the fabric, leaving a perfect image of her shape, full breasts and hips, slim legs.

Then, just as quickly, the light went out.

Leaving John panting in the darkness.

Dear God. How long did Miss O'Halloran plan to stay at the plantation?

Yet, even as he thought the words to himself, he realized that the answer could be both a blessing and a curse.

The sun beat down on his head and shoulders, but he remained as still as possible, staring at a spot behind Tanaka's ear.

He was stronger now, but that strength brought its own brand of attention. Attention that he could ill-afford.

From the moment he'd entered the camp, he'd become a target for the Japanese soldier in charge of the camp. Partly, because the other men looked to him for their orders. Partly, because he was tall, and Tanaka, a small man, had a grudge against tall men.

Today, they were all in for the Sun Treatment. Tenko *had been called at dawn. It was already past noon, and they had yet to be dismissed. Tanaka was in a surly mood, looking for a fight. There would be someone in the pit before the day was over, he'd bet.*

But it wouldn't be him.

He didn't think he could endure another week in the pit.

So he fixed his gaze into nothingness, allowed his shoulders to slump in submission, and pinned his mind on the only thing that had the power to steel himself to standing upright one more minute. Enduring one more day.

Rosemary. Sweet, sweet Rosemary.

The flower in his pocket—one that he'd pinched from her birthday corsage that long ago night when they'd first made love—had long since lost its perfume. But if he closed his eyes, he was sure that he could smell the scent of violets and feel the soft silk of her hair between his fingers.

Could she sense his thoughts? The way he continually hung onto her memory like a drowning man clinging to a life raft? Or had she given him up for dead?

Even worse, had she been captured herself?

A wave of despair threatened to swamp him, but he pushed it back. He wouldn't think like that. He couldn't.

Because if he allowed himself to believe, even for an instant, that she wasn't out there, safe…

He wouldn't be able to survive another day.

"Hey, Petey," he said under his breath as Tanaka began his daily diatribe on the evils of America and the cowardly nature of its soldiers.

"Yeah?"

"You think Kilgore would recognize that kid the padre *used as a messenger."*

"Yeah. Why?"

"I want to try and smuggle a letter out. Think we could do that?"

Petey's grin was slow and wide. "I think it's worth a try."

Chapter Five

December 8, 1941

Rosemary padded out of Ward Two and made her way to the nurses station. After making a quick note on Pvt. Reynolds's file, she arched her back and looked at the watch pinned to her chest. Four-thirty. It wouldn't be long now before dawn began to blush against the horizon. And once it did, she would have only a few hours left in her shift. Then she could go home to bed and sleep away the hours until Gilhouley returned.

The thought brought a rush of heat to her cheeks, but she patently ignored the sensation. She refused to be embarrassed, refused to second-guess herself or her actions. She was a grown woman—forty, to be exact. She wouldn't think about the disparity in their ages or their ranks—or the fact that Gilhouley went through women like the hospital went through bandages. Like Scarlett O'Hara, she would think about that another day.

"I'm going to go prep the surgical room for Private Adams," she said to Lt. Kaminski who shared the night shift with her. The only surgery scheduled for the day was routine, a hernia repair. Most likely, the operation would be over within an hour or two, and beyond that, there was nothing pressing on her agenda. She might even be able to leave a little early if Alice didn't mind taking part of her shift.

When Neala Kaminski didn't respond, Rosemary looked up from her chart.

"Lieutenant?"

Neala turned, flushing. "Sorry." Her brow furrowed. "Any idea what's happening on at headquarters? They've had their lights on for a couple of hours now."

Rosemary stepped to the window, lifting one of the slats from the blinds. Just as Neala had said, the squat multi-story building was the hub of activity. A half-dozen Jeeps were parked haphazardly near the door and despite blackout precautions, every light in the building was ablaze.

"Something's going on," Rosemary murmured.

A sudden clatter from the end of the hall caused Rosemary and Lt. Kaminski to whirl and offer a combined "Shh!" to the soldier who came barreling through the side door.

But the soldier didn't bother to temper his headlong dash. Instead, he leaned against the desk, panting, and said hurriedly, "They're bombing Pearl Harbor."

The words were so alien, so nonsensical, that Rosemary couldn't even process them.

"What?"

"They're bombing Pearl Harbor."

Her brow creased. "Who's…what?"

"The Japs! The Japs are bombing Pearl Harbor. In Honolulu! They could be on their way here!"

Leaving the women reeling with as much confusion as when he'd appeared, the soldier bolted out the way he'd come.

The door slammed behind him, a thundering silence reverberating in its wake.

"Do you suppose that was a joke?" Neala asked, her tone curiously hollow.

"At four-thirty in the morning?"

"Maybe it's a drill."

Rosemary shook her head. They'd had plenty of drills in the past few months, but this…

Unsure what to think, she said, "I'll be in my office. I'm going to make a few calls."

* * *

Gilhouley burst through the door of the control tower at Clark Field and eyed the pair of men who sat hunched at the desk rammed up against the wall of windows overlooking the runway. It was early, damned early, but he'd been summoned by a call telling him that if he wanted to see the action at the field, he'd better haul his ass over here pronto.

The small round room was already thick with cigarette smoke and the sharp stench of sweat and nerves.

"What's up?" he asked as he entered the room.

One of the men, Burt Suznovich motioned for him to take a seat in one of the battered office chairs scattered around the room. Anderson, a blue-eyed Swede from the Midwest chewed nervously on the butt of his cigar.

"All hell's about to break loose," Suznovich said. A cigarette dangled from his lips. Nearly a half-inch of ash threatened to fall at any moment, but he didn't notice. "You hear the news?"

"What news?"

Burt thrust his feet out, rolling his chair toward a radio located on one of the filing cabinets in the corner. With a flick of the switch, the dial glowed red, throbbing into the gloom. After several long seconds, the tubes warmed up enough for Gilhouley to make out a familiar deep voice intoning, "…is KZRH, the voice of the Orient, keeping you abreast of the news developing here at our news desk. As we reported earlier, at 7:48 Hawaiian time, the Japanese launched a sneak attack on the naval yards of Pearl Harbor, located on the island of Oahu. Sources declare that the attack was malicious and destructive. Casualties are officially listed at 18 dead, and more than 100 injured, but it is believed that such estimates are only the beginning. Eyewitnesses are claiming that the naval yard is all but destroyed. Fires rage from wounded ships and bombed out buildings. Resources are stretched to the limit as medical personnel and fire crews struggle to cope with the aftermath…"

Suznovich twisted the switch again, plunging the tower into an icy silence.

"Goddamn Japs," Anderson muttered.

Gilhouley didn't pretend to misunderstand the import of what he'd heard.

"We're next," he said lowly.

"Hell, yeah," Anderson rasped. "They called up them flyboys about four in the morning and rolled their machines onto the runway thinking we'd get permission to make a retaliatory strike at Formosa. But Sternberg won't give 'em the go-ahead. So our pilots are sitting in the dispersal hut waiting."

"Do you think they'll be sent up?"

"Got to, whether or not it's for a strike." Suznovich leaned forward and the ash finally fell from his cigarette, spattering across his neatly pressed uniform, but he didn't notice. "See, we've been told over and over again that the Japs wouldn't even consider striking until late spring in '42. That's what all the build-up in personnel has been for the last few months. But supplies have been trickling over here slower than manpower." He snorted in disgust, swinging to point at the runway and hangers below, the tip of his cigarette glowing blood red in the darkness. "You know what we got out there to protect us? Observation planes, rusty old bombers, and pursuit craft. We've got a crew of pilots waiting down in that dispersal hut—and at least half of 'em ain't got no machines to fly! Just last week, we got a handful of brand new P-40's, but only a couple of 'em are fully assembled. Even if they were, we've got no coolant to put in 'em. And guns? Hell, the guns aren't even out of their crates yet."

He scowled, dragging deep on his cigarette, making the tip flare angrily. "Even if we don't strike out at the Japs, we've gotta get those airplanes up in the air or they're sittin' ducks."

"Hell almighty," Gilhouley breathed. Pushing from the chair, he moved to peer out of the window at the landing field below. As the first thin rays of dawn pierced the sky, he could see the aircraft parked tip to tip like huge bulky birds, their wings clipped and ineffectual. "Why aren't they up in the air already?"

Suznovich stamped out the microscopic butt to his cigarette

before it had a chance to burn his fingers. Even before the smoke had ceased to twine up from the ashtray, he had another one in between his lips. The flint of his Zippo grated into the pulsing silence.

"You tell me," he said, his voice low and rasping from too much nicotine and adrenalin. "You tell me, then we'll both know."

* * *

The phone receiver had barely rattled into place when Rosemary was on her feet and moving into the ward again.

"Lieutenant Kaminski, I want every nurse on the base here in this hospital within the hour." She handed her a clipboard with names and numbers. "Here's a list. Notify as many as you can by phone. Apprise them of the situation." She held Neala's fearful gaze for several seconds. "This is not a drill. The Japanese struck Oahu early this morning and we've been told to expect all hell to break loose here at any moment. Lieutenant Strickland is on her way. She'll help you make calls."

"What about the girls who are on leave? And the new nurses?"

Rosemary squeezed her eyes shut, pinching the bridge of her nose, trying to force the whirling of her brain to cease so that she could concentrate—*concentrate!*

This is what all those drills were for. Remember your training.

"Make the calls first, then draw up a list of anyone we haven't been able to reach. With last night's party, the rest of our staff could be anywhere. Once we have the bulk of our nurses here, we can start worrying about anyone who might be off-base. If need be, we'll send someone to collect them. Our first priority will be prepping the wards. Ambulatory patients are to report to their posts on base. Those who can't be moved need to be gathered together in a single room. Use Ward B. It has the fewest windows. Crowd the beds close together if necessary."

She handed the clipboard to Neala who ran toward the phone at the nurse's station and began dialing. Kaminski's finger was shaking so badly, she was having trouble lining it up with the corresponding holes.

"Private Adams!"

The soldier in question lifted himself on his elbow. "Yes, ma'am?"

"No surgery today. Get your clothes on. I'm going to need your help."

"Yes, ma'am."

* * *

The tower was still thrumming with barely submerged energy when pilots were ordered to get their birds up into the air. From his vantage point at the tower, Gilhouley watched as the men ran from the dispersal hut toward the aircraft lined up on the runway.

"Is this precautionary? Or are the Japanese here?"

His questions melted into the air unheard as Suznovich and Anderson donned their headsets. Within minutes, more controllers thundered up the staircase, manning their positions.

Standing back, Gilhouley tried to make himself as invisible as possible as the men directed the controlled chaos below. The windows were soon rattling from the noise of engines rumbling to life—the deep bass of the bombers, the tremolo of the old fighters, and the roadster-like power of the new P-40's, still unpainted, their shiny silver skins reflecting the sun's glow as it arced over the horizon. One by one, they rolled down the tarmac, moving faster, faster, until the awkward beasts seemed to slowly rise from the asphalt, clawing their way higher and higher, gaining more speed and altitude now that they'd been freed from the earth's grip.

Gilhouley had to forcibly relax his hands as they curled into tight fists at his sides.

Only when the last plane was in the air did the tension in the room ease ever so slightly.

Suznovich exhaled in a rush. "They're up."

"For how long?" Gilhouley asked.

"'Til they're called back or run out of fuel." Now that the

tension had eased, he reached for another cigarette. But after putting it between his lips, he forgot to light it. "Those virgin planes are the ones that need watching. They could have some gremlins that haven't been caught yet."

"Any news about Pearl on your headset?"

Suznovich held his gaze. "Nothin' but scuttlebutt. But it sounds bad. Word is the casualties are a hundred times worse than what they're reporting on the radio." He rolled his shoulders as if to ease a crick. "You stickin' around or headin' back to Stotsenberg?"

In a flash, Gilhouley thought about Rosemary. She would have received the news by now. No doubt she was gathering her nurses together. Just in case. Even if he were back on base, he couldn't interfere with the demands of her command. And with his own posting to the press corps, his place was here, where he could better monitor and report on the day's events.

"No. I'll stick around a little longer. See what happens."

"Suit yourself," Suznovich said, then turned back to the windows. Lifting a pair of binoculars, he began to scour the skies for the first hint of danger.

* * *

A roar overhead startled John from a deep, dreamless sleep. He jolted to an upright position, his heart pounding. Momentarily confused by his surroundings, he squinted into the bright sunlight streaming through his window.

When had he gone to bed? He honestly couldn't remember. At one point, he'd been sitting on the porch with a shotgun resting in his lap. And then…

He raked his fingers through his hair, absorbing the shagginess on top and the closely clipped sides. Inwardly, he cursed whatever had awakened him. He couldn't remember the last time he'd been able to sleep so deeply. No dreams. No nightmares. Just the velvety blackness of unconsciousness.

Stumbling from the bed, he narrowly avoided tripping on the

pile of clothing he'd left on the floor—another unaccustomed habit. He was generally neat to a fault.

Moving to the kitchen sink, he braced his palms on the lip of the counter and turned the taps, waiting for the water to run cold. The light streaming inside pierced straight through to his brain. And his mouth felt dry as dust. Leaning forward, he cupped his hands and drank deeply from the faucet, then stuck his whole head under the water, welcoming the chill. Straightening again, he reached for a towel as a low growl began from the west, growing in speed and volume until it reverberated through his skull like a jackhammer.

Immediately, his body tensed at the memory, the unmistakable sound.

Whirling, he ran to the door, wrenching it open as a plane roared past the house, then another and another, flying so low that he couldn't mistake the red balls painted on the underside of the wings, the helmeted pilots.

What the hell?

He flattened himself against the wall as another plane raced past. This time, the pilot offered a mocking salute.

Not again. Not again.

But even as the words reverberated in his brain, John knew that, this time, he couldn't ignore his instincts to run.

As quickly as they'd come, the planes disappeared from sight. But John wasn't foolish enough to think that a flyby had been their only aim.

Racing into the house, he feverishly donned his clothing. Then he reached for the shotgun propped against the wall by the door. As if the touch of the stock were a talisman, he suddenly remembered everything from the night before. How he'd stayed up for an hour, two. And the longer he'd sat in the darkness, staring up at the inky shape of the Big House, the more foolish he felt. What did he think was about to happen? A raid on the house? The vandalism to the radio had probably been caused by kids who had too much time on their hands or a worker jealous of the Wilmot's possessions. Railing at his hyper-vigilance, he'd finally gone inside, downed a couple of shots of whiskey to help him sleep. And after that...

Well, he didn't remember what had happened after that. He'd never had a head for alcohol. Didn't even drink beer. So it hadn't taken much for him to fall asleep, evidently.

But now, as he ran toward the road and the fields, he cursed himself for not listening to his gut.

Dust rose in puffs from below his boots as he raced full-speed to the ramshackle outbuildings used for plantation business. Already, he saw a crowd of men huddled together, their hands shading their eyes as they watched line upon line of distant planes hovering on the horizon like flocks of birds.

"Hey, boss!" Esteban, a burly Filipino shouted from the ramp leading up to the equipment barn. "'Bout time you got here."

The others turned to face him as well.

Esteban lumbered toward him. "We be next, you think?"

"Next?" John echoed in confusion.

"You didn't hear the radio? The Japs...they bomb Honolulu."

The other men began talking—some in English, some Spanish, some Tagalog—their voices jumbling incomprehensibly. John held up a hand.

"Honolulu?"

"A place called Pearl Harbor. An *Americano* naval base. They're saying it's bad. Real bad."

The men turned to John, but it was Esteban who spoke.

"What we gonna do, boss? We goin' out in d' fields?"

John was under no illusions that it was work that preoccupied their attention. For months, the Philippines had seethed with rumors of a possible assault from the Japanese. It was only logical that an attack would eventually occur. With invasions into China and Manchuria, then French Indo-China, the Philippines were bound to fall in their sites as well. But the Americans had been stockpiling men and materiel for months and it was hoped that with that inherent threat, the Japanese would be deterred.

It would seem that such hopes were futile.

John squinted up at the sky. To the south, he saw a swarm of specks in the sky and wondered fatalistically if it was a flock of birds or something far more sinister.

"Lock everything up as tight as you can. Secure the machinery in the sheds." He glanced at the watch strapped to his wrist. It was just past noon. "The priorities right now are your families. If this is an invasion, the Japanese will probably land north of here and march straight through to Manila. We're right in their path. Do whatever you can to protect your loved ones. As for me, I'll..."

He suddenly broke off, turning around to stare at the house, at the single open window with its fluttering lace curtain. In a flash, he remembered the broken radio and the absence of Kako and Miyoki, both of whom were from Tokyo. Could they have been acting as informants for the invading army?

"What's wrong, boss?"

He opened his mouth to tell Esteban of his suspicions, then thought better of it. Right now, none of that was important. What mattered was getting everyone to safety. "Wilmot's guest arrived last night," he said instead.

"What y' gonna do?"

John grimaced and then said, "Wilmot's got a summer place up in the Sierra Madres. I'll take her there. The Americans will probably have to wait for reinforcements, but they'll drive the Japanese out within a couple of weeks. She'll be safe there until the fighting is over. As soon as the area is clear again, we'll be back. If any of you want to come with us, meet at the Big House in an hour."

Before he could say anything more, a low drone filled the air, becoming louder and louder, until the earth vibrated with the noise. Looking up, John saw a wall of aircraft on the horizon.

Esteban crossed himself.

John, motioned for the men to leave. "Go! Now! Forget about the machinery. Get your families to safety before all hell breaks loose."

"Where do you think they're going, boss?"

John squinted up into the sky, then toward the south. "The American bases. Clark Field. Stotsenberg."

Esteban crossed himself again. "Lord help them," he whispered.

John began to stride determinedly toward the house. "Lord help us all," he muttered under his breath.

* * *

By noon, the planes had been recalled for refueling. From the tower, Gilhouley watched as, one by one, they bounced onto the runway and taxied out of the way, lining up so that the tanker trucks and ground crews could swarm over them. Apparently taking shifts, some of the pilots headed toward the mess hall while others returned to wait in the dispersal huts.

The tower fairly crackled with nerves and anticipation, taking on the acrid smell of sweat mingling with cigarette smoke and the all too real tang of fear, until Gilhouley's head swam with it.

Needing some fresh air to clear his thoughts, he volunteered to go with Suznovich to the chow line and collect sandwiches for the men who stayed behind.

"Head on out, I'll catch up with you," Suznovich called out.

"Fine."

As he took the stairs that circled around the outside of the building, Gilhouley glanced at his watch. It was a little past twelve o'clock. Under normal circumstances the workday would be winding down. Because of the heat, the Army bases had a five-hour workday—from seven in the morning until noon. After that, soldiers would head for the beach to surf or into town for cold beers. The brass would make their way to the officers' club along the coast or to the polo fields. At Stotsenberg, there was a theater, pool, or golf course, or a person could catch a train to Manila.

But today, no one was leaving. As he reached the tarmac and began striding toward the mess hall, Gilhouley shifted his shoulders against the prickling frisson of nerves that started at the base of his spine and crept up, up, until the hairs at his nape stood on end.

Suddenly, he stopped, not knowing what had raised his hackles. A low drone, like the angry buzz of hornets bled into the chaos of the air base. Squinting against the fierce sunlight, he held a hand up to shade his eyes, catching the distant shapes of planes flying in formation.

From what he'd remembered, Clark Field had brought in all of its airplanes for refueling. But Suznovich had said that there were other aircraft from bases throughout the Philippines that were still patrolling the area. As the craft drew closer, the sun glinted off the shiny silver of their skin. More P-40's perhaps? Newer ones that hadn't received their U.S. markings?

The planes were flying in a strict V-formation, growing larger and louder, rushing toward the airfield with frantic speed. Frowning, Gilhouley noted that something was falling from the planes, a twinkling metallic confetti that spun and drifted down toward the ground.

Too late, Gilhouley realized what he was witnessing. He tried to turn, tried to head for cover as the first blast threw him into the air. He landed with a thud against the tower walls as everything around him grew silent and black and slow. Fading...fading...

Fighting the sensation, he clawed his way back to awareness, pushing away the need to sink into unconsciousness, knowing that if he did, he would be defenseless against the onslaught around him.

The ground was heaving, dirt and debris pelting him like hail. Gilhouley shook his head, then rued the movement when his brain slammed against his skull. Bit by bit, the tinny ringing in his ears subsided and the thundering noises of the attack assaulted him full force.

Fighting to breathe against the stench of smoke and burning fuel, he dragged himself to the stairs and clawed his way to his knees, his feet. Staggering forward, he fought to gather his bearings in a world that was suddenly alien to him. Huge holes pockmarked the runway. Outbuildings and hangers were on fire. Men raced frantically toward planes that were yet undamaged, while other machines lay like crippled starlings that had been torn asunder.

Horrified, he realized that it wasn't just the equipment that had been blown to bits. His eyes fell on a figure a few feet away. Gorge rose in his throat as he saw the mangled torso, curiously devoid of its legs and one arm. Leaning over, he threw up as he realized that the body was all that was left of Burt Suznovich.

"Hey! Help me! Help!"

Looking wildly for the source of the voice, Gilhouley finally saw a figure sitting with his back against the side of a nearby hanger.

Gilhouley ran toward him, shuddering to a stop when he saw that the man's leg was a bloody unrecognizable mass.

Pushing aside his horror, Gilhouley unhooked his belt and knelt beside him, wrapping the leather strap around his upper thigh. "Hold on, I've got you."

The man gripped at him with bloody fingers. "Patch me up as best you can. I've gotta get to my plane."

Startled, Gilhouley didn't know what to say. God himself couldn't have put the mangled mess back together. He squeezed the man's shoulder reassuringly, then looped the belt through the buckle and pulled the leather strap as tight as he could before wrapping it around again.

Another bomb landed nearby, causing the ground to shudder. Debris flew through the air, and Gilhouley bent over the wounded man, trying to shield him as scraps of metal, rocks, and chunks of asphalt whistled through the air. A few yards away, a plane fought its way down the runway, trying to gain speed even as it avoided the larger craters. But just as it was about to lunge off the ground, a round of strafing caused it to erupt into a fireball.

Gilhouley flattened himself against the pilot as a piece of the propeller whipped through the air like a deadly boomerang, slicing through the sheet metal walls of the hanger.

From somewhere in the distance, Gilhouley heard the clang of alarms, then the sweet, sweet sound of ambulances in the distance.

"We've got to get you out of here," Gilhouley said. "If I help, do you think you can stand?"

The man gritted his jaw, his teeth flashing white against the black soot coating his face. His nod was curt.

Bending low, Gilhouley wrapped the pilot's arm around his

shoulders and hauled him upright. Trying to take as much of the man's weight as he could, he half-walked, half-carried him away from the runway toward a transport truck being loaded with wounded.

"You, there!"

Gilhouley straightened to see a man kneeling over a prostrate figure further into the truck. He wore what had probably once been a white lab coat, but it was now covered with blood and soot and gore. "I need you here. Right now!"

Gilhouley climbed into the truck, weaving his way among the wounded to crouch beside him.

"Give me your hand."

Confused, Gilhouley reached out.

The doctor took his fingers and yanked them toward the neck of the soldier at their feet. Before Gilhouley knew what the doctor meant for him to do, he pressed his fingers deep into a gash that was spurting blood.

"Press down here, tight as you can!"

Then the doctor was gone, leaving Gilhouley amid a jumble of men with broken bones and gashes as well as those who hovered near death.

The chaos outside was so loud that Gilhouley didn't realize the truck's engine had rumbled to life until a jolt signaled that they were underway. Bending even closer to the man whose pulse he could feel knocking against his fingertips, he met the soldier's wide-eyed stare. Gilhouley had seen that look of abject terror before, on a horse that had broken its leg after stepping in a gopher hole.

Crouching low, he murmured, "You'll be fine. You'll see. It's only a few miles back to the hospital in Stotsenberg. They'll fix you up good as new."

But the wide-eyed stare of the soldier didn't abate. Clearly he didn't believe Gilhouley.

And Gilhouley couldn't blame him.

• • •

Rosemary was pulling supplies from the infirmary when an explosion nearly rocked her from her feet. Gripping the medical cabinet, she scrambled to keep the bottles from rattling off the shelves as another bomb hit, then another, and another. Finally, she grabbed a nearby basin and scooped the vials of morphine into a shivering pile, then slammed the door closed, not bothering to lock it. If they received the flood of wounded she was anticipating, she didn't want anyone needing to search for the key.

She ran to the main ward, just as the doors opened and the first wave of men began to stream in.

At first, the injuries were not serious—cuts, scrapes, burns, a broken arm. But even as she and her nurses began scrambling to help the doctors who had arrived only moments before, the ambulances began to disgorge the more dire patients. In less time than she would have thought possible, the hospital took on the grim hellishness of shattered limbs, gaping wounds, and death.

"Dodd! Take some of your nurses outside and set up triage! I don't want anything but the most critical cases in here until we can get a system going."

"Yes, sir."

Triage. In her twenty years of nursing, Rosemary had never been asked to put the skill to use.

Signaling to three of the new nurses who stood wide-eyed next to the door, she motioned for them to follow her outside.

"We'll set up on the lawn under the trees over here," she said, ignoring the roar of planes flying overhead. She didn't even have time to see if they were from the base or something far more sinister.

The ratcheting sound of strafing caused them all to dive to the ground, but the bullets hit on the street and not on the grass.

Scrambling back to her feet, Rosemary motioned for the corpsman to bring the patients to her rather than into the hospital. "I want the three of you to sort the wounded according to the gravity of their conditions. Put anyone who's still ambulatory here, next to the hospital, where they can help us with the incoming injuries. Those who can wait but can't walk go there, in that shady patch. Those needing immediate attention will be here, near the side door. Arrange them according to severity as much as you can." She hesitated before saying soberly, "Those who are mortally injured need to be taken over there, beneath the acacia trees to the rear."

To their credit, the women she'd chosen shook off their shock, one of them bellowing instructions like a drill sergeant as all manner of vehicles began converging on the hospital—Jeeps, ambulances, farm trucks, and even a motorcycle with a side car laden with a pair of burn victims.

For a moment, Rosemary stood stock still at the base of the stairs, unable to take in the horrific scene. But then an explosion from somewhere near the parade grounds roused her from her stupor and she hurried back inside, knowing she couldn't stop, couldn't think. She could only try to stem the tide of suffering and help as many as she could.

Her morning soon became a hazy blur of blood and carnage, shattered limbs and men's screams. With so many needing attention, she ordered one of the nurses to fill a pail with water and morphine to distribute the painkiller more efficiently to the wounded. Another group was assigned the task of ripping up towels and filling buckets of water so that they could attempt to wipe away the debris from those who'd been blinded when they'd dived into earthen trenches, only to be pummeled by the shockwave of the blasts.

Finally, delegating her authority to Alice, she paired up with Dr. Grimm in one of the surgical rooms. Soon, she was witnessing trauma that she'd only ever read about in books—ruptured spleens, decimated limbs, severed arteries. As if the force of the bombs and shrapnel weren't bad enough, pulverized bones had become a weapon of their own, driving into men's bodies like shards of glass. And with each soldier, there seemed to be an invisible clock ticking over Rosemary's head, warning her that time was precious and dozens of men still awaited attention.

Try as she might to retain her humanity, Rosemary's body and her mind soon became numb. She worked by rote, experience, and gut instinct, refusing to allow herself to think about the dead and dying, the ruined lives.

But, when a nearby blast caused her to throw herself over her patient's body and squeeze her eyes closed, for an instant, one fleeting instant, her mind flashed back to Gilhouley's arms, his kisses, the warmth of his body driving into hers…

May God forgive her for that selfish second when she prayed that last night's brief interlude of happiness wouldn't be their last.

• • •

"Get up!"

Glory Bee had barely processed the harsh command before the covers were stripped away and a rough hand shook her shoulder.

She came up swinging, but by the time she opened her eyes and squinted up at John Macklin, he was already striding toward the opposite side of the room.

Her fury was instantaneous. "What the hell do you think you're doing?"

He ignored her, taking her largest suitcase from where it stood, still packed, near the door to the closet. He punched the locks open, then upended the case, dumping everything in a heap on the ground.

"Hey!"

He looked at her then, his eyes dark and so cold, so singularly focused on his own goals, that she shrank back against the headboard, scrambling to tug the sheet up to her chin. Then, he turned to the smaller case she'd left open on the chair, upended it as well, and threw the suitcase onto the foot of the bed.

"Get dressed. Now. You need practical clothes—trousers if you have them—and sturdy shoes. We might be forced to do some walking."

Her mouth opened in stunned disbelief. "Now look here…I don't know what's come over you since last night, but—"

He continued on as if she hadn't spoken. "As soon as you're dressed, I want you to take the larger case downstairs and fill it with food from the larder. Tinned goods are best, since they'll keep as long as we need them. Get as much as you can, and don't forget an opener—"

"Stop!" she interjected forcefully, flinging the covers aside to spring from the bed and advance toward him, unable to contain her anger any longer.

John took her hand, dragging her to the window, where he flung the curtain aside and pointed. "Do you see that?"

"What is it?" she whispered when she saw roiling plumes of inky black smoke boiling into a pristine blue sky. From somewhere came the distant boom of thunder—or maybe it was fireworks.

John was standing so close to her, she could feel the tension radiating from him in shivering waves.

"If I were to guess, that's what's left of Stotsenberg and Clark Field."

She stared at him in horror. "But…"

"The Japanese bombed one of the naval yards in Hawaii. Now, they've come here."

Glory Bee's stomach dropped so suddenly that her teeth suddenly pounded with the thrum of her own heart.

"All those boys…"

Instantly, she remembered the raucous servicemen that she'd entertained. In her mind's eye, she could see them tumbling up to the stage in an effort to catch a glove, a stocking, diving for the discarded items like puppies scrambling for table scraps. Their exuberance had been infectious, exhilarating.

How many of them now lay hurt, bleeding?

"The Army will take care of their own," John said softly, drawing her back to the dangers at hand. "But we've got to head somewhere safer. Wilmot has a hunting lodge in the hills. We'll stay there for the duration. I doubt the Japanese will head that way."

He pointed to the empty suitcases. "Fill the small one with clothes," he said, more gently than the first time he'd issued his orders. "Bring only the necessities. With luck, American reinforcements should arrive in a couple of weeks and drive the Japanese out of Luzon."

"A couple of weeks?" she echoed faintly. "But…"

Sensing her confusion, he held her shoulders, bending until she looked him straight in the eye. She could see the absolute need he had to make her understand the gravity of his concern.

"The Japanese won't be content with a few air raids. They will launch a land invasion—today, tomorrow, who knows. When they do, the Americans won't be able to hold them for long. Not with the contingent they have on the island. They'll retreat to Manila and send for reinforcements, but until then, we have to take care of ourselves."

She frowned. As much as she wanted to process what he was saying, her brain lagged behind like a phonograph needle stuck in a scratch.

"But they'll have reinforcements soon. They can hold Manila until then, can't they?"

John straightened again. "Not if their air fleet has been severely damaged."

Her gaze ricocheted to the smoke in the distance, then back to John, whose eyes had turned from brown to black.

"B-but h-how can you know all this? I-I mean, the Army has probably planned for this. I'm sure they have measures in place to protect…American civilians…and…"

He didn't answer, merely backed away.

Glory Bee's arms crossed protectively in front of her, her palms gripping the warmth left by his hands moments before.

"Ten minutes," he said sternly, quietly. "You have ten minutes to pack your things. We leave in twenty."

She nodded, jerkily, feeling suddenly numb and clumsy.

Sensing her compliance, John turned and disappeared down the hall. And even though she knew that she should hurry, Glory Bee couldn't keep from turning to look out of the window at the billowing black smoke staining the sky.

"Hey, Mickleson, you got any papers?"

"Why?"

"'Cause I need it, that's why."

The other soldier eyed him suspiciously. "Whatcha gonna do with it, wipe your ass?"

Petey bent close, his eyes taking on a feral gleam that caused Mickleson to rear back. "Y' got any paper or not?"

"What if I do? Whatcha gonna give me in exchange?"

Petey's hands curled into fists. "I ought t' beat it outta you but..." He pulled his shirt aside to show a peek of two bananas.

"Where'd you get those?" Mickleson asked, his gaze riveted to the fruit.

"I know somebody who knows somebody."

Mickleson looked carefully around to make sure none of the other prisoners were watching. He licked his lips.

Petey leaned in to ask him again, "Do...you...have...some...paper?"

"No, but I know how you can get some."

"Tell me."

Mickleson's brow puckered. "Do I still get the bananas?"

"Only if I get paper. And a pencil."

"Shit, you didn't say anything about a pencil."

"What good is the paper if I can't write on it?"

Mickleson scowled, then motioned for Petey to follow him. They skirted around the rough bamboo huts until they came up on the corner of the structure used by Tanaka's interpreter, a short squat Jap that they'd nicknamed

Putzy-sahn.

"What the hell?" Petey asked. "You want me to steal from the Japs? You think I gotta death wish?"

"Ol' Putzy will never notice. Whenever Tanaka's around, he can't tell his ass from his elbow. Wait here until the boys come in with the goods from the garden. He'll go up to inspect the cart and you can slip in and grab it."

"You'd better not be blowing sunshine up my ass, Mickleson."

"Hey, if you get caught, I don't get the bananas."

They waited, Petey's stomach twisting with nerves and dysentery until he feared he would have to make his way to the latrines. But finally, the cart rattled into view, the prisoners waiting at the gate while the guards searched them.

Just as Mickleson had said, Tanaka jumped to his feet. Placing rocks on his papers to keep them from blowing away in the breeze, Putsy-sahn hurried after the officer striding toward the cart and the guard who accompanied the prisoners.

"Now!" Mickleson whispered.

Petey crept toward the desk, his heart thundering in his ears, his limbs trembling so badly he could barely move. He snatched the pen first—a pen, a real mother-fucking fountain pen!—shoved it into the pocket of his shirt, then reached for a piece of paper from the pile at the corner of Tanaka's desk. But as he tugged a sheet free, the rock dislodged and the breeze caught at the flimsy papers, lifting them into the air.

"Shit, shit, shit!" Petey whispered, dodging back toward Mickleson and cover, throwing himself to the ground, praying that none of the Japanese would notice him as they rushed to capture the wayward pages. Then they scrambled to their feet and ran back in the direction of the hut. As they dodged into the relative shade, Petey began to laugh, a wild laugh filled with equal measures of glee and remembered terror.

"Shit, Mickelson. You nearly got me killed!"

"You all but sent up a flare to let 'em know you were there, Petey."

The two of them looked at each other, then dissolved into giggles again. But soon, the merriment proved exhausting, so they sat in silence, eyes closed.

"I hope it was worth the effort," he said to Petey.

Petey grinned. "Me too."

"Can I have my bananas now?"

"Sure."

Petey unbuttoned his shirt and reached inside, paused, then began to giggle again.

"What the hell, Petey?"

Pulling his shirt aside, Petey revealed the crushed bananas.

Mickleson's face was a study in disappointment. But he ignored Petey's laughter and said dejectedly, "What the hell. Hand 'em over."

Chapter Six

John glanced at his watch and sighed. He'd given Glory Bee ten minutes and it had been nearly twenty. They needed to leave. Now.

He was about to turn toward the house and drag Glory Bee outside by her hair if necessary when the door swung open and she rushed outside, carrying the smaller of the suitcases in one hand and her make-up case in the other.

He opened his mouth to insist she leave her make-up behind when she dropped the bags on the ground and lifted a silencing hand.

"Before you start yelling at me for not following your orders, I made a dozen sandwiches with all the bread, meats and cheeses I could find and stuffed them in my make-up case. Once we've eaten everything, we can ditch it somewhere."

He grabbed the bag with her clothing and stowed it in the bed of the truck. "Put the sandwiches up in front with us. They'll stay cooler there. Did you get the rest of the food supplies gathered up in the largest suitcase like I asked?"

She nodded. "It's inside the house. And it's heavy. Really heavy. All the canned food weighs a ton. I also threw in some bags of rice, flour, and sugar…uh, matches, utensils, and a half dozen tin plates."

"Good girl."

John whistled to Esteban who stood a few feet away next to one of the other farm trucks. His wife Maria—who was nearly eight months pregnant—was already ensconced in the cab with two of their smaller children. Another three youngsters sat in the bed.

Around them were heaped blankets and bags, two goats, and a crate of chickens.

"Glory Bee O'Halloran, this is Esteban Morales, one of my fellow workers." He pointed to the truck. "That's Maria, his wife. She's got Luis, who's two, and Pepe, who's three. In the back are the older kids, Estella, who's six, Gabriella, who's eight, and Angelo. He's the oldest, at ten."

Glory Bee offered them a wave and a smile. "Hello, everyone. You can call me Glory Bee."

"Can you get the last of her luggage, Esteban? It's in the kitchen, I think?"

John cast his eyes toward Glory Bee for affirmation, and she nodded.

"I dragged it to the doorway, but that was about as far as I could get it alone."

As Esteban hurried back to the house, John scanned the drive for any sign that there were more employees on their way to join them. But there were no telltale plumes of dust. Around him, everything was quiet. Too quiet. And that was nearly as unsettling as the Japanese planes that had flown overhead hours before. John was so used to noise—men, machinery, women singing, children playing. It was as if the farm had already become a ghost town.

Realizing that they couldn't wait any longer, John slowly went to the passenger door.

"Get in," he said, too curtly, most likely. After the way he'd treated her this morning, he didn't suppose Wilmot's guest would want much more to do with him.

But, to his surprise, she touched his hand as she slid inside. The gesture was so simple, a moment's connection, a wordless vote of confidence.

John slammed the door shut, then moved to help Esteban lift the last suitcase into the truck. "Good god, Glory Bee," he called out as he and Esteban staggered under the weight. "What all did you pack?"

"Anything and everything I could fit inside," she yelled back.

He could see her grin in the side mirror of the truck. "We may have been exiled from the plantation, but I don't aim to go hungry."

Esteban laughed, a huge rolling belly laugh. "Let's go, *padre,*" he bellowed.

John climbed behind the wheel. After checking the lane leading down to the worker's huts, he shifted into gear and rolled away from the house. Even then, he couldn't help taking one last look at the Wilmot estate as it grew smaller in his rear-view mirror.

Why did he feel like he was leaving so much more than the house behind?

* * *

The hours soon became a blurred montage of sounds and smells that had hitherto been unfamiliar to Rosemary. In the artificial cocoon of the operating room, she was cut off from any views to the outside world, so the passage of time was marked with the thick odors of burnt flesh and blood, smoke, diesel, and aircraft fuel. At times, she could hear the clang of alarm bells, the roar of engines, distant explosions, and over it all, a symphony of screams and moans.

The surgical suite held its own orchestral arrangements as well. The rubbery *squish* and *hiss* of a blood pressure cuff, the clink of tools on the tray, the *zzz, zzz, zzz* of a saw cutting through bone.

With only three surgeons available and about that many general practitioners, the medical staff was pushed to its limits, but still they plugged on, sensing that there were more men waiting in the hall, and even more beyond that. They'd filled the wards within the first half hour, the halls minutes after that, then the lobby, the veranda, and now the lawn beyond. Neighboring medical facilities had been contacted in a plea for help, but Clark and Stotsenberg weren't the only bases that had been hard hit. More personnel would eventually come, but it could be days. In the meantime, Rosemary and her girls had to hold on as best they could.

All thought to traditional nursing duties had long since been abandoned. Besides triage, her nurses were administering painkillers and anesthesia, cauterizing wounds—anything they could manage by themselves in order to help relieve the doctors for more serious medical procedures. Gauze and bandages were already running low, so Rosemary had sent a few of her nurses to neighboring barracks to collect towels, sheets, and whatever else they could find that would be useful.

But even with the monumental efforts, the wounded continued to arrive until Rosemary had forced herself not to think about what lay beyond this room. There was only this moment, this patient, and she would do her best and move on.

"Done," she said to the corpsmen, motioning for them to take the latest amputee from the table and bring in the next one. This soldier couldn't be much more than nineteen with a shock of red hair and freckles spattered over his nose.

"I got hit," he said when Rosemary bent over him.

She offered him a reassuring smile. "We'll take care of you, don't you worry. Dr. Grimm is the best."

As she spoke, she wrapped the blood pressure cuff around the boy's arm. Squeezing the bulb, she placed her stethoscope in the hollow of his elbow and listened, automatically watching the sweep of the second hand on her watch.

"Ninety over sixty-seven," she murmured to Dr. Grimm.

"He's going to need blood."

She checked the soldier's dog tags, then shook her head. There was no blood available for this patient.

"Put him out," Grimm said wiping his forehead and rolling his aching shoulders.

As Rosemary moved to place the mask over the boy's mouth, he caught her hand.

"If I don't make it, tell my mom I did okay. And I love her."

Rosemary offered him a wide smile that she hoped didn't appear too false. "You can tell her yourself. Once you wake up, you can write her a nice, long letter." Then she quickly put the mask in place and began administering anesthesia. It wouldn't be long before they would be out of that too.

She squeezed the boy's hand as his eyelashes fluttered. If there was one thing she'd learned in the past few hours, it was that the dying all offered the same request. They wanted their mothers, their wives, their sweethearts to know that they'd been loved.

Reaching out, she laid a gentle hand on the redhead's forehead, stroking his hair back from his clammy brow as she waited for the anesthesia to take effect. With a little luck, he'd get that chance to write to his mother.

She could only pray that her own luck would hold and she'd see Gilhouley again.

* * *

Dust spewed behind them in a cloud as John and Glory Bee left the Big House behind. In order to make their way to the hunting lodge, they would have to travel north, then east.

Without the radio in Wilmot's office, John felt as if he were flying blind. The wireless in his own cottage had been full of news of the airbases being bombed, but John knew that the broadcasts were being carefully couched not to cause alarm in the outlying areas. For all he knew, a land invasion had already begun and the airstrikes were only a precursor to the day's events. Without the short wave radio in Wilmot's office, he'd been unable to check with the plantations along their route for a more accurate accounting. And so, with his hands tight on the wheel, he kept one eye on the road and the other on the horizon ahead, looking for the telltale smudges of smoke.

"Are you sure this is the right thing to do?" Glory Bee asked, breaking the silence. "I mean, I'm an American citizen. I could go to…I don't know, the consul, the embassy, whatever they have here at Luzon. Or maybe I should go back to Stotsenberg. That's where I spent my first—"

"They can't help you. Not now. They've got enough on their hands without worrying about stranded tourists." Too late, he realized that his words had emerged much too harshly. Grimacing, he offered a gruff, "Sorry."

"No. Really. I appreciate your honesty. But I'm sure that you have…more important things to do as well."

For a moment, she looked as if she were on the verge of tears, and John hastened to reassure her. "It's not a problem. Really. You're a friend of Wilmot's—"

"A friend of a friend."

"Doesn't matter. You're with me. I'll see to it that you're safe."

He held her gaze for several long seconds, until finally, she accepted his words. Then he returned his attention to his driving.

"How long will it take us to get there?" Glory Bee asked.

He reviewed the route in his head, then quickly hedged his bets. "That depends on what conditions we find ahead of us."

"Do you think the Japanese could have already landed?"

He heard the panic in her tone, but another quick glance assured him that she was outwardly calm. The last thing he needed on his hands was a hysterical woman. "I don't know. But I doubt they mean to bomb us and leave." Again, he skipped a quick look in her direction, wondering how honest he could be with her. "They need the Philippines. And judging by the attack at Pearl, they mean to take control of the Pacific."

"But why?"

He shrugged. "The long answer is cultural: they feel a superiority, that their emperor is descended from deity and all of Asia should be under their control. The short answer is oil. Their fuel supplies have been cut off due to the recent embargoes and they need the rich reserves found further south. In order to get them, they have to make sure that no one has a toehold in the Pacific. So they take out the Americans by destroying the fleet at Pearl and the bases here in the Philippines. Then they push out the British and Dutch in the East Indies."

"It seems impossible," she whispered. "They're such a little country."

"Don't underestimate the Japanese. Behind that 'little country' is a fanatical will."

He felt her gaze upon him. It was a disturbing sensation, like the caress of a hand down his spine. Too late, he realized that he'd cracked open the door to a part of himself that he didn't want examined.

"You sound as if you've had personal experience with that fanatical will."

John's fingers tightened reflexively around the wheel and his jaw hardened.

"Sorry," she said quickly. "I guess that falls under the heading of *personal* again. I warned you that I have a hard time keeping my nose out of other people's—"

"I was at Nanking," John blurted, surprising himself with the outburst. But where he'd always felt shame in admitting that part of his life, this time, he felt…relieved. "I was at Nanking when the Japanese invaded," he said again.

He wasn't even sure if she knew where Nanking was, let alone the significance of his confession, but her whispered, "Dear God," reassured him that she was fully aware of the horrors suffered by that city when the Japanese invaded. "The Rape of Nanking" the newspapers and newsreels had called it. And as horrific as the media had portrayed the event, the reality had been worse, so much worse.

"How did you make your way here?"

"The Church negotiated with the Japanese and eventually arranged for us to leave."

"Us?"

He glanced at her only briefly. "I was a priest."

It was clear that she didn't miss the past tense, but to his surprise, she didn't press for details. Instead, she muttered, "You must think I'm a heathen."

John couldn't help a bark of laughter. "Why?"

She rolled her eyes. "I strip. I swear. I even drink on occasion. I'm sure you're used to much more…refined company."

This time, he couldn't help smiling. "Your company is more than enjoyable."

Glory Bee was less than mollified. "Let's hope you think that once the Japanese arrive. Because if they get too close, I'm going to be cursing like a sailor."

* * *

It was growing dark by the time they arrived at Wilmot's hunting lodge. As she peered through the trees at her first glimpse of the building, Glory Bee discovered that it wasn't nearly as grand as what she'd been expecting. The term "lodge" had given rise to visions of a huge log building decorated with animal horns and wagon-wheel chandeliers. But then, she supposed she should have known better. Wilmot was from England, where, evidently, the term meant something different.

Instead, the drive opened up to a clapboard bungalow like dozens of others she'd seen lining the streets of Manila. Low, squat, and built on stilts to aid ventilation, it had once been painted a brilliant white. But the color had been dulled by time and the woodwork was in need of repairs. Nevertheless, the building looked sound, and as long as there was a bed, a bathroom, and bathing facilities somewhere on the premises, Glory Bee wouldn't have cared if it was a bamboo hut.

Their journey had probably not been terribly long if calculated in miles. But they'd had to traverse a series of roads that had grown increasingly more primitive, until the final stretch had been made on a track of wheel ruts etched into the earth. Even more disturbing had been the chaos of traffic. The attack had put the entire island on alert and the roadways had been cluttered with all manner of vehicles—carts, bicycles, and wagons. Horses and oxen had vied for space with luxury vehicles and rattletrap farm trucks, all of them intent on getting somewhere other than where they'd started. And there was no rhyme or reason to the migration. Some moved north, some moved south. Most brought only what they could carry and their desperate need to avoid an imminent invasion.

As John eased to a stop in front of the wide veranda, Glory Bee breathed a sigh of relief. She needed to use the facilities something fierce and had been debating whether or not she should ask John to pull over.

Gathering her purse and the make-up case that held the last of the sandwiches, she waited as John gave instructions to Esteban on where he and his family could stake out the goats and quarter the chickens. As if they were as eager as Glory Bee, the children jumped from the bed of the truck and disappeared, squealing, into the trees.

As soon as John headed back in the direction of the house, Glory Bee darted from the truck, following closely on his heels.

He stopped at the threshold, running his fingers across the top of the lintel. "There's usually a key kept…" He sighed, kneeling to check beneath the rug. "Damn."

"I thought priests weren't supposed to swear."

"I'm not a priest anymore."

Turning, he jabbed his elbow at one of the panes of glass inset into the door, causing it to shatter. Then he reached inside and turned the knob. "After you."

Stunned by his response and the suddenly harsh expression that settled over his features Glory Bee followed his orders, her physical discomfort forgotten. Stepping inside, she discovered that the house was indeed compact. To her left was a sitting area with a door that led into a small bedroom. To her right was a dining room and beyond that a narrow kitchen.

John strode inside, weaving his way around lumps of furniture covered in dust covers. Flinging open the draperies, he revealed a huge picture window that looked down upon the valley below. It was an imperfect view of the world they'd left behind, but Glory Bee supposed that they would see something to warn them if the Japanese began advancing south.

"Make yourself at home," John said, reaching into a cupboard below the window seat and removing a pair of field glasses. Bringing them to his eyes, he said distractedly, "There's no electricity up here, but there's a wood stove for cooking and heating water. I'll get a fire started as soon as I can, but I need to make some radio calls first."

"Okay."

"Up the stairs, there's an attic bedroom. You can take that one or the one through there." He pointed to the door that led off of the sitting room. "There's a small bathroom off the kitchen if you need it."

"Thanks."

Glory Bee made her way through to the kitchen, setting her things down on the table. After availing herself of the facilities, she stood in front of the tiny sink and twisted the taps. The water, when it emerged, was tainted with rust, so she waited until it ran clear before washing her hands and splashing more liquid on her face.

As she straightened, she caught her reflection in the mirror.

Had it really only been a couple of days since she'd arrived in the Philippines? Her supposed haven?

A bitter laugh bubbled from her throat. If Michael only knew what had happened to her…

Word about the Philippines had probably reached the United States by now. He must be worried sick. That first afternoon on the island, she'd managed to send him a telegram stating that she'd arrived safely. But that had been before Pearl and the attack here in Luzon.

Would he be wondering if she was in harm's way? Or would his duties as a congressman be even more pressing now that American holdings had been threatened? He'd told her several times that it was only a matter of time before the U.S. was drawn into war, but he'd always mentioned the Germans, not the Japanese.

Still, he must have known there was a threat brewing in the Pacific. How could he not have known? Sgt. Wilcox had told her that the wives and families of the personnel on Luzon had been evacuated months ago.

So why had Michael sent her here? Right into the mouth of the dragon?

Shaking her head of such thoughts, she straightened and left the bathroom, intent on gathering the rest of their things from the truck.

Michael couldn't have foreseen the imminent danger in the Far

East, that was all. He would never do anything to harm her. He loved her. He just couldn't afford for her to be seen around Washington in her current condition. A discreet affair could be tolerated. A love child with a stripper could not.

Unconsciously, her hand strayed over the roundness of her abdomen beneath her un-tucked shirt. Since abandoning her girdle, the kid had spread out. There was certainly no doubt that she was pregnant, even though she still couldn't accept the fact. She felt no excitement, no fear, merely a curious detachment from the whole process. To date, her only real emotions over her situation had been a sense of inconvenience and an overwhelming loneliness at being parted from Michael.

But now, she found herself plunked in the middle of a Japanese offensive, hiding in a mountain lodge with a man who was an ex-priest. She was thousands of miles away from home, unable to contact Michael in any way. She was tired, frightened...

And pregnant. Very, very pregnant.

If that pregnancy hadn't already gone away by being ignored and denied, it wasn't going to go away now. It was only a matter of time before she would have to tell John about her...condition.

She could only pray that American reinforcements had arrived by then.

Frowning, she went outside in search of wood for the stove. She might not be much help with the radio or in keeping their group hidden from the Japanese. But she could at least get the stove fired up so that they could have something warm to eat for dinner.

Nevertheless, as she began gathering twigs and sticks, she couldn't help staring down into the valley below where the smudges of smoke could be seen in the distance.

"Damn you, Michael," she whispered under her breath with sudden vehemence. "Damn you for sending me here."

* * *

Rosemary didn't know how long she'd been in the hospital, moving from one hellish injury to another. She couldn't have said if it was day or night, or how much time had elapsed while she'd been shut away in the operating room. She only knew that when Dr. Grimm asked for a clamp, she stared blankly at the array of tools on the tray for several long moments, her mind frozen.

"Major Dodd!"

Dr. Grimm's gentle command jerked her back into motion and she quickly grasped the clamp and turned to slap it into his hand.

Grimm's eyes were gentle above the edge of his mask. "How long have you been on duty, Major?"

She shrugged. "A while."

"Ten hours? Twelve?"

"Since before the attack."

"How long before?"

He wasn't going to take an evasive answer so she said, "Since eleven last night."

Grimm pointed to another nurse. "You. Take over the instrument tray." He then pointed the clamp in Rosemary's direction. "You. Take twenty minutes. No duties. None. I want you to get something to eat, drink, take a ten minute nap, then get back."

"Dr. Grimm, I appreciate your concern but—"

"That's an order, Major. Then I want similar rotations passed out among the other women. We're in this for the long haul, and we all need our wits about us."

When it became clear that he wouldn't resume his surgery until she complied, Rosemary nodded and backed away so that Lt. Wakely could take her place.

Moving wearily, she crossed into the hall, blinking at the brilliant sunlight streaming through the gaping windows and glinting off the shattered glass that was strewn across the tile floor like diamonds.

She'd been so sure that it would be nighttime.

She'd thought she'd been a hundred years in the operating theater.

A glance at her watch told her it was barely seven-thirty. Soon, the long shadows of evening would appear. But not yet. For now, the buttery stream of sunlight illuminated the crushed, broken, and maimed men filling every bed, every gurney, every possible inch of floor space. She was forced to weave her way among them like a drunken man, until finally, she was able to dodge through the door to her office.

Surprisingly, the room was empty. Since it was too small to be of much use for the wounded, the space had been crammed with odd pieces of furniture, boxes of books, and superfluous equipment.

Picking her way through the medical flotsam, she went to her desk, only to discover that her chair had already been filled with containers of tongue depressors and surgical tubing. But the window in this room, miraculously, was intact.

Unable to summon enough energy to lift the boxes away, Rosemary tipped her chair, sending the boxes tumbling to the floor. Then she collapsed onto the seat, resting her head on folded arms propped on top of a desk cluttered with cleaning supplies and file folders.

She needed to close her eyes. Just for a few minutes. Enough to ease the pounding ache in her head and shoulders and the numbness that had invaded her brain.

But as soon as she blocked out the chaos around her, she was flooded with images: the ride in Napoli's seaplane, a corsage of violets, the cornflower blue of Gilhouley's eyes.

The thought caused her throat to grow tight.

Had it only been a day and a half ago? It felt like a lifetime since she'd been in his arms.

Rubbing the spot between her eyes, she couldn't keep her brain from looping into her most pressing concern. Where was Gilhouley now? He'd gone to Clark Field—and judging by the casualties they'd received from the airbase, the area had been one of the prime objectives of the Japanese. At first, when Rosemary had encountered some of the pilots, she'd asked if any of them had seen Gilhouley. But as the injuries from Clark became more and more severe, she'd stopped asking.

* * *

Glory Bee woke slowly, by degrees—not really sure how she had fallen asleep in the first place. But as she surfaced from a swirl of hazy, unsettling dreams, she realized that she was lying on the sofa, a soft lap blanket tucked around her waist.

Vaguely, she remembered coming back into the sitting room after all of the tinned food had been stowed safely away. By that time, John had dragged the kitchen table into the sitting room next to the radio by the window. As he spoke with other plantation foremen in the area, he made notes on the map with a red carpenter's pencil.

At first, she'd tried to listen in on the conversations, moving silently around the room as she stripped the furniture of its dust covers, folded them, then set them in a pile on one of the chairs. But with her task finished and no other useful occupation apparent, she'd sunk onto the sofa. Soon, her weariness had overtaken her to the point that the static and the garbled transmissions had hissed around her like an incomprehensible symphony. And somehow, through it all, she must have fallen asleep.

The shadows had all but overtaken the room. Except for a pair of hurricane lamps, one on the table and the other on the mantel, she might not have been able to see at all. But the flickering glow illuminated the man who sat looking out the window into the blackness beyond.

John Macklin could have been carved from stone. His features were harsh, his posture still and stiff. A faint muscle pulsed in his jaw as he contemplated the valley below. Yet, even with his forbidding appearance, Glory Bee couldn't help staring at him.

Glory Bee had always been a sucker for wounded strays. As a child, she'd brought home birds with broken wings, lost puppies, and half-drowned kittens. Once she'd matured, things hadn't changed much. She'd transferred her affections to wounded boys from abusive homes, then men. Even her affair with Michael had begun because of the abject loneliness she'd seen in his eyes. Of course, she hadn't known at the time that his melancholy was due to an unhappy marriage rather than a checkered past.

But with John, there was a difference. Even if she'd wanted to take him on as one of her projects, she couldn't fix him. Nor was there anything that she could do to alleviate the turbulence that lingered behind his steady gaze. No, this was a man who warred with his own inner demons, and she'd learned long ago that such pain couldn't be alleviated with a kiss and a cuddle. Only John could come to terms with the things he'd seen and experienced.

But even knowing that on a logical level didn't prevent the emotional tug she felt every time she was with him. A part of her longed to draw him into her arms until some of his pain faded away. But the more practical part was dying to know why he'd left the priesthood, even though she sensed that she might find the knowledge even more disturbing than her imagination. It was clear that whatever had happened still warred within him. And she knew enough about John to rest assured that he hadn't made his decision lightly.

So what vagaries of fate had brought him here, to the Philippines, to this lodge, to this moment, where his path tangled with hers?

As the last few wisps of sleep faded away, Glory didn't move, didn't make a sound. She stared at her unwitting companion, trying to understand why she was so drawn to him despite all the reasons why she should leave him alone. She was already in more trouble than she could imagine. She didn't need to borrow more.

As if he'd heard her thoughts, he suddenly turned and met her gaze.

"Feeling better?"

Glory Bee nodded, feeling her cheeks flush. How long had he been aware of her stare? "I don't know what came over me."

"You're still getting your land legs."

"Perhaps." Or perhaps, it was the fact that pregnancy exhausted her.

The silence blossomed in the air between them, thick and fraught with danger. Glory Bee told herself to keep all conversation light and casual, but before she knew the words had even been formed in her head, she blurted, "What did you do in China? As a priest?"

He didn't answer right away. Instead, he all but skewered her to the chair with his dark gaze.

"Sorry," she said hastily. "*Personal.* I really didn't mean to—"

"I taught school."

"What did you teach?"

"I taught English at a Catholic grammar school."

Her brows knit together. "I didn't think there were many Christians in China, let alone Catholics."

She thought his lips tilted in a hint of a secret smile. "There weren't many. But there were lots of children who longed for an education."

"Did you teach boys and girls together?"

He shook his head. "What few girls were allowed to attend school were taught in a different section by the nuns. Co-education is primarily discouraged in China."

"Did you enjoy it?"

His eyes took on a faraway sheen, as if he were picturing himself in another time, another place.

"Yes. Yes, I enjoyed it very much." Abruptly, he stood, putting an end to the current tack of their conversation. "Are you hungry? We can poke at the fire you started in the stove."

She shook her head, disappointed that he hadn't been willing to tell her more. "No. I'm fine. You go ahead if you want."

When he moved into the kitchen, she raised her voice to be heard. "Where are Esteban and his family?"

"They've set up under the trees out back."

"Wouldn't they rather sleep in here where it's more comfortable? Especially with the children? We could lay out blankets on the floor. I'd be happy to take the couch and give Esteban and his wife my bed."

John returned carrying a sandwich. "I made the suggestion and was politely refused. They tell me it's too hot inside."

"But—"

"Esteban is proud, and I'm his boss. He doesn't feel comfortable sharing quarters with us yet. Not with his whole family in tow. In time, maybe, but not tonight."

Glory Bee nodded. She could understand precisely what Esteban was feeling. She felt like an interloper herself. John didn't know her from Adam, and yet he'd taken it upon himself to see that she'd been taken out of harm's way. No one would have faulted him if he'd left her at the plantation or dumped her off at the nearest American base.

Standing, she moved to the map where John had been plotting the information he'd received over the radio. When she saw that it was studded with bright red x's, she gasped. "All of these areas were attacked?"

He nodded. "Stotsenberg, Clark Airfield, Iba, Manila…They hit most of the key areas, airfields, fuel dumps, the docks."

Until that moment, the reality of the attack had been an ephemeral thing, ink blots of smoke against the brilliant blue Filipino sky. But looking at the splashes of red, the danger of their situation hit her full-force. If John had not brought her here, she would have had no one to turn to for help.

"How long do you think it will be before the Japanese bring troops onto the islands?"

He hesitated, trying to decide if she could handle the truth. Then he offered quietly, "From what I've been able to gather, it's already begun."

She gasped, her stomach wrenching as if she'd dropped twenty floors in a too-fast elevator.

"I think they've begun amphibious landings on a few of the northern islands. Bata is the only one I've been able to confirm so far."

She wrapped her arms around her middle, suddenly chilled. "But they're being fought off, aren't they?"

John shook his head. "Not officially. I'm sure there's opposition from the Filipinos, but no one could tell me if the Americans are involved yet. With their limited resources, they might be waiting until the Japanese land on Luzon."

Her gaze strayed to the map.

"The Americans will have their hands full, won't they?"

He nodded.

"They might even be overrun."

John sighed. "That is a very real possibility."

"What will happen if reinforcements don't arrive as soon as anticipated?"

John pointed to the map. "From the rumors I've heard amongst the Filipinos, the Americans plan to draw back to the south, here, around Manila. If Manila is overrun, part of the American forces will evacuate across the bay to this strip of land called Bataan. It's primarily jungle, heavily wooded, and easy to dig in for a siege. Everyone else will be sent here, to this island."

"Corregidor," she said. "Our boat passed by it on the way into Manila. It was beautiful."

"The Americans have built a series of tunnels into the rock. It should be fairly impregnable."

She absorbed the information on the map for several long seconds before asking, "What about us? What do we do if the Japanese decide to head in our direction?"

She saw by the glimmer in John's eyes that he hadn't expected her to catch the vulnerability of their position. They had retreated to the mountains, but there was nothing to keep the Japanese from going coast to coast, especially if the Americans retreated to the south.

"We'll head higher into the hills and hope that they don't follow."

"And if they do?" she pressed.

He pointed to a range of mountains. Beneath his finger she saw the words "Sierra Madres".

"We're here." He moved slightly north and east. "Esteban's wife is from this area. That's why they're travelling with us. They're hoping to link up with her relatives somewhere in this area. About here is a thick forest—mostly bamboo, vines. It's fairly impenetrable.

If need be, we'll hide here. As a last resort, we can make our way to the eastern coast here. There might be a chance we could radio for help. Since you're American, that could work in our favor. If not, we could try to get hold of a boat and make our way south down the chain of islands to a safer spot."

"Providing the Japanese haven't moved in and set up shop there as well."

His head dipped in assent.

Glory Bee curled a hand around her neck, massaging the ache that settled at the base of her skull. "In other words, if the Americans fail to defend the island, we'll be in a great deal of danger."

She blinked as the red markings on the map swam in front of her. Her lungs grew tight, making it difficult to breathe.

John sighed. "Maybe I shouldn't have told—"

"No! No, you *should* have told me. I might make my living as a stripper, but unlike what most people think about me, I'm not stupid."

"I never said—"

"No, but you wouldn't have been the first to have assumed I have the brains of a gnat." She took a deep breath and planted her hands on her hips. "I have a right to know. And frankly, I'd rather have the truth from the beginning rather than having someone blow smoke up my skirt."

"I would never do that to you or to anyone else in this situation."

As quickly as her anger had flared, it fizzled away. She eyed John with something akin to wonder, realizing that what he'd said was the truth. John had been honest with her from the moment he'd awakened her in the Wilmot plantation house.

She couldn't remember another man ever having been so up-front. Just as she'd told him, she'd grown accustomed to men discounting her intelligence…

Or deciding that she should blindly obey them when they decided she should travel halfway around the world in order to avoid gossip.

The moment the thought was formed, Glory Bee felt a pang of disloyalty. But it was true. She'd tried to talk Michael out of sending her away. She'd begged him to let her stay in the States. But he'd been adamant that she have the baby far from home where no wind of scandal could taint his career.

Oh, he'd done his best to convince her that the arrangements were for her own good, that she was being treated to an exotic vacation…

Nevertheless, Glory Bee had known the truth. She was being banished. And there was nothing she could do about it.

Without really thinking about her actions, Glory Bee reached up to cup John's cheeks in her hands. His chin was covered in dark stubble that abraded her palm and she was instantly aware of his masculinity. Her femininity. Hard to soft.

Lifting on tiptoe, she pressed a kiss to his cheek. "Thank you, John Macklin."

He reared back as if he'd been burned. But when she would have drawn away, his fingers snapped around her wrist, holding her there, her palm against his face.

For a moment, his eyes flared wildly, and too late, she realized that this man had been a priest. In such a capacity, he probably wasn't used to casual kisses or even more casual caresses. Dear sweet heaven, the man might never have been kissed at all.

Never been kissed.

Before she could think twice, she leaned into him again, her body resting against his, her mouth brushing his once, twice, three times. He remained totally unresponsive, even though his breath suddenly rasped in his throat. But when she would have drawn away, he suddenly plunged his fingers into her hair, drawing her tightly against him, his mouth taking the initiative, tentatively at first, then more hungrily, until the two of them were tangled together, legs, hands, mouths.

Then, abruptly, John tore himself away, backing toward the window. She could hear him struggle to right his breathing as he leaned hard against the casing.

"I'm sorry," he said dipping his head. "I shouldn't be kissing any woman, let alone—"

She quickly interrupted him, her smile wide enough to rival the Cheshire Cat's. "Yes, John, you should. You most definitely should. You should kiss women and kiss them often."

Then, ignoring her own whispers of conscience at the fact that she'd been kissing someone other than Michael—and thoroughly enjoying the experience—she turned and walked out of the room.

He waited until it was dark, until most of the hut was asleep, until he had the only shred of privacy available to a man living crammed into one spot with hundreds of other men.

It was far from quiet. The moans of the injured and the rattle of breathing from those who were ill warred with the constant whine of cicadas and the god-awful drunken singing coming from the barracks on the other side of the fence. But he tried to block them all out.

One piece of paper.

One piece of paper and the hope of a miracle.

He carefully set the paper on his thigh, slipping the stolen pen from his pocket. The blank sheet was at once terrifying and powerful. In it lay the hope of not only making contact with the outside world, but of getting a message to the woman he loved.

And it was at that moment that he realized that the rest of the world could hang themselves. If he had only a few lines, a few hundred words, they were for her, no one else.

So even though his hand still trembled from the after-effects of the latest malaria attack, even though he could barely see to form the words, he began, making his script as small as possible, knowing that space was limited and there was oh, so much he needed her to know.

Chapter Seven

December 9, 1941

Darkness hung low over Fort Stotsenberg when Rosemary stepped outside for the first time in hours. A glance at the watch pinned to her chest assured her that dawn was only a few minutes away.

Sinking onto the top step, she closed her eyes and dragged air into her lungs, needing to wipe away the stench of blood and scorched flesh and fuel. But out here it wasn't much better. The breeze was heavy with the scent of smoke. Smoke and death.

They had long since run out of room for all of the wounded who needed attention, so makeshift beds had been fashioned on the grass. She could see her nurses moving among the wounded like fireflies in the darkness. Their bright white uniforms and gleaming pearl hose had been soiled with blood and soot and worse. But in the dim blushing light of dawn, the women still glowed like little beacons of hope.

Her girls had served her proud. Even the new recruits had thrown themselves into their work until finally, finally, they seemed to be gaining the upper hand on the situation.

Just as Grimm had ordered, Rosemary had begun rotating rest periods, knowing that a mistake made out of weariness could be cataclysmic. At first, those breaks had been brief, twenty minutes every four hours. But now, they could afford to send a pair of the nurses who'd been on duty for more than twenty-four hours back to their quarters for an hour of precious sleep. *If* their quarters were still standing.

Rubbing her eyes with the flats of her palms, Rosemary wondered if her own bungalow had gone up in flames. She was in one of the rows closest to the parade grounds where several shells had landed. But she didn't have the will or the energy to look, and she certainly didn't have the time.

Grasping the iron railing, she hauled herself back to her feet. She felt as if each limb weighed a hundred pounds as she descended the steps and moved onto the grass.

Alice was the first to see her approach and met her halfway. "You need to get some sleep," she said disapprovingly. "You ordered Kowalski and Brennen back to their quarters. Don't you think you should do the same?"

"Not yet. There's still so much to do."

"You've trained the girls well. Let them do their jobs. You're no good to us if you're staggering on your feet."

"Not yet. I've sent Wilson to the mess hall in search of coffee and sandwiches. I'll wait until she's back first."

Alice scowled, but didn't argue.

"Have you seen anyone from the press corps?" Rosemary asked, keeping her tone carefully bland.

"Why? Are you hoping to get an interview?"

"Hardly."

"Then why…?" Alice's look became suddenly all-knowing. "You're looking for Gilhouley, aren't you?"

When Rosemary opened her mouth to demur, Alice waved aside her response. "Don't bother answering. I saw the pair of you leaving the dance together." She lowered her voice to murmur, "Are the two of you…involved?"

Rosemary hesitated before saying, "I don't know."

"But you've been out with him. Danced with him." She paused, lowering her voice to a murmur, "Kissed him?"

Rosemary was too tired to lie, so she nodded.

"Sweet day in the morning," Alice muttered with something akin to wonder, then she laughed. "You and The Great Gilhouley. Now there's something I never would have imagined possible. Not in a million years."

She broke off when Rosemary bit her lip and looked away.

"Ah, sweetie, I'm sorry. No. I haven't seen him. But that could be a good thing, right? If he's not injured, then he has no reason to be at the hospital."

"It's that…we arranged to meet. Hours ago."

Alice touched her hand. "He's probably busy. Look at us. We haven't had a minute to breathe."

Rosemary nodded. "You're right. I just…"

Unbidden, her gaze strayed toward the trees where row upon row of soldiers had been lain out of the way, their faces covered with canvas tarpaulins. But the impromptu shrouds were too short, leaving their feet exposed in a myriad assortment of shoes—some scuffed and worn, others polished and new.

And some of the feet were bare and vulnerable.

Try as she might, she couldn't remember what Gilhouley's shoes looked like, didn't suppose that if he were resting beneath those trees that she could recognize him by his shoes alone.

"Don't think that, Rosemary," Alice warned.

But her words were cut short as the rumble of transports cut through the early morning air. At least six trucks barreled toward them, laden with the latest batch of injuries. Shaking off her melancholy, Rosemary rushed to greet them.

"I want anyone who can still walk over there, on that patch of grass next to the stairs," she said to the first medic who jumped from the rear of the vehicle. "We'll get to them as soon as they can, but first we need to separate them from those who are critical."

As her own nurses rushed to join her, Rosemary lowered the tailgate, then began helping the more mobile men to the ground. "Over there, please. Over there. We'll get to you as soon as we can."

Soldiers from the surrounding area swarmed around the trucks, helping to unload makeshift stretchers made from tarps, ladders, even doors that had been removed from their hinges.

"This one needs to be taken inside. Take him straight to the operating room. This one can wait a little, but I still want him inside."

She was so intent on giving orders, that when a man jumped from one of the last trucks and staggered toward her, she nearly didn't recognize him.

"You! Over by the..."

Her words died in her throat as he straightened, and suddenly she recognized him—not by his face, which was so smeared with oil and dirt he appeared like a shadow in the dimness—but by the square cast of his shoulders, the familiar narrowness of his hips.

"Gilhouley?" she breathed. "Riley?"

His clothes were covered in blood, and he must have sensed the panic that washed over her because he said quickly, "It isn't mine."

But before he could offer more of an explanation, Lt. Wakely appeared on the steps.

"Major Dodd! Dr. Grimm needs you in the operating room. Now."

Pointing a finger at Gilhouley, Rosemary said. "I want you in the hall outside my office. Lieutenant Strickland will find you a spot. You wait there until I can get to you, understand?"

Then, unable to even wait to hear his response, she hurried back into the hospital.

* * *

After falling asleep earlier that evening, Glory Bee found it nearly impossible to settle back down again. So after tossing restlessly in bed, she gave up trying and rolled into a sitting position. She'd left the lamp burning low, so she twisted the wick until a warm glow flowed into the corners of the room.

She couldn't account for her restlessness, an itchy, inexplicable need for...

For what?

John?

Raking her fingers through her hair, she shook her head in disgust. Had she really stooped so low that she couldn't even remain faithful to the man whose baby she carried?

Sighing, she stood, crossing to a narrow bookcase on the far wall. Maybe if she could find something to read she could…

A scream suddenly split the darkness and Glory Bee rushed toward the staircase, staring down into the dark abyss at the bottom. But even as her foot stood poised over the top tread, she hesitated, her heart pounding in her chest, her pulse knocking so loudly she could hear it in her ears.

Dear God, had the Japanese managed to sneak up on them in the middle of the night?

Another cry split the darkness and she flattened herself against the wall, taking one step then another. Slowly, she crept down the narrow stairs, wishing that she had a weapon. The moans came again, followed by two barking shouts that sounded like, "Back! Back!"

Once in the kitchen, there was enough moonlight stealing in through the windows for Glory Bee to see the shape of the counters and the huge wood burning range. Spying an empty coffee can that held spoons and utensils, she slid a large wooden rolling pin free, wincing at the faint clink of cutlery. Immediately, she froze, but there wasn't a response from the other room, so she tiptoed forward until she could peer around the corner into the sitting room.

Here, the picture window offered even more light. A silver puddle of moonlight illuminated the center of the room and rimmed the shape of the desk with the radio and the tufted sofa where she'd fallen asleep earlier.

John's voice slid into the darkness again. He mumbled lowly under his breath before shouting, "Mary Francis! Let her go! Mother of God, are you animals?"

Creeping forward toward the bedroom, she relaxed infinitesimally when she realized that there were no intruders in the room. John was having a nightmare.

Setting the rolling pin on the sideboard, she hurried toward him. The covers were tangled about his waist and above them, his chest and face gleamed with sweat.

"Blast," she whispered softly to herself, grasping the matches left at his bedside. As soon as a flame appeared, she touched it to the hurricane lamp on the nightstand and replaced the chimney. Then she sat on the side of the bed and said softly, "John? John! You're having a bad dream."

His hands dug into the sheets, twisting them violently as he wrestled with an unknown demon. Not sure what to do, she gingerly reached forward with two fingers, poking him in the shoulder.

Before she even knew what had occurred, John flung her onto the floor, straddling her thighs and leaning over to press his forearm against her throat.

"John!"

His eyes suddenly blinked open and he shuddered, gazing around him uncomprehendingly. Then, in a rush, he took in the room, his bed, before his gaze finally met hers.

"Shit," he rasped, springing away so that he sat with his back braced against the wall, knees up, his chest heaving as he sought to catch his breath.

Slowly, Glory Bee eased into a sitting position, one hand rubbing her neck.

"Did I hurt you?"

He was so horrified by the idea that she hastened to reassure him. "No. Just startled me."

"Sorry."

He raked his fingers through his hair and swore again, tipping his head back and closing his eyes. Even in the dim light of the lamp, she could see the pulse knocking at his neck.

"You were having a bad dream," she whispered.

He wiped a hand over his face.

"I'm sorry I woke you so suddenly. I didn't know what else to do." She folded her legs in front of her and rested her elbows on her knees, willing to stay until he'd calmed down, sensing that he needed something to divert him from the aftereffects of his dream.

"I'm not surprised that you had nightmares tonight," she said. "Not really."

His brows lifted in an unspoken question.

"With all that's happened, it's bound to cause...bad memories to surface."

He didn't respond, but she could see that the vein at his neck was beginning to relax.

Not sure how to proceed, Glory Bee asked, "Who's Mary Francis?"

He looked startled.

"I know...*personal,*" she said quickly. "You called out to her in your sleep. I got the impression that you thought she was in danger."

His jaw worked for a moment before he said, "She was, uh... one of the sisters who worked at the...the girls' school."

"Were you in love with her?"

Rather than being annoyed, John laughed. "No. Sister Mary Francis was at least fifty, but she was...a dear friend."

"She was...hurt?"

His amusement faded and he nodded. "She was raped and killed by the Japanese."

Glory Bee felt a shiver of horror. "They raped and killed a nun?"

He nodded. "She was ordered to make her students available to...entertain the needs of the soldiers. When she refused, the soldiers scaled the walls of the convent. Then they tortured and killed her. As an example." John stared down at his hands, drawing them into fists, then releasing them again. "Afterwards, they... mutilated her, then hung her naked body outside the school as a warning to others who might try to disobey their edicts."

Glory Bee shuddered. "No wonder you have nightmares."

As if suddenly realizing that he sat wearing nothing but his undershorts, John rolled to his feet, turning his back to her as he stepped into his trousers and buttoned them. Then, he stood, leaning against the windowsill, loath to being alone again, but not sure how he should proceed.

"Is that why you left China?"

He shook his head. "I left because I was ordered to do so. I wanted to stay behind. To help. But the diocese was given permission by the Japanese for its staff to board a boat headed for Shanghai and we were all told to be on it. I would have forced the issue, but after what had happened to Sister Mary Francis, I was afraid that if I ignored the Japanese's none-too-subtle hint to leave, they would turn on my students in retribution."

He bowed his head. "In the end, it didn't matter. Since my students were young and male and could conceivably fight against the Japanese, they were taken out into the woods and executed."

"Dear God," Glory Bee whispered.

"That's the reason I left the priesthood. What kind of God could allow that to happen to children?"

Glory Bee didn't know how she could even respond to that, so she stood and moved toward him, laying her hand on his back. He flinched but did not step away.

"So you came here?"

"Eventually."

Again, she was at a loss for words, so she wrapped her arms around him and laid her cheek against his back.

"I'm sorry. So, so sorry." Too late, she realized that, again, she had allowed herself to get too intimate with a man who probably wasn't accustomed to such physical outpourings of comfort. So with one last squeeze, she released him and turned.

"Would you like some coffee? Or perhaps tea. I saw tea in the cupboard."

"Tea, thanks."

She padded into the kitchen and busied herself with stoking the fire in the stove, filling the kettle with water, then setting it over one of the burners. While the water heated, she gathered thick mugs and set them on the table along with spoons and a small sack of sugar.

Minutes later, John joined her. He'd donned a shirt, but left the top two buttons undone. He was rolling the cuffs up to his elbows as the teakettle began to shriek. After dumping the leaves into the pot, Glory Bee grasped a strainer from the coffee can on the stove, then set everything on the table. Taking a chair opposite, she said, "Have you managed to shake the wiggly woolies away?"

His brows rose and she laughed. "When I was small, I was

deathly afraid of the little wooly caterpillars in the garden—wiggly woolies, my Nanna called them. So when I had a nightmare, she would ask if the wiggly woolies had come to get me."

John's smile was rueful. "I'm doing much better, thank you."

Setting a strainer over his cup, she poured his tea, then did the same with her own. Sensing he remained unsettled, no matter what he might say to the contrary, she continued her prattle.

"I spent most of my time growing up with my grandmother—Nanna Sue, I called her."

"You had no mother?"

Glory Bee grimaced. "Oh, I had a mother. She just wasn't sober long enough to be much good at the job. So by the time I was two, I was living with Nanna Sue." She laughed. "She was a rip-snorter, I'll tell you that. She had only two things in life that she hated. The demon alcohol and Yankees. But she was sweet with me. If I'd asked for a star of my own, she probably would have found a way to pluck one from the heavens and pin it on my shoulder." She shook her head. "We didn't have a lot of money, but there was love and laughter in that house, I'll tell you."

"What happened to her?"

Glory Bee shrugged, stirring a scoop of sugar into her tea. "Kicked by a mule, can you believe it? Nearly ninety-five at the time, but it was the ornery animal that brought her down, not her age. Still, I couldn't complain. Her worst fear was that she'd become an invalid and a burden to those around her—not that she could ever have been a burden to me. But this way her death was quick, just like she wanted."

"So that's when you…when you became a…"

"A stripper?" she supplied with a laugh. "Lord, no. I wanted to be an actress. Didn't matter how poor we were, Nanna Sue and I still found money for the pictures every single week. I knew I wanted to go to Hollywood someday."

John took a sip of his tea. "I take it that things didn't work out."

She shook her head. "I got work in the theater right away, first in Richmond, then Washington, D.C.. But it wasn't long before I realized that I'd never get past the chorus. Never had enough schooling to put on airs the way some of the other girls did, and that didn't sit well with the men in charge. So, after a time, I found something I was good at. It so happened that meant taking off my clothes." She pointed her spoon at him. "But, mind you, I've got class and I've got standards. I never take everything off, at least not so the men in the audience can see from London to France. No, I put most of my emphasis on the tease, rather than the strip. And it's served me well. Men prefer a little mystery, even though they don't come right out and say it."

John laughed, the first time she'd ever heard such a thing from him. "Yes, I suppose you're right." He took another gulp from his mug, then said, "So how did you end up in the Philippines at the outbreak of a war?"

She sighed heavily. "Damned if I know. I needed a little… time off. I was told that if I came here, I could have a vacation in paradise." She grimaced. "Some paradise. If it weren't for you, I'd be in a hell of a fix, wouldn't I?"

"I'm glad I could be of help."

Glory Bee stirred at her tea, then said more seriously. "We're in a bad spot, aren't we, John?"

When she looked up, his eyes were dark, quiet. He didn't bother to lie. "Yes."

"But we have a chance of staying away from the Japanese, don't we?"

His thumb rubbed over the edge of his cup. "I think we have a good chance, Glory Bee. With luck, we'll only have to hide for a few weeks. By then, if all goes according to plan, the Americans should be landing in Manila."

She heaved a deep sigh. "I hope you're right. I really hope you're right."

Because, after hearing what John had been through in Nanking, the alternative was far too horrible to contemplate.

• • •

It took much longer to process the new batch of wounded than Rosemary had expected, and she was afraid that in that time Gilhouley would have left—or that the encounter in the yard had been a mirage. But as she rounded the corner of the hall, she saw him sitting where she'd told him to go, his back against the door to her office, his wrists resting loosely on his up drawn knees. She would have thought he would have fallen asleep since she'd been gone for so long, but he sat staring at the wall. Staring, but not really seeing.

It wasn't until she knelt beside him and gently touched his head that he jerked back to awareness. Then he smiled, a slow, weary smile. And in his gaze, she saw it all—his exhaustion, an echo of the horrors that he'd seen, and an overwhelming joy at seeing her again.

Tears threatened again, but she pushed them away. She cradled his face in her hands and kissed him, not caring who might see, grateful that he was here. He was safe.

"Come on. I can't leave the hospital yet, but I've got a short break." She pressed a palm to his chest to help push herself upright, then frowned when it came away wet with blood.

"It's not mine," he said again.

"Gilhouley, this is fresh. You're bleeding."

Taking his hand, she pulled him upright, leading him through the pallets of the injured to what had once been the supply room and was now a makeshift treatment room. She motioned for him to get up on one of the tables, then gathered water, soap, and antiseptic. Since there were no available towels, she took a pair of bandage scissors and cut a chunk of her slip free.

"Take off your shirt."

Rosemary quickly moved to help him. After tending to so many wounded, she couldn't help lingering over the task, needing to reassure herself that Riley was all right, that he was here, he was safe. After pushing the fabric aside, she hissed, seeing several gashes in the fabric of his undershirt.

"You must have been cut by shrapnel."

He looked down at himself in surprise. "It doesn't hurt. I didn't even know I'd been hit."

"It will. You've still got a lot of adrenaline running through your system, but you'll be crashing here pretty soon."

Not wanting to pull at the wounds until she could see them more clearly, she took the scissors and cut him free of his undershirt. He was covered with several pockmarked abrasions, but two of the gashes were giving her the most concern.

"These will need stitches, but we've got to clean you off first." She thought for a moment, then said, "Can you stand?"

He shot her a sharp look.

"Some people don't react well to the sight of their own blood."

He grimaced. "I've seen enough blood to last a lifetime today."

On that point, she had to agree. "Bring your things."

She gathered a few medical supplies, then led him to the nurses' locker room, which was a few doors down from her office. "There's a shower in there. Wash yourself off as much as possible. I'll stand out here to make sure no one comes in. Then we'll go to my office and I'll stitch you up."

Rosemary snagged one of the last remaining sheets that her nurses had gathered from around the base. "Clean towels are long gone, but you can wrap yourself in this."

Gilhouley hesitated. "Are you sure—?"

"Just go."

He disappeared into the locker room and a few minutes later, she heard the sound of running water. To his credit, his shower was brief, barely more than five minutes. Then he emerged with his filthy clothes in one hand and the sheet wrapped tightly around his middle.

Rosemary ushered him into her office, locking the door behind her. Then she slid the boxes of supplies off the desk so that he could perch on the edge.

After a quick examination of the gashes, she said, "You're going to need about two dozen stitches."

He looked wary. "Don't you need a doctor for—?"

"I've been doing it all night," she said. "Right now, the doctors are busy with more serious cases." She shot him a soft smile.

"I'll hurry."

He nodded, but she saw that his knuckles grew white as he gripped the edge of the desk.

"Do you have a problem with needles?"

"I don't think so."

"Good."

She withdrew a syringe and filled it with Novocain, then carefully deadened the areas around the deepest gashes. Glancing up, she saw that Gilhouley had pinned his stare on the opposite wall.

"Okay?"

He nodded and she worked as fast as she could to draw the edges of the wounds together. When she carefully snipped the thread and straightened, he let out his breath in a whoosh.

"Not too bad, I hope."

He gingerly fingered the wounds.

Now that she was finished, Rosemary couldn't help but admire his physique in the harsh light. He looked battered, bruised, and weary, but otherwise fit for duty. The fact brought a rush of relief that nearly brought her to her knees.

"What happened?" she asked, her words so soft they were barely audible.

"I was coming down from the control tower when the first wave hit." He shook his head. "It was…"

She squeezed his hand, moving closer, and without a word, he drew her between his legs, his arms pulling her close so that her head rested on his shoulder. The warmth of his body seeped into hers, easing a place deep inside her that had been cold and afraid and fearful since she'd known he'd been caught in the thick of things.

"Next thing I knew, I was helping with the wounded, carrying them to trucks, taking care of them while they were transported here. I don't know how many trips I took or how many bodies…" His voice grew husky. "A lot of good men died today, Rosemary."

She nodded against him. "I know."

He pressed a kiss into her hair. "The Japs will be back."

She wound her arms around him, holding him as tightly as she dared. "I know."

Rosemary felt him shudder against her. "I felt so damned useless out there. I'm from the goddamned press corps. What good am I in the middle of a war?"

"You can tell people the truth about what happened."

"That's just it. I can't. There is no way that I could ever put into words what I've seen today, Rosemary. And even if I did, the brass would never allow me to publish it. We were caught with our pants down—and why? We knew about Pearl, we knew the Japanese would strike us as well, and yet..." A sob caught in his throat. "Those pilots, Rosemary. They were under fire, most of their aircraft exposed, yet they were still running toward their machines, willing to do anything to get into the air in order to save their fleet or at least down a Jap or two. There was this one guy..."

Rosemary waited, as Gilhouley shuddered against her.

"His...uh...He was thrown free from his plane when a shell went off." Gilhouley swallowed hard. "When I got to him and rolled him over...Geez, Rosemary, there was nothing left of his chest, these...these white strips of rib and...the zigzag of intestines. But he was still breathing, still...begging me to help him get to his plane while he gripped my hand and his blood bubbled from his gut."

Sobbing, Rosemary drew back, cradling his face in her hands, sweeping the tears on his cheeks away with her thumbs. Then she kissed him, again and again—and as if the dam of his control had finally broken, he covered her lips with his own, drawing strength from her passion as she drew hers from him. The events of the day, their weariness, the horrors that they had seen and their gratitude that they were together, alive, added fuel to the fire until neither of them could deny their overwhelming need.

Rosemary wrenched at the sheet wrapped around Riley's waist just as he grappled to bring her skirt up. Frustrated, wanting him with her, in her, she helped him with her underthings until he was sliding into her, pounding against her with the same frantic need that yawned within her. With a measure of adrenaline still pumping through her system, her climax was quick and powerful, and Riley joined her almost instantaneously, his body shaking with the intensity of his release. Then they sank against one another, exhausted, spent, their bodies momentarily sated, but their minds and hearts still hungry for the closeness.

A knock came at the door, startling them both.

"Y-yes?" Rosemary called out, her voice garbled and husky.

"Major Dodd?"

"Yes?" Rosemary quickly tore herself out of Gilhouley's arms and began hastily gathering her clothing.

"Dr. Packard needs your help with an amputation."

"I'll be right there. Tell him I've got to…wash up first."

The whisper of crepe soles against the floor moved away from the door.

"I've got to go," she said to Riley, turning to kiss him, once, twice, wishing, more than anything, that she didn't have to leave him.

Not yet.

Not now.

Judging by the expression he wore, Riley was equally torn.

"I know. I've got to find my own staff and then see what we're supposed to do. Somehow, I don't think that finishing the latest base newspaper is going to be a high priority."

They stood frozen, their eyes taking in what their hands had enjoyed only moments before. Then Gilhouley turned away. He scooped his filthy clothing off the floor and began stepping back into them. Rosemary wanted to protest, but she didn't have anything clean for him to wear and he couldn't make his way around the base in nothing but a sheet.

As soon as he'd turned back again, she whispered, "Find me. When you're free, find me."

Still, she hesitated. And then, knowing that she was needed elsewhere, she smoothed her hair with her hands, replacing the pins and righting her cap. "I don't even know if my house is intact, but if it is, let yourself in."

She had her hand on the door, hesitated, then ran back for another kiss.

"Watch after yourself, Gilhouley. Whatever happens next."

"You too."

Then, after one last quick kiss, she unlocked the door and hurried back to the operating room.

He'd sent the letter each day with Kilgore when he'd gone out to garden. And each day, his friend had returned, imperceptibly shaking his head.

Not yet.

Not yet.

If not for the quinine bottle he'd hidden under his bunk, he would have thought that the mention of a person called padre *sending help from outside had been a figment of his imagination. Certainly, with every day that passed, the likelihood of making contact again had become more and more remote.*

But whenever Kilgore returned, he would retrieve the letter, put it in his pocket until the next day. And the next. And the next.

Until Kilgore had run afoul of Tanaka. This time, it was Kilgore who was sent to the pit. He'd been eating food from the garden. For that, he'd been beaten so severely that he'd been unconscious for three days now.

Volunteering to take Kilgore's place, he'd begun his own daily trip to the garden. As far as work details went, it was better than most. But the sun was scorching and water breaks were few. Even so, there was some satisfaction to digging his hands into the earth and watching things grow. There was a rhythm to each day as seeds were planted, watered, tilled, and harvested that helped to soothe his soul and make him think he could last a little longer. Best of all, when the guards weren't looking, it was possible to sneak some of the smaller fruits and vegetables into their pockets or shirts to be eaten during their midday break.

The days soon faded to weeks. His spot in the garden detail remained permanent—even after Kilgore recovered enough to stagger out to his duties.

Then, one morning, when he least expected it, Kilgore tugged on his pant leg.

"There's the kid."

"What?"

"There's the kid that gave me the quinine."

The boy hung back, hiding in the trees.

He started to rise, but the kid quickly shook his head, holding up a hand.

The guards. The guards were closely watching their captives.

The boy backed into the foliage and disappeared, leaving him wondering if he should celebrate or cry.

Chapter Eight

December 23, 1941

The days spent at Wilmot's lodge began to take on a surreal quality for John Macklin. Each morning, as soon as he'd dressed, he would make a series of calls to several plantation owners around the island. Then he would add the information he'd gathered to the map. In time, the red marks grew more pronounced, the x's of air raids joined by arrows that showed amphibious landings.

Usually, Glory Bee would join him as he finished his calls, her wide eyes studying the gathering swarms of red. To her credit, she rarely needed an explanation. He could see by the worry darkening her gaze that she knew their situation was growing more perilous each day. Even if she hadn't, when the wind was right, John knew that she'd caught the hint of smoke in the breeze.

It would be so easy to pretend that things weren't so bad, if only for Glory Bee's sake, John thought. With a little imagination, he could convince her that the boom of artillery was really thunder. But each time a swarm of planes appeared in the sky, the sudden pallor of her skin would give little credence to the lie. They both knew that the Japanese had begun their march. They could only pray that they wouldn't decide to head this far east.

"Bee! Bee!"

John turned from where he'd been studying the valley below with a pair of field glasses. He hid a smile when Esteban's youngest son, Luis, toddled toward Glory Bee.

In the past few days, the children had become Glory Bee's

constant companion. They were fascinated by her pale skin and fire-red hair. She was uncomfortable in their presence at first, but after several days, she'd begun to treat them with resigned acceptance—although she still tended to talk to them as if they were mini-adults.

Grasping his rifle from where he'd propped it against a tree, he slung the strap over his shoulder, then collected the rod and reel that he'd taken from the shed behind the lodge.

As soon as Glory Bee saw that he meant to move away from the house, she sidled up beside him.

"Where are you going?"

John saw no reason to lie, even though he sensed Glory Bee's intent.

"Fishing. There's a stream a couple of miles down the slope. I thought I'd catch something for dinner."

"Can I come with you?"

He opened his mouth to refuse. The last thing he needed was more time spent in this woman's company. But she looked so hopeful, that he knew he couldn't disappoint her.

"Very well."

She fell into step beside him, and once again he was struck by how small she was. She might have curves in all the right places, but she was no bigger than a mite.

"Thank you," she breathed as soon as they were out of earshot.

"Getting a bit much for you? The kids?"

She rolled her eyes. "Being a woman, I'm supposed to be endowed with all these…maternal instincts."

He would have laughed at the statement, but she was curiously serious. More so than she needed to be.

"I suppose there's something wrong with me," she sighed, biting her lip.

Her chin wobbled and John was flummoxed. He couldn't imagine why she was so worried about the way she interacted with Esteban's children.

"Maybe you need practice."

Her brows lifted curiously. "You think so?"

"Sure. I'd say you don't give yourself enough credit. Esteban's little ones have always been a handful." He added encouragingly. "Luis has taken a shine to you."

He loved the way that she gave him a one-sided, rueful smile.

"I haven't decided if that's a blessing or a curse."

This time, it was John's turn to laugh. "You really are something, do you know that Glory Bee?"

She grimaced. "Is that a good thing or a bad thing?"

"A very, very good thing."

Too late, John realized that they'd come to a stop in the middle of the path, and that he'd turned to face her. Of its own volition, his hand lifted to cup her cheek. Her skin was so soft, so smooth, so velvety—and he had only to touch her for warmth to travel from that point of contact through his whole body. The suddenness of the effect astounded him.

"Don't."

The word that escaped her lips was a mere puff of sound. But contrary to what she'd said, her eyes grew dark and she took a tiny step forward.

John knew that he should back away—run away. He hardly knew this woman, and yet, she'd managed to crash her way through barriers that had taken him a lifetime to erect. And he honestly didn't know what would happen if he didn't repair his defenses as soon as possible. His whole sense of worth relied on denial and sacrifice. Yet, here she stood, ready to pin a lie to everything he'd once thought would make him happy.

"You're a dangerous woman, Glory Bee."

He didn't realize that he'd spoken the words aloud until her lips parted, and she took another step, so that they stood toe to toe, with an electric awareness thrumming between them. This close, John could smell the sweet fragrance of her hair and the faint scent of roses. Dear God, how did she manage to smell like roses in the middle of this mess?

"I think you're the dangerous one, John," she murmured, her own gaze painting a path of fire over his skin, from his eyes, to his chest, and lower, before lifting again to zero in on his lips. "I can't do this, you know."

He grimaced. "I know. It isn't the right time."

"Or place."

"Or—"

Suddenly, he couldn't bear the temptation any longer and his control snapped. Bending, he savagely took her lips with his own, crashing into her, taking her, sweeping his tongue into her mouth to taste her one more time.

Her hands slid around his waist and she pressed herself to him, the softness of her breasts flattening against his chest. His own hands swept around her hips, pulling her tightly against him, against that part of him that wanted her, needed her.

He shuddered, kissing her again and again, allowing himself to drown in the storm of sensation that she inspired.

Dear sweet heaven above. He'd never known that he could feel this way. Yes, he'd fought against the temptations of the flesh. His vows of celibacy had not been taken lightly—nor had they been easy to maintain. Even after leaving the priesthood, he'd battled with his own basic, human needs. But he'd never given into them. Not before now. Partly because everyone at the plantation knew that he'd been a priest, and he thought that they secretly hoped he would return to his earlier vocation. But even more than that, he'd been too embarrassed, thinking that any woman who might join him in lovemaking would find his inexperience laughable.

But with Glory Bee, he didn't think. He surrendered to the insanity of it all, allowing his body to revel in emotions and sensations that he'd never thought possible.

Lifting his head, he stared down at her in wonder—meeting her own bewildered gaze. Then, as if the storm had passed, when he kissed her again, it was with more tenderness. While one arm stayed around her waist, the other hand swept over her back, her hips, taking in her womanly shape, before straying up, up, to cup her breast.

She shuddered against him and he quickly altered his course.

But before he could stray too far, she took his wrist, guiding him back to her taut, straining nipple. Then, to his infinite amazement, her fingers shifted to the buttons of her blouse, slowly releasing them, before guiding his hand inside, beneath her brassiere.

He shivered as he touched the softness of her breast, flesh to flesh. Such incredible, incredible softness, and then the hard nub of her nipple rubbing against the sensitive hollow of his palm.

Their kisses became even slower, filled with an aching need that radiated between them.

And yet…

And yet…

Pulling away, John rested his forehead against her own, struggling to drag air into his starved lungs. The need of the moment warred with years of discipline and dogma nearly crushing him beneath their weight.

As if sensing the change in his mood and its cause, Glory Bee didn't demur when he moved his hand back to the safety of her waist. Instead, she wrapped her arms around his neck and held him. Tightly.

His pulse was rushing through his ears with such noise and fury that he thought, but couldn't be sure, that she gentled him like a startled child. "Shh. Shh. It's all right."

Then, when he was calmer, and his heart thudded dully in his chest, she drew back. Turning away, she fastened the buttons to her blouse, then bent and retrieved the fishing equipment that he'd dropped onto the ground.

After that, she looked at him from beneath her lashes for several long moments. There was no recrimination, no annoyance, just a gentle understanding. He could drown in those deep blue eyes.

"Come on," she said softly, taking his hand and turning back in the direction of the lodge. "It might be better for both of us if we have beans for dinner again tonight."

* * *

Gilhouley stepped into Col. Ross' office and snapped to attention, offering a quick salute.

The older man wearily returned the gesture, then said, "At ease, Lieutenant."

As Gilhouley settled into the more informal pose, Col. Ross shuffled through several folders on his desk. Then he leaned back, wearily scrubbing at his eyes with the palms of his hands.

Gilhouley was shocked by the man's appearance. In the space of a few days, Col. Ross had grown haggard and gray. Dark circles carved hollows beneath his eyes and his normally pristine office was a study in chaos. Evidently, the rumors that Stotsenberg could be evacuated soon had some credence, because file drawers were open, their contents disgorged onto the floor in haphazard piles. On his way indoors, Gilhouley had seen Ross's aides tending to huge smoking oil drums filled with papers.

"I've got a special assignment for you, Gilhouley."

"Sir?" Gilhouley couldn't keep the confusion from his tone. He would have thought that the last thing Ross needed at the moment was someone to write a press release.

Ross pulled one of the folders closer and rifled through the pages. "Says here that you spent some time in the Aleutians."

Shit. Hopefully, it didn't say why he'd spent time in the Aleutians.

"Yes, sir."

"It also states that you have a talent for radio communication."

Gilhouley felt heat rise into his cheeks. His "talent for radio communications" had not been strictly official and he'd received a reprimand for his unauthorized use of the Army's equipment to order beer, hotdogs, and fireworks for an impromptu Independence Day party for the rest of the schmucks in his barracks. But since he wasn't sure how in-depth the report might be, Gilhouley decided it might be best not to comment.

Ross leaned back in his chair again, causing the spring at its base to offer a weary whine.

"How the hell did you end up in the press corps?" Ross asked bluntly.

Gilhouley shrugged. "I was told that my…communication skills were above average." Which meant he'd said the wrong thing to the wrong officer. "So when I was transferred to the Philippines, I was sent to the press corps." The colonel behind his transfer had probably thought it would be a further demotion. But Gilhouley had liked the assignment. Liked it a lot.

Ross made a huffing noise. "That means you can string a sentence together—which, I might add, is more than most of my aides can do."

"I suppose so, sir."

Inhaling sharply, the colonel straightened again. "Well, you're about to be reassigned."

Gilhouley nodded. Most of the non-essential personnel were being absorbed into the infantry as quickly as they could be supplied, so he wasn't at all surprised by the information.

"What I'm going to ask you to do will be strictly voluntary. But it's a job that will draw on your special skills." He slapped Gilhouley's folder shut and stood, rounding the desk. "Quite frankly, I need someone who's a goddamned idiot, and I think you'll fill the bill. You'll be drawing upon your ability to communicate, but even more importantly, your talents for larceny and quick thinking."

Gilhouley shifted uncomfortably. "Sir?"

"I'm organizing a few select teams of men to take some supplies into the hills. It won't be long before the Japs will be knocking at our back door. Before that happens, we intend to hide radio equipment in various spots around the island. A few of the radios will be buried until later, even more will be distributed to key Filipinos that are already mounting guerrilla offensives against the Japs. Unfortunately, most of those locations will soon be behind enemy lines, so we need to act swiftly. I'd like you to lead one of those groups of men."

Gilhouley was surprised that he'd even be considered for such a mission. His training was solid, but it had been years since he'd done anything but man a typewriter.

"Any questions?"

Gilhouley shook his head. Even with the colonel's brief

explanation, he didn't need anything else spelled out to him. It was obvious that the colonel thought their positions would be overrun. Soon. Weeks from now, these radio stations might be the only means of gathering intelligence until reinforcements from the States could come. These missions could prove vital when it came time to push the Japanese back off the island.

But Gilhouley also wasn't stupid. In order to make the information they gathered as valuable as possible, they would have to move deep into what already was, or soon would be, enemy territory. If they were caught, they would be killed.

Gilhouley felt a moment's hesitation. Not because of the job that needed to be done or the dangers involved. No, his only twinge of resistance came from whom he would be leaving behind.

Rosemary.

But then, even as his body was sufficed with the memory of their stolen moments together in her office, his body pounding into hers, he knew that he couldn't refuse Col. Ross's offer. If there was any chance in hell of driving the Japs off the Philippines, he had to do it. Because the alternative—the thought of Rosemary becoming a prisoner to those animals—was unthinkable.

"Will I be allowed to pick my own team?" Gilhouley asked.

"That's up to you. We're sending out squads of five. But this is a need-to-know operation."

"When do you want us to go?"

* * *

If Rosemary had dared to hope that the Japanese meant to bomb the Philippines and then leave—as it appeared they'd been content to do with Hawaii—she was soon disappointed. Day after day, the planes returned. Sometimes the Zeroes were seen in the distance, and at other times, the sirens would sound and the women would be sent to the nearest shelters.

She always felt like a coward when they were forced to head for the basements or the outer trenches. Most of their patients weren't allowed the same luxury. At best, they could only crawl beneath their cots. And after one particular day, when the nurses had been sent to the trenches a half-dozen times, it became apparent that trying to maintain the uniform of crisp white hose, white dress and cap, was pure folly.

Speaking to the quartermaster, she arranged for the girls to receive two sets of the same one-piece coveralls that the pilots wore. But as she handed out the new "combat" uniforms, as the girls had dubbed them, they soon realized that the only size available was a forty-four long.

So the women donned their coveralls, rolled up the sleeves and cuffs, belted the waists, and slogged away at their jobs during their shifts, then spent their few precious off-duty hours with needles and thread, sewing feverishly in the hopes of making their new clothes look a little less like clown suits.

Rosemary secretly found the coveralls liberating. So many of their duties had expanded to include jobs once delegated to doctors and orderlies. The one-piece garments were more practical, if a little hot. Soon, she insisted that their shoes be replaced with the men's hardier boots as well, since it was clear that luck was not going to turn in their favor any time soon. The Japanese had begun their amphibious landings. First, in the far north. Then, barely four days after the first attack, at Legaspi and Albay in southern Luzon.

Less than two weeks after the first attack, Rosemary received the order to begin transporting the wounded south to Manila. With the invasion force advancing toward them, medical personnel would either be moved to Corregidor or the Bataan Peninsula where the troops would hunker down and wait for reinforcements from America to relieve them.

If Rosemary had thought her women were being pushed to the brink before, the logistics involved in moving so many patients belied her assumptions. With very little sleep or relief from their duties, they began the newest phase of their responsibilities: evacuation.

They started with those who could weather a journey by truck and ambulance first. Once again, the walking wounded were enlisted as makeshift medical staff to help those who were more seriously hurt. Convoys of trucks were loaded with as many men as possible. A pair of nurses went as well, one each in the lead and rear vehicles, and the rest of the patients were closely watched by their comrades.

By the time that two such convoys had departed for Manila, Rosemary received word that the more gravely injured would be taken south by train. She and the other nurses were to be on that train, no exceptions. Their retreat would be permanent. It would fall to the doctors to see that any remaining patients were sent south as well.

After passing on the word to her nurses, Rosemary began packing boxes and crates with all of the medical tools and supplies she could manage to gather in the time remaining. She'd be damned if she'd leave anything useful behind for the Japanese. To hell with her own belongings. She'd pack the most necessary personal items into a duffel bag—clean coveralls, an extra pair of shoes, underthings, her only remaining white uniform, and her last unopened pair of alabaster hose, toiletries and sanitary items. While other women dithered over whether or not to pack their evening gowns and hats, her only indulgence was the violet corsage Gilhouley had given her, stowed at the top of her duffel.

The trip to her bungalow to gather her things had taken less than fifteen minutes, but in that time, she'd been able to see that Gilhouley still hadn't made an appearance. Except for a shattered window in the sitting room, her residence had remained relatively unscathed. But a fine layer of grit and dust covered everything after the attack, and the only footprints to be seen were her own.

She was rushing down the stairs with her bag when a Jeep screeched to a stop in front of her. Her heart slammed against her ribcage as she recognized Gilhouley, gaunt and a little pale, his face retaining only a few scratches from the first attack.

"Get in," he said abruptly.

"I've got to—"

"I know. You're getting ready to be evacuated, but there's something we need to do first. It'll only take a few minutes."

Since the nurses had been given an hour to pack their things, she didn't suppose it would hurt to spend the remainder of her time with Gilhouley. Especially since she didn't know when she would see him again.

The moment she'd taken her place in the Jeep, he punched the accelerator, weaving his way through base traffic and bomb craters. As soon as he'd taken the curve onto the main road, he increased his speed even more until she had to grasp the dash to steady herself.

"Where are we going?"

"Just a few miles away. I need to take you out into the hills."

Her brows rose and he laughed. "Not for that." He thought better of his answer because he hastened to add, "But, trust me, if we had time, I'd insist on that too—although I'd rather do it on a bed, if you don't mind, much as I enjoyed our encounter in your office."

Rosemary's pulse knocked against her throat. She supposed she should be embarrassed or appalled at her own forwardness, but she didn't care. Gilhouley was safe; he was here with her. At the moment, nothing else mattered.

"How are you?" she said, using her free hand to stroke his cheek.

"Tired. Sore."

"Are the stitches holding?"

"They're fine. I'm fine. How about you?"

"Exhausted."

"I bet."

"What have you been doing since I saw you last?"

He caught her eye, debating how much he should tell her. "Training," he said vaguely. "I've been reassigned to a combat unit."

"Which one?"

"I'll be under Colonel Ross."

"He's Cavalry, isn't he?" Her brows rose. "Can you ride? Most of the cavalry from Stotsenberg are still mounted, aren't they?"

"I doubt that will become an issue."

He swerved around another crater, then turned sharply right, heading down a dirt track toward a field of cogon grass that dipped and swayed in the wind like a verdant sea. Once he'd reached a stand of trees, he pulled to a stop. "We've got to hurry."

Still mystified, she watched as he withdrew a small canvas pouch and a bulging sock, then a grocery sack filled with what looked like empty beer bottles. "Stay here for a minute."

He strode through the grass about twenty yards to where a set of rough wooden posts had once anchored a fence. Digging into the grocery sack, he set a bottle on each one, then returned, motioning for her to get out of the Jeep and stand next to him.

For several seconds, debated his words, then said, "Despite what they might be telling you, things are going to get rough, Rosemary."

She touched his arm. "I know that."

"It could be weeks, maybe even a month before relief troops arrive."

She nodded.

"So I want you to be prepared."

Gauging her reaction one last time, he reached into the pouch and removed a revolver much like those she'd seen in Wild West movies.

"This was given to me by my father, and to him by his father. It's old, but it's reliable. And since it's not Army issue, I can do with it as I please. You're going to take this with you on the train."

She opened her mouth to object, but he immediately silenced her.

"You can't change my mind, so don't even try. We're not leaving here until you know how to shoot it. It's a weapon of last resort, up close, understand?"

Rosemary nodded, at once touched and terrified.

He handed her the sock and she realized it was filled with cartridges.

Holding the revolver in both hands, he showed her how to release the cylinder from its firing position.

"Slide a cartridge in all of the chambers but one. You'll keep one of them empty as a safety measure."

She nodded, doing as she'd been told.

"You're going to make sure that the empty chamber is opposite the hammer."

Rosemary watched carefully as he showed her how to do it, then made her practice the procedure several times.

"This revolver has a sensitive trigger, so I want you to hold the gun like this in both hands. Forget what you've seen in the movies. If you ever need to use this, you're going to be scared and nervous and you'll need both hands to hold it steady enough to aim."

He stood behind her, wrapping his arms around her. "Don't pull the hammer back until you have your arms up and in position so that you can site down the barrel. Like I said, the trigger is sensitive and you don't want to accidently shoot your foot rather than your target."

"Okay."

With his hands in position over her own, he gently pulled back on the hammer.

"Close one eye and look down the length of the gun. Aim at the bottle over there. The first one. There's a notch near the hammer and a little vertical piece of metal at the tip of the gun that looks like a post. Line it up so that the post is right in the center of the notch and both of them are dead center over the bottle. Then gently squeeze the trigger."

The gun recoiled in her hands, the sound of the shot scaring her more than anything. But Gilhouley held her steady.

"Good job."

She opened her eyes to see that the bottle still stood on the fence post.

"I missed."

"That's because you closed your eyes. Now you know what to expect. Try again."

This time, he made her pull back the hammer and carefully aim. "Keep one eye open and don't hold your breath."

The air rushed from her lungs in a whoosh.

"Take aim, then gently squeeze the trigger when you're ready. The revolver will do all the work."

This time, she concentrated on keeping her arms level and one eye open.

Bam!

The noise and recoil was still unsettling, but a burst of splinters from the fence post told her that, this time, she was at least hitting in the proper area.

"Good girl!"

"But I only hit the post."

"Yes, but if that were a Japanese soldier, you would have hit him in the gut rather than the chest. Either way, you'd probably stopped him in his tracks. Now do it again."

By the fifth shot, Rosemary winged the bottle. At Gilhouley's insistence, she emptied the barrel twice more, destroying a half dozen bottles before he called it quits.

"That's enough for now. We can't afford to use up any more ammunition, and I think you've got the hang of it."

"You should take it, Gilhouley," she insisted as they made their way back to the Jeep. "I can't exactly wear a holster with my uniform."

He tucked the pouch with the gun inside her duffle along with the sock containing her ammunition. Then he pulled her tightly against him. "No, but you can have it next to your bunk at night. Just in case."

Unspoken between them were the horrors that had occurred to the women of Nanking—the gang rapes, the torture, the mutilations.

Her throat was tight as she asked, "When will I see you again?"

He shook his head. "I don't know. The Japanese are closing in fast. Once they take the base…I don't know where I'll be." He rested his forehead against hers. "But as soon as I can, I'll find you. Promise."

When he kissed her, his lips were soft and gentle, his tenderness more bittersweet than she could have imagined only days earlier. She opened her mouth against him, desperately clinging to him, knowing that time was flowing through their fingers like sand.

When Gilhouley backed away to bury his face against her neck, she whispered next to his ear, "Promise me, you'll stay as safe as you can."

"Only if you'll do the same."

"You know I will. It won't be long. You'll be in Manila soon."

But too late, she realized that in order for that to happen, the Japanese would have pushed the defending forces south across Luzon.

"We've got to go," Gilhouley murmured against her skin.

"I know."

And yet, they continued to stand, locked together for several long moments before Gilhouley finally stepped away, kissing her hard and full on the mouth, then released her to stride around the front of the Jeep to the driver's seat.

After climbing inside, she reached across the gear shift to grip his thigh. Then, he was turning sharply, heading back the way that they'd come.

Soon—much too soon—he brought the Jeep to a halt in front of the hospital. Here, there could be no desperate public embrace, no feverish last kiss, so he touched the hand that still lay on his thigh. "Take care of yourself."

She nodded, her throat tight. "You don't have anything of mine to take."

He smiled, digging into his pocket. "Oh, but I do." He removed a tiny flower and she realized it was one of the violets from the corsage he'd given her. "I stole it as I was leaving, the first time we made love. No one on earth could have a better talisman than that."

She blinked at the tears that threatened to spill free, but seeing the curious stares of her nurses as they loaded crates onto a nearby truck, she settled for, "So long, Gilhouley."

She slipped out of the Jeep and gathered her duffel. As she slung it over her shoulder, Gilhouley threw her a salute. "See you soon, Major."

Then with a growl of the Jeep's engine, he made a wide U-turn and headed in the opposite direction.

• • •

Glory Bee stepped onto the porch that wrapped its way around the Wilmot's hunting lodge, making her way to the back where John and Esteban were splitting wood for the stove. She couldn't be sure, but his posture seemed somehow...lighter, looser. Since the night she'd awakened him from his nightmare, he'd begun to smile more. And laugh. Maybe by talking to her about his experiences in Nanking, the load of anger he carried had eased.

Glory Bee could only wonder what would have happened if he'd been allowed to unburden himself without the threat of war breathing down their necks.

"I can help carry those up to the pile," she called, gesturing to the cut pieces lying on the ground.

"No need, Missy," Esteban said with a grin. He whistled and his children barreled out of the trees and scooped them up, racing to be the first to place them in the pile.

Glory Bee laughed. "You've got them well-trained, Esteban. I think—"

A low drone caused her to grow suddenly quiet, and she froze.

Lifting a hand, John motioned for them all to remain still as they cocked their ears toward the sound.

Planes.

The rumbling grew louder and louder, like a growing thunder that did not end.

"Glory Bee, get the children into the house. Esteban, get your wife."

"Come on, kids. Inside. Inside!"

Glory Bee rushed to scoop Luis into her arms, then began herding the other youngsters into the lodge. Once there, they hurried to press against the large picture window and peer down into the valley below. Dozens of shiny silver planes flew in formation, the red circles gleaming like dots of blood on their wings. In the valley below came the telltale sign of smoke and dust.

Her heart slammed against her ribs. Had the invasion forces arrived in the valley? Or were the villagers below fleeing as the Japanese planes made another run at the American bases?

Maria scurried into the house, calling to her children in Tagalog. Esteban quickly followed. Then John strode across the room to a door that had remained closed and locked. Lifting a foot, he kicked at the flimsy barrier, breaking it, then reached inside to unlatch it. There, in a specially made cabinet, weapons of all kinds lined the walls.

Removing a rifle, he tossed it to Esteban along with a box of ammunition. Then he took a pistol, checked the chamber, and shoved it into his waistband.

"Is it the Japanese?" Glory Bee asked. "Have their front lines progressed this far?"

John's expression was grim. "We'd be fools to think otherwise."

A chill passed through her system. Sweet baby Jesus, it was happening. It was actually happening.

"Do you think they'll be coming up here?" Glory Bee asked in alarm.

John shook his head. "No. Not yet, anyway. But from now on, we're going to be armed at all times." He eyed Glory Bee. "You said you were from Virginia. Is that in the country? Are you a country girl?"

She nodded.

"Can you shoot?"

Her shoulders lifted helplessly. "I shot birds and squirrels with a BB gun when I was little, but..."

John took a small pistol from the shelf along with a handful of cartridges. Taking her hand, he dropped them into her palm. "Load it."

Sensing this was a test to see if she could handle the weapon without shooting herself in the process, she checked the cylinder, then slid the shells into position and locked everything back into place.

"Good. That's yours. Keep it with you at all times."

As she met his turbulent gaze, she sensed he was thinking of Sister Mary Francis and the other poor girls at the convent school, so she didn't argue. Instead, she tucked the weapon into the back of her waistband.

"What do we do now?" she asked.

"We wait. We watch for smoke. If it gets too close, we head deeper into the hills."

He waited in agony for three days. Three impossible, agonizing days.

And then, when he hadn't even expected it, he turned to find the Filipino messenger boy crouching in the dust next to him.

"You...Gilhouley?" he asked.

He nodded.

The boy handed him a small package—matches, cigarettes, quinine, and a folded scrap of paper.

He quickly shoved the items into his pockets, then withdrew the letter. He had no envelope to put it in—had no way of knowing if it would ever get to Rosemary—or if she was even alive. But for the first time in years, he had a flare of hope.

"Give this to the padre. *Tell him to send it to Major Rosemary Dodd."*

The boy looked at him blankly.

"This..." he pointed to the paper. "For Major Rosemary Dodd. A nurse."

The boy glanced up, saw the guards returning and snatched the paper from his hand. Then the kid scampered away, disappearing into the brush as if he'd never been there.

As he watched him go, he felt suddenly weak with relief.

Dear God, let his letter get to her.

Let her be alive.

Chapter Nine

December 24, 1941

Rosemary was one of the last to board the hospital train. She'd inspected each of the cars, double-checked the supplies they'd managed to pack away, and conferred with her nurses. Then, with a nod to the stationmaster and a salute to Dr. Grimm—who would remain behind for another few days—she climbed up the steps of the final car and stowed her duffle next to the rear exit.

There was barely any room to move. Except for the first four seats, the rest of the train had been converted with something akin to shelving where the wounded men on their stretchers had been laid as tightly together as they could manage without endangering their care. IV bottles and tubing swayed in the air as the train jerked and trembled, then began a slow roll. A pair of orderlies had taken position by the exits, each of them fully armed.

Alice sidled up beside her. "I think everything has been strapped down as best as possible."

"Keep an eye on Sergeant Kearney in the middle. He was carried out of surgery only an hour ago. I want his vitals taken every fifteen minutes."

Alice nodded and moved forward, pausing now and then to talk to the men as she went. Rosemary followed a little more slowly. She would take the back half of the car and Alice would take the front—just as the rest of her staff had done throughout the train. Hopefully, by dividing the space up, they could keep things as efficient as possible. The journey wasn't incredibly long, less than fifty miles, but due to the injured, they would be travelling at a slower rate of speed. Rosemary estimated it would be about ninety minutes before they reached Manila.

"Hey, Major, you got a light?"

She smiled at a young cavalry lieutenant and reached into her pocket for the lighter she kept there.

He puffed until the tip grew red, then asked, "Where you from, ma'am?"

"Nebraska."

"Nebraska, huh? I'm a Philly boy, myself."

She raised her brows. "Good to know. I've been warned about fraternizing with those Philly boys."

Rosemary tried to soothe her nerves by settling into a familiar routine. Granted, until a few weeks ago, she'd never been confronted with the dire injuries that surrounded her before, but the job was still the same. Check vitals, adjust IVs, administer medication, repeat. And through it all, she smiled and chatted while keeping the men at arm's length.

But even as she immersed herself in tasks that were second nature to her, she couldn't prevent the tension that gripped her shoulders and the way she continually listened for the slightest sound—a rumble of artillery, the growl of an aircraft engine—that would warn her that trouble was on its way.

Just before they'd left Stotsenberg, they'd received word that two other air bases were under aerial attack and American forces on the ground were heavily engaged. The battle for Luzon had begun in earnest.

If not for her work, Rosemary wasn't sure how she would have coped. At odd moments, thoughts of Riley would pop into her head and she would be overcome by her need to know that he was safe. But with all that she'd already seen, she couldn't kid herself. The odds were stacked against the Americans and their Filipino counterparts. Their arms were dated, their air force decimated. And the Japanese would throw everything they had at them. The forces of the Rising Sun needed the military positioning that the Philippines would offer them. They would not accept defeat.

It was while she was checking the bandages of an amputee that she heard it, a low growling hum that cut through the rhythmic clacking of the train. Bending low, she scanned the horizon, then instinctively took a step back as she saw the nose of a zero heading straight in her direction.

The plane screamed overhead as an explosion rocked the train, dirt and debris shooting up into the sky several yards away from the car. As the chunks of rock and grass pelted the windows, the zero pulled up and began a slow turn, coming in for another try.

Rosemary swore. Each car on the train had been marked with a red cross to label it as a hospital transport, but the pilot didn't care.

Before Rosemary knew what was happening, she had more to contend with than the pilot of the plane. Men who had already suffered through several air attacks reacted instinctively, jumping into the aisles and scrambling for the nearest exit. The roar of the plane and the ratcheting of its guns caused many of the men to scream in fear and rage.

"Get back in your seats!" Rosemary shouted. Then as loud as she could, "Get back! Now! That's an order!" She pointed to the orderly. "I want you to shoot anyone who tries to get off this train!"

Just when Rosemary thought she would have a mob on her hands, the shocking intent of her words tapped into the training the men had been given and the noise died down as they turned to stare at her in disbelief.

"We're as safe on this train as we would be anywhere else. The only thing that can hurt us now is panic." She pointed to the bunks. "Get back where you were!"

Slowly, the men began to comply. With some, the burst of energy had exhausted them, but with others, they kept a nervous eye on the windows. But the Zero that had targeted them had either run out of ammunition or had tired of his game, because he did not return.

Alice and Rosemary spent the rest of the journey checking on torn stitches and twisted IV lines, but thankfully, no real damage had been done.

They rolled into Manila with a palpable sense of relief. But that relief was short-lived as Rosemary stared out of the windows into a decimated city. Beautiful old buildings had been reduced to rubble and fires raged on the outskirts of town.

"It doesn't look much better than Stotsenberg," Alice said lowly, before turning to help unload the wounded.

It took over an hour to transfer all of the wounded onto the waiting trucks. In that time, the temperature within the cars became unbearable, so much so, that Rosemary worried the wounded would soon be suffering from heatstroke as well. But, at long last, the last man was taken away and she and her nurses gathered their things. Wearily, they climbed into their own waiting transport and traveled the short distance to Sternberg Hospital.

It was with mixed feelings that Rosemary turned over her command to the senior nursing staff.

"You and your girls have done a fine job, Major Dodd."

"Thank you, Colonel Willmington."

"I'm sure you need something to eat and a place to wash up, so my assistant will take you to the nurses' quarters where arrangements have been made. The Japs have made a mess of it, I'm afraid. But at least you'll have a few minutes of privacy."

"Thank you, Colonel."

"Anything else we can do for you?"

Rosemary hesitated before saying, "Most of my nurses have been working round the clock, Colonel. A few hours' sleep would do them a world of good."

Col. Willmington nodded. "Unfortunately, a few hours are about all I can spare. They'll probably have to bunk on the floor, but tell them to get some rest, then report to the hospital at 1800. You'll be on duty at the hospital tonight. Tomorrow, you and your nurses will report to the docks at 2000."

"Thank you, Colonel." Rosemary offered the woman a crisp salute, then went to the far end of the platform where her nurses waited next to a pile of luggage. "We've got until 1800 to rest, get something to eat, and change for duty. We'll be buddying up with the nurses who are already here. Grab your gear."

Now that the promise of a few hours of sleep hung in the air, the energy seeped from Rosemary's body like grains of sand through an hourglass. By the time she'd reached the nurses' quarters and helped her staff settle in, her legs felt as if they'd been encased in lead.

Finally, an older woman with black hair mixed with strands of gray motioned for Rosemary and Alice to follow her to a room at the back of the first floor.

"I'm Major Cooper. You two are with me."

She opened the door to a small room with two narrow beds. "My roommate escorted a batch of nurses to Corregidor this morning, so she won't be back. I'm on duty until late this evening, so the bunks are yours." Her eyes grew gentle. "I hear it was rough at Clark that first day." She hesitated before asking, "You wouldn't have happened to run into a Major Walter Beidermeyer would you? He's a crew chief at Clark. We're supposed to be married in February."

Rosemary was so weary, she couldn't honestly remember any of the names of the wounded that had poured through her hospital doors. "I-I don't think so."

She looked at Alice, who also shook her head.

"I'll ask my other nurses after they've rested," Rosemary said.

Major Cooper offered them a sad smile. "Thanks. I'd appreciate that. Pleasant dreams."

As soon as she'd closed the door, Rosemary sank onto the bunk.

"I think I could sleep for a hundred years," Alice said as she collapsed onto the opposite cot.

"We don't have a hundred years. We only have until 1730. Then we'll need to change into fresh uniforms, get something to eat, and make our way to the hospital to be reassigned."

"Don't remind me."

Alice kicked off her shoes and lay down, not even bothering to pull back the covers. She simply turned her face to the wall and fell instantly asleep.

Rosemary carefully removed her shoes, then pulled her duffel bag close. Reaching inside, she stroked the delicate petals of her corsage as if they were rosary beads. *Please, keep him safe.*

Although her family was a church-going one, it had been years since Rosemary had darkened the door of a religious building, but she brushed that thought aside. At the moment, she was helpless and alone, and she had no other means to come to Gilhouley's aid, but to pray.

Please, please…keep him safe…

• • •

Glory Bee was roused from her sleep by a hand against her shoulder. She discovered John standing over her in the darkness.

He held a finger to his lips, gesturing to the children.

Blinking sleep away, Glory Bee realized that little Luis had crawled into bed beside her and had burrowed into a spot next to her back.

"What is it?" she whispered.

"The fires are getting too close. I need you to pack up everything you can. Esteban has arranged for some local *cargadores* to carry our things. We've got to be out of here within the hour."

A wave of icy fear swamped her body and for several long seconds, Glory Bee couldn't move.

"Where will we go?"

"Into the mountains."

She nodded. "I'll…I'll get all my belongings together."

"Don't forget the pistol."

"I won't."

John gestured to a rucksack he'd placed on the floor. "I found that downstairs. It will probably be easier to handle than your suitcase."

"Th-thanks." She cleared her throat. "John?" she called before he was about to disappear down the stairs. "Will this work? Can we keep ourselves hidden in the hills?"

John's expression was grim. "It has to work."

* * *

Less than twenty minutes later everything had been packed up and they were ready to leave. John made one last round of the house. He'd already cleaned out the weapons' cupboard for arms and ammunition. He'd added tins of matches to their stash, and blankets and tarps. Then with Esteban's help, they'd carried the radio into the nearby woods, wrapped it in tarpaulins, and hidden it. It was too bulky to take with them, but there might come a time when they would need it.

The truck had also been hidden, but John had little hope that it would remain unseen if the Japanese headed this way. No, the rest of their journey would have to be taken on foot.

He surveyed the motley group assembled on the veranda—Esteban, his pregnant wife and five children, the four *cargadores* from a nearby village, and Glory Bee. None of them were in the best shape for a rigorous hike into the hills. But it was their only chance of staying away from the Japanese.

"I think we're ready."

John shook himself free from his thoughts as Esteban approached. Slinging his rifle over his shoulder, he called out, "All right, everyone. Let's go."

* * *

Gilhouley motioned for the driver of the car to stop and cut the engine. As the hot motor ticked in the sudden silence, he cocked his head out the window, listening to the distant *boom, boom, boom* of the heavy artillery and the staccato *ackety-ack* of machine gun fire.

"They're getting pretty close," the driver, a gangly kid of nineteen, murmured, a cigarette hanging from his lips untended while his fingers gripped the wheel. Despite his age, he'd proven to have a cool head and quick wits.

"How much fuel have we got?" Gilhouley asked.

Kilgore thumped on the dial. "Barely enough to get us back to

Manila from where we are now. We're either going to have to hike in the rest of the way into the hills to find Santo Tomas, or hike part of the way back to Manila once we've run out of gas."

Gilhouley squinted up at the tree line, knowing that regardless of what they did, they would not be able to travel very far without threat of exposure. The dry season had settled over the Philippines, and the roads were choked with telltale dust. Even at slow speeds, the passage of a car would be clear to anyone who might chance to look toward the hillside.

"How much farther to the rendezvous point?"

"At least five miles. Maybe six. We could hike it, easy."

Gilhouley pondered that point for a moment. With the Japanese approaching, they didn't have much time. Ross had arranged for them to meet with Felipe Santo Tomas, one of the Filipinos who'd been trained under the Americans not so long ago. Word had it that he'd already mustered a band of men willing to fight. Col. Ross wanted to get a radio into their hands before they moved to a new position.

"Petey, stay here with Kilgore," Gilhouley murmured to the curly-headed teenager who sat in the back, his rifle trained out the back window. "I'm going to have a look around."

"Yes, sir."

Grasping his rifle, Gilhouley opened the door, slinging a small pack over his back. Motioning for the men who sat in the rear rumble seat of the beat-up Model A that they'd commandeered from one of the camp cooks, Gilhouley pointed for them to move toward a clearing a few yards ahead of them. Beyond that was a bluff that looked down on the valley below.

Moving carefully, he and his companions walked forward, their rifles at the ready, their footsteps measured to minimize the noise.

Not for the first time, Gilhouley was grateful for the men he'd chosen as part of his team: Doug Kilgore, their driver, was a fellow member of the press corps. He had the mind of a mathematician and skills on the radio that put even Gilhouley's to shame. Josiah Tecumseh Peterman—or Petey as they called him—had barely been relieved from the brig for decking his superior officer when the other man had run away during the bombing at Clark. Ernie Berman, a cavalry officer and a farm boy from Iowa, could fix anything mechanical or electronic with a stick of gum and some twine. And Elian Baptiste was a native to the Philippines. The son of a French planter and a Filipino mother, he was fluent in English, Spanish, Tagalog and French.

It was their third foray into the Filipino forest. So far, they had delivered or hidden seven radios. They had one to go before returning to base.

Nearing the edge of a bluff, Gilhouley motioned for his men to stay low. Removing a pair of binoculars from his pack, he trained them on the valley.

"Shit." The roads he could see with his field glasses were clogged with tanks, military personnel, and trucks.

"What's up, boss? Are those our boys or theirs?" Berman whispered, crouching in the brush beside him.

"Theirs."

Gilhouley squinted through the binoculars again. It was too far away to catch many details, but even at this distance, he could see that the Japanese were advancing toward a line of trees where, no doubt, the American forces were hunkered down, waiting.

"What do y' wanna do?"

Gilhouley turned to Baptiste. "Can you get us to the rendezvous point on foot, without using the road?"

Baptiste offered him a cocky grin. "Yes, sir."

"All right. Go tell the others. We're going to hide the car as best we can in those trees up ahead. Then we'll load up with our supplies and hoof it to the rendezvous point. Then, as soon as we've dumped off the radio, we'll try to get back here in time to drive out."

The men nodded and crept back to the waiting vehicle. As their hushed voices relayed the instructions to Kilgore and Petey, Gilhouley lifted the binoculars back up to his eyes for one last look.

They would be cutting things close. There was a single bridge leading across a ravine at the base of the mountains. If they didn't reach it before the Japanese Army…

Hell, he didn't even have the time to think about the shit they'd be in then.

• • •

Glory Bee panted as the path ahead of her grew steeper still. They'd been climbing steadily now for nearly an hour and her knees and calves were beginning to burn and tremble from the unaccustomed exercise.

Lord, she'd never realized that she was so out of shape. With her dancing and performing, she'd always considered herself fit—she had to be if she planned to parade on stage with very little clothing. But this…this was torture.

Looking behind her, she could see that the children were also beginning to flag. At first, they'd considered their hike a big game. Rather than trailing the adults, they'd darted in and out of the trees, playing tag and hide-and-seek along the way. But as the trail became steeper, their games had ceased, and now they shuffled wearily in a line between Maria and Glory Bee, their features flushed and beaded with sweat.

Swatting away the gnats that swarmed around them in clouds, Glory Bee returned her attention to the front of the line. Unlike the women and children, John was completely unfazed by the exercise. He climbed easily, ever vigilant.

As if he'd heard her thoughts, John stepped to the side of the trail and pointed up above them. "We'll go as far as that rocky outcropping, then we'll take a break in the shade. Just a little further now."

Although the landmark that he'd pointed to was only a few hundred yards away, it seemed like a million miles to Glory Bee's trembling muscles. And as much as she wanted to rest, she was afraid that if she did, she wouldn't be able to get back up again.

As she approached the spot where he stood, John held out his hand. "Grab hold, Glory Bee."

Confused, she took his hand, then was relieved as he fell into step ahead of her and began pulling her up the rest of the incline, until, finally, they reached the rocks.

Glory Bee didn't even bother to hide her weariness. She sank onto the ground, panting.

John knelt beside her, handing her a canteen. "Not too much. Just a few sips at first."

She nodded, unable to speak, and swallowed the tepid water.

"You're doing really well."

Her laughter was wry. "And you're an excellent liar."

His quick grin was so startling that she nearly didn't catch it before it was gone again. In the hike, his hair had become mussed, falling from under his hat to spill across his forehead in a way that made her fingers itch to touch it.

"Find yourself a shady spot," he said. "We'll stay here until the heat of the day has passed, then start up with some fresh legs. Esteban knows of a village a ways down that ridge. We'll stay there for the night."

Glory Bee nodded, buoyed by the news. If they were going to a village, there would be a level of civilization. One of her greatest fears had been that they would camp out in the middle of the woods.

John offered her the canteen again and this time she couldn't keep from gulping the liquid.

"We need to find you a hat."

She gingerly touched her nose and winced at the slight stinging sensation.

"Am I turning red?"

"I'm more concerned about sunstroke. You haven't had time to acclimate to the heat of the Philippines, let alone the sun." He took his own field hat from his head and settled it over her brow. It fit so loosely, she felt like a child playing dress-up. "Use this until I can find you another one."

"But don't you need it?"

"I'll manage until we can find you something that will work better."

Again, a ghost of a smile toyed with the corners of his lips. But just as quickly, he looked out over the valley, and the lightness was gone, replaced by a brooding worry.

Following his gaze, Glory Bee gasped. Far below them, the fields of cogon had been set ablaze. Fueled by the hot, dry winds, a wall of flame leapt and danced. Black smoke roiled upwards to stain the azure blue sky.

"Why?" she whispered. "Why would they set the whole island ablaze?"

"To drive out anyone trying to hide."

"Like us?"

He nodded. "And to prevent the Filipinos from forming guerrilla bands. Many of the men on the island have been trained by the American military in the past few years just for this event. Others are determined to defend their homeland."

Which meant that it could only be a matter of time before Esteban and John might decide to join them.

John squeezed her shoulder, then stood. "Drink a little more and rest. Now more than ever, we need to reach that village by nightfall."

* * *

A hand touched Rosemary's shoulder and she awakened with a jolt. For several long moments, she stared at an unfamiliar wall, an unfamiliar bunk, and a rumpled set of blankets. Then Alice stepped into view and every fear, every worry, every heartache rushed back, slamming into her chest like an anvil.

"It's 1730. I let you sleep as long as I dared. There's a bathroom down the hall, water's hot. You'd better take advantage of it while you can. I'm going to make sure everyone else is up and ready to go."

Nodding, Rosemary forced her aching body into a sitting position. Then, taking clean clothes and a towel from her duffel, she stumbled to the showers, washed as quickly as she could, and dressed. A glance at her watch showed her that there would be no time for a meal.

After stowing her things, she went into the main room where her own nurses were gathered in a knot.

"All here?" she asked, her gaze scanning the women present.

"Wilson and Juarez are on their way. Emerson and Todd have already gone to the hospital," Alice reported after checking the clipboard in her hand.

Lt. Wakely approached Rosemary and handed her a sandwich wrapped in waxed paper.

"Merry Christmas, Major."

Rosemary stared at her blankly.

"It's Christmas Eve, don't you remember?"

In a few hours, it will be Christmas Day.

For a moment, she was flooded with images of snow and mistletoe, a big tree in the parlor and the smells of her mother's homemade pumpkin pies. But with a rush, reality returned, and those memories could have been from another lifetime.

"Thanks."

As if reminding her that several meals had passed since she'd eaten, Rosemary's stomach growled. Normally, she wouldn't have eaten so casually in front of her staff, but since many of them were also taking advantage of the sandwiches and fruit provided, she unwrapped one corner and took a bite.

She could have wept. Peanut butter and strawberry jam. So simple, so…American. Again, she was inundated with memories of the farm and sitting at her mother's freshly scrubbed table for lunch when she was little.

Tears pricked her eyes, but she pushed them back, refusing to become sentimental. Not now. Not when the *boom, boom* of artillery echoed the thudding of her own heart.

The last two nurses scurried down the staircase and Rosemary gestured to the others.

"All right, then. Let's go."

As they walked out of the nurse's quarters into the hot, humid air, Rosemary realized that in the scant hours that they'd been resting, the mood on the base had deteriorated even more. Traffic was congested with troop transports, Jeeps, and ambulances. Offices were being emptied, important papers burned. Anything of military value was being stacked ready for transport.

They were still yards away from the hospital when Col. Willmington motioned for them to join her next to a long line of trucks with canvas tops.

"Major Dodd."

As Rosemary approached, she handed her a sheaf of papers.

"Here are the new assignments. Your staff has now been divided into two groups." She handed another set of papers to Lt. Wakely.

"Lieutenant Wakely, you'll be escorting the women listed here to a steamer waiting at the docks. At 2030, you'll be picked up by several cars and taken to the quay where you'll be in charge of evacuating as many men as we can load on the ship to Corregidor."

Vera Wakely nodded, her mouth tightening as she surveyed the names.

"Major Dodd, you and the rest of your staff will have the evening shift in the hospital. Then, at 2100 tomorrow evening, you'll take the ferry *Sea Spray,* which has been commandeered to take food and medical supplies across the bay."

Col. Willmington removed another set of papers from her clipboard. "Here's the manifest list. Once you reach Bataan, I want you to make sure that everything is taken off that ferry and loaded on the waiting trucks. Don't leave so much as a pin behind on that ship. We're already running short on supplies and we don't have anything to waste."

"Yes, Colonel."

"Very well, then. Go to your assigned duties before any more air raid sirens can go off."

Without even waiting for a salute, Col. Willmington turned and strode toward the next group of nurses heading toward the hospital.

"All right, everybody. You heard the Colonel," Rosemary said, lifting her voice to be heard over the din of artillery and the rumble of trucks. "Lieutenant Wakely is going to read off the names on her list. If you're called, head back to the nurses' quarters and grab your gear."

Rosemary noticed that Vera's hands were trembling as she read through the roll. Although Vera had been in charge of shifts before, it was the first time she'd been asked to take such an important leadership role. But Rosemary didn't doubt for an instant that she could handle the responsibility.

"Anderson…Call…Faberge…"

As each of the women dropped away and returned to their barracks, Rosemary offered them quick encouraging words, a hug, a shake of the hand.

"Gudmandson…Hillary…Hubbard…"

Alice joined her in offering their goodbyes until Lt. Wakely finished with, "Zimmerman!"

As the last woman hurried away, Rosemary quickly counted heads. Fifteen women were being sent to Corregidor.

Lt. Wakely paused before taking her place among them.

"Major." she said with a salute.

Rosemary returned the gesture, then pulled Vera close with a quick hug.

"Godspeed, Lieutenant."

"Godspeed to you, Major."

Then, blinking away the moisture that suddenly gathered in her eyes, Lt. Wakely marched into the gathering gloom.

Rosemary stood for several minutes, watching them go, trying to push away the uneasiness that came with her group splitting up. Except for the girls who'd arrived right before the attack, she'd worked with most of the women for years. And although her staff had swelled and waned with transfers, marriages, and girls going home, they'd never been torn apart by the violence of war. As she watched them go, Rosemary felt suddenly vulnerable. Smaller.

At her side, Alice shivered.

"Why do I suddenly feel like a goose has walked over my grave?" she whispered so that the other women wouldn't hear.

"I don't know," Rosemary admitted slowly.

Alice eyed her thoughtfully. "You feel it too?"

Feel what? The helplessness? The uncertainty? The absolute certainty that she would never see these women again?

"Yeah," Rosemary finally said. "Yeah. I feel it too.

He bent over the row of squash, hoeing at the ever-present weeds.

Even though he technically wasn't allowed to eat the bounty he grew, he was inordinately pleased by the harvest they would have in a few weeks. He'd worried that after being forced to endure another week in the pit, the plants would have suffered. Kilgore was conscientious enough, but the other men…

Well, they were either too weak or too filled with hatred for the Japs who would eat from the garden to take much care. But he didn't see things that way. Although he had to be careful, there were ways to smuggle some of the fruits and vegetables back into camp.

He pushed himself to his feet, wincing. His ribs hurt like a sonofabitch and he'd been pissing blood for days. But a return to the garden had been like a homecoming in many ways.

In the past, he'd never planted so much as a front lawn. He was a city boy through and through. But he was proving to have an innate knack at growing things. Lately, he'd even begun to wonder if that's what he would do after the war. Heaven only knew, after his last bout in the pit, he didn't want to be closed in ever again. The thought of working in an office gave him the willies.

Not for the first time, he remembered that Rosemary came from country folk. What would she think of him if he stated that he wanted to buy a little farm? Or at least a place with room for a garden? Who would have thought it? The Great Gilhouley puttering in the dirt. But then, he would do anything to have a chance to snag the fruits and vegetables straight from the source and eat his fill, instead of torturing himself by tending to produce that rarely ended up in his stomach.

"You need to take it easy," Kilgore said, sidling up beside him. "You've only been out of the pit two days, and they want us to clear that patch they've staked out in all that cogon. If you don't pace yourself, you'll be passing out.

He knew Kilgore was right. He shouldn't have even come back yet. But he was afraid that if he didn't, he would miss seeing the boy.

If the boy ever came again.

It had been six months. Six months since he'd passed the letter to the kid.

Dammit all to hell. How much longer would they have to wait for some outside contact? They'd given up on any official help. Clearly, the American government had abandoned them and left them for dead.

But the padre…

Surely he could trust him.

"The guerrillas are taking a beating in the hills," Kilgore said, reading his thoughts.

"How do you know?"

"Heard the guards laughing and talking about it. They said they caught one of the leaders. Beheaded him. Disemboweled him. They were bragging about it like they'd caught themselves a fish in the lake and gutted it for dinner."

His stomach lurched. "Any specifics on who it might be?"

Kilgore shook his head. "Nope. But things sure as hell don't seem to be getting any better."

He stood for a moment, panting, trying to get air in his system without jarring his ribs. But even as the despair threatened to wash over him, he pushed it away. As long as there was a chance, a miniscule chance, that Rosemary would know he was alive…

He still had a shred of hope.

Chapter Ten

Gilhouley lifted his hand, motioning for his men to stop as he neared the rendezvous point. Issuing a signal, he sent Baptiste and Petey wide to circle the clearing while Berman and Kilgore waited behind, the heavy packs of radio equipment strapped to their backs.

Glancing down at his watch, Gilhouley noted that they'd made good time. They were right where they needed to be.

So where the hell was Santo Tomas?

The barely imperceptible rustling of foliage signaled the arrival of his men.

"Anything?" he murmured.

"Not a thing," Baptiste said with a shake of his head. He dragged his hat from his head and swiped at his brow. "On the way back, I looked for broken vines, bent grass, anything that might give a hint that someone has been here. Nothing."

Gilhouley swore under his breath again. "Dammit all to hell. Where's Santo Tomas?"

He glanced at the watch strapped to his wrist. The second hand made a jerky sweep around the dial, a none-too-subtle reminder of the need for haste.

"Tell Kilgore to break out the radio and get in touch with home base. Apprise them of the situation and ask for new instructions. Baptiste and I will scout up the slope a ways and see if we can get a better look around."

Petey nodded and jogged back to the men with the packs.

Motioning for Baptiste to follow him, they skirted the tree line, heading farther up the trail. After about two hundred yards, Baptiste pointed to an outcrop of rocks jutting out of the forest.

"How about there?"

Nodding, Gilhouley led the way, grasping at vines and roots, scaling the steep slope, then flattening himself against one of the boulders. Taking the binoculars from his pack, he scoured the surrounding hillside, looking for the slightest hint of smoke from a cook fire, movement, swaying grass—anything to signal that Santo Tomas was in the area.

He handed the binoculars to Petey. "You see anything?"

Baptiste took his time, so Gilhouley uncapped his canteen and took a quick drink. Damn, it was hot. Even this late in the day, the heat was unrelenting.

"Shit, I don't see any sign of 'em," Baptiste said, handing back the binoculars.

"Let's get out of here."

The trip back down the slope was more hazardous. Gilhouley found it hard to find footholds in the dry, dusty earth, and he ended up skidding the last dozen yards to the bottom. Baptiste, who was close behind him, fared no better. But they didn't even bother to brush themselves off. Instead, senses prickling, they hurried back to the other men.

As soon as he caught sight of Kilgore, Gilhouley knew the news wasn't good.

"What's up?"

Kilgore glanced at Berman, who nodded for him to speak.

"Santo Tomas' body was found about an hour ago. Those sick bastards beheaded him, then nailed his body to a tree about five miles north of Clark Field. We are to maintain control of the equipment and get the hell out of Dodge."

Baptiste crossed himself, then let out a string of curses that would have made a sailor blush.

Gilhouley heaved a frustrated sigh. "Why the hell didn't they let us know sooner?" But before anyone could scramble for an answer, he waved them away. They'd been told to limit radio contact to a minimum. And just because Santo Tomas was dead, that didn't mean that some of his men couldn't have showed up at the rendezvous point.

"Let's get out of here."

"Uh, Lieutenant, there's one more thing."

He was almost afraid to ask.

"Manila is being evacuated. MacArthur wants all military personnel out of the city by New Year's Eve. Therefore, we are to head straight to Bataan."

Bataan. Even if the roads were passable, they would run out of fuel miles before they got there—which meant a good thirty, forty miles by foot. And he had no doubts that if the Americans were retreating that quickly, that meant that most of Luzon was crawling with the Japanese.

Shaking his head, Gilhouley said. "Pack up. We need to get out of here. Now. If we don't, we probably won't be able to get across that bridge at all. Ditch everything that isn't absolutely necessary. We're going to make our retreat as quickly and as quietly as we can. Got it?"

His men didn't even bother to respond. They knew as well as he did that the likelihood of making it to the bridge before the enemy's arrival was nothing short of a Hail Mary pass. And if they were caught by the Japanese…

Well, Santo Tomas's body had been left as a warning. Who knew what they'd do to a group of American soldiers?

• • •

Glory Bee had thought that the journey down the slope would have been easier than going up, but her leg muscles were screaming by the time they made their way into the valley below. Despite the use of John's hat, her head was soon pounding and no amount of water could slake her thirst.

As they left the scrub and moved into the denser trees, she

welcomed the lengthening shadows that at least gave her protection from the sun's heat. As a natural redhead, she'd always been prone to burning and her skin felt as if it were on fire.

It soon became apparent that while she had been expecting a small, rural town, the village they were moving toward was little more than a congregation of bamboo huts that circled around a shared well. But her disappointment was tempered by the promise of water. If it had been Glory Bee's lead, she would have rushed forward. Their canteens had been drained long ago, and Glory Bee's thirst rivaled only that of the children who whimpered at the need for food and rest.

But yards away from the village, John held up a hand and motioned for everyone to be still.

It was then that Glory Bee became aware of the silence.

Gesturing for everyone to stay where they were, John and Esteban grasped their rifles in front of them and began to move slowly toward the huts.

Shivering despite the heat, Glory Bee knelt in the cover of bamboo and vines, pulling Luis tightly into her arms.

He rubbed at his eyes and rested his cheek against her shoulder. His body shook with exhaustion. Although he'd done only a little walking—spending most of the time on his father's wide shoulders—it was clear that he too was at the end of his endurance.

"Shh, shh," Glory Bee whispered against his hair, meeting Maria's wide, worried stare as the woman gathered the other children close.

Not for the first time, Glory Bee found her eyes straying to Maria's pregnant form. If Glory Bee's weariness was nearly overwhelming, what must it be like for Maria? Esteban had said the baby was due in less than a month. Surely, this headlong rush into the forest couldn't be healthy for the woman.

But what else could she do? She couldn't stay behind. Just like Glory Bee, she was fleeing for her life.

Glory Bee's eyes closed and she shook her head. How had things come to this point? How had a relaxing few weeks in the tropics disintegrated into a hellish journey of fear? And how much more would they be required to do before finding safety?

Her arms wrapped around Luis more tightly and she rocked him, feeling him sag against her. To their credit, all of the children sensed how important it was to remain as quiet as possible while John and Esteban crept toward the first hut.

Peering over the foliage, Glory Bee watched as John lifted aside a length of cloth being used as a makeshift door, then dropped it, shaking his head. They moved on to the next domicile, then the next and the next, until it became clear that the village had been deserted.

Glory Bee felt a prickling at her nape as she wondered what had happened to the inhabitants. Had the Japanese skirted around the mountain somehow and arrived here first? Or had the villagers, warned by the scent of smoke in the air, moved further into the forest?

As they returned, John and Esteban were far less cautious, but they maintained their grip on their weapons.

"We'll stay here for the night as planned," John said as he approached.

"Where has everyone gone?" Glory Bee asked, even though she knew the question was useless.

"There's no sign of violence or any other indication of the Japanese. I suppose they've moved on to a safer spot."

"Are you sure we should stay here? I-I mean, they left for a reason."

John touched her arm reassuringly. "We'll be fine. Esteban and I will take turns guarding the area. The children can't go on any farther."

Unspoken was the fact that Glory Bee and Maria were in no better shape than the kids, so despite her misgivings, she trudged along behind the men as they led the way back to the well.

The *cargadores* settled their packs onto the ground and moved to begin drawing water up to refill their canteens, while Maria sent the older children looking for any bottles or buckets that might have been left behind.

Glory Bee moved to the suitcases, which still held their supply of food. She might be a detriment on the trail, but she'd be damned if she wouldn't contribute something.

Since they couldn't light a cooking fire for fear of the smoke being seen over the ridge, she laid out a small buffet of SPAM, pork and beans, and fruit cocktail. Her stomach lurched a little at eating the meat cold, but she knew that she would need all the strength she could get, so after everyone had gathered a portion, she sat down on a rock and forced herself to begin.

In the end, she needn't have worried. Her body was so tired and hungry she wolfed most of the food down within a matter of minutes, slowing only when she got to the fruit and decided she would savor the last few bites.

John sat down next to her, eating the remains of the pork and beans directly from the can. "You and I will be taking that hut right there." He gestured to the one closest to the well. "Esteban and his family are taking the larger one next to us."

"What about the *cargadores?*"

He sighed, looking at the clump of men who huddled in a knot a few yards away. "They're frightened by the empty village. I told them they could sleep in the forest if they'd like and return at first light." He shrugged. "But they may decide to abandon us altogether."

"What will we do if they leave?"

"We'll carry what we can and bury the rest. We can always come back for the supplies."

"Provided the Japanese haven't taken up residence."

He nodded curtly. "But there's no sense borrowing trouble. Right now, we all need a good night's sleep, and this place is better than most." He gestured to her plate. "Finish up, then you'd better turn in. I'll see if I can't find something for your sunburn, but I'll wait until you've had time to wash up first."

Glory Bee did as she was told, rinsing off her utensils before putting them back into her rucksack. Then, grabbing her things and a pail of water, she headed into the first hut.

Overall, it wasn't a bad place to spend the night. The structure had a packed earthen floor and bamboo walls with a bamboo shelf, which had probably once held a mattress for sleeping. Laying her rucksack on the ground, she spread a blanket over the bamboo shelf before sitting wearily. If she hadn't known that John would be joining her soon, she would have stretched out and gone straight to sleep. But unsure of how much time he meant to give her, she untied her shoes and peeled off her socks, wincing when she pulled at the raw blisters that had formed on her heels and toes. Standing, she stripped off her clothes until she was clad in only her bra and panties, then turned her back to the door. Using the pail, she washed quickly, hissing as the water hit the fiery skin of her arms and face. Since she was usually so careful with her skin, she couldn't remember a time when she'd been so sunburned.

Although it seemed a bit incongruous considering her surroundings, she removed her underthings and pulled on the embroidered cotton nightgown she'd worn the first night to the Philippines. After using the last of the water to rinse out her clothes, she draped them over the windowsill to dry.

She was settling onto the blanket again when John called out, "Glory Bee? May I come in?"

"Yes."

John slid through the curtain carrying a small bottle filled with a bright blue liquid.

"What's that?" she asked with a frown.

"After shave."

When her brows rose, he hastened to add, "One of the main ingredients is witch hazel. It should help with your sunburn."

At the moment, her face and arms radiated with their own inner furnace and the pain was building, so she nodded. She was game for anything at this point.

John took a seat on the bench beside her and unscrewed the cap.

"Good lord, I'm going to smell like a barber shop on Saturday night."

John chuckled, and again, she was struck by the way she clung to that sound like a miser gathering gold.

"Maybe it will keep the mosquitoes away."

She only grunted.

John poured some of the liquid in his palm, then handed her the bottle. After rubbing his hands together, he began to smooth the aftershave over her skin.

She hissed, the pressure of his calloused hands enough to cause a stinging pain. But as the witch hazel sank into her pores, she felt a small twinge of relief.

"Good?"

"Mm-hmm."

He poured more of the bright blue liquid in his palms, then began to work on the back of her neck and shoulders.

And suddenly, it wasn't the pain that was causing a reaction, it was the feel of his hands gliding over her skin, the whispering caress of his fingers, the frisson chill of his breath against her nape.

Inexplicably, despite everything that had happened, every moment that had led up to her being in the Philippines, she found herself wanting to close her eyes and absorb the sweet friction of his palms against her.

Michael's skin was soft and his nails well manicured. And he was smaller than John—only an inch or two taller than Glory Bee, as a matter of fact. But she'd always felt comfortable with him.

John, on the other hand…There was nothing comfortable about John. He was a curious mixture of planes and angles—and his personality was a veritable land mine. He simmered with barely submerged anger whenever the Japanese were mentioned, but at times, she caught glimpses of the joyous man he must have been as a priest. Most of all, there was his hunger whenever she was in his arms. But she knew his desire warred with his conscience and a code of conduct he found difficult to shake.

If things were different…if *she* were different.

As if he sensed her disquiet, John handed her the bottle and rose to his feet. "I'll let you finish doing your face."

He was about to leave the room when she said, "John?"

John turned in the doorway and the last rays of the sun slid over his features. Once again, where Michael's features were round, his coloring fair, John had been carved from a block of granite, his hair dark, yet flecked with gray. It was obvious that he'd spent most of his time working in the sun because his skin had the ruddy tan.

"Thank you," she said simply.

"No problem. Hopefully the burn won't bother you tonight."

She opened her mouth to clarify that she hadn't been thanking him for the aftershave. No, her gratitude extended much farther than that. But the curtain dropped and he disappeared.

Settling down on the bunk, she reached into her pack and removed the mosquito netting. After fixing it to a nail in the wall that had probably been used for the same purpose, she settled the fabric around her, then arranged her pack beneath her head for a pillow.

Her body thrummed with exhaustion and she closed her eyes, trying to sleep. They would probably be hiking further into the woods tomorrow and she needed every ounce of strength that she could muster.

But as the camp settled into silence around her, a prickling unease skittered down her spine. The forest around them was rife with sound—the whisper of bamboo fronds, the scurry of animals. From far away came a screeching noise. An animal?

A human?

Despite the heat, she shivered beneath the blanket. She'd grown up in the country, so she was well aware that the night was rarely silent. But here…here, the noises were ominous and unsettling. There was a reason why the villagers had deserted the area. The rustling that she heard could be the footfalls of dozens of Japanese soldiers creeping toward them. What if the dark undergrowth that they had welcomed only hours earlier had become a verdant trap?

Her throat grew tight with terror. Unbidden, the sting of tears caused her to blink the moisture away.

Dammit. She wasn't a hysterical child to be frightened by wiggly woolies, no matter where she might find them. She refused to become a cowering ninny because of a few nighttime noises.

But even as she railed against her weak emotions, the tears

came harder, faster, spilling down her cheeks until she sniffed in her effort to control them. Her chest constricted and she sobbed, then damned herself for the telltale sound. She couldn't let John see her this way. Not after everything he'd done for her.

Too late.

The curtain twitched and he peered inside.

Glory Bee quickly closed her eyes and tried to remain perfectly still, pretending sleep. But her shuddering inhalations gave her away.

John moved toward her, then sat on the edge of the bunk. Reaching down, he removed his boots, then wordlessly, he slipped beneath the mosquito netting and drew her tightly against him.

Although she knew she should keep her distance, Glory Bee melted against him, gripping his waist and burying her face against his chest as the tears continued to fall.

"D-don't y-you need to g-guard?"

"Esteban is going first."

He ran his hand over her hair, then swept his fingers down the length of her spine. Up and down. Up and down. Until she began to regain her composure.

"I-I'm sorry."

She felt his lips against the top of her head. She thought she sensed his smile.

"You don't need to be sorry." His low voice proved to be as much of a caress as the tips of his fingers.

"I-I don't know wh-what's come over me."

Again, she thought she felt him smile.

"You're tired, hungry, sore, and frightened. I think you have a right to cry."

"B-but I don't w-want to s-seem weak."

"Ah. In my experience only the weak refuse to cry."

"How's that?"

"If you don't feel, if you don't care, you'll never cry."

The statement was so powerful in its simplicity. "Do you ever cry, John?" she whispered.

The silence that pounded between them was warm and fraught

with meaning.

"Yes."

The admission was so painful that she gripped him tighter.

"Is it the loss of your students and your friends that makes you cry?"

He nodded against her. "Sometimes. Sometimes I wonder how I can go on when they're all gone."

She wiped at her cheeks, absorbing that statement. "I envy you a little, I think."

"How so?"

"Except for my grandmother, I've never had anyone in my life who left me so…empty when they went away. I've certainly never had anyone who would miss me if I were gone." The words spilled from her lips without thought and she immediately wished she could retrieve them.

That wasn't true. She had Michael. Michael loved her.

But Michael also had a wife. A wife he wasn't willing to divorce, no matter how smitten with Glory Bee he might be. He'd proven that fact time and time again. Glory Bee wasn't a priority in his life. She fell somewhere below his career, his reputation, and his family name.

"It isn't true that no one would miss you, Glory Bee," John murmured against her.

"Oh?"

The noises of the night filtered around them for several beats before John said, "I'd miss you."

The words hurt more than she could have ever imagined, because they were uttered by a man who was a near stranger. One who had no reason to rue her absence after such a short acquaintance.

And yet, more than anything on earth, she wanted his statement to be true. She wanted John Macklin to care for her enough to miss her once this was through and she'd made her way back home.

Because heaven only knew, she would miss him too.

• • •

John waited, feeling Glory Bee's body slowly becoming lax against him, knowing that as soon as she fell completely asleep, he would have no legitimate reason to stay.

But he did. Even long after he knew she was completely unaware of his presence, he continued to hold her, absorbing the warmth of her body seeping into his side. The weight of her head pressing into his chest.

The curl of her fingers against his waist.

Was this what it felt like? Not just to hold a woman, but to be held by her in return? Not only in passion, but in friendship…affection?

He closed his eyes, breathing deeply, trying to calm the frantic beat of his heart lest she hear it under her ear and know the effect she had on him.

Dear Lord above, he shouldn't be doing this. He shouldn't be playing with fire. He'd only known Glory Bee for less than a month, and their situation was far from conducive to building any kind of emotional relationship. She was grateful for his help. She'd made no secret of that. And he would be a fool to take advantage of her faith in him. More than that, he would be a fool to believe that any intimacy developed between them during such a time of fear and privation could last.

His fingers curled into the soft strands of her hair and he allowed the tresses to twist and twine around his knuckles like lengths of silk.

True, he'd only known her a short time. And yet…

There was something about her that felt timeless and familiar and oh, so right.

Knowing that to remain any longer at her side would add fuel to the unwanted fire of his attraction, John forced himself to slide free. She frowned, uttering a soft moan—a sound that was nearly his undoing. But he resolutely turned his back on her and sat up, reaching for his boots.

Tomorrow, they would need to delve deeper into the woods. The village was situated at the edge of a bamboo forest, and he knew from experience that even a hundred feet in, the foliage would become nearly impenetrable. Once there, it would be easy to hide from the Japanese patrols. Even if the soldiers tried to make their way into the forest, John and Glory Bee would hear their approach in plenty of time to hide. It shouldn't be too difficult to build a rough shelter. The primary problem would be water.

After tying his laces, John reached for the rifle and moved outside.

As soon as he stepped down onto the ground, he became aware of a single hulking shape in the darkness. Crossing to Esteban, he sat down beside him next to the well.

"The *cargadores*?"

Esteban sighed. "Gone. I couldn't keep 'em here, Boss."

John nodded, not really surprised. The men had been spooked by the distant fires. When they'd found the empty village, their fears had magnified.

"I tried to offer them more money, Boss, but they kept sayin' these woods are haunted."

John squinted into the darkness that surrounded them. Now more than ever, the foliage loomed like a black, yawning maw.

"Maybe they're right."

"Don't you be talkin' that way, Boss." Esteban shivered and crossed himself.

"And what will you be doing, Esteban?"

So far, it was Esteban who had been leading them up the mountain. His wife had family nearby. One of her brothers, a man named Pascal, was rumored to be gathering men to fight.

Esteban dropped his gaze, studying a mosquito bite with abject fascination. Then he admitted slowly, "Maria is tired. Afraid. She thinks her family can keep us safe."

John nodded. "Her brothers are strong and know the area well."

"My children are also strong but…" Esteban lifted his shoulders helplessly. "They're children. They make noises. And once Maria has the baby…"

John reached over to clap Esteban on the back. "You don't have to apologize for taking care of your family, Esteban. You need to do what is best for them."

Esteban still looked glum. "You could come with us, *padre.*"

For a moment, John considered the idea, if only because Glory Bee might need the feminine companionship. But he soon shook his head.

"It wouldn't be safe, Esteban. If the Japanese stumbled upon Maria's clan, they'd most likely continue on. But if they found you harboring a couple of whites…" He gave Esteban's shoulder one last squeeze. "I think we'll take our chances in the woods. Hopefully, it will only be a couple of weeks."

He couldn't be sure, but he thought Esteban's eyes gleamed with unshed tears.

"You have been a good friend, Boss."

"As have you, Esteban."

Esteban jerked a thumb toward the hut that sheltered Glory Bee. "You're sure you don't want to send her with us?"

Something in John's gut clenched at the idea. If he were honest with himself, he would have to admit that she would have as much a chance staying safe with Esteban as with himself. But besides the danger that her presence might bring to Maria and her family, John found that he didn't want to leave her well-being up to anyone else.

"No. I'll take care of her."

Esteban suddenly grinned. "You like her, boss?"

"I think she's a nice lady," he answered diplomatically.

"'Cause you keep saying you're not a priest anymore," Esteban said slyly.

"No. I'm not a priest any more. But I think she already has a fellow in her life."

Esteban dismissed that idea with a wave of his hand. "Even if she does, he's not here, is he?"

John laughed. "I don't think that's a particularly honorable sentiment, do you?"

"Hell, he ain't here to protect her. What's so honorable about that?"

Grinning, John hitched a thumb toward the hut behind him. "Go get some sleep. I'll take over the watch. You and your family will want to make an early start."

Esteban hefted himself to his feet and shuffled toward the hut. But at the doorway he paused.

"It sure is good to hear you laughin', Boss. Maybe that girl's got a fellow. But maybe you need her a little more than he does."

Before John could think of a suitable reply, Esteban disappeared into the hut, leaving John to wrestle with his own manner of temptation.

• • •

The night was inky black as Gilhouley and his men carefully made their way to the spot where they'd hidden the car. As Kilgore and Berman rushed to remove it from its hiding place amid the trees, Gilhouley and Baptiste crept to the same lookout point where they'd checked on the progress of the Japanese, not so long ago.

Grabbing the binoculars, Gilhouley tried to make out something—anything—in the darkness that could help him see the progress of the Japanese. But other than the fields that had been set ablaze, it was too dark to make an assessment.

He handed the field glasses to Baptiste.

"Judging by the fires, I'd say they've made it as far as—"

Without warning, the valley below glittered with light and heat, firecracker sparks and flashbulb pops. Then several beats later came the sound of machine gun and mortar fire.

"Poor bastards," Baptiste said.

Gilhouley watched for a moment, a rock seeming to lodge in his throat. Then he said, "Let's get going. They're heading in the direction of the bridge, and I don't want to be caught behind enemy lines."

They ran back to the car, helping to push it out of the brush onto the road.

"Keep your eyes peeled. If you see anything—anything at all that could be a Japanese patrol—you give the alert." He turned to Kilgore. "Be prepared to maneuver if you have to."

Kilgore nodded.

He motioned to Berman and Baptiste who would be taking the spot in the rumble seat again. "I want you wearing the packs with the radio equipment in case we have to abandon the car and head for the hills. I'll be damned if I'll leave it to the Japanese." He met each man's gaze. "Double check your weapons, then let's go."

Within seconds, the men had all piled back into their previous positions. Kilgore gunned the engine.

"You'll be running without lights, Kilgore, so take it easy. But get us the hell out of here as quick as you can."

"Yes, sir."

The car jolted, rocks spewing from beneath the back tires as Kilgore punched the accelerator. Then they were barreling down the mountain, gravity adding as much to their speed as fuel.

"Shit, Kilgore, can you even see what you're doing?" Petey called from the back seat.

"We're still on the road, aren't we?"

As if to refute him, the tires skidded off the rutted path into a patch of scrub, tree limbs and vines smacked the hood of the car as Kilgore adjusted his course.

Gilhouley glanced over his shoulder through the rear window to make sure that Baptiste and Berman were still in their places. He grinned when he saw that they'd hunkered low against the rear window, swearing.

The car bounced and bucked, squeaking and groaning at the unaccustomed speed and hard ride, threatening to come apart at the seams. But as they skidded down the last final turns, it looked like they would be able to make it. The bridge loomed ahead of them, a strip of lighter gray in a black, black night.

But then, when only a few dozen yards separated them from their goal, the darkness erupted in gunfire.

Kilgore swore, slamming on the brakes and wrenching the wheel to one side so that the car skidded into a half-circle. Then, gunning the engine again, he turned wide through the brush, jouncing his way back to the road while Baptiste and Berman returned fire.

"Who the hell's shooting at us? The Americans or the Japanese?" Petey shouted as he twisted in his seat and returned fire through the window.

Distant shouts from the opposite side of the bridge peppered the air.

"That sure as hell doesn't sound like English to me," Kilgore ground out, his hands fighting to maintain control as the car now headed back up the mountain from where they'd come.

"Anybody hurt?" Gilhouley barked as the sound of gunfire faded.

When no one responded, Gilhouley relaxed infinitesimally. But then, just when he thought they had a chance of escaping, Kilgore slammed his fist against the wheel.

"Shit! Shit, shit, *shit!*"

Gilhouley twisted from looking out the back window to staring at Kilgore.

Still wrestling with the wheel, Kilgore pointed ahead of them. "They must have fucking hit the fucking radiator!"

Gilhouley heard the telltale hiss. Vapor was pouring from the front of the car and the Model A began to shudder. Since the vehicle had already been running hot, Gilhouley knew that it was only a matter of minutes before the motor failed.

"Take it as far as you can, Kilgore. That patrol will be heading after us and we'll need as much of an advantage as we can get."

They jounced and shimmied for about five miles before the steep incline and the loss of water from the radiator was more than the little car could handle. As it shuddered into its death throes, Gilhouley motioned for Kilgore to pull off the road next to a shallow ravine.

"Grab your gear," he said as the car rolled to a stop.

The men climbed out, quickly strapping on packs and grasping the ammunition canister they'd brought with them.

Petey kicked at the tire, then began to wrestle with the lid to the gas tank.

"What the hell, Petey?" Kilgore demanded.

After finally managing to wrestle it free, Petey whirled, throwing the lid deep into the trees. "I'll be damned if I'll leave it for the Japs to patch up and use," he grumbled as he scooped up a handful of dirt and pebbles and poured it into the tank, repeating the process twice more. "I'd set it ablaze if it wouldn't give away our position."

"Put it in neutral, Kilgore. We'll roll it into the ravine. Hopefully, they won't find it there until daybreak."

The men braced themselves against the car, heaving until it began to roll down the slope, picking up speed. The Model A careened into the underbrush. At the last minute, one of the front tires butted onto a rock and the car tipped. Then, in slow motion, still rolling down the hill, it fell sideways and skidded to an ungainly stop.

For several long seconds, Gilhouley and his men stood looking down at the car, knowing that it had been their last chance for an easy getaway.

Shaking himself loose from such thoughts, Gilhouley grabbed his rifle.

"Let's go."

"Which way?"

"The Japs will probably expect us to head north, sticking close to the road." He pointed east. "So we're going that way. Straight up the slope."

"Lieutenant, come quick!"

He barely glanced up as Petey ran into the hut. Instead, he bent low over Kilgore, spooning the rice water gruel—what passed for a meal lately—into the other man's mouth. The quinine they'd been smuggled was gone and Kilgore's body was wracked with fever. Clenching his jaw shut, the man tried to turn his head away, but he forced a little of the liquid into his mouth.

"What is it?"

"A plane!"

"So what, Petey?" Mickleson complained from the corner of the hut.

Petey grinned. "You'll wanna see this one. Hurry!"

He almost didn't go. His body ached and his gut was twisted with dysentery. But distractions were few and Petey was more worked up than usual.

The low growl of a plane grew near again and Petey waved at them. "Come on!"

It took more effort than he possessed to rise to his feet, but he finally managed to stagger toward the doorway. Clinging to the lintel, he peered out into the hot, searing sky.

At first he didn't see what had Petey all worked up. The last thing he needed was a Jap Zero deciding to strafe the camp—or the garden. Don't let them tear up the garden. But as he squeezed his eyes shut against a white-hot sun and the waving heat, he caught the speck in the sky that became a bird, then a plane. And then, as it swooped low, he felt a sense of déjà vu *as he remembered standing next to the control tower at Clark Field. He remembered the tinsel falling from the sky, only to explode when it hit the ground, then the blood red circles painted on the wings.*

But this time, as the plane screamed past and the sunlight glinted off its wings, it wasn't a circle he saw but a star.

"Shit, almighty, it's one of ours," he managed to rasp before the familiar glitter of bombs being released caused him to throw Petey to the ground. As the explosions rocked the camp, radiating from the strike zone barely a half-mile away, he added, "And they don't know it's us."

Chapter Eleven

December 25, 1941

Rosemary was the last of the nurses to climb up the gangplank to the ferry.

"Everyone aboard?" she asked Alice, who waited at the top.

"Everyone, everything…this boat has been loaded so full, I'm afraid it will sink before we even get away from the dock."

Rosemary grimaced. "Don't say that out loud. It's bad enough that everyone's thinking it."

"Here's your vest."

Rosemary glanced at her clipboard and made a final tick on her list, then set her things down on a crate to accept the life vest that Alice extended to her.

"And your Christmas dinner," Alice said, handing her a sandwich wrapped in waxed paper.

One of Rosemary's brows rose questioningly.

"According to the cooks, before the Japanese arrived, they'd had an elaborate meal planned with all the trimmings: mashed potatoes, turkey, stuffing, pies, rolls." She shrugged. "They're handing out cold sandwiches instead. At least they spread a little cranberry jelly on the bread."

As Rosemary unwrapped the offering and took a bite, Alice shivered, despite the heat.

"You know that song, with Big Crosby…*I'm Dreaming of a White Christmas?*"

Rosemary nodded. *Holiday Inn* was one of her favorite movies.

"The nurses at Sternberg have begun calling this our Black Christmas."

Alice stood silently for a few minutes while Rosemary finished her sandwich. Then, as if the scene of the docks was too much for her, she backed away and returned to sit with the other women.

Rosemary didn't follow immediately. Instead, she leaned against the railing of the ferry as it pulled into the choppy waters of the bay. They were running without lights, guided only by instruments, she presumed, since the water was thick and inky, the sky only a shade lighter. There was little moonlight tonight, but there was no need for it. The fires caused by the approaching Japanese army had cast a ruddy false twilight that was so bright, a few of her nurses had used the glow to read the inventory lists they'd been given at the dock.

The ferry vibrated ominously as it moved away from its moorings, but Rosemary's attention wasn't on the water they would navigate. Instead, she continued to watch the receding sight of Manila with its shattered docks and decimated skyline.

Was this what it was like to watch the death of a city? Despite blackout conditions, she could see the docks teeming with refugees screaming for help.

The noise rose up around the pier, nearly drowning out the sound of the air raid sirens and the distant drone of planes. The ferry was already loaded past what it had been designed to handle, and the old wood creaked ominously as it headed out toward the open waters of the bay.

The air raid sirens sounded again, their whooping wail one of the most mournful noises in the world.

"Major, we've had a warning of planes headed this way. You really should go below deck."

She turned to find a seaman eyeing her with concern. But when she thought of being trapped below deck should they be hit…

"I…I'd rather stay up here, if you don't mind."

He opened his mouth as if to argue, then changed his mind. Obviously, she wasn't the first to refuse the offer.

"Then you'd better take this." He handed her his helmet. "I can get another one below deck."

"Thanks."

She jammed the helmet over her head, fastening the chinstrap. Then she stood hugging her life vest as the ferry inched away from land at a snail's pace.

How many days had it been since Gilhouley had brought her here? Since they'd boarded Napoli's seaplane and toured the island? Was he out there, somewhere in the darkness, trying frantically to help with the evacuation? Or was he at the front lines fighting against the Japanese?

Both scenarios caused her stomach to wrench so violently that, heedless of who might see her, she bent over the rail and purged herself of the sandwich that she'd only just eaten. Then, realizing that it would be torture to stand here and listen to the waves of noise coming from Manila, she resolutely turned her back and moved toward the little clump of nurses huddled in a knot near a pallet of beans.

"Are you all right?" Alice asked as Rosemary sank down beside them, resting her back against the bags.

"Just a little seasick."

But both of them knew that she was lying.

"He'll be all right," Alice murmured, briefly squeezing her hand. "You never know. He might be on Bataan waiting for you."

Rosemary prayed that Alice was right. She honestly didn't know how she would get through the next few weeks if she didn't have the hope that Gilhouley was out there, somewhere, thinking about her.

• • •

Dawn was streaking the sky when the ferry docked at a rough wooden pier.

Bataan.

Rosemary knew little about the area, even though she'd lived in the Philippines for years. It was a nearly uninhabited peninsula of swamps and jungles, a ripe breeding ground for malaria, and apparently, the best place on the island to dig in and wait for reinforcements.

Rousing her nurses. Rosemary ordered them to gather their things and follow her as she descended the gangplank to the sandy beach beyond.

"Set your things there, next to those bushes. As soon as the transport trucks arrive, we'll begin unloading the medical supplies." She reached for the clipboard that Alice held toward her. "To help make this as efficient as possible, I'll be dividing you into teams. Each team will be responsible for a section of the ferry. Make sure that you get everything, absolutely everything. Once the item has been unloaded from the boat and placed on a transport truck, you will cross it off the list and make a note of the vehicle number at the side. Once you've finished, bring your lists to me for a final check. Any questions?"

The women shook their heads.

The low drone of engines wove through the stillness, and Rosemary glanced toward the road that led up to the beach. It was little more than wheel ruts etched into the foliage. But as the noise grew louder and louder, she realized that the noise wasn't coming from the lane, but from overhead.

"Take cover!" she shouted as a half-dozen planes beelined toward them.

As she threw herself onto the sand, puffs of dirt kicked up inches away from her. The *phut-phut-phut* of machine gun fire followed a half second later as the Zeros roared over the beach, strafing the sand.

Sailors and soldiers who had already begun to unload the ferry dived for the water as the planes swooped overhead, banked, then returned.

"Into the trees! Into the trees!"

Scrambling to her feet, Rosemary helped to pull her nurses to their feet, pushing them into the cover of the trees. As another Zero zoomed above her, she dived in after them, then rolled when sand spit at her from the spray of bullets.

A bomb exploded mere yards away, the blast throwing them to the ground again as dirt and debris pelted them like searing hailstones.

Looping her arms over her head to protect herself, Rosemary pressed her face into the moist foliage, panting against the waves of heat and noise, the smells of cordite and smoke. Already, she could hear the cries of the injured from the beach screaming for help.

Another explosion rocked the air, then another, and another. Then, with one last burst of machine gun fire, the Zeros climbed high, banked, and were lost from view behind the canopy of the trees.

Rosemary's limbs trembled as she pushed herself away from the ground. After glancing at the other women huddled in the bushes, she rolled to her back.

At first, she couldn't bring any sense to the world around her. Her hearing was curiously muffled and tinny, and her eyes couldn't pierce the strange blackness that met them. But then, as she blinked, she realized that it wasn't her eyes that failed her. It was smoke. Thick, black smoke.

"No," she muttered to herself. "No, no, no!"

Pushing herself to her feet, she ran out to the beach, scarcely crediting that this idyll could so quickly be changed.

Writhing figures were scattered across the ground. Like her, some of them were able to push themselves to their feet. Others had grasped their weapons and were pointing them upwards in case another set of Zeros flew overhead. But these images barely touched her mind as Rosemary staggered through the sand to the beach, her mouth opening in horror.

"No!"

The splintered remains of the ferry had become a raging inferno. The water bubbled and hissed as the heavily laden ship split in the middle with a horrendous crack. Then, amid smoke and shooting flames, it sank beneath the churning water with such speed that Rosemary could scarcely believe the credence of her own eyes.

Gone. It was all gone. Food, medical supplies, fuel. All of the supplies that they so desperately needed were now heading to the bottom of the bay.

Then, just as quickly, the water grew still again, flaming bits of wreckage bobbing on the surface, moving concentrically away from the ferry's watery grave.

* * *

Glory Bee woke with a start, then moaned as every muscle in her body protested. Hell itself could not have devised a more torturous bed than the bamboo shelf. If she hadn't been more afraid of the bugs that made their paths across the floor, she probably would have slept there.

Easing herself into a sitting position, she winced as her sunburned skin screamed in protest. Glancing down, she nearly moaned aloud when she saw that she closely resembled the hue of a boiled lobster.

Moving as gingerly as she could, she applied another coating of aftershave, hissing in relief at its cool sting. Then she donned her brassiere and a fresh shirt. Slipping her legs into her trousers, she frowned as she struggled with the fasteners. It wouldn't be long before she wouldn't be able to wear them at all. Please, please, let the Japanese be routed before she had to admit to John that she needed to go in search of maternity wear.

Jamming her feet into socks and then her shoes, she ignored the sting of yesterday's blisters and tried her best to hobble outside.

She had expected the compound to be a hotbed of activity. Judging by the slant of the sun through the window in the hut, she'd known that she'd been allowed to sleep late. But there was no sign of the children or the *cargadores.* There was only John who sat by the well, carefully oiling one of the pistols he'd stashed into his pack.

"Where is everyone?" she asked as she walked toward him.

He looked up, obviously choosing his words with care. "Gone."

"Gone?"

He sighed, returning the pistol to his pack. "The *cargadores* left during the middle of the night, claiming that the woods were haunted. Esteban and his family moved out early this morning."

Glory Bee couldn't account for the rush of loss that she felt. "Why?"

"Maria has family nearby. They've gone to join them."

"So why didn't we go with them? Why didn't you wake me?"

John stood and walked toward her, taking her elbows. "Because the presence of white people in their camp would endanger their whole family. I couldn't let them take that risk."

Glory Bee shuddered, and he must have felt the telltale tremor because he wrapped his arms around her waist and drew her close.

"You understand, don't you?"

She nodded against his chest, gripping his shirt in her fists. For a moment, she felt so alone, so vulnerable, that she could barely breathe.

"We're going to head into the woods. Esteban thought there was a stream a few miles in. If we can find a source of fresh water, then we can build a shelter and wait out the next few weeks. It's probably one of the safest places on the island for us."

We. He'd said *we.*

She wasn't alone. She had John to help her.

"Are you up for this, Glory Bee?"

"I guess I have to be."

"I can take you to Esteban if you want."

She tipped her head to meet his gaze. "No. I wouldn't want to do anything that could hurt Maria or the children. As long as I'm with you, I'll be all right."

• • •

It was nearly noon before John and Glory Bee left the village. John had loaded their packs and one of the suitcases with as many tins of food as they could carry, then had hidden everything else beneath a tarpaulin just inside the tree line.

"I'll find a place for us to make a shelter, then I'll come back for the rest of our supplies later," he said.

Glory Bee could only nod. Her disquiet about being in the empty village hadn't eased with the daylight hours. The bamboo around them seemed to be full of eyes, and she would be glad to leave this place behind. So far, they'd seen no fires or smoke behind them, but she didn't trust the Japanese not to be lying in wait.

John filled the last of the canteens with water, slinging one of them on a string around her neck. Then he took her hand and pulled her forward.

"Let's go."

Slowly, they followed the tree line down a natural slope to where the thick of the forest began less than two miles away.

At first, Glory Bee doubted that she would be able to walk even that far. The blisters on her feet screamed in protest and her muscles were stiff, her sunburn raw. But soon, she was able to push through the pain with a dogged sense of will. She would not disappoint John. She would not let him down.

Once at the edge of the forest, John was forced the let go of her hand.

"I'll go first, you follow right behind me, yeah?"

"Yes."

Stepping into the thick forest was unlike anything Glory Bee had ever experienced. She felt as if she were being swallowed whole as the heat of the sun disappeared and they plunged into a green, primordial world.

Trees and tangled roots vied for space with choking vines. The ground beneath their feet became softer, sucking at their shoes as they moved. Where before they had been able to cover several miles in an hour, now they fought for each precious yard of ground. Soon, John was forced to pass the suitcase to her so that he could use his machete to hack at the undergrowth in order to give them enough room to pass.

At first, Glory Bee was nervous about the way they were forced to cut a path, sure that if a Japanese soldier were to see it, they would surely follow. But when she glanced behind them, it was as if they had never been there. The jungle sprang up around them, obscuring all evidence of their passage.

As they plunged deeper and deeper, Glory Bee could see why John had thought this would be an ideal hiding place. Visibility was less than a few yards. And if a person were to huddle low in the vines, she doubted they would ever be noticed.

Glory Bee couldn't have told how long they fought their way into the interior. Time had been swallowed up as completely as the sun. Soon, she began to believe that she was locked in a never-ending loop.

Hack, hack, climb, crouch, slog.

Where before, she'd been overcome with the sense of being watched, now the jungle was closing in on her, threatening to suck the very air from her lungs with its moist dankness.

"Not much farther," John said, glancing over his shoulder.

He'd become her anchor in this sea of green and she latched onto his familiar frame as if it were a beacon in the wilderness. Dear God, if he somehow got too far ahead of her to see, she knew she would never find her way out of this place again.

Without warning, the jungle suddenly parted. Glory Bee would have stumbled headfirst into the clearing if it weren't for John's steadying hand.

In front of them lay a small trickling stream lined with rocks, and while they were still in the thick of the woods, weak sunlight filtered down through the trees overhead. Flat boulders led up a small slope back into the heart of the jungle. But here, the bamboo was thinned out enough that they could make a shelter without too much trouble.

"We'll set up a structure over there, against the hill. There's probably enough space between those boulders that we can fashion a hut to sleep in. The stream will provide us with water and the foliage should give enough cover that we can build a small fire if necessary.

John set the suitcase on one of the rocks, then slung his rucksack to the ground where he began unpacking.

"What are you doing?" she asked as she sank wearily onto one of the boulders.

"I can probably make two…maybe three more trips before darkness sets in. I'd like to bring back as many of our supplies as I can. Especially the ammunition."

Glory Bee stared at him uncomprehendingly. "You're going back to the village?"

"Yes."

"But…" When she thought of making the journey yet another time, Glory Bee could have wept. She'd made the last few hundred yards through sheer grit alone. She didn't think she could do it again…and again…

Although she steeled herself against her despair, her chin wobbled, betraying her.

John moved to crouch in front of her. "You're going to stay here, Glory Bee."

"No! I—"

He stopped her with a finger on her lips. "Glory Bee, you've been a trooper. Really. I'm proud of how you've met every task head-on. But you can't push yourself much farther and we both know it."

Tears flooded her eyes but she resolutely blinked them away.

"If I go on my own, I can move more quickly, and let's face it, right now, time is of the essence."

"I-I can do it. I won't be a burden."

He slid his hand around her neck, sweeping his thumb gently across her cheek.

"I know that. I know you'll give me your all. But I need you to stay behind."

The thought of being here alone without John was even more terrifying than pushing herself to take a journey she knew she wasn't physically capable of making.

"No, I—"

"You'll be fine. Really."

"But—"

"You're going to stay here and set up our camp. We need a ring of stones to contain our fire and somewhere to stash our foodstuffs. Clear out the area between those two boulders there and use the last tarpaulin we have to form a roof. You can probably stretch it across the gap and weigh it down with rocks. Can you do all that for me?"

She was well aware that he was giving her busy work to keep her occupied, but staring into his deep coffee-colored gaze, she also knew that he would not let her come with him. She would have to find the courage to remain here on her own.

"Promise me you won't get lost."

His smile was so sudden, so sweet, that it took her breath away.

"I promise."

Then, before she knew what he meant to do, he bent to place a quick kiss on her lips.

"I'll be back soon."

She was still reeling for that brief, unexpected caress—one that he had been the one to instigate—when he stood, grabbed the empty rucksacks, and disappeared back into the jungle.

* * *

Gilhouley pushed his men hard and fast, taking only a few breaks for rest and water. Although he was sure the Japanese would look for them along the road, now that the sun was high, he was also sure that they would have found the car. Although they'd scaled the face of the mountain at one of its steepest points, he didn't doubt that the Japs could follow them just as easily.

They had climbed high enough that the foliage was thinning, and with it, their cover, so Gilhouley altered their course to the south where he could see a rocky outcropping. With a little luck, they could take a longer break there, wait out the heat of the day, then begin moving again once darkness fell. Even more importantly, if the Japanese happened to track them, the rocks would give them cover to make a stand.

"Over there," he panted, pausing at the side of the trail and allowing his men to pass. In doing so, he noticed for the first time that a dark stain was beginning to soak through Baptiste's fatigues from a spot at the top of his shoulder.

"Baptiste! Why didn't you say something?" Gilhouley grasped the man's arm and pulled him aside.

"I'm okay, Lieutenant. The bastards winged me."

"As soon as we get to those rocks, you get patched up, you hear?"

"Yes, sir."

They slogged the last few yards, and then hoisted themselves and the equipment up into the lee of the rocks. Then they hunkered down, panting.

For long moments, none of them moved. Then, bit-by-bit, they slid out of their packs and reached for canteens.

"Berman, Kilgore, I want you on watch first. Petey, you and I will take the second shift." He glanced at his watch. "We've got about six hours until the sun starts to go down. I want everyone to grab something to eat, then get as much rest as you can."

Keeping low, Gilhouley scrambled closer to Baptiste.

"Let's see what's under your shirt, Baptiste."

The men glanced at Baptiste curiously. Then Petey groaned when the other man shrugged out of his sleeve. A ragged gash ran across the top of his shoulder. It was now caked with dried blood and dirt.

"Shit, Baptiste," Petey exclaimed. "Why didn't you say something?"

Baptiste hissed when Gilhouley probed the wound. Just as he'd suspected, the bullet had winged him rather than lodging into bone or muscle.

"Damn, damn, *damn!*" Baptiste cursed as Gilhouley checked the depth of the wound.

"You'll need stitching," Gilhouley announced.

"Shit, damn, and hell! You've gotta be kidding!" Baptiste blurted, his skin growing pale.

"Relax. I was taught by a professional." Gilhouley dug into his pack, removing a first aid kit that he'd stashed inside as well as his small grooming kit. After washing the wound as best as he could with water, Gilhouley doused the area with Mercurochrome.

Baptiste hissed, slapping his hands against the rocks.

Petey dug into his pack. "Here, drink some of this."

He handed Baptiste a silver flask.

Baptiste took a sip, two.

"Drain it. This is going to hurt like hell," Gilhouley said as he removed a needle and a length of thread from the sewing kit tucked next to his comb and razor.

Baptiste's eyes widened and he tipped the flask back, taking deep gulps of the liquor.

"What you got in there?" Gilhouley asked Petey.

"Some of my bunkmate's homemade stuff. It tastes like shit, but it packs a wallop."

"That oughtta do the trick."

Gilhouley waited until Baptiste had passed the empty flask back to Petey. Then he motioned to Berman and Kilgore. "Help hold him down. The last thing I need is for Baptiste to be bucking against the needle."

The two men nodded, taking his knees while Petey grasped Baptiste's good shoulder.

Gilhouley took a lighter from his pocket and held the flame to the tip of the needle for long seconds.

"Ready?"

Baptiste nodded, but his eyes were wide and dark, like a spooked horse.

"Here we go."

Bending low over the wound, Gilhouley tried to remember everything that Rosemary had done when she'd stitched up his own gashes. As gently as he could, he pushed the gaping flesh together, then plunged the needle into Baptiste's flesh.

Baptiste hissed, instinctively bucking against the pain, but his buddies held him tight, so Gilhouley plunged the needle through the opposite side of the wound, then pulled the thread taut.

Again and again, he repeated the procedure, moving as quickly as he dared. The needle soon grew slippery with blood and his fingers fumbled with the unfamiliar task. He was sure that if Rosemary saw his efforts, she would be horrified since his stitches were ragged and uneven. But at least he'd managed to close the gaping wound. And here, in the forest, infection and insects could cause much more havoc than an open wound.

Finally, he reached the end. After fashioning a semblance of a knot, Gilhouley leaned down and bit the thread free. As he straightened, he felt his muscles suddenly relax, trembling. His breath emerged in a shuddering whoosh.

Done. All done.

Looking up for the first time, he saw that Baptiste's head lolled to one side and his eyes were closed.

"What the hell?" he asked.

Petey laughed. "He was out by the second stroke of the needle."

Gilhouley pushed himself away, leaning his back against a boulder and dragging air into his lungs. In the space of a few hours, he'd been confronted with one SNAFU after another. He'd been frustrated, shot at, and marooned behind enemy lines. But nothing had taken as much out of him as sewing up another man's flesh.

Around him, the other men eased into position. Berman and Kilgore settled their rifles against the boulders, one of them grabbing a pair of binoculars from his pack to sweep the forest below for any sign of movement. Petey arranged a folded up shirt beneath Baptiste's head, then settled down on the ground next to them.

After taking a swig from his canteen, Gilhouley braced his hands against the ground to rise, but Petey opened one eye and pointed a finger at him. "No, sir. I don't mean to be disrespectful, Lieutenant, but Berman and Kilgore have got things covered. You've already got the next shift with me." His lips spread into a wide grin. "As for him?" He hooked a thumb in Baptiste's direction. "Hell, we'll be lucky if Baptiste is conscious by nightfall tomorrow after drinking all of that rotgut."

Gilhouley opened his mouth to argue, then realized that Petey was right. If he was going to lead his men, he needed his wits about them. They would be moving through unfamiliar territory in the dark, evading Japanese patrols. Even Filipino guerrillas in the area would shoot first and ask questions later. And somehow, through all that, he and his men would have to find water and a clear path south.

Grabbing his pack, Gilhouley shoved his things back inside, then lay down on his back, propping his head on the lumpy canvas. Now that he was still and the adrenalin seeped from his body, he was tired. So tired.

Nevertheless, before sinking into sleep, he reached into his pocket and fingered the fuzzy violet.

Somehow, someway, he and his men would find their way back behind American lines.

* * *

There was still no sign of John by the time Glory Bee had finished setting up their camp—not that she had expected him to return so quickly. Without a watch or a clear view of the sun, she had no way to estimate the passing time. So, she began searching out nooks and crannies between the boulders that would serve as natural hiding places for the tinned foods they'd brought with them. It wasn't until everything had been carefully put away that she realized their supply would be limited at best. Barely a couple of weeks, if they kept their meals to a minimum. If John was able to bring the rest of their things, they might have a month's worth.

A noise from the bushes alerted her and she quickly crouched behind one of the boulders until John's familiar shoulders appeared through the vines.

Rushing toward him, she helped take the packs while he set the suitcase on the ground.

"You made good time," she said as she handed him a fresh canteen.

John nodded, trying to catch his breath. His skin, already tanned from his work outdoors, was growing even ruddier from the sun. Sweat ran from his hairline down the sharp angles of his features. Throwing off the rest of his gear, he tipped his face back and poured the canteen over his head. Then handing the empty container to Glory Bee, he braced his hands on his knees and bent low gasping for air.

"Sit down," she urged. "I'll get you something to eat and—"

"I can't," he gasped. "I've got to get back as soon as possible."

Glory Bee grew still. "Why the rush?"

He inhaled deeply and looked up, his eyes dark and turbulent. "I hiked up the hillside just to see how far the Japanese are from the village. If they don't stop on the way, they'll reach it by dark."

Despite the thick tropical heat, Glory Bee shivered. Somehow, she had convinced herself that now they had a spot to hide, the Japanese would go away, that they would find other terrain easier to traverse, that they would concentrate their energies on the American military bases rather than the indigenous people who were fleeing into the jungle. But the news that John brought shattered those pipe dreams.

"I've got to get the rest of our food and supplies. It might be the only chance we have."

Glory Bee picked up one of the empty rucksacks. "I'll go with you. I'm more rested now. I won't hold you back."

John shook his head. "No."

"Dammit, John! I can't leave you to take all the risks!"

He stood, towering over her. "And I'm not letting you take any risks at all!"

His pronouncement shuddered into the trees around them.

Glory Bee stood absolutely still, stunned by the depth of feeling in John's words, and more. He was looking at her, not as a friend, but as a man. A man who wanted her. Cared for her.

"You…stay…here," he said, spitting out each of the words as if they were nails.

Then, denying what thrummed between them, he scooped up the packs and the suitcase and disappeared into the jungle again.

Leaving Glory Bee rooted to the spot in stunned disbelief. A disbelief that soon shivered away beneath a mountain of regret.

Rumors were rampant after that first sighting of an American plane.

The Japanese were being routed by American soldiers.

The Americans had been rebuffed, no help was coming.

Days bled one into another. Weeks became months. As he staggered back from garden detail, he knew that if help didn't come soon, there wouldn't be anyone left to rescue. They'd begun their life in camp with thousands of men and slowly, disease, starvation, labor details, and Tanaka's punishments had thinned the herd. They were down to fewer than five hundred men.

Worse yet, Tanaka was growing nervous. His daily diatribes had become screaming matches so filled with hate and vitriol against his captives that if the Americans were to miraculously make their way onto the island, he feared that the he and his fellow prisoners would be killed by Tanaka out of retribution.

As he saw Petey shuffling up beside him, he noted the telltale bulge of his shirt.

"Whatcha got?"

"A couple of bananas, is all."

He looked at their guards. It had been especially hot today and the men looked tired and angry. Spoiling for a fight.

"Leave 'em here."

"Come on, lieutenant. I'm so hungry, I could gnaw on a piece of bamboo—and our shitty rations aren't even worth shitting out anymore."

"Leave 'em here."

Petey wanted to disobey, but the kid stepped behind him, surreptitiously dropping the fruit into the dust. Then he sidled up beside him again, casting one last longing glance at the bananas which would soon wither and brown in the hot tropical sun.

They had almost made their way to the front gate when a disturbance from the front of the line alerted them. One of the guards began shouting. He pushed a prisoner out of line, leveling his rifle. Shaking, the man reached into his shirt, taking out a fistful of green beans. He held them out in surrender, clearly trying to placate the guard. The Jap screamed at him and the prisoner sank to his knees whispering, "Please, please."

But the guard was beyond being soothed. Ratcheting a shell into position, he fired.

The prisoner dropped to the ground, what was left of his head digging into the sand while blood poured out onto the greedy earth.

Beside him, Petey let out his breath in a shuddering half-sob. Then the kid looked at him, his eyes filled with terrified tears, before they all ambled forward, trying hard not to stare at the figure that had been left in the dust.

Chapter Twelve

December 26, 1941

It was already growing unbearably hot as the Rosemary and her nurses climbed into the transport trucks. Rather than carrying the cargo from the ferry that had been so carefully packed in Manila, the trucks were now filled with the wounded.

Since they had only a few basic supplies, Rosemary and her nurses had done the best they could to patch up the men who'd been injured. Thankfully, except for three serious cases, most of their new charges sported minor burns and scrapes. A half-dozen had gunshot wounds, but they were all grazes or through and through shots. Using pressure bandages that the soldiers had stowed with their gear, the nurses had been able to ready everyone for travel.

Rosemary was the last to climb into the truck. After picking her way to the spot that had been left for her, she slapped the side of the bed in a signal that everyone was ready to go.

The truck lurched, searching for purchase in the soft sand, then finally shuddered forward, building speed as they headed into the surrounding trees. After a few hundred yards, the transport turned south on a dusty road that followed the line of the bay.

Around them flowed the current of a defeated army searching for purchase on the peninsula. Weary columns of soldiers carrying outdated weapons trudged alongside refugees with carts heaped with bedding and suitcases and crates of chickens and ducks. Cavalry horses plodded next to oxen and goats. And the children…barefoot, wide-eyed children who looked as if they carried the weight of the world on their shoulders, moved listlessly forward. The sight was heart-rending and discouraging.

"They're calling it a 'fighting retreat'," Alice murmured next to her. "Since the main Japanese forces landed days ago, the entire Army is falling back into Bataan."

"MacArthur's men will be able to hold them off once they dig into the jungle."

"I hope so. Right now, it doesn't look like they can hold off much of anything."

The truck veered off the road, leaving most of the foot traffic behind. Rosemary had been told that they were being taken to the hospital complex at Limay, and she took heart from that brief piece of information. Once they reached proper medical facilities, she would be back on familiar ground. True, they may have lost a good portion of their supplies from Manila. But more than two weeks had passed since the war had begun, which meant that help was on its way.

Not for the first time, she tried to do the calculations in her head. If reinforcements came from Pearl, it would be at least two more weeks before any aid could arrive. If they came from 'Frisco or San Diego, it could be upwards to a month. Maybe six weeks.

Or six months...

Closing her eyes, she tried to still the panic that swelled in her chest. They could last that long. If worst came to worst, they could all be evacuated to Corregidor. The defenses there were impregnable, the hospital facilities deep underground in a series of tunnels. The Americans could hold off there for months and months.

The truck drew to a squeaking halt. Rosemary stooped, slowly weaving through the tangle of bodies to the back of the transport. She grinned when a familiar face was there to unlatch the tailgate.

"Dr. Grimm!"

"Welcome, welcome," he called out. "It's so good to see you all. We're in dire need of your assistance."

He helped Rosemary jump down, then reached for the next girl and the next.

As the truck emptied, Rosemary quickly scanned her surroundings. Almost immediately, her heart sank. This was no modern hospital with a surgical wing and comfortable wards. Instead, it was a series of bamboo huts with thatched roofs.

Dr. Grimm must have caught her dismay, because once the weary women had all gathered their things, he motioned to a pair of nurses scrubbing equipment next to one of the huts.

"Major Dodd, this is Major Woolsey and Lieutenant Daan. They'll help you get settled in." He offered one last wave. "Good to see you all."

As he strode away, the two nurses hurried toward them, offering wide smiles.

Maj. Woolsey took charge, calling out, "Grab your gear and we'll show you to your quarters, ladies. Then, once you've stowed your things, we'll take you to Colonel Nester for your work details. Right now, the whole hospital is in crates, so we've got to get everything unpacked."

As they fell into step behind the two women, a memory of a day not so long ago flashed into Rosemary's head: Lt. Wakely leading the new nurses down the steps of the hospital at Stotsenberg. At the time, Rosemary had thought that the women in white had looked like baby geese trailing after their mother.

And now, she was one of those baby geese. But rather than gleaming figures in white, she and her nurses were bedraggled, weary, and shell-shocked. And rather than being led around a modern medical facility, they were being led to an era of medicine which could only be described as primitive.

• • •

It didn't take long for Glory Bee to find new hidey-holes for their supplies and pack them away. Then she was left to her own devices.

It was at that moment that the unfamiliar sounds and the dancing shadows of the jungle began to settle around her so heavily that she felt as if she were being crushed by it. Finally, she had to move, or she knew she would go completely insane. Her imagination was going wild to the point where she vacillated between imagining the Japanese hiding in the bushes, to believing she'd been plunked down into some Vernian lost world and dinosaurs could crash through the foliage at any moment.

Needing something to keep herself occupied, she decided that she would take the opportunity afforded by John's absence to wash the grit and grime of her travels from her skin.

Grabbing clean underwear and her robe, she removed her clothing and set it on one of the boulders near the cooking area she'd formed. As soon as she'd finished with her bath, she would come back and rinse them out, then hang them up to dry.

Wading down the stream a few yards, she found a spot where the water came up to her knees. Slinging her clean clothes over a branch, she sat in the shallow pool and splashed water over her face and arms.

The cool liquid was heavenly against her heated flesh, and she felt a measure of control return to her as she was able to scoop it over her head, rinsing her hair of the sweat and grime. And the chilly kiss against her sunburned skin provided an instant relief.

Was this how Eve had felt after having been driven out of Paradise? Alone, afraid, inestimably weary, wondering how she would cope for a day, let alone a week, a month…a lifetime?

A rustling in the undergrowth whispered into Glory Bee's musings, scattering her thoughts and causing her eyes to open. In an instant, the menace of her surroundings came crashing back as she strained to hear what had alerted her. The crackling came again, this time, in a measured cadence.

Quick, quiet footfalls.

It was too soon for John to have returned. Even with her dawdling and daydreaming, he couldn't be back. Not yet.

Her limbs were suddenly frozen, her breath coming in shallow pants.

Should she dodge for cover, or stay and pray that whoever was out there would move past without seeing her?

Another step.

Two.

Glory Bee slowly reached up, trying to grasp the hem of her robe. But in order to grasp it, she would have to stand up, and that would cause a splash.

Shivering, she crossed her hands over her breasts, waiting, waiting…

Without warning, the furtive rustling became an all-out crash and Glory Bee jumped to her feet, grabbing at her clothes as a shape came barreling out of the foliage toward her. But it wasn't a man who bounded toward her, but a horrible monster with scaly skin and dark slitted eyes.

Before she could even think of the consequences, Glory Bee screamed, then screamed again. Rather than being startled, the huge lizard hissed, flaps of skin forming a halo around its face until it truly seemed a relic of some primordial time.

Another scream tore from her throat and another and another, until she heard more crashing coming through the bushes. Fearing that the lizard was part of a herd that would attack, she turned to scramble toward the camp just as John burst through the trees, his rifle lifted and aimed in her direction. Seeing no other threat than the lizard, he lowered the weapon and ran toward her as Glory Bee rushed into his arms.

Sobbing, she tried to explain what had happened, but John needed no explanation. Instead, he dropped his packs and rifle onto the ground, then held her tighter still, absorbing her terror, wrapping her in the strength of his arms. And then, somehow, his lips were pressed against her temple, her cheeks, her jaw, until she had only to shift her head ever so slightly.

The kiss was an explosion of passion, a grinding of lips and of bodies, hands reaching, clasping, holding, as the world faded around them beneath a wave of white-hot need. The adrenaline rush caused by her fear heightened her senses. She was overcome with the desire to absorb each sensation, to draw him so close that they ceased to be two separate beings.

She sobbed against him, as much from relief as from fear. When she'd needed him most, John had appeared, and it was at that moment that she was struck with the horrible realization that no man had ever really put her first. Until now.

John scooped her into his arms, carrying her back to the boulders where she'd left her clothes. Then he sank down onto the ground, still cradling her in his arms, his hands framing her face as he searched her features.

"Are you all right?"

She nodded, managing to gasp, "L-liz…lizard!"

He laughed. "I saw."

She punched him in the shoulder. "It scared the bejeezus out of me!"

"I'm sure it did."

Glory Bee opened her mouth to tell him to go to hell, but as she met the dark twinkle of his eyes and the rich amusement that lightened his features, she was struck suddenly dumb.

When he looked like that, happy and…and carefree…

He was beautiful.

He was the most beautiful man she had ever seen.

Her anger and fear rushed from her body, and flooding into its place was a warmth and certainty unlike any she had ever known before. This man cared for her. He would do anything to protect her. And that realization made her feel invincible.

Bending toward him, she wrapped her arms around his neck. She'd only closed half the distance before he was rising up to meet her. This time, when their lips met, the caress was slow and sweet.

Threading her fingers through his hair, Glory Bee melted against him, strained against him, hard to soft, male to female. And the heat that rose within her was unlike anything that she had ever experienced before…because she knew that it didn't matter if she spoke her mind, asked personal questions, wore bright red lipstick, or cursed in public. The light of affection in John's eyes wound not dim in disapproval. He cared for *her*, Glory Bee, with all her faults and foibles. He didn't crave the stripper.

He craved the woman.

The thought alone was enough to fill her with a sense of power and femininity unlike any she had ever known. Without releasing him from her kiss, she shifted in his embrace, moving to sit with her legs straddling his waist so that she could press herself against him more tightly.

He shuddered against her, his arms wrapping around her back to pull her tightly, tightly against the bulge of his want, and she smiled against his lips, reaching to unfasten the buttons of his shirt one by one by one.

John released her only long enough to shrug free of his sleeves, then, he was bending toward her, his lips closing around one taut nipple. Drawing her deep into his mouth, he alternately suckled and nipped until she gasped against him, her hips unconsciously rocking against him.

Drawing back, he smiled. A slow, hot smile that held nothing of the priest, only of the man. A man who wanted her more than air.

Then, he was laying her down on the rock, sliding the wadded up ball of his shirt beneath her head as he bent over her, kissing a blazing path down her neck, down, down, straying to one nipple. The other.

Glory Bee's eyes flickered closed, her arms flinging above her head as she surrendered to the passion roiling through her. She couldn't think. She could only feel. And never in her life had she experienced anything so heady and arousing.

One of John's hands slid down her side to rest on her thigh. Drawing deeply on her nipple, he allowed his thumb to stray toward her feminine nest, teasing the delicate hair before parting her and pressing against her most sensitive point.

She gasped, her back arching. And as she did, he continued the intimate foray of his lips down, down to where he placed a kiss against her belly.

It took several long moments before Glory realized that he wasn't moving. He was barely breathing. Then her eyes flickered open and she caught him staring at her stomach…

At her stomach.

Before she could speak, he suddenly rolled to his feet.

Instantly conscious of her nakedness, she jumped up, reaching for her robe, as he grasped his shirt and rifle.

"John, I—"

But he made no indication that he even heard her. He stormed off into the jungle, leaving her shivering and alone and nearly torn asunder by her regrets.

* * *

John had nearly reached the abandoned village before the screaming of his lungs and the stinging welts caused by the thick underbrush brought him up short. Dropping his pack onto the ground, he tugged on the shirt that was still wadded up in his fist and thrust his arms through the sleeves, buttoning it to his neck, then jamming the tails into his pants.

He was about to reach for his rifle again when his legs buckled beneath him and he crashed onto his knees. Tipping his chin back, he fought the unmanly sobs that tore at his throat and chest. But when he felt as if his lungs would burst, he finally gave in to the storm of emotion that swept through him.

Dear God above.

She was pregnant.

Glory Bee was pregnant.

The wracking sobs came harder and faster, tearing down the painful defenses that he'd built so carefully around his emotions. And like the sudden bursting of a dam, his weariness—not only from the last few days, but of the weeks and months and years of denial—swept the walls down, and grief stormed through him, leaving him utterly vulnerable to its attack. He cried, not just for Glory Bee and what might have bloomed between them, but for the fall of his adopted homeland, for his students and Sister Mary Francis. And as the tears fell, they fed upon themselves weakening him even further. Images of Nanking that he'd meant to block forever stormed over him, emasculating him, until finally, he collapsed onto the ground, shaking with the fury of his emotions.

He could not have said how long he lay there or how long he grieved for those who were lost to him forever. He only knew that the late evening shadows were beginning to fall.

It would be dark soon.

And as much as he dreaded his next meeting with Glory Bee, he could not leave her alone in the jungle at night.

Pushing himself to his feet, he staggered forward toward the village. There were only a few things left to carry back to their camp. Pails and pans that could prove valuable in the jungle. And the fabric he'd removed from the windows and doors. They could serve as covers while they slept. He'd piled everything neatly at the edge of the village so that he could quickly collect them and be gone.

He was so deep in his own thoughts that it wasn't until he heard the *ca-chick* of a rifle round being chambered that he realized he wasn't alone.

Automatically, he lifted his own weapon to his shoulder, but a curt, "Put it down!" cut him short. "Now!"

Damning himself for his carelessness, John carefully set his rifle on the ground and straightened, holding his hands up, hoping that in the shadows, the pistol in his waistband wouldn't be seen.

Then, just as quickly, he suddenly realized that the voice that had spoken to him in English. English with an American twang.

"My name's John Macklin," he said into the gathering shadows. He wasn't sure how many men were hidden behind the bamboo huts. "If you're a Yank, I mean you no harm."

There was a beat of silence, then a man stepped around the edge of the first hut. Even in the shadows, John couldn't have ever mistaken him for a Japanese soldier. He was well over six feet tall with a shock of red-gold hair. That combined with his bright blue eyes screamed "American."

The man continued to hold him in the sites of his rifle and John had no doubt that there were others nearby.

"Where you from?" the soldier asked curtly.

"New Zealand, originally. But I've spent the last few years as foreman to the Wilmot Plantation about fifteen miles north of Clark Field."

He couldn't tell if the soldier found that to be good news or bad.

"What are you doing out here?"

John offered a short mirthless laugh. "Same as you. Avoiding the Japanese." He let his hands drop a few inches. Then, when the soldier didn't object, he brought them all the way down to his sides. Still moving slowly so that he wouldn't startle the Yank, he crossed to the pile of belongings he'd left near the last hut and began to shove them into his pack.

When he straightened, the American no longer had his gun pointed at him, but held it at the ready against his chest. Clearly, he didn't intend to stop John from collecting his things and leaving.

John was backing away when he suddenly stopped.

"You can't stay here," he said when it became clear that the soldier was more than willing to let him go. He pointed to the ridge he'd climbed earlier. "Last time I checked, there was a patrol heading in this direction. As soon as they top that rise and see the village, they'll be coming down that hill to investigate."

The soldier's eyes narrowed. "How do you know that?"

"That's where I came from. The Japanese have been burning their way up that slope, hoping to flush out refugees and guerrillas. It's only a matter of time before they show up." Lifting the pails that he'd stacked one inside the other in his left hand and his rifle in his right, John said, "If you want someplace safe for the night, you'd better follow me."

• • •

If Rosemary's mother had envisioned her daughter's career to entail taking temperatures and distributing reading materials, Rosemary wondered what Elise Dodd would have thought if she could have seen Rosemary's activities for the day.

She and her girls had begun by pumping water from the well so that they could scrub down every bed, every table, every piece of equipment before it was taken into one of the many huts that made up the medical complex. They had assembled and lined up cots in the wards, helped stock cabinets with medicines, and unrolled linens and mosquito nets by the handful.

Soon, Rosemary had the sense of being back on the farm—not that the duties were the same. But the backbreaking physical labor was similar and their shifts were long. What meals they had been given were taken on the run, and any thoughts of taking breaks or enjoying the sunset were completely forgotten.

Even more reminiscent of her work at home was the need for adapting to the materials at hand. Since their sterilizing equipment had gone down with the ferry, Rosemary and Alice made a raid on the kitchen, absconding with a pressure cooker and an outdoor electric ring, which they installed in the center of the surgical pavilion—a fancy name for several huts which had been arranged to face one another in order to better utilize shared equipment.

Then, when Rosemary thought that they were beginning to get a handle on things, an ambulance arrived, disgorging its patients, several of whom needed surgery.

So it was dark when she staggered toward the beach where she'd been told that the other nurses had gone to cool off.

Seeing Alice's familiar shape in the dim light, Rosemary slogged through the sand toward her. Alice sat with her hems rolled up, her feet extended toward the bubbling surf.

"There you are," Alice said warmly as Rosemary settled down beside her. "How was surgery?"

"Long," Rosemary said with a sigh, rubbing the back of her neck. Following Alice's example, she removed her shoes and socks and rolled up her pants. As soon as the cool water of the bay bubbled over her feet, she sighed in delight.

"We're supposed to report the quartermaster first thing in the morning. They've given us permission to replace the pilot's coveralls with a set of tans. The new uniforms should be much cooler."

"Thank heavens." Rosemary tipped her head back so that the breeze would dry the sweat on her face. When she opened her eyes, she could just make out the figure of a nurse lying spread-eagle in the sand. "Is that Lieutenant Reyes? What's going on with her?"

Alice chuckled. "Some idiot covered all of our equipment with this…greasy lubricant to keep them shiny and new." Her brow creased. "Cosmoline, one of the orderlies called it. Anyway, the only thing we had on hand that would clean it off was ether." She nodded to the woman lying prone in the sand. "Rita, there, spent a little too long on the task and nearly knocked herself out. A couple of the orderlies carried her out here hoping that the fresh air would help her come to her senses."

"I can hear you, Alice," Lt. Reyes grumbled.

"Keep breathing deeply, Rita," Alice called.

Rosemary shook her head in disbelief. "Good lord. It's not bad enough that we're being shot at by the Japanese, now we're being gassed too."

A tipsy-sounding giggle came from Rita's direction.

"Hey, I have some news," Alice said suddenly.

Rosemary's brows rose. If it was another rumor about approaching ships or sightings of far off formations of American bombers, she wasn't sure if she wanted to hear it. Rumors ran rampant here on Bataan, even worse than at Stotsenberg.

"I worked on a fellow from the press corps this afternoon."

In an instant, Rosemary was at attention. "Did you ask him about Gilhouley? Were they together? Was Gilhouley all right?"

Alice lifted a hand to stop her babbling. "I asked, but he hadn't seen The Great Gilhouley. Not since Stotsenberg."

Rosemary sagged in disappointment.

"He said Gilhouley wasn't with the rest of the press corps when they were absorbed into the Cavalry unit."

"How can that be?"

Mindful of Lt. Reyes, Alice leaned closer. "He said Gilhouley was put in charge of a special team. One of the other men was from the press corps as well. He didn't know the details, only that they were heading north in a car they stole from one of the cooks."

"North? Are you sure?" Rosemary asked, her heart thudding with fear.

"That's what he said. But who knows if that's true or not. He said the men were being pretty hush-hush about what they were doing."

Rosemary stared out into the darkness, remembering how vague Gilhouley had been when she'd questioned him about being reassigned to the Cavalry. Evidently, he hadn't been free to relate the details to her.

Which meant that what he was doing was probably dangerous.

"Hey, maybe I shouldn't have told you," Alice said quietly.

Rosemary quickly shook her head. "No. I'm glad you did. I'd rather know the truth than be wondering."

She didn't know quite how to interpret the information. If Gilhouley had headed north, that meant he hadn't been caught in Manila or the stream of a retreating army. But it also meant that, unless he'd found a way to get back to the front, he could be stranded somewhere behind enemy lines.

* * *

Glory Bee hardly moved the whole time that John was gone. After dressing in trousers and a fresh shirt, she sat on one of the boulders by the stream, waiting, waiting, hardly knowing what she would say to him when he returned, but certain that she owed him an explanation.

As the jungle began to come alive with its eerie night noises, she wrapped her arms around her middle, wishing that she dared to light a fire. Not for the heat. The air was sticky and hot, so thick with moisture that it felt difficult to drag it into her lungs. No, she longed for the brightness it would provide as the shadows lengthened around her.

Resting her forehead on her up drawn knees, she wished with all her might that she could erase the hours to that point when John came crashing through the underbrush, ready to save her from whatever had frightened her.

She couldn't imagine Michael ever doing that.

Glory Bee sighed.

A rustling alerted her, and she jumped to her feet, swiping her cheeks dry with her palms. Her pulse suddenly beat in her throat like a startled bird and her mind scrambled for something to say.

But when John pushed his way into the clearing, he wasn't alone. Glory Bee instinctively shrank back as three...four...five men melted out of the forest. All of them were armed, grim-faced, and exhausted.

She wasn't the only one who was surprised, because as the soldiers came to a halt, they suddenly stared at her, becoming even more still and alert.

"It's the stripper!" one of them blurted.

"Shut up, Petey," another muttered out of the side of his mouth.

The leader scowled at them. "Berman, put Baptiste down over there by the stream."

For the first time, she noted that one of the strangers was being supported by a soldier with hair so short it was nearly non-existent. The two of them stumbled across the stream. Then the fellow named Berman carefully settled the other man on the ground. Immediately, Baptiste—who she suspected was Filipino—closed his eyes and fell asleep.

"Is he injured?" she asked.

The short blond kid that they'd called Petey offered her a wide grin. "Partly. But partly, he's drunk." The soldier had a drawl, but thicker than her own. He was from somewhere in the Deep South. By the Gulf, she'd guess.

When she frowned in confusion, the leader explained. "He was shot earlier and needed stitches, so Private Peterman, here, offered him some homemade alcohol. It's taking longer than expected for the effects to wear off."

"Does he need anything?"

"No. But thank you all the same." The tall leader quickly made introductions. "Sorry, I'm Lieutenant Gilhouley. These men here are Privates Berman, Kilgore, and Peterman."

"But they call me Petey," the curly-haired kid inserted with a grin.

Gilhouley gestured to Baptiste who had begun to snore. "That's Sergeant Baptiste." He hitched a thumb in John's direction. "We happened to meet up with John here at a village not too far away. He offered to let us stay here at your camp for the night."

"Of course." She wove her hands together, enduring a beat of awkward silence before saying, "You must be hungry."

It was clear from the way the other men looked suddenly hopeful that they were in need of something to eat, but Gilhouley quickly said, "We don't want to use your rations. I'm sure you've only got enough for yourselves."

Glory Bee looked at John, but he continued to avoid her gaze. "Don't be silly, Lieutenant. I'm sure that we can come up with something." Gilhouley clearly intended to refuse, but Glory Bee insisted, "It shouldn't take long to heat something up."

At long last, Gilhouley nodded. "Berman, Kilgore, take the watch. I'll relieve you after dinner. Petey, look through our packs and see what we have that can be added to the meal."

In the end, Glory Bee took the cooking pots that John had brought and quickly made rice, which they topped with tins of chipped beef taken from the soldier's packs. Since Glory Bee wasn't accustomed to making rice at all, let alone over a small flame, the fare was sticky and bland, but the soldiers ate hungrily and she soon followed suit. Thankfully, she hadn't taken into account just how much the rice would swell up, so there was more than enough to go around, even with a group of hungry men.

As she washed out the pots, mess kits, and utensils, Petey quickly moved to help her, then laid out their gear on a rock to dry. Then, with a grin, he took a candy bar from his pocket and handed it toward her.

"Here, ma'am. A little something for later."

She tried to demur, but he pushed it toward her. "Come on.

I can get more at base once I get back. It's just gonna melt into a puddle if things get much hotter."

Since it was important to him that she take it, she smiled. "Thanks."

Standing, he returned to the spot where the men had set out their packs. The four younger soldiers quickly settled down for the night, leaving Gilhouley and John to sit keeping watch.

When it became apparent that she was in the way, Glory Bee indicated the shelter she'd formed earlier that day. "I think I'll turn in," she said to no one in particular.

As she walked toward the split in the rocks, she prayed that John would follow her, that he would say something, anything—even if it was only goodnight.

But her only response was silence.

* * *

John pulled his gaze away from the dejected slant of Glory Bee's shoulders, refusing to watch as she settled down to sleep. Instead, he returned his attention to Gilhouley and poked the fire with a stick in order to scatter the coals and extinguish the flame.

"How familiar are you with the area, John?"

He glanced up, still fiddling with the glowing coals.

"I'm more familiar with the western slope of the Madres, but I can find my way around. Why?"

Gilhouley debated what to say before finally explaining. "I need to get my men back behind American lines as soon as possible."

John considered the lieutenant's words carefully. "It's too dangerous to head back the way you came."

Using the stick, he began to draw a rough map of Luzon in the dirt. He put a "C" in the approximate spot where Clark Field could be found, an "M" for Manila, then a series of "X's" to show the location of the Sierra Madres.

Gilhouley bent low to point to the range of mountains. "Is there a way to go south, maybe even on the eastern slope of this range?"

John considered it for a moment. "Anything's possible." He hesitated, then added, "I don't know if I would recommend it over other routes."

Gilhouley's gaze was suddenly attentive. "Other routes?"

John held the other man's look for long seconds, trying to read him, then finally said.

"I know some people who could help you. Filipinos. I think that if I explained your situation, they might have a way to get you there faster."

"How?"

John drew a line east to the coast, then circled the bottom half of the island. "By boat."

Gilhouley stared at him in astonishment. "Boat?"

"It would be risky, but not as risky as trying to make your way over land. You'd have to take a small craft so that you could dodge anything the Japanese have out in the water. But if you hugged the coastline, you could probably make the trip in a couple of days, a week at most. It would beat the hell out of walking."

"And you could arrange this?"

John shrugged, thinking of Esteban and Maria. One of Maria's brothers, Pascal, was rumored to have been forming a guerrilla band for several months now. John wasn't sure that he'd even be given the chance to talk to Pascal. But if he could talk to Esteban…

"I might. If the people I know are agreeable to the idea."

For the first time, a slow smile spread across Gilhouley's features. "What if I offered them something valuable as a sort of… trade for their services?"

"I suppose that would depend on whether they feel you've got something worth the risk. I'd be happy to pass on the message."

This time, Gilhouley's eyes fairly snapped with excitement.

"Then tell them I've got a radio and codes to connect directly to the U.S. armed forces."

"They're here," Kilgore said, dodging into the hut, his voice ringing with urgency.

He barely heard him. He was shaking so hard from malaria that he truly thought that he would rattle apart at the seams. He was cold and hot and his joints ached as if he were a hundred years old. And he was thirsty, so thirsty. But when he'd tried to drink the water Petey had brought him, his stomach had rebelled and he'd thrown it all back up again.

"Who's here?" Petey said listlessly. He was so emaciated that he was little more than a walking skeleton. He'd long-since lost most of his curly hair, and what was left was a curious gray color. He'd aged decades in the last few weeks.

"The Americans," Kilgore said, his voice low and filled with excitement.

Petey offered a mirthless laugh. "And so's my Aunt Fannie."

"No, honest. They're here!"

Kilgore dug a piece of crumpled paper out of his pocket. "They flew over the garden, over the camp, and threw these out the windows. I saw 'em. I saw 'em close enough to make out the fucking bars on the pilot's uniform.

Petey was the only one with enough energy to take the bait. He grabbed the leaflet Kilgore held and squinted, trying to make out the words.

"I'll be damned." The kid leaned toward him. "Lieutenant, would you look at this?"

But he couldn't take it. He couldn't take one more false hope. He wasn't even sure if he could take one more night.

Chapter Thirteen

December 27, 1941

It wasn't even dawn yet when Glory Bee gave up all pretense of trying to sleep. Her rest had been fitful, compounded by the hardness of the ground. Despite the netting, she'd been plagued by mosquitoes—and who knew what other kinds of nipping, biting insects. Her back ached and her own food didn't agree with her. Most of all, she was heartsick in a way that she would never have thought possible. She had to try to talk to John, if only to explain.

But there had been no real opportunity. Whether it was due to the soldiers or the knowledge of her pregnancy, he'd slept close to the stream, his shape a barrier between her and the other men, nevertheless.

Not long ago, she'd heard him stirring. Although she'd kept her eyes closed and feigned sleep, she knew he'd approached the soldier who was on guard and offered to take his place. Then, the camp had grown quiet again.

After carefully folding up her blanket and slipping her feet into shoes and socks, Glory Bee nervously wiped her palms down her slacks, then moved to sit by him on one of the rocks.

He glanced up at her only briefly, his features an impassive mask, and she mourned the fact that he'd become the man she'd first encountered at Fort Stotsenberg. Quiet, forbidding, radiating a quiet, private pain.

"I want to explain," she said quietly.

John returned his gaze to the impenetrable forest around them.

"That's not necessar—"

"Yes. It is."

She curled her hands in her lap, staring down at her nails. She'd always been so careful with her appearance—especially around Michael. Perfect hair, perfect makeup, perfect outfit, perfect nails. But now, as she stared down at the chipped polish and the skin marred by scratches and bug bites, she realized that perfection had been an overwhelming burden.

"I-I know, that…being a priest and all—"

"I'm not a priest."

"But you were," she insisted softly. "And you can't deny that having been a priest, you were faithful to a certain…set of standards."

When he tried to interrupt her, she continued. "I'm not saying that I have an excuse for the things I've done." She grimaced. "Even though I'm realizing that I don't much like the person that I've become."

He would have spoken, but she held up a hand to stop him.

"I'm not making excuses," she began again. "But I would like to explain some of the reasons."

John dipped his head in a curt nod.

"I envy you, you know. I'm sure that you made a lot of sacrifices to become a priest. I would never want to discount that. But I would have given anything to be able to be immersed in a life that encouraged a person to make honorable choices. Me?" Her laugh was bitter. "I grew up poor in the South with a drunk for a mother."

She rubbed at one of the bug bites on the back of her hand, concentrating all her energies there rather than the censure she feared she would see in John's eyes.

"I told you about my Nanna Sue. But what I didn't say was that I spent only a few years with her. Every few months or so, my mother would show up, pack up my things, and insist that she needed me, couldn't bear to be without me. She'd swear she was off the booze and ready to be a real ma." Her breath hitched at the remembered pain. "But invariably, that meant there was a new man in her life. It wouldn't be long before the romance had worn off and she was back to drinking and fighting.

"Some of the men were nice to me. A few even treated me like I was their own kid. But some of them…Some of them wanted to do things to me that no child should have to endure."

She felt John grow still and quiet and suddenly remembered that he'd been in Nanking. He knew all about the depravity of dishonorable men.

"That's why I loved my Nanna Sue. With her I felt safe."

Glory Bee shifted, wedging her hands beneath her thighs. "I was only sixteen when she died, but I swore that I wouldn't go live with my mother. Never again. So I ran off to Richmond, determined to become an actress, but even that was a disaster. I managed to snag a couple of roles in the chorus, but soon discovered the stage managers weren't much better than my mother's boyfriends. As soon as they realized I wasn't about to play their games, I'd find myself back on the street. After a while, it got harder and harder to find work—and I was willing to try anything. Waitress, maid, even a cooch dancer for the circus. But finding a job with so many people already out of work was tough. So by the time I got a chance to audition for the Burlesque Revue, I didn't care if I had to take my clothes off. I was hungry and tired and wanted a job that would last more than a week or two.

"It was tough, but after a while I got used to it. And as I became better known, I developed a bit of a following. Men would send me flowers and gifts—even jewelry—just to get a chance to meet me. I let a few of them take me to dinner. Not many. I don't know…there was always something about them, a hint of lechery, that reminded me of my mother's male friends."

She bit her lip.

"Then I met Michael Griffin, Senator from the Great State of Texas." Her lips twitched. "That's how he introduced himself."

She took a quick breath. "He was different, or so I thought. He took his time, courting me, spending time with me. He never pressured me for anything more than my company. In time, I convinced myself that he truly loved me and we could have a future together. So when he offered me an apartment and a huge diamond ring, I believed that he wanted to marry me."

Even now, the pain was sharp and raw. "I was a fool," she whispered. "I didn't know he was married. When I did find out, I convinced myself that Michael loved me, and in time we could be together. Somehow."

A streak of moisture hit her cheek, and too late, she realized it was a tear. She swiped it away angrily, refusing to cry for Michael Griffin.

"Then I found out I was pregnant."

She sobbed, looking at John again. And this time, she saw a hint of compassion in his gaze—and it was that, more than anything, which was her undoing.

"How could I have been so stupid? It's only been in the last few days that I've realized that when I refused to get rid of the baby, he planned and plotted a way to get rid of *me.* He wanted me away from Washington and his precious career. So he sent me here, halfway around the world.

"Then I met you, John. I met *you.* And in the space of a few short weeks, you've shown me that what I shared with Michael was an illusion, a pack of lies wrapped up in pretty paper. But when I'm with you…"

She couldn't continue, knowing that she'd already lost whatever might have been between them.

Just when she feared that she couldn't take another breath, John's hand slipped around her shoulders and he drew her to him. And her relief was so shattering that she buried her face in his chest and sobbed, huge piteous sobs that came from the depths of broken dreams and betrayal.

As she clung to him, she knew that his act of comfort was by no means a statement that things would go back to the way that they'd been between them. But at least he knew the whole sordid truth. There were no lies between them, no secrets. And the purging of those burdens erupted in his arms until she lay quiet and quivering against him.

"Can you forgive me, John?" she finally whispered, exhausted.

"For what?"

"For everything…for the person I've been…the secrets I've kept."

She thought, but could not be sure, that his lips pressed against the top of her head.

"There is nothing to forgive."

* * *

The air raids over Bataan began soon after dawn and continued unabated for hours—to the point where Rosemary no longer knew what time it was, or how long she'd been in surgery. The wounded were pouring into the hospital quicker than they could treat them. It wasn't long until, much like Stotsenberg, every cot, every inch of floor space had been used and more injured waited beneath the trees out of doors.

At one point, bed sheets had been lain out in the clearing, and someone had painted a big, red cross in the center, but if the Japanese saw it, they gave it no heed. The bombs that fell were close, far too close, to have been an accident. Thankfully, the bamboo and thatched roofs provided them with some shelter from the rain of shrapnel, but with each blast, the doctors and nurses would crouch low to the ground or fling themselves over the open wounds of their patients. Then, when the reverberations had passed and the roar of planes faded away, they would return to their tasks.

Arching her back, Rosemary lowered her mask and stepped into the sunshine. As least with more surgeons and nurses here than what they'd had in Stotsenberg, they were able to see to the wounded more quickly. The huts had been assigned specific specialties, which had also helped with the turn-around. But it was still a far cry from the medicine she'd practiced before. "Battle medicine", Dr. Grimm called it, and she had to agree.

"We're out of surgical caps," she said as she approached Alice who was manning the sterilization pot that they'd rigged up the day before.

"Check with Lieutenant Reyes."

Rosemary laughed. "You mean she's conscious?"

"Conscious and ready to spit bullets. When she discovered another crate of supplies needing to be scrubbed with ether, she nearly blew a gasket." Alice leaned low. "Apparently, she now has the mother of all hangovers."

"I heard that," Reyes said as she marched past, "and I am not amused."

Alice giggled. "See what I mean." She tipped her head toward the beach. "This time, she got smart about it and insisted that the work be done in twenty-minute shifts out on the beach where the breeze can help push some of the fumes away. As for the hats, she was even more livid when she discovered that they'd gone down with the ferry, but the cook had received three cases of chef's hats. So she stole two of the boxes, and she's been cutting them down for us to use in surgery."

"Smart girl."

"You have no idea. I wouldn't cross with that one. Especially in the mood she's in."

Unfortunately, Alice made the remark as Lt. Reyes stalked toward them, her arms full of white chef's hats.

"I heard that too, Alice."

"At least your hearing's not affected," Alice grumbled good-naturedly.

Even Reyes had to smile at that.

"There's someone in the examination hut asking to see you, Rosemary," Reyes said.

Rosemary's heart flip-flopped like a landed fish.

Gilhouley.

"Who is it?"

Rita shrugged. "Don't know. Dr. Grimm told me to get you."

Stripping the bloodstained surgical gown from her shoulders, Rosemary hurried toward the first long hut. But when she stepped into its shady confines, there was no sign of Gilhouley, merely dozens of wounded waiting for attention, soldiers and nurse's alike. But then, just when she was about to cross to the far side of the room where Dr. Grimm was setting a plaster cast on a little girl's arm, she saw a familiar, grizzled leprechaun, and she knew immediately who'd asked for her.

"Napoli!" she said as she approached the man. "What are you doing in this neck of the woods? I heard you were headed for Australia."

He looked up, a grateful grin immediately spreading over his features. But the smile didn't reach his eyes. Instead, he looked pale and clammy, his body racked with shivers.

"I t-tried to t-tell 'em to wait for you, Major. I d-don't want 'em t-touching me until I t-talked to you."

Rosemary slid her stethoscope from her pocket and looped it around her neck. "What's the problem?" she asked, looking at him, then at the nurse who hovered behind him. Immediately, she recognized the girl as one of the new nurses.

"That one d-doesn't know what she's t-talking about," he grumbled. "She keeps t-telling me I can't f-fly. But I keep t-telling her I g-got to get my plane repaired and g-get out of here before the Japanese b-bomb it out of the water."

Rosemary tipped her head, silently giving the other woman permission to leave, while she slid the earpieces to her stethoscope into place. "You've got your plane here?"

He nodded, gripping his waist as if he were chilled. "It's h-hidden in a cove a c-couple a m-miles from here."

His heart was steady, if fast, so she looped the stethoscope around her neck again.

"You must be one of the last people on the island with a plane, Napoli. Last I heard, the Army Air Corps was down to a few dozen machines. Word has it, they're flying in formations of one."

Napoli chuckled, then coughed. "Well? T-tell me I can f-fly. It sh-shouldn't take too long to fix my bird up."

Rosemary shook her head. "I'm going to have Dr. Grimm take a look, but I'm pretty sure you've got malaria and you've got it bad."

"But—"

"No buts, Napoli. We'll give you some quinine, but the best thing for you right now is rest." She tipped his head back. "You're pretty jaundiced. You've got fever chills. If you were airborne, I doubt if you'd have the strength to man the controls. And if a Zero came up behind you, you wouldn't be able to react quickly enough. There's a ward right next to my tent. I'll have them put you there, then I can check on you throughout the day. As soon as it looks like you're on the mend, I'll have Dr. Grimm give you the go-ahead."

Napoli nodded reluctantly. "Thanks, Major."

"Rosemary, please."

His eyes sparked a little when she urged him to treat her as a friend rather than one of the many medical officers.

"How's G-Gilhouley?" Napoli asked. Now that he'd been told he would have to stay for treatment, he didn't bother to try to hide his symptoms, sagging in on himself, his arms wrapping even tighter around his body.

"I don't know. I haven't seen him since we were forced to evacuate Stotsenberg."

She urged Napoli to lie down.

"He's a good fella, G-Gilhouley is."

"Yes. I think so too."

"And h-he's t-taken a r-real shine to you."

She smiled. "I know."

"I-it's the first t-time I've s-seen him looking so happy. H-he was a bit of a h-hellion when I knew h-him in D-dago."

"Oh?" Rosemary had heard the rumors, but she'd never had them confirmed before.

"T-that's how I m-met him. In a b-bar r-room brawl. H-he had a ch-chip on his shoulder big as the G-golden G-gate." He shivered violently before continuing. "H-his d-daddy was in the freight business, y'see, an' he h-had money. W-when Gilhouley announced he was g-goin' t-to West Point, h-his daddy came unglued. S-said G-Gilhouley had betrayed him, by not t-takin' over the family b-business. He said Gilhouley would never amount to nothin' but bein' a drunk and a bully." Napoli laughed. "And for a t-time there, G-Gilhouley was determined to p-prove him right."

Rosemary took a blanket and drew it over Napoli's body. He clutched at it gratefully, drawing it to his chin.

"B-but then, after h-he got in some trouble, he ended up here in the Philippines," Napoli said, his eyes closing. He turned onto his side on the narrow examining table and drew his knees up to his chest. "T-then he musta met you."

The man's voice dwindled away as he fell into a fitful sleep.

Rosemary drew the covers more tightly around him, motioning for Dr. Grimm to come her way when he had a chance. Then, with her own mind whirling to absorb all of the information she'd been given, she perched on the edge of a chair, keeping watch over Napoli.

"Come back to me, Gilhouley," she whispered beneath her breath. "Please come back to me."

* * *

For the first time, Glory Bee understood why there were some folks who truly loved their religion. She'd never really had much experience with it herself. Her mother wasn't concerned about the hereafter, and her grandmother had been a simple woman who read her Bible and prayed over her food, but did not attend any organized sect.

But after pouring her heart out to John, Glory Bee could see how confession was good for the soul. If the kindness and compassion that John had extended to her was an example of his days in China, he must have been adored by his students, whether or not they were Christian. In speaking to him, Glory Bee felt curiously cleansed, as if all the poison of the past hurts she'd endured had been leeched from her body, leaving her lighter. Cleaner.

She still didn't know quite where things stood between them. When the soldiers had begun to rouse, John had put plenty of distance between them. She wasn't sure if that was an effort to protect her from gossip, or to tacitly inform the men that they were to keep their distance too. But at least she'd known he wasn't angry with her. She couldn't have borne it if he'd thought that she'd been trying to manipulate him.

Petey, the soldier who'd given her the chocolate, offered her a reassuring smile when she suddenly bolted upright, her gaze searching the clearing.

"Your friend isn't here," Petey said.

Her pulse slammed against her throat, her stomach dropping like a lead weight. She'd been wrong, so wrong. John couldn't bear to be around her. He'd foisted her off on the soldiers to keep her safe.

Sensing her panic, Petey hurried to add, "The lieutenant's gone too. They went further into the jungle to find one of John's friends."

Her fear lessened slightly, but not completely.

"Esteban?"

Petey nodded. "You know him?"

Glory Bee whispered, "Yes. We traveled together for the first few days."

Petey was oiling one of his pistols and he glanced up from the job, his brow furrowed. "If you don't mind my askin', ma'am... How the hell did you end up in the middle of the jungle behind Japanese lines?"

So they were behind enemy lines now? For some reason, she'd never really thought of her situation in that light.

When she didn't answer, Petey hurried to say, "I mean, I was at Stotsenberg when you...uh...when you..." His cheeks flushed. "When you gave your performance. How the hell did you end up here?"

Glory Bee sat up, sitting cross-legged, her elbows on her knees. Wiping the last of the sleep from her face, she said, "I left the base that night. I'd been invited to stay at a nearby plantation." *Invited?* More like sentenced. "I was there when the attack began."

Petey pursed his lips together thoughtfully. "So, you and John. You've been friends for a long time?"

Glory Bee shook her head. "No. He was the foreman at the plantation where I was staying. He knew we wouldn't be safe there, so he brought us to another house in the hills." She pointed in the general direction of Wilmot's lodge. "When the Japanese advanced, we were forced to keep moving."

Petey's hands had stilled over his task and his jaw dropped. "Geez, you've had a time of it, haven't you?"

She nodded.

"Still, this seems like a pretty good place to hide out for a while."

This time, it was Glory Bee's turn to press for answers. "How are things? At Stotsenberg?"

His gaze grew dark, his expression grim. "It got pretty bad. Heard tell that they've evacuated south, to Bataan."

"So soon?" Glory Bee whispered.

"That's where we're headed."

She plucked at her pant leg. "Then things are serious, aren't they?"

He debated whether or not to tell her the truth, then said, "Yeah."

"How long do you think before more American reinforcements arrive?"

"That, ma'am, is the million dollar question. Scuttlebutt around camp was that it would take at least a month. Maybe six weeks."

Her stomach clenched. "That long?"

"'Fraid so. Some of the big brass were saying it could be about 'one hundred and eighty days'. Why the hell don't they say six months?" He shook his head. "One hundred and eighty days sounds like a lifetime."

"So does six months."

Petey grimaced in acknowledgement. "S'pose you're right."

"Do you think that y'all can hold out until then?"

"We don't have a choice. If the Japanese overrun us, they either push us into the sea or take us prisoner." Petey snapped his pistol together and eyed her grimly. "Word has it that the Japanese don't believe in taking prisoners."

* * *

Gilhouley trailed a few feet behind John, alternating between scanning the path ahead and checking behind them as well.

When they'd stepped out of the bamboo forest, he'd sensed the smoke in the air immediately. It was stronger than it had been the day before.

John pointed to a line of hills in the distance. "Looks like there's more Japanese just over the ridge north of here. They must be following the western slope of the mountain. Far as I can tell, they haven't crossed over into this valley yet, but it's only a matter of time."

Gilhouley removed his binoculars, scanning the area as they crouched low behind a clump of bushes.

"We'll have to stay in the foliage as much as possible," John continued, his brow furrowing as he studied the terrain ahead. "If we're in luck, they'll continue north, out of the area. But it won't be long before the Japanese send patrols this way. If so, it might be a day or two before Esteban can get word to Pascal."

Gilhouley nodded. "I suppose we could camp close to your contact."

John shook his head, removing his canteen and unscrewing the lid. "I'd rather you didn't. Esteban and his family are non-combatants. His wife is due any day, and there are little children present. If you and your men are found anywhere nearby…"

"I understand."

John drank deeply, then recapped the canteen. "You can stay where you are, for now. Esteban can send a runner once he has news."

Gilhouley eyed him thoughtfully. He hadn't missed the strain between John and Glory Bee—nor had he been unaware of the sexual tension that radiated between the two of them like a hot electrical wire.

"As long as you don't mind the company," he offered carefully. If it were Rosemary back in that forest and Gilhouley had a chance of being alone with her…he didn't think he'd let anyone short of Franklin Delano Roosevelt share his camp.

"I think that would be best."

There was such a rueful ring to the words that Gilhouley wondered if he'd misinterpreted the emotions between John and the stripper.

"This Esteban fellow. You can trust him?"

"With my life," John said, standing again. "Let's go. I want to make sure we're back by nightfall."

They continued with their hike, moving slowly through the trees, trying to make as little noise as possible. Until finally, somewhere on the breeze, Gilhouley thought he caught a hint of something other than smoke. Something succulent and meaty…

Fried pork?

"It's up ahead," John said, pointing.

Following the direction of his finger, Gilhouley saw a wisp of smoke emerging from the trees, and unbidden, his stomach grumbled. It had been a while since last night's meal.

John held up a hand, gesturing for Gilhouley to wait. "Let me go in first. I don't want to scare them."

Gilhouley nodded, but his finger continued to rest over the trigger of his rifle.

John brought two fingers up to his lips, issuing a mournful sound much like a bird. Then, lifting his hands, he stepped into the clearing below.

For an instant, Gilhouley couldn't see anything to warrant the need for caution. But then, several men melted out of the shadows—one of them, a huge, broad Filipino who grinned so broadly that Gilhouley could see a flash of a gold tooth.

"*Padre!*"

As if the word had unleashed a torrent, the area was suddenly full of squealing children who clambered around John until he hugged each of them in turn, then scooped a little boy onto his shoulders.

"I've brought someone with me, Esteban. A friend."

"Come, sit, sit!"

John motioned to Gilhouley and he cautiously stepped forward.

He'd expected to be met with suspicion, but evidently, John's word was good enough for the men who had only moments ago emerged carrying rifles and shotguns. They eyed Gilhouley curiously, but made their way through the trees to a settlement of huts. In the center, a cooking fire held several pots, one of them rattling from the heat.

If the men with Esteban paid him little attention, the children were wild with excitement, clustering around him like slippery fish, all of them wanting to touch his hand, his clothes.

"*Americano! Americano!*"

John laughed and motioned for Gilhouley to follow, but with the children scampering under his feet, he finally gave up, clicked the safety on his rifle and scooped a pair of the giggling youngsters into his arms and carrying them to the clearing as if they were a pair of footballs.

Esteban laughed, a huge belly laugh that shook his entire body like a Filipino Santa Claus.

"This is Lieutenant Gilhouley, Esteban," John said as Esteban took a seat on a felled log.

He held out his hand. "Aren't you too far north, Lieutenant?" he said with a wide grin.

Gilhouley couldn't help laughing. "Yes, sir, I am."

"Esteban! Call me Esteban."

A woman walked toward them, carrying a pile of plates. She waddled with the stooped posture of a woman who had endured nine months of pregnancy and did not wish to endure any more. She smiled shyly at Gilhouley before turning to ask John, "How is Glory Bee?"

John's smile was curiously tight. "She's doing well, thank you, Maria."

"Not sick?"

"No."

"Good."

Finished with what she had to say, Maria used the edge of her skirt to lift the lid from the pot, revealing a simmering concoction of meat and vegetables in a thick broth. From another vessel, she scooped out rice, and from another, stewed greens.

The first plate was passed to John, the second to Gilhouley.

When he tried to demur, Esteban waved away his concerns. "We caught a wild pig so there's more than enough to go around. Eat, eat. It's hard work getting through the forest, eh?"

Gilhouley laughed at the understatement of that remark. Even though he felt a pang of guilt at eating when the rest of his men were still back at the camp, he began scooping the hot food into his mouth, knowing that meat of any kind would be a luxury in the days to come. He wouldn't have begrudged his men eating if they'd come across such bounty, and he doubted that they would look askance at him.

"Lieutenant Gilhouley needs your help, Esteban," John began after they'd had several mouthfuls.

"My help?" Esteban grinned. "How can that be?"

"I take it you've had a chance to contact Maria's brothers?"

Esteban waved to the group lining up to receive their portions. "These are their sons, their daughters, their wives."

John chose his words carefully. "But Pascal and his men are elsewhere?"

Esteban's eyes narrowed, his expression becoming carefully bland.

"We all take turns looking for game and supplies," he responded vaguely.

"Do you think you could get a message to him?"

The large man chewed thoughtfully. "Perhaps."

John gestured to Gilhouley. "Lieutenant Gilhouley and his men would like to propose a business arrangement with Pascal."

"How many men?"

"Five altogether."

"And what sort of business would Pascal want with the *Americanos?*"

John set his plate aside only half eaten and sat with his elbows on his thighs, his hands loosely clasped in front of him.

"They need to get to Bataan. *If* Pascal would be interested in helping them get to the coast…and *if* they could supply a small boat…"

"Ahh," Esteban drawled. "You want to circle the island to Bataan."

"Could it be done?"

Esteban's lower lip jutted out as he thought carefully. "You would have to go at night to escape the patrols, but yes, I think it could be done." He set his own plate aside and slapped his thighs. "But you said that this would be a…business arrangement."

John nodded. "Lieutenant Gilhouley has something that he thinks would be of use to Pascal."

Esteban grimaced. "Guns? Ammunition?"

"Not exactly."

This time Esteban turned to Gilhouley, asking him directly. "Then what have you got, *Americano?*"

Gilhouley's gaze bounced to John, who imperceptibly nodded in encouragement.

"I've got a radio that Pascal can use to coordinate his efforts with the U.S. military."

Esteban stared at him in astonishment, then began to laugh his Santa Claus laugh. Grabbing his plate, he stood, leaning over to slap Gilhouley on the back, his ham-sized palms nearly unseating Gilhouley before the large man strode toward his wife for seconds.

"Do you suppose that means he's interested?" Gilhouley asked under his breath.

John's smile was more restrained than Esteban's, but still encouraging.

"He's interested."

"*Padre!* Bring the lieutenant over here and fill your plates again. There's more than enough and you'll need your strength for the hike back."

He grew stronger after seeing the leaflet. Especially when the distant sound of mortar fire was heard only days after the papers were dropped.

Unfortunately, news of an offensive was a mixed blessing. On the one hand, it was the first tangible proof that the Americans weren't just flying planes over the island. They had invaded.

But the noise made the guards antsy, and Tanaka was especially frantic. He'd dispensed with communicating at all with his American prisoners. Instead, he played his own vicious game of Russian roulette. On a good day, he stayed in his hut, drinking saké *and listening to his damned collection of Jap opera. On a bad day…*

On a bad day, the man strode outside, picked a prisoner at random, and shot him.

More and more, he and his men had begun to depend on their time outside the wire. The garden had become the closest thing they had to a refuge. The guards, as if sensing the encroaching battle, had become more lax.

They spent their time speaking in low voices, huddled together as they mulled over the latest news from the front. Their control of the prisoners slipped enough that a few of the villagers dared to approach the Americans during their midday break, bringing rice wrapped in newspaper or bundles laden with fruit.

He'd become obsessed with his garden, obsessed by the only thing he could count on for sure—that nature would ignore the chaos and desperation around her and the laws of the harvest would apply.

He was so intent on his hoeing, that he barely noticed the little boy who sidled up beside him. It wasn't the same youngster he'd seen before. This was a child, no more than five. The kid looked up at him with wide eyes, tugging on his trouser pocket. Then he turned and ran into the jungle.

It wasn't until later, when he was crawling into his bunk, that he realized a scrap of paper had been slipped into his pocket.

Glancing over either shoulder, he lifted the paper free, squinting at it in the darkness. The message was simple and chilling.

Take care. J's exterminating POW's as A. Army advances.

Padre

But it was the postscript that caused his hands to tremble so fiercely, he could hardly keep hold of the paper.

P.S. Letter to R. received and forwarded.

Chapter Fourteen

Darkness was falling when John and Gilhouley approached the camp. After Gilhouley's offer of radio equipment had been made, Esteban's mood had brightened even more. Just as John had projected, once they'd eaten their fill, the Filipino had told Gilhouley that he would extend the offer to Pascal, but it could be days before he managed to contact his brother-in-law. As soon as he had an answer, he'd send a runner back to John's camp.

As they slogged through the underbrush, John suspected that they wouldn't have long to wait. Somehow, he wouldn't be surprised if the guerrillas knew everything that happened in the surrounding area. He'd bet that they'd had a man watching Gilhouley and him make their way through the jungle. But he could also understand their need for caution. Especially when Gilhouley had explained to Esteban what had happened to Santo Tomas.

John shook his head in regret. He'd encountered Santo Tomas several times when conducting business for the plantation. He was a good man with a reputation for fairness and honesty. He'd once bragged about his daughter Chica with such pride that the little girl had blushed and squirmed in his arms with embarrassment. His death served as a reminder to John of how dangerous the Philippines had become.

They were nearly a mile from their goal when John reached out to snag Gilhouley's arm, bringing him to a halt.

Gilhouley automatically raised his weapon, thinking John was issuing a silent alarm, but John motioned for him to keep his rifle at his shoulder.

"Before we get back into camp, I need to ask you some things, and I need you to tell me the truth."

Gilhouley's eyes narrowed, but he said, "Fine. What is it?"

"How bad are things here on Luzon?"

There was a beat of silence as Gilhouley obviously debated how candid he could be without giving away military secrets.

"I don't think they could get much worse," he finally said. "Our army is retreating to Bataan, our airfields and bases are destroyed."

"How strong do you think your defenses will be on Bataan?"

When a flash of suspicion entered Gilhouley's gaze, John hastened to explain. "What I need to know is whether a civilian would be safer with you or with me."

Gilhouley's posture relaxed and he glanced in the direction of the camp. "You mean would Miss O'Halloran be safer?"

"Yes."

He considered the situation, shifting slightly. "Would you be coming with her?"

Until that moment, John hadn't really thought that far. But now that he was confronted with the possibility of entrusting Glory Bee's safety to someone else, he was forced to think things through.

"I don't think so."

And it wasn't because of the way things had changed between them or his own confusing emotions. It was because, in that instant, he realized that by coming into the hills, by allying himself with the local guerrillas, he had done the one thing he had not been able to do in China. He was fighting back.

Again, Gilhouley weighed the matter carefully. Then he said, "Things will get rough on Bataan before they ever get better. It could be weeks, even months before reinforcements arrive."

"But she would be surrounded by the military. She could be with other women. Women who could help her if she…if she got sick."

Gilhouley had said it could be months before help came. How

far along was Glory Bee's pregnancy?

"The evacuation plans include medical facilities, even the participation of some of the nurses."

Again, John thought of the possibility of a baby. One that would cry and fret. A baby who might even need medical attention—all of which would be dangerous here in the jungle.

"Is there a possibility that American civilians could be evacuated to safety?"

Gilhouley's gaze grew sad. "Right now?"

John nodded.

"I'd say the chances are slim to none. There are literally only a few dozen aircraft left. The Navy is decimated. Any evacuations that might occur would probably have to be done by submarine or seaplane, and I'm sure that officers and the wounded would be taken out first."

John grew quiet, knowing that there were no real answers. Whether she stayed with him or went to Bataan with Gilhouley, the future held untold risks.

Gilhouley dragged his helmet from his head and wiped his brow with his arm. "Do you want my personal opinion?"

"Yes."

"If it were me—" he pointed in the direction of the camp "—if it was my girl back there…I'd keep her here rather than take her to Bataan." He settled his helmet back in place, leaving the chinstraps dangling. Then he offered John a cock-eyed grin that made him look, oh, so American—big and brash and cocky. "But then, if it were me, I'd also let her make the decision. Otherwise, you might never hear the end of it."

Then, with a laugh, he turned and resumed their hike through the forest—leaving John to wonder if Gilhouley's answer would be the same if his girl were pregnant with another man's child.

* * *

Rosemary had been given the evening shift off—which meant, that for the first time in weeks, she would be allowed to sleep, uninterrupted, until 0800 in the morning.

If the Japanese cooperate, she thought as walked to the tent that she and Alice shared.

Just before reaching the row of shelters reserved for the nurses, she dodged into the last ward. As promised, she went to one of the far cots to check on Napoli.

Although he still lay shivering in his bunk, she thought his color looked better. But she knew it would be some time before the quinine could take effect.

"Hello, Major," he said gruffly.

"You're going to call me Rosemary, remember?"

He smiled and she grabbed an empty crate, tipping it on its side so that she could use it for a stool.

"How long have I been out?" His voice was gravelly and shaky.

"A few hours. Have my nurses been treating you well?"

Napoli's eyes became suddenly bright, and he swallowed hard before speaking, "You've been really kind. You've all been really kind."

She felt his forehead with the back of her hand. "I'm glad. I'd have to discipline them something fierce if I thought they weren't spoiling you."

He sniffed and scrubbed at his eyes. Then, he clutched at her hand, squeezing it.

"Gilhouley's a lucky man to have found you, Maj…Rosemary."

Rosemary smiled. "I think I'm the lucky one."

Napoli sniffed again, then said, "Remember, he's not quite as tough as he seems."

"Oh?" she said lightly.

A chill caused Napoli to shudder and his eyes grew heavy. "That father of his hurt him. Hurt him to the core." He fought against his weariness, his lashes opening wide for a moment before beginning to droop once again. "Never had a mother. She died when he was born. I think his dad always…blamed Gilhouley…for that…"

Napoli's jaw grew lax and he sank back into a fitful sleep again.

Tucking the covers more tightly around him, Rosemary reached overhead to pull the mosquito netting over his wizened frame.

Then, after she'd done all she could to make him comfortable, she eased from between the rows of cots.

She'd learned more about Gilhouley from her chance encounters with Napoli than she had in the months that she'd known Riley. And yet…

And yet…

The things she'd learned hadn't convinced her she was making a horrible mistake by becoming embroiled in a wartime romance.

They'd only made her love him more.

* * *

Since Maria had given him a huge packet of rice wrapped in newspaper and a bottle of her pork stew to carry back to the camp, John waited until everyone had eaten their unexpected banquet and the soldiers were gathered in a circle playing cards before daring to approach Glory Bee. Moving as casually as he could, he walked to the spot where she had made a place for them to sleep only the day before.

He saw the way she tensed as he approached, but she didn't bother to look up. Instead, she sat in the lee between the rocks, running a comb through her hair as if the task would keep the earth spinning on its axis.

His throat grew dry as he watched the tresses flow through her fingers like molten copper. Not sure if he could trust himself so close to her, he nearly retreated. But he didn't know when Esteban might return with a message, and if Glory Bee wanted to go with the soldiers, she would need to be ready.

Hesitating, he knew he had to choose his words carefully. Just as Gilhouley had suggested, he had to make sure that she had all of the information needed to make her decision. Even so, he couldn't influence her. Not if he was going to live with his conscience afterwards.

But as he watched the gleam of her hair in the darkness, he was forced to admit that he was taking the coward's way out. As long as he foisted all responsibility onto Glory Bee, he didn't have to examine his own chaotic emotions.

Did he really want her to go?

The thought settled into his stomach like a lump of lead.

Could he live with the temptation if she stayed?

John sank onto the ground beside her. "How are you feeling?"

His question took her by surprise, because she stared at him blankly, then suddenly realized why he was asking.

"I'm fine."

"Not tired, or...I don't know...nauseous?"

She scowled. "My feet are blistered, my skin is broiled, my thighs, my calves, and my back are killing me, and I have bug bites on every inch of my body. Oh, and I ate a whole candy bar that Petey gave me in about twenty seconds flat, and now I have an overwhelming urge to find myself some more, a lot more, but other than that...I'm peachy."

Against his will, his lips slid into a quick grin. "I think I might have a possible solution to the chocolate problem."

Her brows lifted. "Really?" There was a slight tinge of suspicion to her to her tone.

John felt as if he were about to walk into a minefield wearing hobnailed boots. He probably should have taken more time to work out the best way to approach her with the idea. But there wasn't time. There simply wasn't time.

"I talked to Gilhouley about your predicament."

She stiffened, the color leeching from her skin, and too late, he realized how his words might be misinterpreted.

"No. No! Not...*that* predicament," he said hurriedly with a waving gesture toward her stomach. But she didn't look mollified. Instead, she bristled even more.

"And what predicament would that be?"

"You, me...I mean...No, that's not what I mean, I..." He swore softly under his breath and blurted, "Look, I spoke to Gilhouley, and if you want, they'll take you back with them to Bataan."

He wasn't entirely sure how he'd expected her to react, but he was mystified when her eyes suddenly filled with tears.

"When do you want me to leave?"

She was so suddenly docile, so…emotionless, that he couldn't help needling her.

"It's not about what *I* want. This is your decision, Glory Bee."

"Is it?" she suddenly hissed, anger blazing from her eyes. "Or do you want me to believe that so no hint of blame can ever be laid at your door."

When he would have responded, she held up a hand, palm out. "Never mind. I get it." Her laugh was bitter. "You'd think that after playing this same scenario time and time again that I'd learn my lesson—and you know what, I have. I have definitely learned my lesson. So I'll pack my bags and be ready to go."

She stood and moved deeper into the lee away from the prying eyes of the soldiers, shoving things hastily into her bag. When he caught her stuffing a rock and his shaving kit inside the pack along with one of the fabric pieces he'd brought from the abandoned village, he dodged to take her by the elbows. But she fought against him, trying to wrench away.

It was then that he saw the tears that fell from the dam of her lashes. Her chin crumpled, her skin growing blotchy and red, even beneath her sunburn.

He cupped her face in his hands, trying to understand. He only wanted to do what was right. If she could find safety with the Americans, he couldn't stand in her way. But she looked at him as if he'd ripped the heart from her breast and crushed it in his hands.

"Don't send me away," she whispered, her voice so choked and filled with emotion that he nearly didn't understand her. "Please, don't send me away."

And then, in one crashing moment, he realized that she thought, with his cautious words and carefully coached argument, that he was attempting to abandon her, to banish her—to throw her away.

Her mother, the men in her life, even the father of her baby…they had all tossed her aside the moment she'd become inconvenient to them. They had used her for their own selfish pleasures and motives without a care in the world as to what would make her happy or complete. And unwittingly, he'd been about to do the same.

He felt a rush of shame, acknowledging that he'd been no better than any of the other people she'd cared about. Shocked and confused by her pregnancy, he hadn't wanted to deal with the repercussions. He hadn't wanted to examine his own shortcomings too closely. He hadn't wanted to admit that her condition had shocked him to the core. That he'd been angry—and a yes, jealous—of the way she'd been so comfortable with her sexual history. Rather than deal with his chaotic emotions, he'd sought a way to circumvent them without telling her the truth. And no matter what had happened, no matter what decision she made, she at least deserved to know that he had grown to care for her.

Because he did care for her. More than he knew he was willing to admit.

Swiping the tears away from her cheeks with his thumbs, he stared deeply into her eyes, eyes that reminded him of dark rain-kissed pansies. And in that instant, he knew that whatever his shortcomings might be, he couldn't hurt her. Not now. Not ever.

"Don't cry," he urged, his chest tight. "Don't cry." Then he bent to brush his lips across hers, softly, sweetly, and then, because he couldn't help himself, he lingered, the caress growing more demanding, more intimate, until his tongue begged for entrance. When her lips parted, he pressed closer and closer, his arms sweeping around her waist to draw her tightly against him.

She sobbed against his lips, but when he drew back, thinking he might be hurting her again, she blinked up at him, her eyes wide with disbelief.

"You don't hate me," she whispered.

"Hate you?"

"Y-yes…I was so sure that you…that I…"

He stopped her with a finger on her lips.

"I could never hate you."

"B-but you could hate what I've done."

"I could never hate you or anything you've done," he stated more forcefully. "Never." Then he kissed her again.

"You won't send me away?"

John couldn't account for relief that eased the tension gripping his chest. "Not if you don't want to go."

"I don't want to be a burden."

He kissed her cheek, her nose. "You could never be a burden." He drew back to eye her with concern. "But I want you to think carefully about what you're saying. It could be months before the Americans arrive, and even then, driving the Japanese back off the island—"

"I don't want to go."

"Glory Bee, have you thought about when the baby—?"

"I don't want to go. Please don't make me go."

He drew her into his arms, settling her cheek against his chest, wondering if she could hear the way his heart thumped against his ribs—in joy, in panic. It wouldn't be easy. The fact that Glory Bee was pregnant would complicate their situation immeasurably. But if she needed help, Maria was near.

"You'd best unpack your things, then," he whispered against her hair.

When she gripped his waist, he settled his back against a rock, bringing her with him. Spreading his legs out in front of him, he cradled her between his thighs, drawing a blanket around her shoulders.

She shuddered against him, exhausted, emotionally and physically.

"You won't leave me."

He stroked her hair, and the tresses wound around his fingers like molten copper. Just as he had imagined.

"Esteban will send a runner as soon as he has news. I don't know if I'll need to go with the Americans, to make sure they get to Esteban's camp safely. But if they need my help, I'll make sure you know when I'm going."

"Even if…" her words were interrupted by a shuddering yawn, "…it's the middle of the night?"

"If it's nighttime, I'll wake you first. But I'll be back as soon as I can. I promise."

"You're sure?"

"I'm sure."

Her fingers curled into his shirt.

"I'm sorry, John."

"I told you. There is nothing to forgive. You are an incredible woman, Glory Bee. With everything that you've been through, you remain so…filled with joy. That's a gift. A gift you've shared with me."

"How so?"

He continued to stroke her hair, feeling her body relax against his.

"Because you've taught me how to live again." He added more quietly. "And to love."

He waited for her response, barely able to breathe. He couldn't believe that he'd allowed himself to think the words, let alone utter them.

But as the silence continued—much longer than he would have liked—he leaned down to gauge her reaction, then laughed softly.

He'd bared his heart and soul to her—something he never would have thought possible mere weeks before. And Glory Bee, this incredible, maddening, joyful woman…

Was fast asleep.

• • •

There was no sign of a runner from Esteban for a day…two …three…

When a week passed, Glory Bee could see the tension in the soldiers beginning to increase. They alternated between fanning out on patrols and prowling around the camp, oiling their weapons to keep them in prime working condition.

In order to make their rations stretch further, the men had begun eating one meal a day. Glory Bee would have been happy to follow suit, but John forbid her from cutting back on her calories any more than she already had. But he also knew she didn't want to be caught eating in front of the men, so he would bring her a little rice left from the night before or a precious tin of fruit from their supplies.

So far, the soldiers hadn't made too serious of a dent in their cache of canned foods. At least once a day, one of the soldiers would return to camp with something for the dinner table—whether it was fish from the stream or birds they'd caught with the snares that Petey had fashioned from shoe laces and woven twigs.

For the first time in her life, Glory Bee found that growing up poor had its advantages. As a child, she'd eaten squirrel, raccoon, and even snake. But as she did her best to make their offerings palatable with her limited culinary skills, she couldn't control the cravings that besieged her. She wanted ham and greens and bread with rich creamy butter. And chocolate.

But food wasn't her only craving. After a week where every waking moment had been spent with someone guarding the camp or ensuring she was well protected, she needed privacy.

Privacy and a real bath.

Finally, when the itch of bug bites and the lank texture of her hair became more than she could bear, she carefully chose a moment when John was standing away from the other soldiers and made her approach.

Things had been better between them for the past few days. The mood between them had become warm. Friendly. He'd taken to sleeping next to her at night when he wasn't assigned to guard duty. But other than stretching out next to her, or drawing her onto his shoulder, he didn't touch her. Didn't kiss her. At times, he was so careful, so solicitous, that she could scarcely bear the way he kept her at arm's length. Since discovering her pregnancy, he'd begun to treat her as if she were made of spun glass, refusing to let her carry anything heavy or strain herself in any way. She supposed that with the other men so near, he didn't want to give them anything to gossip about when they returned to the base.

Nevertheless, while he remained outwardly calm and unaffected, his actions had the opposite effect on her. By denying her emotions and impulses, the sexual tension had built up inside her with such force that her frustration had become pique, her pique, anger, until she felt as if she were a powder keg about to blow. And, by heavens, if she couldn't satisfy her raging need for John Macklin, at least she would satisfy the need to wash her hair.

John must have sensed at least a portion of her mood because he frowned as she approached and his posture stiffened, as if he were bracing himself for whatever storm she might bring.

But Glory Bee had no wish to make a scene. She'd never been that kind of a woman. Instead, she said lowly, "I need to take a bath. A real bath. Sometime today."

He regarded her uncomprehendingly for a moment, then understood the gist of her request. He didn't speak, but nodded.

Without another word, she returned to the lee in the rock and gathered up their blankets so that the insects wouldn't find new places to hide. Then, knowing that John would somehow grant her request, she dug into her pack for fresh clothes, her comb, and the small precious cake of soap. If only she'd known she would be marooned in the jungle for weeks. Then she would have brought bars and bars of the stuff.

It was only after she'd gathered everything together in a pile that she became aware of a stillness in the camp. Peeking around the edge of the rocks, she discovered that the clearing was empty except for John, who stood poking at the fire underneath a pair of pots.

Confused, she rolled to her feet and approached him. "Where have all the men gone?"

John offered her a soft smile—and again, she was struck by the way that hint of tenderness made him look so much more approachable. Young. Attractive.

"When I explained your need for privacy, they decided to

head downstream a mile or two and take advantage of the water themselves." He glanced at his watch. "They've given me their word they won't return for at least an hour."

An hour.

One hour alone with John.

Her hands twisted together. "You didn't want to go with them?"

He scowled. "I'm not leaving you here alone. I'll keep an eye on things while you wash up."

For a moment, she felt a flare of hope. What kinds of things did he intend to keep his eyes on?

Feeling suddenly free, like a hostess who'd finally rid herself of persistent houseguests, she hurried back to collect her things. Then, returning to the same deep spot in the river where she'd bathed once before, she kicked off her shoes.

"Promise me that you'll watch for lizards," she said breathlessly as she dragged her shirt over her head and kicked out of her trousers.

Just in time, she peered over her shoulder to see John look in her direction. Unable to dampen the wicked voice that whispered in her ear to tempt him even more, she reached behind her to unfasten her brassiere, then allowed it to drop to the ground unheeded.

He swallowed. Hard. And she couldn't help but laugh.

"Dear God, Glory Bee." His words begged her to stop, but his eyes clung to the fullness of her breasts like a dying man being offered salvation.

"After the last few days, I was beginning to believe that you didn't want me anymore," she whispered, surprising even herself with her boldness.

"Nothing could be farther from the truth."

She considered pushing things even farther. But she feared that if she forced him to admit how much he desired her, he might decide to flee and finish his guard duty from the safety of the woods. So, instead, she slipped the silken tap pants down over her hips. For several long moments, she stood still, allowing John to see what she had never exposed onstage. And then, when she feared he might bolt, she stepped into the stream and sank down into the water.

She had thought that he would turn away, that he would pretend to guard her from Japanese and forest animals alike, but he continued to face her, watching, his expression at once rapt and horrified.

Sensing that he warred with the values that had made him a priest, she didn't say a word. She reached for the soap, dipped it into the water, then began to rub it over her arms, her neck, her breasts, until her skin was shiny and slick. Then, sitting back, she ran the bar over her legs, her belly.

At that point, John didn't even pretend to keep guard. He set his rifle on the ground and faced her more directly, his elbows on his thighs as he leaned toward her. But his posture couldn't hide the effect she was having on his body.

"You're killing me, Glory Bee."

"Then come join me."

He shook his head.

"Why not?"

He looked heavenward for a moment, then back at her. "You know why not."

"You're not a priest anymore," she reminded him, shocking herself with her brazenness.

"No, but I…"

Her head tipped to one side. "Have you ever been with a woman before, John?"

The forest pulsed for several long seconds before he shook his head.

"Not even when you left the priesthood?"

"No."

"Why not?"

Personal. Very, very *personal.* But Glory needed to know the answer, needed to know what made this man so different from any other male she'd ever encountered.

"It always felt…wrong."

"Sinful, you mean?"

"No." He looked up at her then. "More like I hadn't found the right partner yet."

The words caused a slow heat to spill through her veins. He'd never felt tempted. Until he'd met her. The idea was so powerful, so overwhelming, that this time, it was her turn to shift in discomfort.

Wrapping her arms around her up drawn knees, she regarded him carefully as she asked,

"Does it bother you that I'm pregnant?"

He chose his words carefully. "It concerns me."

She wasn't quite sure what he meant by that, so she asked, "Does it bother you that I've been with other men?"

"A little. But only a little."

Again, she was astonished by his honesty.

"Does it make you want me less?"

He shook his head. "No. Nothing could ever make me want you less."

When he stood, she was sure that he meant to come to her, to draw her in his arms, to kiss her—and her body trembled from the need of it. Instead, he moved to the fire, and she frowned until she saw that he'd taken hold of one of the pots and now carried it toward her.

Warm water.

Here in the midst of the jungle, surrounded by the most primitive conditions, he had thought far enough ahead to supply her with warm water. John stepped into the stream and crouched beside her.

"Undo your hair, Glory Bee," he said, his voice low. "I love your hair."

Lifting her arms, she began to remove the precious pins from the braids she'd looped over the top of her head. The action caused John's gaze to slip down to the fullness of her breasts as they swayed from the movement. And sensing the slender control he had on his emotions, she prolonged the task, removing her hairpins with infinite slowness, then using her fingers to unwind the plaits, until the tresses hung over her shoulders, teasing the taut tips of her nipples.

Standing, John began to pour the warm water over her head, and she couldn't help the moan of pleasure that escaped from her throat. She felt as if she were being bathed in liquid sunshine as the liquid sluiced down her throat, between her breasts, then down, down, to the part of her that ached for John's possession.

When she thought she could bear no more, John knelt beside her again. Reaching for the bar of soap, he rubbed it against his hands, then plunged his slick fingers into her hair, massaging her scalp until she thought that the pleasure building within her might come to a climax then and there.

Only after the strands were squeaky clean, did he stand again, rinsing the soap away with the rest of the warm water. Then, when she thought that she could bear no more, he reached for her, pulling her upright into his arms. Heedless of the way she soaked his clothing, he lowered his head to kiss her, tenderly, slowly, then with increasing fire until Glory Bee wasn't sure where her body ended and his began. She only knew that it felt so good, so right, to be with this man, to have him strain against her, his mouth ravishing hers.

Her own hands clutched at his waist, tugging his shirt free until she could spread her hands wide over his bare flesh. She wanted him more than anything she'd ever wanted in her whole life. More than air itself.

She tunneled between them, searching for the buttons to his shirt, needing that contact, flesh to flesh, heart to heart. But he drew away from her to hold her hand.

"Not yet," he whispered hoarsely. "Not here."

She whimpered against him with her need—and she knew that she'd finally managed to crash her way through his emotional barriers because he whispered, "They'll be back soon. Gilhouley and his men."

She mewled in distress. Why hadn't John sent them away for a day, a week?

John kissed her again, his own desperation and want so palpable that she was slightly mollified.

"They won't be here for much longer. Esteban is bound to send a runner soon. Then, as soon as they're gone and we're alone…"

He kissed her again, so powerfully that common sense was

nearly overruled.

But from some distance away, she heard noisy footfalls and knew that their idyll was about to be disturbed.

Breaking away from her, John quickly handed her the clothing she'd set out—a dress this time, since her trousers were already growing uncomfortable. She'd barely managed to put on her underthings and pull the frock into position before Petey appeared, then Gilhouley, Berman, Kilgore, and Baptiste. She knew them well by now, knew where they were from, why they'd joined the Army, what their specialties were.

But in that instant, Glory Bee couldn't wait until they were gone.

"Lieutenant, come quick!"

He looked up from his attempts to repair his pants. They were literally falling apart at the seams, and since he'd cut them off at the knees long ago, he was pulling frayed threads from the edges and using a bit of bent wire as a needle in order to patch up the holes.

Kilgore's expression held such terror that he immediately dropped the pants and staggered toward him on trembling legs.

"What is it?"

"Petey. They caught him bringing a handful of greens in from the garden."

"Shit, shit, shit!" He'd told Petey to watch himself in the next few days. Tanaka had been foaming at the mouth with fury earlier that week, and so far, he hadn't come out into the compound, gun cocked.

"Who caught him? Putzy-sahn?"

Kilgore nodded.

"That won't be as bad. He'll—"

"He's already gone inside to tell Tanaka."

The sound of screams came from the compound and he dodged outside. Petey was being held by two guards while Tanaka charged toward him, beating him with a cudgel.

He lunged toward his friend, but Kilgore and another soldier held him back as Petey was struck again and again. Even from this distance, they could hear the bones crack, until his face became an unrecognizable, bloody lump, and his body crumpled to the ground. Even then, Tanaka continued to kick him—head, ribs, crotch—until Petey no longer moved. Then, offering a torrent of barely intelligible syllables, Tanaka ordered the prisoner strung up from a pair of poles in the center of the compound.

"At least Tanaka didn't shoot him," Kilgore whispered, his features pale.

Was it better? Or would a quick death have been more merciful than the vicious beating and days spent hanging by his arms in the sun?

"Is he breathing?" he whispered desperately. When no one answered, he shouted, "Is he breathing!"

"I don't know, Lieutenant."

They watched in horror as Petey's body was strung up by his wrists. His head lolled forward, blood dripping into the dust beneath him. His arms strained beneath the burden of supporting his dead weight, looking as if they might separate at the shoulders.

"Come on, Lieutenant. We gotta back off. If we stay here, Tanaka will come at him again."

"No."

"Lieutenant?"

"No! I'm not moving. Not until I know he's breathing." He sank into the dust, sobbing again, "Not until I know he's breathing."

Chapter Fifteen

January 9, 1941

Rosemary sat wearily on the beach, nursing a precious bottle of Coca-Cola. There had been a bodega in one of the barrios a few miles away and the nurses had begun congregating there between shifts. It was so easy to sit on the wide stoop, sipping sodas and pretending to be at a mom-and-pop store back home. But earlier that afternoon, the little shop had received a direct hit and all that was left was a few scattered bottles of cola, dented tins of food, and splintered wood.

The scuttlebutt floating through camp was that the Powers-That-Be were already looking for another location for the hospital.

In one respect, Rosemary would be glad for the move. This close to the bay, the facilities were too exposed, and the Japanese had no respect for the bed sheets painted with red crosses that had been laid out in the clearing and on the roofs of the huts. If Zeros weren't flying overhead and strafing the staff who wandered into the clearing, the Japanese Artillery was lobbing shells over their heads.

On the other hand, the move might cause problems of a different nature. The only logical alternative to their current site would be a spot further inland where the jungle would provide better cover. And the interior of Bataan was known for its inhospitable conditions. It was the perfect breeding ground for malaria, dysentery, and dengue fever.

Even more concerning, it was one step farther away from Gilhouley. If the hospital were repositioned, would he be able to find her if he ever had a chance to break away from his duties?

A shadowy shape slowly made its way toward her, and she smiled when she recognized Napoli.

"I see you're feeling better," she said with a smile.

He grunted, standing above her, his hat in his hand. "Good enough t' give my bed up to someone else who needs it."

She nodded. "I'm glad. I was worried about you for a day or two."

Napoli's smile was disconcerted and he shuffled his feet like a shy teenager at his first dance.

"I want t' thank you, Rosemary."

She stood, brushing the sand from her trousers. As promised, the women had been issued army tans—and the uniforms were cooler than the coveralls. But after a day spent wading through a sea of death and destruction, there were times when she longed for the femininity of a dress and the sweet scent of perfume.

"Promise me you'll take care of yourself."

He nodded, gripping his hat in his hand.

"Where are you headed?"

"I've got a little camp a few miles down the coast. Not too bad of a place. Got a supply of food, even a radio. My plane's hidden in a cove there while I try to scrounge up a part I need. I'll spend some time fixin' her up. Then, maybe in a week or so, I'll try to make a run to Australia."

"Have you got enough fuel to get that far?"

He shrugged. "Probably not. But there's plenty of islands where I can ditch if I have to. Hopefully the Japs haven't got control of all of 'em."

To Rosemary, his plans for fleeing the Philippines didn't seem much safer than sticking around, but she couldn't blame him for trying.

"I wish you well, Napoli."

He nodded. "I'll come and say goodbye before I go, just to check and see if you've heard anything from Gilhouley."

"I'd appreciate that."

"Well..." Running out of things to say, he held out his hand for her to shake, but she ignored him, and drew him close for a quick hug and a kiss on the cheek.

When she stepped back, she was sure he was blushing, but his grin was pleased.

"You're a good lady, Miss Rosemary. Gilhouley's lucky to have found you."

Then, with a quick salute, he jammed his hat on his head and began to trudge through the sand toward his camp.

Rosemary watched him until he was completely swallowed by the darkness. Then, wrapping her arms around her waist, she turned her attention back to the bay, hoping, praying, that the promised reinforcements would show up soon.

* * *

Dawn had barely begun to color the sky when Glory Bee felt a hand on her shoulder. Immediately, she was awake and struggling into a sitting position. Rubbing the sleep from her eyes, she looked up into John's features.

"Esteban sent a runner to say that the guerillas are ready to escort the soldiers east. We'll be leaving in a few minutes. I don't know how long I'll be gone. It may only be to Esteban's camp, it may be as far as the coast."

Glory Bee swallowed beneath a sudden irrational fear. Even though she trusted John to come back to her, she couldn't shake the terror of being alone, in the jungle, wondering when he'd return.

"Take me with you," she said suddenly, grasping his arms. "Please." She remembered the fear she'd felt when she'd been confronted by a lizard. How much greater would her terror be if something else approached her in the darkness?

When John meant to refuse, she added quickly. "Please. Only as far as Esteban's camp. I could stay there with Maria and the children until you come back. Please." She admitted in barely a whisper, "I'm afraid to stay here on my own."

"Take a light pack—only a few changes of clothes, your pistol, and some water. Better hurry. We're leaving as soon as the soldiers have gathered their gear."

The moment he'd left, Glory Bee upended her rucksack and filled it again with a nightgown, brush, extra shirt, and a loose cotton dress. Near the top, she put the pistol that John had given her when they'd still been at the Wilmot's lodge. She had only one pair of trousers, which she quickly donned, along with her only long-sleeved button-down shirt. Then, after braiding her hair into two plaits, she wound them over her head and secured them with pins.

When she emerged, ready to go, she noted that the soldiers were still double-checking the radio equipment and she felt a surge of self-satisfaction that she hadn't kept the men waiting.

"Ready?" John asked, his dark gaze gleaming in approval.

"Yes."

"Do you think you could help carry a rifle?"

She nodded and he handed her the weapon.

"It's loaded, so be careful. Leave it slung over your shoulder, pointing up."

"I can do that."

For a moment, his hand lingered in the hollow of her back, and that simple, unconscious caress was as precious to her as a full-blown embrace.

"Let's go," he called out.

Immediately, the soldiers filed into position, Gilhouley and Baptiste up front with John, the other three hanging back with Glory Bee. It was Petey who kept within arm's length of Glory Bee, his attitude curiously protective.

She couldn't help saying, "Thanks again for the chocolate bar you gave me, Petey."

Petey grinned. "You liked it, huh?"

"I don't think there's a woman alive who doesn't like chocolate."

His brows rose, and she was reminded again that he was probably only nineteen.

"Really?"

"Uh-huh."

"That's good to know."

"We also love flowers—simple bouquets, not those horrible, tacky ones that arrive in big containers like funeral baskets—and men who listen, really listen, when we talk to them."

Petey's eyes widened. "How about movies?"

"I love the movies."

Then, because the way through the forest was becoming thick with trees and vines, Glory Bee returned her attention to the path ahead.

Petey, on the other hand, hung back a little until his fellow soldiers caught up to him. "Did you hear what she said, Berman? Women like chocolate and movies and flowers. And, oh, yeah, they like it when we shut up and listen and don't interrupt."

Glory Bee had forgotten how difficult it was to make a path through the dense bamboo forest. Even though John and the other soldiers had made several trips to the clearing beyond, the vines and foliage were still so thick that their progress was slow.

Although her sunburn had subsided to a dull ache, the slap of leaves and the tug of vines soon brought a new collection of scrapes and cuts despite her long sleeves. And the insects were determined to eat her for lunch, then carry her off.

But Glory Bee didn't complain. She didn't think she could have spent a night alone in the camp. And if John had been gone for longer than that, she would have been a stark, raving loony by the time he returned.

So she slogged along with the men, the rifle bumping against her thigh, until, without warning, they stepped into a clearing beyond.

The unexpected sensation of the hot sun beating down on her face was so startling, that she stopped dead in her tracks and Petey nearly ran into her. Taking a few steps, she felt a breeze brushing over her cheeks that was hot and dry, not muggy and smelling of rotting vegetation.

As the men fanned out around her, John managed to step into place beside her and she began moving again, following the trampled grass to a rocky slope that led down and east.

"It's like stepping into a different world, isn't it?" he said.

She nodded.

"You doing okay?"

Glory Bee reached out to briefly touch his arm. "I'm fine."

"We don't have much farther to go. Only about a mile up—"

John suddenly held up a hand and the soldiers immediately came to a stop, bringing their weapons up.

In the same instant, Glory Bee caught a whiff of smoke. Then, from far off, came the firecracker *pops* of gunfire and what sounded like the screech of birds…or screams.

John turned to her, his features grim, his eyes dark and filled with that same determined anger she'd seen in them when he'd spoken of wanting to stay in Nanking to help his students.

"Get back into the forest. Not too far. Just enough so you can't be seen in the open. You stay there, understand? You stay there until I come for you."

She nodded, handing him the extra rifle.

"Do you have the pistol I gave you?"

"Y-yes. It's in my pack."

"Make sure it's loaded. But don't shoot unless someone gets close. Otherwise, you stay hidden as much as you can."

"Yes."

The soldiers were already creeping forward, their rifles held high. After one last glance in their direction and a squeeze of John's hand, she turned and ran back into the gloom of the forest, crouching low behind the bamboo and vines. But she didn't go in so far that she couldn't peer out of the foliage at the men making their way down the hill.

All too soon, they disappeared from view, and as they did so, her heart thumped so loudly in her ears that she couldn't hear. She strained to catch the slightest noise that might reassure her that it had really been birds making the cries.

Not Maria.

Or the children.

Perhaps Esteban and the others had been shooting game for food.

But as the smell of smoke became more pungent, she knew that such foolishness would only get her killed. She needed to be alert. Ready.

Slowly taking the rucksack from her shoulders, she laid it on the ground, trying to avoid even a hint of noise. Then, with the soughing of her breath overly loud, she reached inside for the pistol.

Her fingers trembled violently as she lifted it free—and now that she might need to use it, the weapon seemed suddenly small and ineffective.

Slipping the chamber open, she double-checked to make sure that it was loaded, then snapped it shut again and waited.

Even though she'd been expecting something to warn her that John and the soldiers had reached the camp, she wasn't completely prepared for the sudden sound of gunfire—much closer now. John and the other men must have intercepted the Japanese coming toward them. She heard shouts—in English and Japanese, then another burst of gunfire.

Then, without warning, a figure burst through the trees. Glory Bee had only a few seconds to grasp the fact that it wasn't John or one of the Americans. She saw only a flash of dark hair, an unfamiliar uniform, before he crashed into the thicket, heading straight toward her.

Too late, she realized that she should have stayed utterly still. If so, he might not have seen her at all. But when he was nearly upon her, she stood up, her pistol whipping into position as he lifted his toward her. Explosions filled the jungle. Then, horrified, she watched as a blossom of red appeared on his chest and he whirled and fell into the underbrush.

The whole encounter could not have lasted more than a few seconds, but to Glory Bee, each tick of the clock had been an eternity. She was shaking so badly that the pistol wobbled in front of her, but she carefully pulled back the hammer again, just in case.

She stumbled toward the Japanese soldier, her limbs so unsteady she feared that she might fall. But she finally managed to reach him and nudge him with her foot.

He didn't move. He didn't breathe.

She'd killed him.

Again, tremors wracked through her body, but she still kept the pistol leveled at him, wondering what she was supposed to do. John had said to wait here until…wait here…until…

Glory Bee frowned as her eyes suddenly crossed and the forest tipped crazily. She stumbled toward a stand of bamboo, hoping to find something to brace herself against. Dragging air into her lungs, she fought the dark spots that gathered at the fringe of her vision. But it hurt to draw breath and she had a stitch in her side as if she'd been running…or...

She pressed a hand to the ache, then drew back in horror when her fingers came away wet and slick with blood.

Her blood.

The thought brought an inexplicable urge to giggle, but at the same moment, the trees began to spin around her like a carousel.

Closing her eyes, she swallowed hard, praying that John had heard the shots, that he would come to find her. Now.

But she heard no sounds, no footsteps. Only the strident rasp of her own breathing.

Glancing down again, she tried to wad up her shirt and press it to the wound, but there was something wrong with her hands. She felt so weak.

Lurching forward, she fought to remain conscious as she stumbled her way out of the thick trees. Her progress was so slow that, at times, she feared that she wasn't moving at all. But she kept her gaze trained on the path ahead. She couldn't have said why it became so imperative that she leave her hiding place—even if she might be in danger of encountering more Japanese soldiers.

John. She had to find John.

Even if it meant breaking her promise.

• • •

John surveyed the remains of Esteban's camp, his stomach lurching at what they'd found. A slow simmering anger filled his veins.

After surprising the Japanese patrol on the path and killing them, he and the American soldiers had carefully made their way to the small gathering of huts where Esteban and his wife had fed them less than a week ago.

But when they'd arrived, it had been to a scene of utter carnage. Esteban had been brutally murdered. The three guerillas who had arranged to meet with the soldiers had been beheaded, then set ablaze. The women and children…

Kilgore bent low over a patch of bushes, vomiting. But John stood rigidly, taking in the scene, images of Nanking popping like flashbulbs in his head. A chill settled deep into his bones and he tasted the coppery tinge of hate on his tongue.

How could anyone be so savage? What kind of person could murder innocent children? A pregnant woman? And for what?

But he already knew why they'd been murdered. Somehow, the Japanese had known that guerrilla forces were in the area. And they'd viciously decided to flush them out.

"A few of them have been dead for a while," Gilhouley said after bending to check Esteban's body for any sign of life.

John's stomach churned. "They kept the women and girls alive the longest," he said, his voice raspy. Rage spilled into his bloodstream, demanding retribution. If the Japanese soldiers hadn't been killed on the path, John knew he would have hunted them down without mercy.

"Shit," Gilhouley whispered under his breath. "They're animals."

John shook his head. "Even animals wouldn't do this."

"Hey, John!"

John turned, meeting Petey's gaze. The soldier turned and pointed.

"Look."

Glory Bee appeared at the top of the rise. She paused for a moment, breathing hard, then began to hurry toward them, nearly running down the path.

"Dammit all to hell! I told her to stay in the forest," John rasped, rushing to intercept her. He couldn't let her see Esteban and Maria. The children. Little Luis.

"Glory Bee, what in God's name do you think you're doing here!" he demanded. "I told you to hide until I came to get you!"

She suddenly stopped, looking at him with such a panicked expression that he damned himself for speaking too harshly. But without warning, she dropped to her knees.

It was then that John became aware of the patch of red at her side and the sheen of blood on her fingers.

In an instant, his world fell out from under him. He rushed toward her, catching her as she collapsed completely, her eyes closing.

"Lieutenant!" Petey shouted.

Gilhouley and his men quickly gathered, forming a protective circle around Glory Bee, their weapons pointed out.

John drew her tightly against him as Gilhouley pressed two fingers to her neck.

"Is she…?"

"She's fainted, that's all. Her heart's beating fast."

Gilhouley pushed her hand aside and pulled up her shirt. A bullet hole oozed above her hip.

John recoiled, not from the blood, but from the fact that she'd been injured while following his instructions. He'd been the one to tell her to stay behind. But he'd thought she would be safer there.

"There was one soldier who ran," Petey said quietly.

Gilhouley grew grim. "She must have met him head on when he decided to hide in the forest." He glanced up. "Berman, Kilgore! I want you to follow his trail and make sure he doesn't have a chance to report our position to his buddies."

The two men quickly disappeared.

Ripping open his pack, Gilhouley brought out a wad of bandages and gauze.

"The bullet's still in there. She needs medical attention, real medical attention. Not the first-aid shit I know."

He pressed a thick handful of gauze to the wound, then began wrapping the bandages around her waist. "Hold her steady. I want this as tight as I can get it."

John swallowed hard before saying, "She's pregnant. Do you think that…is the baby…?"

Gilhouley met his gaze, then shook his head. "I don't know. My medical skills could fit in a thimble. But I'd say that now, more than ever, we've got to get her to a doctor, *pronto*."

Since Gilhouley had finished dressing the wound, John carefully lowered her shirt, then held her close.

"Estebañ was my only contact to the guerrillas. I don't have a way to get you a new set of guides."

Gilhouley thought for a moment, a muscle working in his jaw.

"How far to the coast?"

"About another ten, fifteen miles."

"Do you think you could find us a sheltered cove somewhere?"

John tried to picture the map he'd been carefully marking since they'd left Wilmot's plantation. In his mind's eye, he could remember something along those lines due east.

"I could try."

Gilhouley looked up at Petey. "Break out the radio."

Petey looked confused. "Colonel Ross already told us they can't send anyone to get us."

"We're not calling the base. I'm going to see if I can pull in a favor."

* * *

Rosemary was on duty when Alice sidled up next to her.

"There's someone here to see you."

For an instant, her heart quickened, and she looked up, searching for Gilhouley amid the personnel who wandered among the extra cots being set up outside the medical huts. But it wasn't Gilhouley she found, it was Napoli. He stood a few yards away, crushing his hat in his hands and eyeing her apprehensively.

Rosemary gestured to the bandage she'd been winding around

a soldier's arm. "Finish up for me here." She threw a quick smile at the gangly kid. "You'll be good as new in a few days. Keep the area as dry and clean as you can. If possible, change the bandage once a day." The instructions were issued automatically, even though she knew that as soon as he went back to his unit, he would be sent to the front. Once there, it would prove impossible to follow her orders.

"Yes, ma'am. Than you, ma'am."

After washing her hands in a nearby basin, Rosemary hurried toward Napoli.

"Are you having chills again?"

Napoli glanced over each shoulder, then handed her a scrap of paper. "I need these things."

Mystified, Rosemary opened the note. "Morphine, sulpha, bandages, gauze." She shot Napoli a quick frown. "You know I can't supply you with these things. If you're not feeling well, I—"

Napoli regarded her with dismay and hurried to explain, "Oh, no, ma'am…I mean, Rosemary. No, no, no. I'm not asking for myself." He bent close to whisper, "It's Gilhouley that needs 'em."

As quickly as she'd felt a surge of disapproval at Napoli's request, she now felt a burst of hope.

"What?"

"He's…well, he's pinned down on the coast. He's got civilians with him. One of 'em, a woman, has been shot."

The hope within her died a little. "Napoli, I don't know what you're—"

"Honest, Major Dodd." He grimaced. "Rosemary." He touched her arm. "See, I still owe Gilhouley a favor and it appears he's ready to cash in. He wants me to fly up there and pick 'em up."

"Can you do that?" she whispered. "I thought your plane needed repairs."

Napoli flushed. "That part I've been needin'? It's been hidden in my sea bag for some time—I didn't want anyone stealing my bird while I was sick. Truth be told, I could have left a while ago. But I figured I'd stick around a little while and wait for the American reinforcements. There was no sense flying into uncharted waters when there might still be a chance you all would rout the little yellow bastards. But…" he slapped his hat against his thigh. "Dammit, Gilhouley is in bad straights and he says the woman needs help now. He's already asked his superiors and they've refused. I'm his last chance."

She quickly gathered the supplies that Napoli had requested and scooped them into a canvas bag along with a precious tin of pudding and the sandwiches that Alice had brought her for lunch.

She handed the items to Napoli, asking, "When will you go get him?"

Napoli slung the strap of the bag crossways over his body. "Some of the flyboys are going to try to make a bombing run tonight with what few planes they have. They've got this plan to attack some of the Japanese ships. I'll volunteer my services for reconnaissance late this afternoon. As soon as I've got permission, I'll be on my way. It won't be a complete lie. I'll just bring them reconnaissance from a little farther afield than they're bargaining on."

Rosemary leaned forward, pressing a kiss to his cheek. "Godspeed, Napoli. Bring them all safely home."

* * *

Gilhouley ordered his men to fashion a stretcher from an old ladder that they found near one of the huts. After covering it with blankets, they began their trek through the dense underbrush. While Gilhouley and his men had been securing the radio again, John had carried the bodies into one of the huts and covered them with the only blankets that were left. When Gilhouley had come to get him, John was praying. He stood with his head bowed, his shoulders rigid. As soon as Gilhouley had cleared his throat to get the other man's attention, he'd genuflected, then turned, jamming his hat on his head.

"As soon as we fail to arrive at the rendezvous point, Pascal will send men to investigate," Gilhouley had said softly. "They'll take care of the bodies."

"I know," John rasped.

But Gilhouley knew the words were little comfort. If not for Glory Bee, John would have stayed behind, regardless of the danger to himself.

Now, however, it was a race against time. Not only was Glory Bee injured, but the window for opportunity with Napoli was very slim. They had miles to go to reach the inlet that John remembered on the map. And with little more than a compass and the information in John's head, they were still running virtually blind.

But all of them were willing to do whatever necessary to get Glory Bee safely to one of the hospitals on Bataan.

Now that they were out of the forest, the sun beat down on them relentlessly, but at least they were headed downhill. The men took turns with the stretcher, joining together to help negotiate the rocky patches. Although it was more dangerous to be out in the open, especially since they knew more Japanese patrols could be in the area, they kept to the edge of the tree line in order to move as quickly as possible.

Without familiar landmarks, it was difficult to gauge the distance they'd covered. They plugged on until Petey, who'd taken the lead, suddenly drew up short, lifting his face to the breeze.

"You smell that?"

Gilhouley thought that Petey was alerting them to smoke, but when he took a deep breath, he couldn't smell anything but dust and his own sweat.

When the other men were similarly mystified, Petey grinned. "That there is the smell of the sea. I'm a Louisiana boy, and I know when we're close to the ocean. Shouldn't be far now. Maybe a mile or two."

As the sound of the surf began to reach them, they moved more cautiously, afraid to burst out on the beach in case Japanese boats might be patrolling the area. But when the foliage opened up to reveal the sparkling blue of the ocean and a stretch of glittering sand, Gilhouley held up his hand.

"Berman, Petey, go scout out the area. We'll hang back here with the stretcher."

The men nodded, stepping cautiously onto the beach, one going north, the other south. They were gone for about fifteen minutes before returning.

"Anything?"

Berman shook his head. "Seems clear."

"Any sign of a keyhole rock formation? That's where Napoli said he'd meet us."

Petey grinned. "It's about two hundred yards up the beach." He slapped John on the back. "That's some damned fine navigating."

John glanced at his watch. "How much longer?"

Gilhouley checked his own timepiece. "It's still early yet. I doubt we can expect to see Napoli for at least another thirty minutes to an hour."

A muscle worked in John's jaw.

"We'll move up the beach into position, get as close as we can to the rocks. Napoli said the drop off in the water is pretty steep there, so he'll use the formation for cover and bring the seaplane in as close as he can." Gilhouley knelt to check the bandage at Glory Bee's side. She was still losing blood, but as least the flow had eased. "I doubt we'll be able to use the stretcher to load her. Someone will have to carry her. We might even have to swim out to him, I don't know."

"I'll take her," John said firmly.

"We can all—"

"I'll take her," he insisted again, his eyes flashing with a dark fire that Gilhouley recognized: a primitive, possessive need to protect what was his.

"Fine. But don't be afraid to ask for help if you need it." Shifting, he grasped the rear rungs of their makeshift stretcher and motioned for Baptiste to take the front. "Let's go."

Compared to the jungle, the walk down the beach took very little time, despite the loose sand. Motioning for Baptiste to head toward the shade beneath some coconut trees, Gilhouley cocked his head. From somewhere in the distance, he heard the sound of a rumbling engine.

"That could be him. Stay alert. The racket caused by an engine could bring every Jap for mil—*Get down*!"

Too late, Gilhouley realized that it wasn't a plane, but a boat that had made the rumbling noises. A small patrol vessel was coming into view at the mouth of the cove, moving north. It travelled slowly, its guns gleaming dully in the sunshine as it cut through the waves.

"Shit, shit, shit!" Kilgore said beside him and Gilhouley turned his head ever so slightly to see that Petey and Berman were yards away from them, spread-eagle in the sand, trying to make themselves as inconspicuous as possible.

"No one moves a muscle," Gilhouley said slowly. But, as he'd feared, something in their alarm must have alerted Glory Bee because she whimpered and twitched.

"Not now, not now," Gilhouley muttered under his breath.

John moved infinitesimally, laying his fingers against her cheek and she stilled.

Gilhouley's mouth grew drier than the sand beneath him and his ears roared with the sound of his own pulse. The boat crept along at an impossibly slow speed. He could only pray that the men aboard were looking out to sea, because if they had a pair of binoculars…

Beneath him, Gilhouley reached to touch his pocket and the spot where the violet lay.

If there was ever a time when they needed a little luck, it was now.

The boat continued to inch along.

Gilhouley inwardly swore as the craft paused, wavered in their direction. But then, it began to move forward again, out of the cove.

His heart slammed against his chest in relief, his breath escaping in a whoosh.

The Japanese were moving on.

The boat was about to make its way around the rocky shoreline to the north, when, from far away, Gilhouley heard the familiar growl of a seaplane—the tone higher than the boat's had been.

"Shit, not now!"

But Napoli had definitely arrived. Just as the boat disappeared around the point, the plane came roaring over the beach, waggling his wings when Napoli apparently saw them. He pointed the aircraft out to sea again, turned, and was beginning his descent, when the Japanese patrol boat shot from behind the rocky outcropping.

"Move, move, move!" Gilhouley shouted.

He and his men threw themselves to their feet as John quickly scooped Glory Bee from the stretcher. As the soldiers formed a protective circle around him, the plane came in steep and fast, slamming into the surf, then turning so abruptly that it threatened to tip over as it came as close as it could to stopping in the bobbing waves.

Gilhouley and his men charged into the water. But the plane was still yards away and the boat was speeding toward them.

Fighting against the breakers and the current, they held their rifles over their heads, grabbing hold of John's shirt, turning him, towing him, so that he could support Glory Bee as the water grew deeper and it became necessary to swim. Kicking furiously, Gilhouley tried to calculate the distance before the boat would be in firing range. They had to hurry. They had to hurry!

Finally, Kilgore managed to hook an arm around one of the pontoons. Seconds later, Berman reached the plane, then hoisted the man up so that he could open the rear door, Gilhouley and Baptiste kicked frantically in order to reach the pontoon as well.

As soon as Berman was inside, he lay on his stomach, reaching down.

"Give her to me!"

The men hauled Glory Bee's limp body into the plane.

"In!" Gilhouley shouted to John.

He could see that John meant to resist, so he grabbed him by the belt and yanked upwards. At the same time, Berman reappeared, reaching down to grasp John and pull him into the plane. Then, within seconds, the two men appeared yanking the rest of the men aboard as bullets hit the water a few feet beyond where they'd been.

"Get out of here, now, now, now!" Gilhouley shouted.

Before they could even latch the door completely shut, Napoli pulled back on the throttle. As the seaplane roared forward, then up, up, and out of range, the Japanese sent off one final volley of bullets, hitting the fuselage with a tinny *thunk, thunk, thunk*. Then they were climbing so steeply that Gilhouley had to grab onto one of the seats ahead of him to keep from sliding to the rear of the plane.

Then, they were leveling out.

"Anybody hurt?" Gilhouley called out.

"Dammit all to hell, would you look at that?" Petey shouted, pointing to a bullet hole in the metal between his legs. "Those damned Japs nearly took out the Peterman family jewels!"

And for some reason, after everything that had happened, that statement was enough to have all of the men laughing and slapping him on the back. Their relief was so palpable, that Gilhouley sagged beneath the sheer intoxication of it all.

But his joy at their narrow escape was short-lived when he looked in John's direction and saw him bending low over Glory Bee.

A glance at her side told Gilhouley the wound had opened again. And this time, it was bleeding like a sonofabitch.

He woke to the sun sliding across his cheekbones and frowned.

There was something different.

Something wrong.

Blinking, he slowly pushed himself up enough to peer through the window. The sun was high in the sky and the camp was quiet. Too quiet.

Leaning over, he nudged Kilgore in the ribs. "Wake up," he whispered.

Kilgore grunted, but his eyes eventually flickered open. Hissing, he moved slowly, his body feeling the aches and pains they all fought. Then he scrubbed his face with his hand.

"What?" He realized how late it was even before the word was uttered. "What the hell? Did we sleep through tenko*?*

"Doesn't look like it. No one else is up either." He peered over the edge of the window again. "I can't see the guards."

"You're shitting me."

"No. I really can't see any guards—not in the tower, not at the gate."

The two men rolled to their feet as the rest of the hut began to rouse. The whispering began, the low curses.

The other huts must have awakened at about the same time, because men began filing into the compound, confused.

"They're gone!" one of them finally shouted. "The Japs are gone!"

Kilgore caught his gaze and the two of them hurried to the door.

"Maybe it's a trap," Kilgore muttered as they stepped out into the sunshine. "You read the note from the Padre*. They wait until we make a move and then—*bam*! They've got the perfect excuse to throw us in a hole and set*

us on fire."

"We don't know if that really happened in the camp north of here or not. The information was gathered from gossip passed on by the villagers."

"Like hell, we don't. Tanaka would do it in an instant."

More men were tumbling into the compound and the whispers were becoming murmurs, then shouts of joy. They were gone. Tanaka and his guards were gone.

"Something's wrong. It's a trap," Kilgore muttered.

But he ignored him, already running toward the figure strung up between the posts.

"Lieutenant, no! It's a trap!"

As if to give credence to his words, there was a low rumble. In the distance a convoy of troop transports appeared.

But he didn't care. He ran to Petey, fumbling with the knots in the rope.

"Help me!" he shouted. "Help me get him down before they get here!" Then, he turned back to his task, swearing when his fingers couldn't work the bindings free.

Then suddenly, Kilgore was there, then another soldier and another. Feverishly, they fought to untie him while another prisoner supported his body. Then, at long last, as a pair of soldiers jumped from the lead truck to open the gates, Petey sagged, the ropes came free, and they dragged his battered body back to the hut.

Chapter Sixteen

Rosemary was about to leave her shift when she looked up to find a tall, grim-faced man striding toward her. He cradled a woman's limp body in his arms, and behind him, trying to keep up, was Napoli.

She rushed toward them, motioning for them to deposit the woman on one of the examining tables.

"Gilhouley got caught by Colonel Ross as soon as we landed. He said to tell you he'll be back when he can."

She nodded and quickly removed the bandages. The gunshot wound was angry and red, but it was the bleeding that concerned her most.

"Alice!" she called to the woman across the tent. "Get Dr. Grimm. This woman is going to need surgery."

Alice sprinted from the tent and Rosemary turned to the man who'd carried the woman into the compound. "What's her name?"

He'd taken a place by the woman's side and now held her hand.

"Glory Bee. Glory Bee O'Halloran."

Rosemary looked up in surprise. "The stripper?"

He nodded.

She took a pail of water and a cloth and began cleaning the area.

"She's pregnant." The man said baldly.

"Do you know how far along she is Mr.…?"

"John. John Macklin." His eyes were dark, nearly black with his concern. "I-I don't know how far along she is."

"Are you family?"

He shook his head. "I…we're…"

"Listen, Mr. Macklin. We're going to have to take the bullet out, then stop the bleeding and check for…any other injuries she might have sustained."

She saw Grimm rushing toward the hut, Alice in tow, so she turned her attention toward Napoli. "Get him out of here," she said lowly.

John's expression grew so fierce she nearly took a step back.

"No. I stay here. With her."

Rosemary knew when she had a fighter on her hands, and she could tell that his reasons for staying would seem to far outweigh hers for having him go. But the medical team would have enough to do in taking care of this woman's wound.

"No, Mr. Macklin. You can't stay here. You'll be in the way—and we have to work quickly. I promise you, I'll stay with her; I'll take care of her. And if she awakens before we give her anesthesia, I'll tell her that you're just outside the surgical compound. But you can't stay here. Not if you want her to receive the best care possible."

She saw the moment her words sank in.

"Napoli will take you outside and find you something to sit on. You can wait right outside the hut or get yourself something to eat. I'm sure Napoli could even scare up a drink for you, if you'd like. But you need to go. Now."

John nodded, bending to place a tender kiss on Glory Bee's forehead. For a moment, his hand lingered there, his thumb stroking her hair. Then he reluctantly backed away.

* * *

It was getting dark when Rosemary emerged from one of the surgical huts, but as she stretched the crick in her back, she wasn't surprised to see John Macklin sitting on an upended crate just outside the door. As soon as she appeared, he jumped to his feet.

Rosemary offered him a smile. "She's doing well. The orderlies are moving her to one of the wards. She'll be weak for a while from the surgery and the loss of blood, but as long as she doesn't catch an infection, I think she'll be fine."

He gripped his hat so tightly that the brim was crushed. "And the baby?"

This time, she couldn't help but laugh in relief. Here, in the midst of all the death and destruction of war, the medical staff had been privy to an innocent spark of life. "Last I checked, the heartbeat was fast and strong. I can't tell you how delighted that made the medical staff. Is it yours?"

"Yes," he said without hesitation and a measure of pride.

"Don't worry. We'll keep an eye on things."

John's expression filled with such joy that Rosemary could scarcely believe the change it brought to his whole demeanor. When a pair of orderlies moved past with the stretcher bearing Glory Bee, his eyes followed them every step of the way to the nearby hut, which had been set up as a post-operative ward.

"Can I see her?" he asked, gesturing toward the structure with his hat.

"Sure. It's pretty crowded in there—and Miss O'Halloran will be moved to a different bed in a little while—but Lieutenant Strickland is on duty. I've let Alice know that you'll be staying with Miss O'Halloran."

"Thank you."

He quickly disappeared inside and Rosemary turned to search the camp. If Gilhouley were with Colonel Ross, it could be hours before…

Her eyes suddenly fell on a familiar figure leaving the chow line. He must have had a chance to shower and change because his hair was still wet and his fatigues were fresh. Even in the short time he'd been gone, it was obvious he'd lost weight and his skin was ruddy from the sun. But as far as she could tell, he was all in one piece.

As if sensing her gaze, he suddenly stopped. Stared. Then, murmuring something to one of the men in line with him, Gilhouley handed the soldier his tray and casually strolled toward her.

Moving ahead of him, Rosemary led the way through the

maze of tents and improvised structures. She was suddenly glad of the lengthening shadows as she stopped behind the supply hut and waited.

The moment he rounded the corner, she launched herself into his arms. He caught her easily, holding her tightly against him, his face buried in her hair.

"I was so worried," she whispered, her hands sweeping over his back, his shoulders, needing to reassure herself that he was here and in one piece.

"It took longer than expected to get back."

She didn't bother to ask where he'd been or what complications had caused the deep lines to etch themselves around his mouth. She doubted he would tell her if she asked. And there was so little time available, she didn't want to waste it with needless talk.

"You're unhurt?" she murmured thickly.

"Yeah." The word was a sigh, but it held such a weight of the world, she sensed that although he was physically unharmed, there were things he'd seen—and probably things he'd done—that he didn't want to tell her.

Pushing back, she took his hand and led him around the corner to the door, then inside. Weaving around the boxes and pallets, she pulled him to the far corner where sacks of rice had been piled in the corner. Reaching into one of the nearby crates, she removed a blanket and spread it out over their makeshift bed.

Gilhouley's eyes lit with a slow fire.

"Why, Major Dodd, are you possibly considering—"

"Shut up, Gilhouley." She reached for the buttons of her tans, unfastening them one by one, until the edges gaped all the way down.

Gilhouley liked the juxtaposition of her very male attire and lacy feminine underthings because he swallowed, hard.

But when he would have reached for his own buttons, she pushed his hands away.

"No. I want to make sure that you're really okay."

She began loosening his shirt, slowly, tantalizingly. And with each inch of flesh she exposed, she bent to place a kiss against his warm flesh, reassuring herself that Gilhouley wasn't a figment of her imagination. He was here; he was alive.

When all of the buttons were undone, she circled around to the back and pulled his shirt from his shoulders. As it dropped to the floor, she wound her arms around his middle and kissed him in the center of the crease marking his spine.

Gilhouley shuddered against her. "You're killing me, Rosemary."

She laughed, reaching for his buckle. But he soon pushed her hands away, fumbling with the catch until he managed to release it. Then he twisted to take her in his arms, and all thought of prolonging the temptation evaporated in an instant.

Rosemary gasped as he pulled her tightly against him, grinding his hips to hers, making her intimately conscious of his arousal, of his need, of his hunger. And her want was no less overwhelming than his own as she kicked off her boots and wriggled out of her trousers, all while he kissed her with such passion that she could scarcely credit that it was directed at her—Rosemary Dodd.

As he shucked his own clothing, she dropped her underthings onto the ground and settled back on their bed of rice. And it was only a moment before he followed, pressing down onto her with a welcome weight, his body hard and roughened with hair and so, so different from her own.

He took her mouth again and again, plundering her sweetness, his hand slipping down to cup her breast, his thumb teasing her nipple into a hard, turgid point. But she gave as good as she got, grasping his heated length, causing him to gasp against her.

"Dear God, how I've missed you, Rosemary."

She kissed him, again and again, her hips straining against him, wanting, needing that part of him that could give her release. Only when they were one, could she truly reassure herself that he was safe. That she was safe. That they were together.

As if sensing her thoughts, Riley settled on top of her. Twining their fingers together, he held her hands above her head, his eyes meeting hers, his body rubbing against her intimately.

"Don't ever forget me, Rosemary."

His words pinged against her consciousness, frightening her.

"Don't talk like that," she whispered. Since he still held her hands, she wound her legs around his hips. "We're going to get through this. We have to get through this!"

Then, fearful of what he might say, she lifted up to kiss him, once, twice, until some of the wildness left his gaze and his attention turned to the rhythm of their bodies, the glide of skin against skin, the rasp of feverish breathing.

Then, when she feared she would shatter into a million pieces, he settled against her, pushing into her sweet flesh with such tenderness that her climax was immediate and powerful, rocking her to the depths of her being. If he was surprised by her reaction, he gave no hint, he merely smiled against her temple, increasing his rhythm, sliding a hand beneath her hips to arch her more fully toward him, then pounding into her with renewed fervor until her breath snagged in her throat and she felt her body drawing tighter and tighter for yet another climax.

This time, her release was so powerful that she cried out and he quickly covered her lips with his own. As her inner walls clenched around him, he spilled into her, his head flinging back with his own ecstasy, their bodies shuddering as one.

Later, much later, Rosemary lay quietly in his arms. Their limbs were tangled together and her hair splayed over his chest.

"You've made a wreck of my hairdo," she said against him.

Gilhouley only grunted.

"And you've ruined my morals."

His eyes remained closed, but his grin was slow and filled with mischief. "Perhaps they needed ruining."

She poked him in the chest, then smoothed away the jab with a kiss. "My mother wouldn't say so."

"What would your mother say? About us?"

Rosemary considered the idea. "She'd say you were young. Probably too young for me, in her estimation."

"And handsome."

Rosemary snorted.

"So how old would she want me to be?" he asked, idly running a finger over her back.

"At least my age."

"So we'll tell her I'm thirty-five."

Rosemary grimaced. "You flatter me. I'm forty, Gilhouley. And my mother's right, I'm definitely too old for you."

His shoulders moved in a shrug. "It's just a number, Rosemary."

She grew still. "Is it?" she asked softly. "Is it just a number? Or will it become a problem?"

This time, his lashes fluttered, and he met her gaze. And in that instant, Rosemary was emotionally naked in front of him, every regret, every fear, blatant in her eyes.

"Do you love me, Rosemary?"

His question took her by surprise. But when she would have put him off by saying they didn't know each other well enough to talk of love, she saw an echo of his own uncertainty. More than that, she saw a haunted sorrow in his gaze and knew that he was thinking of an enemy that was bearing down on them with more speed than either of them could fathom. In that instant, she realized that time was a precious commodity she didn't have. She'd seen enough of the injuries being brought to her hospital to know that they were not going to win this battle with the Japanese. Unless reinforcements arrived soon, they would all be at the mercy of an enemy incapable of mercy.

"Yes." The word burst from her lips before she could even think about it. But to her surprise, she didn't want to retrieve it. By admitting her feelings for Riley, by uttering them out loud, she was freeing herself from the last of her doubts. "I do love you, Riley."

His smile was low and filled with promise. "Then we'll lie to your mother." He sifted his fingers through her hair. "We won't tell her how you seduced and ravished me."

This time, when Rosemary punched him, she wasn't entirely gentle and he laughed. But before she could do it again, he pushed her to her back and settled over her.

"We'll tell her that we were friends, then sweethearts, lovers, then partners."

Rosemary blinked up at him. "Partners?"

"I want you to marry me."

She shook her head in confusion. "But…"

"I might not have control over a lot of things, Rosemary. But I do know what I want, and I want to marry you, if you'll have me."

Her fingers trembled as she touched his cheek—because there was more to his expression than devotion. There was also fear and desperation and a grim acceptance that their relationship might not end in happily-ever-after.

"Will you do that, Rosemary? Will you marry me? Will you at least let me leave things in place for you if something should happen to me?"

She quickly pressed her fingers to his lips. "Don't talk like that."

He shook his head. "I love you, Rosemary, but I can't lie to you. If you marry me, this could be one of the shortest marriages on record. You could be a widow before the ink even dries."

Her eyes filled with tears. "Don't. Don't jinx it. Don't even say the words aloud."

He wiped the wisps of hair from her brow. "Does that mean you'll do it?"

She nodded, knowing that if they weren't in the midst of a siege, marrying Gilhouley would mean that the Army would expel her from the Nursing Corps. But even as the thought came to her, she realized she didn't care. All that mattered was this moment. This man. Her career was nothing compared to her love for him. "Just promise me you'll be careful."

"Ah, sweetheart…you've got to know I'll do everything in my power to make it through this mess."

Since she couldn't speak, she wound her arms around his neck and pulled him close. And this time, when the passion flared between them, she fought to retain each moment, each touch, each whispered endearment, etching it firmly into her memory.

Just in case.

Just in case…

• • •

Glory Bee roused slowly, her eyes flickering open to a surreal sight of lines of cots set out beneath the trees. Mosquito nets hung from overhead branches and fluttered in the breeze, and she frowned, unsure where she was, wondering if she'd been plopped into Alice's Wonderland. If she blinked, would the wide grin of the Cheshire Cat hang in the leaves above her?

But it wasn't the Cheshire Cat that appeared when she twisted her head. Instead, it was John, and his smile was so gentle that she could scarcely believe that this was the same hard-faced man she'd met only weeks before.

Tears sprang to her eyes as she became aware of the burning pain in her side. She sobbed, then held her breath as the sharp movement sent a stab of pain through her abdomen.

"My baby's dead, isn't it?" she whispered.

John quickly shook his head, cupping her cheek with his hand.

"No, sweetheart. The baby's fine."

Alerted by their whispers, a woman stepped toward them. Glory Bee frowned, still not able to process the information being given to her.

"Would you like to hear the baby's heartbeat?" the tall blonde asked, reaching for the stethoscope looped around her neck. She donned the earpieces then, after pulling down the covers and pressing it to the swell of Glory Bee's stomach, she listened for a moment before handing the ends of the stethoscope to Glory Bee.

Tentatively, Glory Bee placed them in her own ears, then gasped when she heard a swift *swish-thump* repeated over and over again.

"That's the baby's heart?" she asked with something akin to wonder.

"Mm-hmm. Haven't you had a chance to listen to it before?"

Glory Bee shook her head. She'd gone to the doctor only once to confirm her suspicions that she was pregnant. After that… she supposed a part of her had thought that if she ignored her condition, it would go away. Not that she'd been stupid enough to think it would. No, the idea of having a baby had been terrifying enough that she hadn't known how else to cope.

It wasn't until the baby's life had been threatened that she'd realized what she might lose.

"Our little girl's a fighter, isn't she?" John whispered, and Glory Bee's eyes filled with tears.

Our little girl.

"What makes you think it's a girl?"

"Because she's a survivor, like her mum. She'll have curly red hair and eyes as bright as blue buttons."

Glory Bee blinked against sudden tears. The more John talked, the more he painted pictures in her mind, the more the reality of a baby sank in.

"I don't know if I can be a mother," she whispered, her throat tight with regret.

"Ahh," John said, cupping her cheek and bending low. "What kind of talk is that?"

"I don't know anything about being a good mom."

He laughed. "I've never heard such nonsense before."

"It's true," she sobbed, tears breaking the dam of her lashes. She scrubbed them away in embarrassment. "My own mother was a mess, and I don't know anything about feeding and changing and taking care of a baby."

"Babies don't come with instructions, Glory Bee. They come into this world needing love and patience." His lips tipped. "You might be a little lacking in the patience department…But there's no one on earth with a bigger heart or a bigger capacity to love."

He bent then, placing a gentle kiss on her lips, and despite the stab of pain from her side, she reached to deepen the caress. But John's kiss was brief, gentle, and when he drew back, he held her hand with both of his.

"There's only one thing I would ask."

He sounded so serious, so…tentative, that her heart flip-flopped in her chest in fear.

"I've tried to shake a lot of my past, Glory Bee. I thought that if I began over, became a new person, all of the hurt would go with it." When he met her gaze, his eyes were dark and stormy. "But you've helped me to see that there are some parts of myself that I shouldn't throw away so hastily. What I'm trying to say, Glory Bee... is that I think we've come to a point where...well..."

He squeezed her hand again, then bent to press his lips against her knuckles. "What I mean is...they've got a chaplain...And with things being the way they are...with the war and Japanese advance..."

Glory Bee was truly confused now, and she vaguely wondered if the morphine they'd given her was making it impossible for her to understand.

"I know I gave up the priesthood...and I'm still wrestling with God...but I'd still like to make things...official between us."

John looked down at her expectantly, but she didn't know what she was supposed to say. She didn't have a clue what he was trying to tell her.

"I-I don't understand," she finally admitted.

His lips twisted ruefully. "I'm making a mess of it, aren't I?" He reached into his pocket and withdrew a small circlet made of what looked like twisted wire. "I got this from Gilhouley—I think he made it out of a grenade pin—but it was the best we could come up with on short notice. As soon as I can, I'll get you a proper one." John held the circlet toward her. "Glory Bee O'Halloran, will you marry me?"

For several minutes, the words bounced in her brain like water on a hot skillet, refusing to sink in. But then, as he held the circlet of metal toward her, she suddenly realized John's intention.

"You want to marry...me?"

His brows knitted. "Of course."

"But...but I'm pregnant."

"I'm well aware of that."

"And I'm not in the least bit...saintly."

This time, it was his turn to look confused. "Neither am I."

"But...I'm pregnant," she whispered. More than anything, she wanted to say, "Yes." But she doubted even a saint would saddle himself with another man's child.

He bent to kiss her again, then again.

"Glory Bee, unless you have some grave objections, I'm going to marry you, and I'm going to be a father for our daughter. I'm not promising that things will be easy between us. We both have our ghosts—and then there's the matter of a war hanging over our heads. But if none of that matters to me, I don't think it should matter to you."

This time, her tears weren't of fear or sorrow, but of joy.

"So," he murmured, holding out the twisted circlet of metal. "Will you marry me?"

"Yes," she whispered, her throat so tight with emotion, she feared he hadn't understood her. But that wasn't the case, because he slipped the makeshift ring over her finger, then bent to kiss her.

Around them came the soft sound of applause, and they lifted their heads to see that the nurses had been watching them all along.

Glory Bee laughed, then winced when she received a sharp reminder from her side. Drawing back, John rearranged his chair and took her hand.

She tried to hold onto consciousness, tried to fight the weariness tugging at her lashes. But soon, she slipped into a blissful cocoon of sleep, knowing that when she awakened, he would be there.

* * *

It was dark when Gilhouley stepped into the ward and found John still seated at Glory Bee's side. Moving quietly so that he wouldn't wake the other patients, Gilhouley stepped up beside him and slapped him on the back.

"I see she's wearing the ring, buddy."

John eyed him sheepishly. "Yeah."

"Congratulations."

Stealing an empty bucket from a spot nearby, Gilhouley turned it upside down and sat on top of it.

"We might have to make it a double ceremony."

John's brows rose.

"Rosemary." Gilhouley pointed to her as she moved from bed to bed, checking vitals. "Major Dodd. Figured that I might as well make things official between us as well."

John smiled. "Have you been together long?"

Gilhouley shook his head. "Not long enough."

John understood the melancholy that tinged his tone because he took Glory Bee's hand.

"Listen," Gilhouley said gently. "Rosemary said you can stay here in the ward as long as you like—although, mind you, as soon as she's off duty, there's a couple of nurses who might not be so accommodating."

John threaded his fingers through Glory Bee's as if anchoring him to the spot.

"But she also said that Glory Bee's going to be out of it for a while. Rosemary doubts she'll wake before morning."

When John would have interrupted him with a refusal, Gilhouley held up a hand. "I'm not saying you should leave for good. I thought—while she's totally out of it—you might want to grab something to eat and a shower. I could even rustle up some clean clothes for you, if you want."

John relaxed, even uttered a soft laugh.

"Am I that bad?"

"Buddy, you are ripe—and I say that with all kindness since I washed the same stink off only a few hours ago."

When it appeared that John was tempted, Gilhouley stood. "Rosemary promises to come get you if Glory Bee wakes up—don't you darlin'?"

Rosemary, shot him a disapproving look at his familiar tone, but since she was the only nurse in the tent at the moment, she didn't chew him out.

"Come on, John. Glory Bee will be out for hours—and frankly, you look like you're going to drop."

"Go, John," Rosemary called from across the hut.

John remained rooted to the spot, his gaze bouncing from Gilhouley to Rosemary, then back to Glory Bee. But finally, he stood, leaning down to place a kiss on her brow. When Glory Bee didn't even stir, he evidently made up his mind.

"I could use a shower," he said reluctantly.

"Hell, yeah."

Leading John through the ward, Gilhouley offered Rosemary a conspiratorial wink, then ducked out the door.

The night was dark and still heavy from the heat, and there was something about the lack of sunlight that made the sounds even more pronounced. The camp was a symphony of low murmurs, the grumble of Jeeps, the moans and sobs of the wounded. From a little ways away, came the whisper of the surf, and a little farther still, the boom of mortars and the chatter of machine guns.

For several minutes, they made their way through the camp in silence. Gilhouley sensed there was something on John's mind, so he didn't immediately speak, merely waited for John to say the first word.

"I want you to know how grateful I am," John finally stated.

Gilhouley wasn't about to get all gooey about it, so he said, "My pleasure. She's a nice girl. I'm glad I could help."

John stopped and Gilhouley did the same, remaining still and quiet as John stared down at the ground.

"I'd like to thank you."

Gilhouley touched his arm. "It's really not necessary."

John looked up then and his expression was so fierce that Gilhouley nearly took a step back. "Yes. It is. I want to help."

"Help?"

A muscle worked in John's jaw.

"I want to help you in your fight with the Japanese."

So that was it. Gilhouley slid his hands in his pockets, rocking slightly. "Listen, John. I know that after everything you've been through and what happened to your friends in the jungle, you feel the need to—"

"Don't!" John interrupted fiercely. "Don't hand me platitudes and tell me that my fight here is done!" he whispered fiercely. "They shot the woman I love. And those friends you speak of so casually... Esteban and his wife were like family to me. I loved his children like they were my own!"

"I'm sure that's true, but—"

"And this isn't the first time I've had to deal with the viciousness of the Japanese. I was in Nanking! I was helpless then, but I'm not helpless now, and I will not bow out of this fight because things look hopeless. I will not be forced to run away again!"

"I can probably hook you up with the Filipino volunteers," Gilhouley began, but John shook his head.

"No. I need you to take me to your superior officer."

"Colonel Ross? Why?"

"Because I know what you were doing in the Sierra Madres. You were looking for Santo Tomas, weren't you?"

Gilhouley glanced around them to make sure no one had overheard. His missions weren't common knowledge by any means.

"I don't know—"

"Don't bother to deny it. I've had a lot of time to think today, and I'm sure I've been able to piece things together fairly well."

At least the man had the sense to lower his voice.

"You and your men have been planting radios and supplies throughout the area, haven't you?"

He didn't give Gilhouley a chance to admit or deny it.

"You'd planned on rendezvousing with Santo Tomas, not knowing that he'd already been killed. By the time you realized that he wasn't coming, you were caught behind enemy lines." John moved even closer, a finger lifting to spear in the direction of Gilhouley's chest. "So you were stuck in unfamiliar territory when you happened to stumble across me. And when I suggested meeting up with Pascal, you must have thought that leaving the radio equipment with one group of Filipino guerrillas was as good as another."

"It wasn't quite that cold-blooded," Gilhouley said stiffly.

"No. But in our haste to get Glory Bee to safety, you didn't bring the radio equipment, did you? What did you do with it? Hide it? Bury it?"

Gilhouley clenched his jaw tight to keep from blurting the truth, but he needn't have bothered. John was proving that he had his own talent for larceny.

"If it were me, I'd have put it near that spot where the children used to play. Esteban had a hidden cache of foodstuffs there—rice, beans…You probably noticed it while they were feeding us. Once Pascal sent someone back to check on Esteban and his family, they would eventually take the food. In doing so, they'd find the radio—and I'm guessing—a few of the codes."

John waited, his gaze so fierce, his finger stabbing in the air accusingly, until Gilhouley was forced to nod.

Suddenly, the anger drained away from John Macklin, leaving him radiating with a fierce sense of purpose.

"Your instincts are good, Lieutenant, and your missions have been sound. But you're only scratching the surface of what you can do, and with that, I can help."

Intrigued, Gilhouley cocked his head. "How?"

"I take it that you've seeded your equipment into the hills, some of it hidden, others given to trusted Filipinos. But I've got contacts that you haven't even begun to touch—Filipinos, planters, foremen like myself, and yes, even the clergy. I want you to take me to your Colonel Ross and tell him that I'm offering my services."

Gilhouley sensed there was something more.

"In exchange for what?"

"If the reinforcements don't come, if there's even a hint of evacuating the nurses or the wounded, I want my wife to be included."

Wife. John was already referring to Glory Bee as his wife—and Gilhouley couldn't blame him. The vows between them might not have been spoken yet, but the commitment, the love, the inexplicable bond between them had been formed long ago.

Gilhouley supposed that he should be shocked by John's request, that he would exchange his services as a none-too-subtle bribe to get Glory Bee off Bataan. But, in reality, he envied him. If there had been any way to send Rosemary to safety, Gilhouley would have done it himself long ago.

"I'll take you to Colonel Ross," Gilhouley said slowly. "But first…" Gilhouley slapped him on the back, urging him forward. "First, you've got to take that shower."

The sound of a plane split through the heavy air, but he ignored it. Instead, he dipped a cloth he'd ripped from the hem of his shirt in a few precious drops of water and placed it over Petey's feverish brow.

Petey winced, his breath rattling in his chest, but then he faded into unconsciousness again with a groan.

He continued to bathe the kid's wounds, wishing he had ice to help the swelling. But then, his breath caught in a bitter laugh.

Ice? Hell, while he was dreaming of the impossible, why didn't he wish for morphine, a clean bed…Rosemary?

He scoured his brain, wondering what Rosemary would do if she were here, but the moment the thought appeared, he pushed it away. Pray God, she'd never had to find out. Let her be safe and not in a camp of her own. Or worse.

The noise of the plane came again, louder this time, flying right over the camp. But he didn't bother to look. Right now, his only concern was for Petey. It had been two days since they'd cut him down. Since then, they'd all been confined to their huts—the first decent thing that had happened in a long while. He'd been able to stay with Petey.

But things didn't look good. Petey needed help. More help than he was able to give him.

The roar of the plane came again.

"Dammit all to hell," Kilgore moaned. He sat with his back against the wall, trying to sleep. Anything to take their minds off Petey's efforts to breathe and the searing heat that had been trapped in the hut.

When the growl came again, the aircraft buzzing the camp, Kilgore rolled to his feet and stalked to the window.

Calling it a window was a bit of a misnomer. It was a hole. A hole in a wall of bamboo with another bamboo flap that the Japanese had insisted that they keep closed. But by jimmying it with his finger, he was able to part the flap enough to peer upward.

The plane roared past again, closer still and Kilgore muttered under his breath, "Shit, damn, and hell."

He only briefly glanced up, then returned his attention to Petey. "What's the matter now?"

"That's one of ours."

"So?" It wasn't as if they hadn't had flybys before.

"So, he waggled his wings. What the hell do you think that means?"

Chapter Seventeen

January 25, 1941

Because of the loss of blood, it took days for Glory Bee to become completely aware of her surroundings. She'd awakened several times to assure herself that John was nearby, but then she would be dragged back into the darkness of sleep again.

But this time, when her eyes flickered open, she became aware of a thatched roof overhead, bamboo walls, and an air of controlled chaos.

John was immediately there, sitting on the side of her cot.

"What's happening?" she asked weakly.

"The Japanese are getting too close. The hospital is being evacuated to a spot further inland." John squeezed her hand. "In a few minutes, they'll be loading you onto one of the ambulances. They won't let me go with you because they've got to use every available inch for the wounded. But I'll join up with you as soon as I can."

Glory Bee's pulse grew uncomfortably quick, but since it was so obvious that John worried she might come unglued, she nodded, biting her lip. "I can do this."

His smile was bright, perhaps a little too bright.

"Of course, you can."

He leaned down to kiss her, hotly, intensely. But she'd no sooner begun to respond to his ardor when they were interrupted.

"They're ready for her John. She's the last to load, so we can't leave them waiting."

John nodded, squeezing Glory Bee's hand. Then he stood, scooping her into his arms and carrying her outside.

Glory Bee held up a hand to shield her face and was surprised at how much effort the action required. A part of her was still groggy and her side ached with a searing pain, but she didn't complain as she was taken to a nearby ambulance and placed in the last available spot near the back doors. As she settled onto the stretcher that had been fashioned for her and a blanket was drawn up to her neck, she heard one of the men whisper, "It's the stripper."

Lifting a hand, she waved and offered a weak, "Howdy, boys."

Then John was bending low and brushing the hair from her brow. "Remember, I'll be with you as soon as I can."

She nodded, whispering, "I know." And this time, there was no fear that he wouldn't keep his promise. Where once, she had been sure that if he sent her away she would never see him again, this time, she had no doubts. "I'll be fine, really."

"They need to get going, John." Rosemary said softly.

He kissed Glory Bee's hand, his lips touching the spot where the makeshift ring encircled her finger. "See you soon."

"Bye."

Then, before she could summon the breath to say, "I love you," the doors closed and someone rapped on the metal to signal that the ambulance was ready to go.

Glory Bee winced as the gears ground and the vehicle suddenly lurched into motion. Pressing a hand to her side, she closed her eyes, holding her breath when the bounce and jostle of the springs felt as if a knife were being plunged into her flesh.

One of the men near her cried out in pain, and forgetting her own discomfort, she reached toward him. "What's your name, soldier?"

"Private Scott, ma'am."

"Well, Private Scott, we're bound to encounter some rough roads ahead."

As if to underscore her point, they were all jolted again, and, this time, Pvt. Scott wasn't the only person to cry out.

"I'm going to take your hand, okay?"

"Yes, ma'am."

She felt along the edge of the stretcher until she encountered his fingers. "If you feel like swearing, go ahead. As for me, if I feel like swearing, I'm going to squeeze your hand, okay?"

"Yes, ma'am."

He was so tense against her that she feared the next bump might shatter him into pieces, but as she squeezed his hand, he began to relax, until finally, he allowed the breath he'd been holding to shudder free.

"Where are you from, Scott?"

"Yuma, Arizona."

Glory Bee turned to one of the men propped in the corner. "And you?"

"I'm from a little place called Burley, Idaho."

"Burley, huh?"

Although her strength threatened to desert her, Glory Bee made sure that she talked to each of the men who were conscious. Then, when her lashes began to flag, she murmured, "I think I'm going to take a little nap, Private Scott. Would you mind terribly if I asked you to keep holding my hand?" The words nearly took more effort than they were worth.

"No, ma'am. I wouldn't mind a bit."

Glory barely heard his answer before her lashes fluttered shut and she fell back asleep.

* * *

Rosemary's group of nurses was one of the last to be loaded up and taken out of what had been called Hospital #1. Even as the trucks rumbled out of Limay, the shelling from the encroaching battle grew ever louder. The constant *boom, boom* of the artillery and the chatter of machine gun fire had now added a new member to its orchestra—the squeaky rattling of Japanese tanks.

For the past twenty-four hours, the injuries they'd been

receiving from the front had been incredibly fresh, giving testament to the fact that the front was closing in on them.

As the trucks moved away from Hospital #1, Rosemary felt a twinge of regret. The new facilities would be further inland, away from the coast—and hopefully the relentless aerial attacks. But that also meant that the landscape would grow ever more inhospitable. They were moving to a region of Bataan that was largely uninhabited—and for very good reason. Long ago, loggers and industrialists had given up on that area of Luzon because it was impossible for their workers to remain healthy enough to get the job done. When it became clear there was no way to fully prevent such maladies as malaria, dengue fever, and dysentery, the area had been declared off-limits.

The truck moved slowly at first, following a faint track that made its way through the verdant greenery. Then, they headed south on a dirt road that had been cut into the jungle. With each mile they passed, the light grew dimmer and the jungle around them grew denser, until they passed through a tunnel made entirely of trees and choking vines.

Trying to peer around the side of the vehicle, Rosemary kept looking for a break in the foliage, but there was none. They were heading back in time to a period when the earth had just emerged from its primordial soup.

The swaying of the truck and the dappled sunlight sweeping over her face soon lulled her. In the frantic measures to move patients and hospital staff, Rosemary hadn't slept well, and after the morning's run-in with a Japanese air raid, exhaustion pressed in on her as forcefully as the hot, humid air. She allowed herself to doze, even as a part of her senses remained alert to the slightest noise, the first hint of trouble overhead.

It wasn't long before the grumble of the truck's engine slowed and she roused, twisting to look around. The truck carefully forded a small stream, then turned sharply to the right. And there, carved out of the jungle, were a series of tents and low bamboo huts topped by metal roofs. Surrounding them all was the chaos of the retreating army—Jeeps, trucks, horses and carts. Everyone seemed to be set to an important task, darting around the compound like bees in a hive.

The truck squealed to a stop and the engine was cut. Before Rosemary could completely get her bearings, a pair of women rushed to lower the tailgate.

"Hello! Welcome!"

These nurses, like Rosemary's, wore ill-fitting fatigues held up at the waist with belts or braided bits of rope. But their eyes were bright and their lipstick red, proving that while they may have been deposited into the middle of nowhere, American femininity could not be completely dimmed.

"Major Dodd?"

"Yes," Rosemary said, bending to make her way through the truck.

One of the women held up a hand to help her to the ground. "Hello. I'm Major Cavendish. This is Lieutenant Vanderlin. Welcome to Little Baguio."

Rosemary shook each woman's hand, then asked, "How far to the hospital?"

The women glanced at each other and laughed, but it was Cavendish who spoke. "This is it, Major. Here at Little Baguio, we practice medicine *al fresco*."

Even as she spoke, several other nurses rushed toward them. On seeing that the trucks contained injured personnel, they quickly snapped into action, calling to orderlies and instructing them to take the men to a series of cots that had been laid out under the canopy of the trees.

Stunned, Rosemary realized that what she'd taken for troop cots were actually makeshift hospital beds, laid out in rows, as if they were wards in a regular hospital. Once more, medicine had taken a huge step backwards in time.

Shaking off her dismay, Rosemary hurried to help unload the patients from the trucks in their convoy. Then, before she could even assimilate the change in venue, the ambulances with new wounded began to arrive and she was back in surgery, her ear again tuning to the distant *boom, boom.* It was fainter than it had been that morning, but never ceasing.

It was dark when she finally emerged from the rough wooden shack that had become one of their operating theaters. Until then, she'd been able to push back her own emotions through work and sheer dogged determination. But as she stepped out into the moist heat of the jungle with its ever-present hum of mosquitoes and insects, she suddenly felt alone. Oh, so alone. She hadn't even had a chance to say goodbye to Gilhouley when she'd left. His unit would probably remain at the front, and she had no idea when she would see him next. Yet, now, more than ever, she longed for his steadying presence.

"Major?"

She started when a voice called to her in the darkness. Turning, she saw John Macklin striding toward her.

"Hello, John. How's Glory Bee?"

He grimaced. "The transfer took a lot out of her, but she's doing well."

"Good. I'm glad to hear it."

John stopped in front of her, the tips of his fingers tucked in his pockets. "I wondered if I could borrow you for a few minutes."

"Sure. What's up?"

His features cracked into an embarrassed grin. "We're getting married. There's a chaplain here that I once worked with in China. He's agreed to perform the ceremony."

"What…*now*?"

This time, John's smile was wide and undimmed. "Yes. Glory Bee was hoping you would stand in as her maid of honor."

"Good heavens! Of course I will!"

Rosemary quickly stripped off her bloodied surgical gear, tossing it into a pile of similar garments left at the side of the hut.

"Can I run a comb through my hair first?" she asked, gesturing toward her tent.

"Sure. We're in ward two."

"I'll be right there—oh, and John…does Glory Bee have

anything special to mark the occasion? A veil? Flowers?"

He shook his head. "It's just us."

"I'll be back. Give me one minute. But I want you to wait outside the ward."

"Wha—?"

"Please. Do what I say. It's bad luck to see the bride before the wedding."

Rosemary ran the rest of the way to her tent. Alice was lying down on her cot, reading a magazine with the aid of a flashlight.

"Can I borrow your bed jacket?"

"My what?"

"You know, your bed jacket. That lacy thing you insisted on packing even though we were heading into the jungle."

"Sure…but I thought Gilhouley was still at the front."

"He is." Rosemary grinned. "Get your shoes on. We're going to a wedding."

"A wedding?"

"Come on, Alice. Judging by the journey she's had and all the blood she lost, the bride is probably only going to be awake for a little while, then she'll be nodding off again."

"Glory Bee and the priest? They're getting married *now*?"

"Uh-huh."

Alice scrambled to her feet, reaching for her own bag. She threw the ruffled silk and lace bed jacket in Rosemary's direction, then reached for her shoes.

"Am I invited?"

"Of course, you're invited. The whole hospital's invited. It's not like they can go anywhere private."

Pausing only to replace the pins in her hair, Rosemary dug into her duffle. After a moment's hesitation, she removed the corsage of violets, the perfumed sachet, and the last of a precious tube of lipstick.

"I've got eye liner," Alice exclaimed, "and a white snood."

Within minutes, the two women were hurrying back to the ward carved under the trees. They brushed by John without explanation, and wove through the cots to Glory Bee's side.

Glory Bee was pale, but glad to see them.

"We've only got a minute before the groom will insist on joining us," Rosemary said. "So let's get you ready to be a bride."

They combed Glory Bee's hair until it shone, fashioning the front with two sweeping barrel rolls and tucking the rest of the brilliant strands inside the snood. Then they applied a little eyeliner, lipstick, and rubbed the sachet at the pulse points on Glory Bee's wrists. Propping her up with pillows, they slipped her arms into the frilly pink bed jacket.

When Alice took a compact from her pocket and showed Glory Bee the effects of their efforts, her eyes filled with tears.

"I look…"

"Like a bride," Rosemary supplied when Glory Bee's voice grew choked.

As a final touch, Rosemary pinned the corsage of violets to her chest. "'Sweets for the sweet,'" she said, echoing the phrase that Gilhouley had printed on the card when he'd given them to Rosemary for her birthday. "Violets symbolize romance and modesty. Perfect for a wedding."

"Where did you get them?" Glory Bee breathed, fingering the delicate silk-velvet blossoms.

"Gilhouley gave them to me for my birthday."

"I promise to return them right away."

Rosemary squeezed her hand. "Not before we snip off a few of the blossoms for you to keep. You need a memento of the occasion. Plus, I've been told, these violets are particularly lucky." She thought of Gilhouley and the flower still tucked in his pocket.

Again, Glory Bee's eyes shimmered with tears.

"Thank you."

Now that the bride had been suitably prepared, John and the chaplain walked toward them. Rosemary helped Glory Bee to her feet, then handed her to John who wrapped his arm around her waist to support her.

Rosemary had attended many weddings. As the commanding

officer of a unit of nurses, she was accustomed to attending the ceremonies of girls who fell in love overseas. But this one was different. There were no decorations, no dress, no cake—no marriage license, no certificate, no mass. There was just the exchange of vows between a man and woman who were clearly in love. And she could honestly say that she had never been to a union that had been more blessed and sacred.

As John bent to kiss his bride, Rosemary felt a sting of jealousy that their marriage had been performed, while hers…

Who knew what would happen between Gilhouley and her. She had no idea where he was or how long it would be before she spoke to him again.

But she wouldn't begrudge the current couple their happiness. Pushing aside her melancholy, she hugged them both, offering her congratulations. Then, she and Alice gathered food from the chow line, coffee and doughnuts for wedding cake, and threw an impromptu reception for the new bride and groom until it became obvious that Glory Bee was exhausted. Borrowing folding screens from the operating room, she and Alice gave John and Glory Bee as much privacy as possible in the crowded wartime ward, then headed toward their tent.

"That was beautiful," Alice murmured.

"Mmm."

"You'll be next, I suppose."

Rosemary didn't answer. She didn't dare say it aloud for fear of jinxing things.

"Is he worth giving up your career?" Alice teased.

"Yes," Rosemary whispered into the darkness. "Yes, he is."

* * *

After the women had left, John sat on the side of Glory Bee's cot. Lifting her hand, he kissed the wire ring on her finger. She bit her lip, thinking a moment, then twisted to dig beneath her pillow. "I have a wedding present for you."

John felt a moment of embarrassment since he hadn't thought of a gift for her, but she waved away his disquiet.

"You're my present, John. You and this wedding and this time we have together. My gift is a little…token. Apparently, a lot of the men around here are superstitious and carry something to give them luck—Petey has a rabbit's foot, Kilgore a bottle cap, Berman a picture of his girl. I thought I'd give you a good luck piece."

She handed him a small bundle that had been wrapped in old newspaper and tied with a length of string.

"How could you find anything to give me while you've been sick?"

"Gilhouley. Apparently, he's able to supply more than just wedding rings."

John untied the string, feeling unaccountably like a kid at Christmas. But when he pulled aside the paper to reveal a chain with a small crucifix, he looked up at her questioningly.

Sitting up, she lifted the chain free from its wrappings and settled it over his head. "You may have left the priesthood, John. But you don't have to leave God. Your faith…it's one of the things I love about you. And even though you don't think that you're on speaking terms with God right now…I figure He can watch over you when I'm not around."

John fingered the cross, then looked up at his bride. "I love you so much."

She nodded, pulling back the covers. "I know. So get your shirt off and get in here."

He looked around. Even with the screens, he could sense dozens of soldiers mere feet away.

"I don't think that's a good—"

"We're married, John. No one's going to care if you lie down next to me."

"Glory Bee, I—"

"Shut up, John, and get into the bed."

When he would have settled uneasily beside her, she shook her head.

"Take off your boots and your socks. And your shirt."

"Glory Bee—"

"No one is going to see or care."

He hesitated, debating the circles under her eyes and the sounds of the men sleeping on the other side of the screen. But then, he decided that they could all go to hell. He might not be able to make love to his bride, but he could hold her in his arms.

Bending, he unlaced his boots and peeled off his socks, setting them carefully beneath the cot. Then, with Glory Bee watching, he began to unfasten his shirt.

Her eyes followed his every move with a hunger that still had the power to bring him to his knees.

"Oh, honey," she sighed when he shrugged out of his sleeves.

John flushed in embarrassment, flicking a glance at the screen. "Stop that."

"Why? We're married. You're mine now. All mine."

"And as my wife, you will behave. You're too weak and tired and I'm not about to…perform in public."

He couldn't be sure, but he thought she looked disappointed.

Moving as gingerly as he could, he slid onto the narrow bunk behind her. The bed squeaked, and he winced.

Glory Bee turned onto her side to give him more room, and he did the same, his arm draping around her waist, his hand splaying over her stomach.

"How's our daughter?"

"Fine. Just fine. She's been kicking up a storm today—probably she's excited by the wedding. I keep asking Rosemary to let me listen to her. I think she's going to be a musician. She has good rhythm."

John smiled into her hair. "I don't care what she does as long as she's healthy."

"You say that now. Wait until she's sixteen and bringing the boys home."

"There will be no boys. Not until she's thirty-two."

Glory Bee laughed, then whispered, "Undo my hospital gown in back."

He groaned. Even holding her with the thin shield of fabric was nearly more than he could bear. With each second he spent holding her, his body pounded. As soon as she fell asleep, he was going to have to head for the showers and hope they were cold.

"No."

"Come on, John," she murmured enticingly. "I want to feel you against me."

He knew he should refuse. He knew that he should insist that she get her rest, but he couldn't control his hand. It moved of its own volition to slip the bow free, baring her spine.

Pulling her close, he shuddered, pushing her hair aside so that he could kiss her. Just once.

But once became twice. Then three times. Four. Her skin was velvety and he couldn't help himself as he trailed a string of caresses down her neck, pushing aside her gown enough that he could kiss her shoulder.

She wound her fingers through his, drawing his hand upwards to her breast, and he hissed as the fullness filled his palm, the taut nipple drilling into his sensitive flesh.

"You're killing me, Glory Bee," he whispered next to her ear. "We have to stop."

"Why?"

"You're hurt."

"But I'm not dead," she gasped, turning her head to meet his lips with her own. "And I'd have to be dead not to want you. Tonight. Right now."

"We can't."

"Why?"

"You're hurt. You're tired. You're—"

"I'm hungry, John. I'm hungry for you."

Summoning every ounce of control he possessed, he shook his head. "No. It's not right. It's not…"

She reached behind her to grasp him through the fabric of his pants and all coherent thought shattered at the exquisite pressure of her touch.

"We'll be quiet," she whispered.

"Glory—"

"We'll be really, really quiet," she said cajolingly. Then she captured his hand and drew it down, down, down, until she'd placed his fingers against the wispy hair at the apex of her thighs. "Touch me, John."

And he was suddenly powerless to resist, his fingers spreading wide, exploring the part of her that he had never touched before—not just with her, but with any woman.

"Unzip your pants," she panted against him.

Powerless to refuse her, he did as she'd ordered, and his manhood immediately sprang free, pressing against her buttocks.

Although he was not completely unaware of the mechanics of lovemaking, he had never dreamed that the softness of her skin against him would fill his body with such fire. He'd been so sure that there would be no wedding night between them that he hadn't bothered to even think about it. He'd figured that he would plan out an elaborate getaway once she was completely on her feet—maybe scrounge up a tent and fill it with flowers. He'd envisioned laying her down, her nightdress still on so she wouldn't be scared, and positioning himself on top of her. Missionary style, isn't that what they called it?

But there was nothing prim and proper about the way she reached back to stroke him, her fingers wrapped firmly around his shaft, her buttocks grinding against his hips.

"I want to feel you inside me," she whispered.

He opened his mouth to protest, then threw all protests away. Why was he arguing? He was in bed with his wife. His wife! There was no need to be prudish or hesitant. This woman wanted him. And sweet heaven above, if she kept stroking him like that, he was going to come here and now.

His fingers returned to her moist nest, sliding into her, fondling, caressing. His efforts must have felt good because her breathing became labored and she held him there with one hand.

"Yes, John, yes," she whispered. "I like that. I really, really like that."

Her words filled him with a surge of power.

"I don't want to hurt you," he said against her ear.

"You can only hurt me by waiting."

"I don't—"

She shifted, reaching between them to pull his shaft down so that it slid between her legs. Wrapping her thigh over his, she had only to tip her hips and…

He slid into her so abruptly, so completely, that he gasped, astonished at the pure bliss of the sensation.

But she didn't give him time to think or react, she began to rock against him, faster and faster. His body grew taut, his breathing labored, his entire being centered on that point of contact, that intimate joining. His senses were completely overloaded, bringing him to the brink, and he fought to hang on long enough to…

Before he knew what she meant to do, she grasped his hand, rubbing his fingers against the spot where they joined. And then, her body clenched around him and she pressed her face into the pillow to stifle her cries.

His own climax came hard and fast and he spilled himself into her, his arms wrapped around her waist as he thrust once, twice, then plunged one last time, holding it, holding her.

And then, bit-by-bit, the strength bled from his body and he collapsed against her, his forehead resting against the nape of her neck.

It was some time later when he felt her shift. Then she laughed, ever so softly.

Immediately, he tried to draw back, but she held onto him tightly until he relaxed.

"If I'd known that's what you were capable of, *padre,* I never would have let you out of the forest," she said teasingly.

"Have I hurt you?" he whispered.

"No. I'm feeling very, very good."

"Honest?"

"Mmm."

He pressed a kiss to her neck. "I think my days of celibacy are over."

He saw her smile in the darkness—a slow, satisfied smile that looked very much like the cat who'd eaten the canary.

"On that, you have my whole-hearted agreement."

The night erupted in gunfire and he immediately rolled toward Petey, shielding the other man's body with his own.

"What the hell?"

Was this it? Was this the end that they'd feared? After all these years of fighting to survive, of enduring disease and starvation and abuse, had the Japanese finally decided to kill them all in their beds?

It made sense—and suddenly, he understood everything that had led up to this moment.

Tanaka's final fury.

Being locked in their huts.

The empty camp.

He could see now how beating Petey nearly to death had probably been a way for Tanaka to purge his frustration at being relieved of his command. He probably would have seen the loss of his job as a demotion, losing face among his peers. No doubt, he'd sat seething in his office, vowing revenge on his American prisoners but knowing that such an honor had been given to the new troops moving up to the front lines. If he'd had his way, he would have shot Petey like all the others. But he hadn't dared. Not when another unit had probably been given the order—and the honor—to execute them all. And the flyby of an American plane had probably only exacerbated matters.

But now that fresh troops had taken over the camp—troops with ammunition and experience—the Japs were going to kill them all.

Moving closer to Petey, he hauled the kid into his arms. If they were going to die, Petey was going to know that he wasn't alone.

As if sensing his thoughts, Petey's eyes opened. The gunfire grew closer, more intense, until he could hear the bullets smacking into the ground outside their hut.

Petey's eyes filled with tears. "I thought we'd make it...Lieutenant." He sobbed, then winced at the pain. Petey's frame grew limp. "Too...late..."

"No, dammit. Don't you die on me!"

But Petey didn't answer. The kid grew ever smaller in his arms as outside, the screams began.

Chapter Eighteen

April 7, 1942

Rosemary had hoped that a wedding at Little Baguio might be a sign of better things to come, but with each day that passed, the situation in Bataan became every more desperate. With food supplies running desperately low, rations were cut, then cut again. Soldiers were being sent to the front with only a few hundred calories a day, barely enough to function, let alone fight. And the men who began to pour into the hospital had injuries that were more devastating than ever before. She began to see "layers" of wounds since the men were patched up by the battle medics, then sent back to the front again and again. In order to be brought to Little Baguio, their wounds had to be horrific.

Surgery took on the appearance of an assembly line, with surgeons and nurses circling the tables while soldiers, one after another, were carried in to be pieced back together. Outside the huts, they'd begun to lay the stretchers on sawhorses, lifting their patients' feet higher than their heads, in order to ward off shock. They were running dangerously low on supplies—bandages, anesthesia, and quinine. Especially quinine. Malaria was rampant among soldiers and medical professionals alike, and the medication was so strictly rationed, that what little they were able to dispense was not enough to be effective.

By February, it was clear that things were growing desperate. Days ran one into another, until Rosemary felt that trying to slow the passing of time was like trying to push back the tide with her bare hands.

Rosemary and her nurses tried to hold onto hope. At least once a day, one of the orderlies would scale a palm tree and gaze out into the distance, hoping to see a wisp of smoke out to sea, a shape, a blip on the horizon that could signify that a convoy was on its way. They'd been promised as much by General Douglas MacArthur, their commander.

By March, their hope was beginning to wane. Then it turned to anger. What was wrong with the men in Washington? They must know the situation here in the Philippines. Didn't they care? Why promise them relief if they had no intention of sending it?

Still, they dug in their heels and refused to think the worse. The men dubbed themselves the Battling Bastards of Bataan, and the nurses borrowed the moniker, becoming the Battling Belles—and Rosemary was proud of the nickname. When they'd begun their careers, they'd been given no weapons' training whatsoever—they hadn't even received instruction on wartime medicine. But now, they were as tough and battle-hardened as the men.

Even so, it was a blow to their morale and their *esprit de corps* when they received word that General MacArthur—Dugout Doug—had left Corregidor for Australia. He'd been spirited away in the middle of the night. It didn't matter that he'd been ordered to withdraw and that he'd considered refusing that order. They'd been abandoned by the man in charge. While he'd maintained his command on Corregidor, they could still believe that the reinforcements might come.

Now, there was no reason to hope.

The end was coming. Rosemary knew this without a doubt. As she saw the boys staggering back from the front, she knew they couldn't hold out for long. In her estimation, it was a matter of weeks, not months. Perhaps even days.

And then what?

They had thousands of patients spread out in the cots beneath the trees. What would happen to these gravely injured men, the soldiers, the nurses? Would they all fight to the last person? Or would they be forced to surrender?

Unable to bring herself to plan that far ahead, Rosemary poured herself into her work, anything to keep from thinking about the future, anything to keep from thinking about Gilhouley at the front. He'd begun to find ingenious ways of getting word to her that he was all right. At times, she would find letters left on her bunk that had been sent through buddies passing through Little Baguio.

But she hadn't seen him in person since the hospital had been relocated.

If there was a bright spot at all, it came through Glory Bee and John. After only a short acquaintance, Rosemary had become very fond of the couple. Glory Bee had grown to care so much for the men in her ward, that, as she'd grown stronger, she'd begun to take on some of the simpler nursing duties. Even more importantly, she'd had made it her personal mission to help with the men's morale. Someone had found her a guitar, and most nights, she would linger in the wards singing songs—some bawdy, some sentimental—until it was late in the evening. The soldiers adored her. And as her belly grew larger and larger, the men took it upon themselves to protect her—especially when stray Japanese shells landed nearby.

"Major Dodd, a moment, please."

Rosemary looked up from the pile of charts she'd been compiling and stood. Ironically enough, there was no tent for the wounded, but one had been erected to protect the paperwork.

Standing, she went outside to where several senior nurses surrounded their commander, Col. Nester.

The mood was grim as they gathered into a semi-circle, and Rosemary's stomach clenched as she sensed they were not about to receive good news.

"A bus will be here in thirty minutes. We're being evacuated."

"A bus?" one of the women murmured in confusion. "What about the wounded?"

Col. Nester's gaze was sad. "The nurses are being evacuated to Corregidor. The wounded are not."

There was an immediate outcry. None of them wanted to leave.

Not now. Not when the men needed them most. But Col. Nester held up a hand to stop their arguments before they could even be made.

"Our orders are coming from the highest level. We're being sent to the hospital in the Malinta tunnels since it is believed that the lines will fail, probably in the next few weeks. We will be on that bus, ladies. Pass the word on to your women. They need to pack their things—only what they can carry in one bag—and meet at the bus in thirty minutes. No exceptions."

Rosemary lifted a hand. "You said the nurses were being evacuated. Does that include the Filipino nurses and the civilians who've been helping us?"

Col. Nester sighed. "I'll check. Right now, they aren't slated for evacuation."

Rosemary glanced at her watch, then hurried to the wards. Alice was the first woman she encountered. "We're leaving. Go pack a bag. They'll have a bus here to take us away in thirty minutes."

Alice stared at her blankly. "What?"

"We're being sent to Corregidor."

"Everyone?"

"Just the nurses."

"But—"

Rosemary held up a hand. "I know. Our arguments were made and rebuffed. We're allowed one bag. Tell anyone you see."

By the time Rosemary had found all the women under her command, she had only ten minutes left to pack her own things. As she ran toward the tent she shared with Alice, she closed her mind to the way her women had been forced to back away from doctors in the middle of their surgeries, patients in mid-procedure. And as the word began to spread, the eyes of the men had begun to follow them. Dear God, would she ever be able to push the image away—soldiers who watched them with a mixture of envy and despair, knowing that if the nurses were being sent away so suddenly, the end was truly drawing near.

She was fastening her bag when Lt. Cavendish ducked her

head in.

"We've got permission to bring the Filipino nurses and a few of the civilian women who've been helping us in the wards."

"Good. I'll get Glory Bee."

Lt. Cavendish shook her head. "We've been looking for her for ten minutes. She's not in her tent."

Rosemary felt a pang of frustration—then a rush of panic. This might be the only chance they had to get Glory Bee to relative safety before her baby was born. She was due in less than three weeks.

"Have you seen John?"

"He was the first person we told. He's looking for her as well."

Rosemary swore under her breath. "She's got to be here somewhere."

"We've checked the wards, the huts, her tent…"

"The showers," Rosemary said, already running out of the tent and rushing down the aisle of makeshift shelters that had been formed over the weeks. Turning right, then left, she headed toward the rough wooden planks that shielded the women's bathing facilities from view. The first set of showers was empty. The second set…

Rosemary nearly didn't see her. Glory Bee was crouched in the corner, her head down, wet hair hanging limply around her face, her arms wrapped protectively against her belly.

"Glory Bee?"

Her head reared up and Rosemary knew from her blotchy face that she'd been crying.

Moving more slowly, gently, Rosemary hurried toward her.

"Glory Bee, what's wrong?"

The woman sobbed. "My baby…my baby…"

"Glory Bee, are you in labor?"

She nodded. "I-I think so."

"How long have you had contractions?"

Glory Bee's chin trembled. "Since dinner."

So an hour. Maybe two at the most.

But then she added, "Yesterday."

As the full import of her words sank in, Rosemary quickly

grasped Glory Bee's towel and wrapped it around her.

"Has your water broken?"

Glory Bee nodded. "And I've been bleeding."

"For how long?"

"A day." Her face crumpled. "Maybe two."

Rosemary drew the other woman tightly against her. "Glory Bee, why didn't you tell us?"

"I didn't want to bother anyone. Y-you've all been so busy and…I thought it would…go away."

Lt. Cavendish burst through the door. "You've got five minutes to be on that bus. Did you find—"

Rosemary didn't even bother to explain. "I need a corpsman or a doctor—someone who can help me get her to one of the huts."

"Dear God, is she—"

"Now!" Rosemary ordered abruptly when Glory Bee suddenly gripped her belly and groaned. "Breathe, Glory Bee. Breathe."

"No! I can't have the baby. Not now. It's too early."

Rosemary couldn't help the mirthless laughter that burst from her throat. "You don't have a choice, honey. Your baby wants to be born—in the next few minutes, I'd wager."

Glory Bee shook her head, grabbing Rosemary's arms as another contraction hit. "It's too soon!"

"Some babies like to make a grand entrance by coming early."

She heard footsteps running into the showers and turned in time to see John rushing toward them.

"Get her into one of the huts, quick!"

Lt. Cavendish burst in on his heels. "Colonel Nester wants you on the bus. She says we're being evacuated from Mariveles to Corregidor by submarine at 0100 and everyone needs to be assembled."

"Tell her I'll be there. I'll hitch a ride with an ambulance or a Jeep or something. But Glory Bee can't make the bus ride right now, and I can't leave her." Rosemary knew she was treading close to disobeying orders, so after John scooped Glory Bee into his arms and hurried outside, she pulled Lt. Cavendish aside. "Please. Tell

Colonel Nester that I can't come right now. Glory Bee is showing signs of hemorrhaging."

Lt. Cavendish nodded and ran in the direction of the main clearing while Rosemary went in the opposite direction. Once at the surgical hut, she donned a gown and cap and hurried behind the screens that had been erected.

Glory Bee lay on one of the tables. At her side, John held her hand.

"Rosemary!"

She whirled toward the door to see Lt. Cavendish gesturing to her. The woman shot her a smile. "You have permission to stay, but Colonel Nester says if you aren't at the rendezvous point at 0100, she can't promise that you'll have another chance to be evacuated."

"I'll be there," Rosemary said.

Lt. Cavendish backed away as Dr. Grimm filled the doorway.

"Now, what's this I hear about a baby deciding to be born?" he asked congenially. "Major Dodd, will you give me a hand?"

• • •

At 2100, Hospital #1 at Little Baguio experienced something that it was not accustomed to hearing…

A newborn baby's cry.

For a moment, all activity in the camp seemed to cease. Even the distant sound of battle was muted as the soldiers turned their attention toward that tiny, lusty wail. There, for a moment, crystalized in that ultimate symbol of life and humanity came a tangible ray of hope. So after John was assured that Glory Bee was fine, that the baby was small, but healthy, he took the tiny swaddled infant out into the last light of the day and held her up so that the men in the wards could see her.

"Gentlemen, I'd like to present Hope Rosemary Macklin."

A cheer rose out of the jungle and John grinned. Never in his life had he felt such a mixture of rich emotions: pride, elation, relief. And love. He hadn't thought that he could ever love anyone or anything as much as Glory Bee, but he was swiftly discovering that the human heart knew no boundaries.

"Congratulations," a deep voice said next to him, and turning, John gaped in surprise when he found Gilhouley standing next to him.

Gilhouley grinned. "Leave it to you to upstage my surprise visit," he said good-naturedly. He bent to stroke the baby's cheek.

"She's got Glory Bee's red hair—and her eyes."

John smiled indulgently. "I knew she would."

Gilhouley slapped him on the arm. "But she's got your lousy sense of timing, Macklin."

John grew still. "So things are that bad."

Gilhouley nodded. "The lines won't hold."

John looked down at his daughter's face. "Then I'd say she has great timing." He felt his throat tighten. "Or I might not have had a chance to see her."

Gilhouley sighed, digging his toe into the dirt. "Then I guess I'm the one with the lousy timing. I hear the nurses pulled out of here about an hour ago."

"Yeah," John said. "But Rosemary's inside with Glory Bee."

He saw the way Gilhouley straightened, the way the abject weariness fell away beneath a surge of disbelief. "What?"

"She didn't leave with the others. She stayed to help deliver the baby. But she needs to find a way to get to Mariveles in the next few hours."

John saw a flash of something enter Gilhouley's gaze, and he knew that look—knew it because he'd felt it himself.

"You still got that chaplain friend here in camp, John?"

John nodded.

"Do you think he'd perform a quick ceremony for Rosemary and me?"

"I think he could be persuaded."

"Then you get the chaplain and I'll get my men finding us more roomy transportation than a Jeep. We all need to be in Mariveles by nightfall."

* * *

As she stood trembling next to Gilhouley, Rosemary could scarcely believe how life could change so drastically in the space of a few hours. She'd become a godmother, a namesake, and now she was about to become a bride.

Reaching out, she gripped Gilhouley's hand, as much to assure herself that he was really there more than to steady herself. This time, there had been no time for primping or makeup or even a minute to run a comb through her hair, but she didn't care. Gilhouley was here, and in a world gone mad, she had a brief moment of happiness with a man who had become more important to her than life itself.

As the priest helped them recite her vows, she couldn't help looking at Gilhouley. She still couldn't believe that he was actually here, in the flesh. Yes, she'd received letters—loving notes where he'd poured his heart out to her. But there had still been a part of her that had been afraid that, once they were together again, they would discover what they'd experienced had been nothing more than a wartime romance that would fizzle and fade.

If anything, the opposite was true. After being parted, their hunger, their affection, their connection had deepened until she couldn't imagine living another moment without him.

As if sensing her thoughts, Gilhouley lifted her hand, pressing his lips to the back of her knuckles.

"Do you have rings?" the chaplain asked.

Gilhouley nodded.

Rosemary laughed, expecting to receive a band much like Glory Bee's. Something made from cast off pieces of wire, a grenade pin, a polished piece of shrapnel. Instead, he burrowed into his pocket and removed a heavy West Point graduation ring, which he slid onto her finger. He'd wound string around the inside to make it a tighter fit, but she'd lost so much weight that it still rolled on her finger. She clasped her fingers in a fist to keep it from falling off.

"I now pronounce you husband and wife," the chaplain said with a smile.

Gilhouley needed no further encouragement. He swooped Rosemary into a searing kiss that left little doubt to his feelings for her. And she responded with equal ardor, needing to assure herself that this moment had actually occurred.

But then, as soon as they parted, reality intruded with a shell exploding so close that the earth shuddered and shrapnel fell like rain.

Rosemary quickly looked around, ensuring that the hospital hadn't been hit. The chaplain offered them a quick salute, then strode back to the men in the wards. With the nurses gone, every available man had been put to work.

"I've got to be in Mariveles by 0100," she told Gilhouley breathlessly.

"Don't worry. We'll get you there. I've got a truck being loaded with equipment and supplies already headed in that direction. That's how I was able to get here." He glanced at his watch. "Petey will be meeting us here at 2220. Kilgore and Baptiste are already in Mariveles with the rest of our cargo."

"And Berman?"

Gilhouley shook his head, his eyes taking on a shadow that she recognized as grief.

"I'm sorry," she whispered, squeezing his hand.

Gilhouley turned to John. "Gather your things and whatever Glory Bee and the baby might need, then rendezvous in the main clearing at 2220. We'll leave at 2230."

"We're taking Glory Bee and the baby with us." Rosemary hadn't uttered it as a question, but Gilhouley nodded all the same.

"She's well enough to travel?" he asked.

Rosemary said, "She can't stay here."

"I know."

As John disappeared toward the surgical hut to be with his wife and child, Rosemary melted into Gilhouley's embrace again, breathing deeply of the smells of man and sweat. She wrapped her arms around him, whispering, "I want to make love to you."

"I know." His whisper ached no less than her own.

"But I can't go with you, knowing that there are soldiers—"

He stopped her with a finger to her lips. "I know. Where are your things?"

She pointed to the row of nurse's tents. "Third one on the left. My duffel's on my bunk."

"Are you all packed?"

"Uh-huh."

"Then go do whatever you need to do. I'll come get you when it's time."

Rosemary reluctantly backed away, holding onto his hand until the last possible moment, then rushed to one of the surgical huts as an ambulance careened into the complex. Within minutes, she was back to the task that had become so familiar to her that, at times, she would shake herself, wondering if the entire encounter with Gilhouley and their impromptu wedding had been a dream.

But then, she would touch the heavy ring that she'd removed from her finger and threaded onto a chain around her neck.

It was real. Her marriage was real.

Gilhouley was out there, somewhere close.

And then, although it felt like only a matter of moments, she looked up to find him beckoning to her from the doorway. She paused, her hands bloody as she attempted to staunch the flow coming from a soldier's gut. Seeing the direction of her gaze, Dr. Grimm jerked his head toward the door.

"You'd better catch your ride, Major."

"But—"

Dr. Grimm eyed her sadly from above the edge of his mask. "We'll be all right. You go. Go while you can."

Slowly, she straightened, and after one more moment's hesitation, she stripped off her gloves.

"It has been a pleasure working with you, Dr. Grimm."

"And with you, Mrs. Gilhouley."

Rosemary blinked against the tears that suddenly gathered in her eyes. There would be no evacuation for Dr. Grimm or any of the other men she'd worked with. They would stay here, wait for the line to fail and the inevitable arrival of the Japanese.

Would she ever see any of them again?

"Go on, now. And good luck to you, Major."

"Good luck to you as well, Dr. Grimm."

Then, knowing that if she stayed even an instant longer, she wouldn't be able to leave at all, Rosemary dodged toward the door and Gilhouley.

* * *

Rosemary wasn't sure how Gilhouley had managed to exchange a Jeep for truck, but somehow, being The Great Gilhouley, he'd done it. Within minutes, Glory Bee and the baby were settled into the back on a stretcher. John and Petey squeezed in beside her amongst the crates of medical supplies, ammunition, and duffels that had been stacked in the back. Then, because it was the only privacy that they would be given as a newly married couple, they all insisted that Rosemary ride up front with Gilhouley.

"I'll be fine," Glory Bee said sleepily. "The baby and I are going to take a nap for most of the journey. John will bang on the side of the truck if we need anything."

"You're sure?"

"Go on."

Climbing into the cab, Rosemary slid across the seat, allowing Petey to stow her own duffle and Gilhouley's pack beside them. After he'd jumped into the back and fastened the tailgate, Gilhouley threw the truck into gear.

He moved as carefully as he could on the rutted track, taking his time to make the journey as comfortable as possible for Glory Bee. But it soon became evident that their trip was not going to be completed as quickly as they'd planned. Once they reached the main road, the lane was choked with the chaos of a fleeing army. Tanks and transports vied for space with refugees and foot soldiers, carabao and carts. The ditches on either side were clogged with discarded ammunition crates, furniture, household goods. The wounded who could walk were bypassing the hospital and continuing on to the coast and Rosemary's heart broke when she saw those who were too exhausted to continue, sitting in the dust and confusion trying to catch their breath.

As if the melee wasn't enough to contend with, shells exploded in the forest around them as the Japanese sought to cut off their last avenue of escape. The truck soon slowed to a crawling pace. Rosemary was sure that if she were to get out and walk, she could move faster, but she didn't. She clung to Gilhouley's thigh, appalled by the desperation around her.

"Can't we let some of those men come with us?"

Gilhouley shook his head. "It took some talking to get permission to take you and Glory Bee. We're carrying…sensitive cargo."

She didn't bother asking. She knew he wouldn't tell her.

"How long," she whispered. "How long before Bataan is overrun?"

Gilhouley's gaze was quiet and sad in the gathering darkness. When he answered her, his voice was husky.

"A day. Maybe two."

Rosemary shuddered. "Are you coming with us to Corregidor?"

He was a long time answering. Releasing the gear shift for a moment, he wove their fingers together. "Those aren't my orders."

She refused to become hysterical, refused to leech his strength in any way.

He wrapped his arm around her shoulders, pulling her close. "We can't control tomorrow or the next day or the next. But we can decide now what we're going to do after the war is over. I'm thinking six kids, maybe eight."

The sound that burst from her throat was half laugh, half sob. "Riley, I'm forty years old!"

"So we'll settle on three. We can adopt them if you're a granny by the time I get back."

She poked him in the ribs and he laughed.

"In the meantime, when you get back to the States, I want you to scout out a little piece of property for us. Doesn't matter where.

I figure I can get a job in radio or sales when I get back. Or maybe construction. I've always liked building things with my hands. I know my dad would probably give me a job if I wanted to take over his business, but I don't want that. I want to build a life for myself."

She rested her head on his shoulder, her palm on the spot above his heart.

"If you want, you could get us a place close to your folks. They'd like that, I'm sure. You said they wanted you to come home. That way you'd have someone with you if…until I get back."

Rosemary bit her lip, silent tears spilling over her cheeks.

"Try to find a place close—but not too close. I don't want to be living with the in-laws. And we need a dog. I'd really like a dog. Not one of those yappy things. I want a real dog with shaggy fur and a tail that never stops wagging."

Since she couldn't speak, she nodded against him. "You could work at a hospital in town, or maybe in a doctor's office if you wanted. Or you could stay home and be a housewife, I don't care. Whatever makes you happy. I want you to be happy, Rosemary."

She looked up at him then, and saw that his own cheeks were wet with tears.

"You make me happy, Gilhouley."

* * *

Despite the unexpected delays they'd made in getting to Mariveles, they arrived in plenty of time to rendezvous with the other nurses. But when Gilhouley brought the truck to a halt at the docks, the quay was further evidence of the devastation of war. What few ships that still remained close to the dock were being scuttled and distant explosions added to the din as ammunition dumps were set ablaze.

"Stay here," Gilhouley said to Rosemary as he climbed out of the truck. They were at the spot where Rosemary was supposed to meet the other nurses, but there wasn't a woman in sight.

Petey ran up to him, his rifle at the ready.

"Go see if anyone at the pier knows where the nurses are

gathering," Gilhouley said as he strode around to the back of the truck. "Everyone okay back here?"

Glory Bee had been propped into a sitting position and now rested against John, the baby held tightly in her arms. The infant wailed at the noise, its cries barely heard above the din.

"We're fine," Glory Bee said. It was clear that she was terrified, but she pasted a smile on her lips.

Petey's boots scrabbled against the rocks and he ran back toward him.

"They're gone," he gasped.

"Gone? What do you mean, gone?" Gilhouley said slowly.

"I mean, they took them over to Corregidor in launches about two hours ago when things got too hot on the docks. The sub never made it through the blockade, so it's hanging back in open waters."

"Shit! Any hope of getting a boat over to Corregidor?"

"I don't know, sir. Anything that's still afloat has either left or is otherwise engaged."

Gilhouley thought quickly, then gestured to Petey. "Get in the truck."

"Sir?"

"Get in the truck. There's been a change in plans."

He ran back to the cab and climbed in.

"Where is everyone?" Rosemary asked, alarmed.

"Gone. They left hours ago."

Her face drained of color. "What should I do?"

"Don't worry, I'll notify your superiors about what happened."

"But—"

He ground the truck into gear and lurched forward. "We'll get you and Glory Bee off the island, Rosemary. You're going to have to take the scenic route, is all."

* * *

Glory Bee waited in the truck, the baby to her breast, as a heated discussion took place on the other side of the canvas. The words were too low for her to make out, but it was clear from the tones and the urgency that the men were trying to find a way for them to get off the island.

Finally, John reappeared.

"Come one, sweetheart. Time to go."

She moved the baby away from her nipple, frowning when Hope made a whimper of distress. But after covering herself, she soothed the baby back to sleep.

After she'd managed to scoot toward the tailgate, John scooped her into his arms and carried her through the trees.

"Where are we going?" she asked.

But at that moment, John broke through the foliage and she saw a familiar plane, a familiar grizzled pilot.

Napoli grinned at her. "How's my favorite redhead?" he boomed.

Glory Bee laughed. "There are two of us now, Napoli."

"Let me see."

John paused long enough for Napoli to peer down into the tiny face swathed in blankets.

"She's a little thing, isn't she?"

Glory Bee nodded in pride.

"Oh, but she's a beauty. What's her name?"

"Hope. Hope Rosemary Macklin."

For a moment, his features softened, and she thought his eyes took on an added sheen before he blinked it away.

"You've named her well." He made a sweeping gesture with his hand. "Let's get you aboard. We need to get going now the sun's down."

Glory Bee looked past him to where Petey and Gilhouley were feverishly unscrewing the airplane's seats and throwing them onto the beach.

"What are they doing?" she whispered to John.

"Making room for you and Rosemary. We've got to get the weight of the plane down as much as possible so that we don't have to leave very much behind."

As soon as the plane had been stripped of everything that wasn't essential to the voyage, Glory Bee was carried to a soft pallet that had been formed of blankets and their packs. Then the cargo hold had been stuffed with more crates and bags until there was barely any room at all to sit. Finally, John climbed in, then Baptiste.

Looking out the window, Glory Bee saw Rosemary and Gilhouley clinging to one another. A little way from them, Petey and Kilgore looked on, their expressions sad.

"What's the matter? Why don't they get in?"

"They aren't coming with us," John said lowly.

Glory Bee looked at him in horror. "Why not?"

"They were never coming with us. They have orders to stay."

Glory Bee's heart ached as she watched Rosemary kiss Gilhouley one last time—and she knew a portion of what that kiss must hold. Desperation, regret, despair.

Rosemary sobbed as she climbed into the plane, and Glory Bee quickly handed the baby to John before drawing the other woman down beside her. She didn't bother with platitudes. They wouldn't have helped. She held the nurse tightly, absorbing some of her pain as the engines revved and Napoli pointed them out to sea.

The water was rough and Napoli swore, fighting with the controls of the aircraft.

"She's a heavy bitch," he muttered to himself. "Come on, come on!"

For a moment, it seemed as if they might have bounced above the waves, but the plane came down again, heavy, causing Glory Bee to gasp. But then, clawing for each inch of clearance, the seaplane began to climb, climb, until the spray of the ocean disappeared and they were lifting up into the night.

Leaving Gilhouley, Petey, and Kilgore alone on the beach.

• • •

Glory Bee didn't know how much time had passed when she felt a change in the rhythm of the engine. Somehow, both she and

Rosemary had managed to fall into a fitful sleep. But now, the plane was descending into the blackness again. It landed hard on the ocean, bounced, then puttered toward what she thought must have been land.

As soon as the pontoons scraped against sand, Napoli cut the engines. Baptiste opened the door and jumped into the surf while John began shoveling supplies to him one by one.

"Where are we?" she whispered groggily.

John glanced at Napoli, then said, "We're on a little island about seventy-five miles south of Mindinao. According to our sources, the Japanese haven't touched it yet. Probably because it's too small to be of much use."

Within minutes the only bags remaining were those that belonged to John, Glory Bee, and Rosemary.

Glory Bee glanced down at the other woman who still lay sleeping, her brow puckered in a frown. Then, she looked up at John, knowing without even having to be told.

"You're not coming with us, are you?" But it wasn't a question. She already knew the answer.

John knelt on the floor beside her, taking her face in his hands.

"I'm not sending you away, Glory Bee. I'm sending you and our daughter to safety."

She nodded, remembering that day in the forest when she'd begged John to let her stay with him.

His eyes were haunted. "I've been working with Gilhouley to set up watchers on these remote islands. If there were any other way—"

She put a finger over his lips. "I know, John. I know."

Glory Bee pulled her husband tightly against her, absorbing his strength, his goodness. And she remembered the man he'd been when she'd met him—grim and angry at the world. He'd once been asked to turn his back on people in need, and she knew that to demand it of him again would destroy him. So she framed his face in her hands and looked deeply into his eyes, needing to sear each angle into her memory.

Then, kissing him, once, twice, she whispered, "I love you John

Macklin. I will always love you. And we'll wait for you. However long it takes."

His own kiss was passionate and desperate, sealing the depth of his own desire and wealth of emotion on her in a way that she knew she would never forget. Then, lifting his head, he said, "Take care of yourself. Of our daughter."

"I will."

"If I knew how to get a letter to you, I'd write—"

"Send word through the Capitol Heights Theater in Washington, D.C.." She grinned. "I won't be performing there any time soon, but I've got friends who work there. They'll let me know if anything comes."

He offered her a smile, then he bent to place a kiss on Hope's forehead, brushed a finger against her cheek.

When he looked at Glory Bee, his eyes shone with tears. "I don't think I ever truly believed in miracles before, Glory Bee. But I believe in them now."

He kissed her again, quickly, passionately. Then, obviously not trusting himself to linger even a moment longer, he grabbed his pack and jumped into the surf, latching the door behind him. Pressing her face against the glass, Glory Bee held her hand up, waving. And then, as her heart lay crumbling in her breast, Napoli once again pointed the seaplane toward open water.

All too soon, the darkness swallowed up John's shape, but she lingered where she was, her hand still lifted, until the island and the surf disappeared from view.

The machine gun fire continued and the night seemed to be lit by a thousand flashbulbs. Bending low, he continued to protect Petey as more explosions rocked the compound, sounding very much like grenades.

Were bullets too personal? Had they decided to blow them up, hut by hut?

From outside, they could hear the pounding of footsteps, shouting. Maybe the other huts were fighting back, because it sounded like a fucking battle was going on outside.

Then suddenly, a figure stormed into their shelter, another, and another.

The men cowered against the walls, but he remained where he was, sheltering Petey from harm, covering his battered body with his own, anticipating the storm of bullets that would finish them off, once and for all. But somewhere, from the confused recesses of his brain, he realized that they weren't shouting at them in Japanese.

"U.S. Army Rangers! We're getting you out of here! If you can walk, follow this man here. If you can't, wait where you are. We'll send someone in to help you."

He looked up, up, wondering if he'd finally snapped, wondering if this was what happened to a man who was about to die. Was he imagining what he wanted most to hear?

But then, as he stared at the man at the door, his brain slowly took in the olive drab uniform, the Army issue rifle. And, all be damned, if the man didn't speak with a southern drawl. A southern, fucking drawl.

He looked at Kilgore. His friend was equally stunned.

"Out, out! Move in an orderly fashion, but head toward the gates as fast

as you can."

Needing no further encouragement, he bent low over Petey. "You hear that, Petey? They're here. Just hold on a little longer. Help is here."

There was no response, but a quick hand to the kid's chest assured him that the kid was still alive.

"Help me, Kilgore."

They wrapped Petey's arms around their shoulders and tried to stand. But it had been days since they'd been fed and the dead weight between them was too much.

"Dammit!" he shouted. "Help us. We need help!"

Another man with a rifle dodged through the door. Hearing his cries, the man changed course, ran toward him, then came to a shuddering halt.

In that instant, his gaze clung to the tall, dark-haired man as if he were a revenant from another life.

"John?" he whispered, sure he was imagining things.

But the figure with the rifle grinned, saying, "Well, if it isn't The Great Gilhouley. I've been hoping to run into you." Then, the man known as Padre *bent to haul Petey up and over his shoulder. "Time to get you all out of here, Lieutenant."*

Chapter Nineteen

December 8, 1944
Washington, D.C., U.S.A.

Glory Bee Macklin hurried up to the next available window of the post office. Around her, Christmas shoppers rushed to mail last-minute packages and letters to sweethearts overseas while Bing Crosby crooned a ballad on the radio from somewhere in the storage bay. She'd been waiting in line for nearly twenty minutes, and a glance at her watch reminded her that she needed to get back to the restaurant across the street where Rosemary was entertaining Hope with a new paper doll book featuring the "Heroes of the Armed Forces."

Not that Hope needed any reminding about the Heroes of the Armed Forces. She'd heard enough stories about her daddy and Uncle Gilhouley and how they'd arranged a daring escape from the Pacific for the women. And with the adults' preoccupation with radio and news' reports, the little girl could school a congressman on Capitol Hill about the current status of the war against the Japanese.

"May I help you?"

Glory Bee slid the slip toward the woman on the other side. "I have a notice about a package."

"Yes, ma'am."

The woman strode toward the back while Glory Bee tapped impatiently on the counter. Rosemary needed to be at the hospital by one and Glory Bee had meetings with the USO committee at three. That left just enough time to finish their lunch, drop Hope off at the sitter's, and return.

Again, her eyes fell on the calendar bolted to the back wall, latching onto the large black letters declaring *Dec. 8*.

America had mourned Pearl Harbor the day before with special religious ceremonies and patriotic speeches. But it was the eighth that Glory Bee and Rosemary found to be one of the most difficult days of the year. For them, the news of Pearl Harbor and the subsequent bombing of the Philippines had occurred on the eighth. That was why they'd decided to meet for lunch.

Especially when no mention had been made of the Philippines at all in the memorial services across the nation.

So Glory Bee and Rosemary had held their own quiet ceremony.

"Here you are."

The postmistress handed Glory Bee a thick manila envelope that had seen better days. The edges were frayed and dirty, the inner wrapping of newspapers visible in spots. But when she saw the stamps and postmarks from Australia, Glory Bee's pulse began to knock in her throat.

Australia.

Several times before, John had managed to get a message to her via Australia by giving the packets of letters to soldiers bound for reassignment or with the sailors on the subs that occasionally brought him fresh supplies.

"Thank you!"

She was turning away when the woman halted her.

"You need to sign first."

"Of course."

Glory Bee's hands were shaking so badly that her signature became an illegible scrawl, but she didn't bother to correct it. She clutched the packet to herself and all but ran out of the building.

She was moving so quickly that she didn't see the man who stood outside the door. She wouldn't have seen him at all if she hadn't barreled into him, nearly sending him to the pavement. But as he righted himself and she turned to offer her apologies, the words stuck in her throat.

Michael.

Senator Michael Griffin.

He was just as astonished to see her, his eyes widening with shock, his mouth dropping as his gaze swept over her head from the perky fur hat poised on her fiery curls, to the rich wool coat, and down to the fur-lined overshoes that protected her best pumps from the snow.

"Glory Bee?"

His eyes flashed with an old familiar heat, and then, so quickly she might have missed it, a hint of guilt.

And in that instant, she knew—she knew without a shadow of a doubt—that he had sent her to the Philippines knowing full well that trouble could erupt.

"Hello, Michael," she said stiffly.

Although it had been years since he'd seen her, his gaze flicked in the general direction of her stomach, and she hated him in that moment. Hated him for not knowing how precious a life she'd once carried there, for being willing to throw Glory Bee and his unborn child into the path of the oncoming Japanese.

No. Not his child.

John's.

Just as quickly as she'd felt the wave of disgust, it flittered away, leaving her feeling…

Nothing.

Absolutely nothing.

"You're well?" Michael asked cautiously.

"Yes. I'm doing very well, thank you."

"I…haven't seen you at the theater."

"No. I work for the USO now."

"You perform for the troops?"

"No, I help to organize the tours that go overseas."

"Oh."

It was beginning to snow. Light, fluffy flakes that fell from the gray sky like downy feathers.

"You're alone?"

She knew what he was asking. In his own roundabout way,

he wanted to know about the baby. But there was no regret in his expression, no melancholy. Nothing that might tell her that he truly cared about what had happened to the child that he'd created. The only emotion she could read in his features was wariness. So she quickly reassured him.

"You don't have anything to worry about, Michael."

"Oh. Oh, good!"

His relief was so immediate that she found herself wondering what she'd ever seen in the man. Had she really been that lonely, that unsure of herself, that Michael's self-absorbed affections had been enough for her?

"We should have a drink some time. Get caught up on old times."

She couldn't help laughing, and when he appeared put out by her reaction, she tugged on her gloves. "I don't think so. I'm married now. To a pretty possessive man. A guerrilla soldier with an enormous amount of experience in jungle warfare. And I really don't think you'd want to tangle with him." Offering him a distracted smile, she said, "Goodbye, Michael."

Then, after checking the traffic, she darted across the street and into the coffee shop where Rosemary and Hope were sitting at a table.

"Did you finish your ice cream?" Glory Bee asked as she took her seat.

Hope nodded enthusiastically, her curls bouncing. "Mommy, who was that man?"

Glory Bee had been trying to work off the string of the package and glanced up.

"What man, baby?"

"The one you were talking to over there," Hope said, pointing across the street.

"Oh. Nobody, sweetie. Nobody at all." And in that moment, truer words could not have been spoken.

"Look what came in the mail, Baby Girl!" Glory Bee managed to wrestle the string free enough to rip open the end of the envelope. Tipping it upside down, she spilled the contents onto the table—

letters, pictures, and a lamb made from rice sacks and stuffed with coconut fibers.

"Daddy!" Hope exclaimed latching onto one of the pictures.

Glory Bee's heart flip-flopped against the wall of her chest as she took the picture, examining the dark-haired man who grinned at her, a rifle slung across his chest. He looked thin and his hair had a few more flecks of gray, but the love shining from his eyes was unmistakable.

"I think this is yours," Glory Bee said, pushing the homemade lamb toward her daughter, wondering if John had traded for the toy or lovingly stitched it himself. Her fingers sifted through the rest of the items, stacking the letters for later when she was alone, then hesitating when one of the envelopes caught her eye. Unlike the others, there was no address, merely one word.

Rosemary.

"I think this is for you," Glory Bee said quietly, handing the envelope to her friend.

Rosemary had been carefully stirring her coffee, trying not to show any emotion, and Glory Bee was immediately contrite. She knew it was hard for Rosemary. John had been able to get sporadic letters to his wife and child, but Rosemary still didn't know if Gilhouley was even alive.

Glory Bee's stomach knotted in fear. "It's John's handwriting," she said, offering Rosemary the envelope.

Rosemary's hands trembled so badly, she nearly dropped the note, but taking a deep breath, she used a butter knife to break the seal and withdraw a single piece of stained, ragged paper. The lettering was spaced so tightly together that, from where Glory Bee sat, it was difficult to discern any words. Instead, it gave the appearance of having been tattooed with a looping, angular design.

Unfolding the paper, Rosemary bit her lip, beginning to read. But then her eyes brimmed. Fearing the worst, Glory Bee was ready to jump to her feet and comfort her friend, but Rosemary sobbed openly, then whispered, "He's alive. John has found him." Tears streamed down her face. "He's alive!"

Epilogue

June 9, 1945
Bluebell, Nebraska, U.S.A.

The taxi pulled to a stop in front of a dusty dirt lane next to a shiny new mailbox. A few feet farther, a stake leaned precariously to one side proclaiming: *For Sale.* Over the bold blue letters, another word had been printed in dark black paint: *Sold.*

Climbing from the back, Gilhouley waited as the driver hurried to grab his duffel from the trunk. There wasn't much inside it—the new clothes he'd been given, a shaving kit, and a couple of books he'd brought with him from the hospital in Hawaii where he, Petey, and Kilgore had recuperated. But there was also a conch shell that he'd carefully wrapped in newspaper. And in his pocket was a shiny gold band that he'd bought in Honolulu before shipping out. He wanted to make sure Rosemary had a proper wedding ring. Especially if they were going to live this close to her folks.

"You see any action?" the driver asked as he slammed the trunk door.

"Yeah."

"Germany?"

Gilhouley shook his head. "No. Bataan."

The cabbie grew instantly still. "You had it rough," he finally said. Word of Bataan had only been released to the public at large a little over a year ago.

"Yeah," Gilhouley said, the word holding a wealth of meaning. He reached for his billfold. "How much do I owe you?"

The man shook his head, handing Gilhouley his bag. "Not a red cent. I don't charge any of the boys coming home from the station. It's the least I can do."

Gilhouley slid his wallet back into his pocket. "Thanks. I appreciate it."

"Are you sure I can't take you up to the house?" the cabbie asked as Gilhouley shifted the bag onto his shoulder.

"Nah. I didn't have a chance to let her know I was coming. So I thought I'd surprise her."

The man grinned. "Good luck to you, then." He laughed, then added, "But I suppose you've already had all the luck you need since you're back in one piece."

Gilhouley couldn't help touching his pocket where he'd carefully tucked the remains of the silk violet.

"I suppose you're right."

He waited until the cab had rolled away, the brake lights flashing in the early morning light as it merged back onto the main road. Then he turned and began making his way down the lane.

According to a letter Glory Bee had forwarded to John once he'd begun getting regular mail through the army, Rosemary had bought this place in April, not long after their third anniversary. The little farm was about three miles away from her folks—near enough that she could keep an eye on them, but far enough away to ensure some privacy. From what Glory Bee had said, the house stood at the top of a slight slope, and down below, there was a creek and forty acres of prime land for planting. She'd rented the land out to a local farmer, and as he walked, Gilhouley could already see the first shoots of corn pushing through the loamy earth.

He'd never been to a farm before. Not really. But after the bustle and noise of troop ships, reporters, hospitals and railway cars, he found the soft soughing of the breeze through the grass was soothing. And somewhere, from the trees up ahead, he could hear birds. Not tropical birds, but the sweet sound of a whippoorwill.

So this was home.

His throat grew tight with unshed tears as the house came into view. It was a large clapboard structure with a wide porch that circled the entire structure. Someone—Rosemary, he'd wager—had hung pots of flowers from the posts and scattered chairs to catch the breeze. Repairs were being made. A ladder leaned up against one wall, and he could see where the weathered white paint had been scraped away and the wooden siding was being painted a pale yellow. A garden had been staked out at the side and a wooden windmill carved to look like a man with a hatchet intermittently filled the air with its chatter.

At the edge of a weathered picket fence still in need of painting, Gilhouley paused, taking it all in, feeling a little out of place yet curiously at peace, as if he'd known about this place for years. He pushed the gate open and the spring whined as he stepped through.

Summoned by the sound, a dog rose from his spot by the front door. He eyed Gilhouley warily, barking a warning. But there was no threat to the sound, simply a notice to those inside that a visitor had arrived.

Gilhouley dropped his bag to the ground and crouched down, holding out his hand. As the dog trotted eagerly toward him, Gilhouley could see that the animal wasn't too big or too small. He was enough mutt and enough collie to be fluffy and soft, with a wide sweeping tail that began to beat excitedly as Gilhouley reached out to scratch his ears. A tag hung from his collar and Gilhouley captured it long enough to read his name: Napoli.

Gilhouley chuckled, but the sound died in his throat as a figure stepped through the door, calling out, "Napoli, get down. I swear, you haven't got the manners God gave a…"

Rosemary.

The words died in her throat as Gilhouley slowly straightened. Then her eyes filled with tears and she launched herself down the steps into his arms.

"Riley!"

He caught her against him, burying his face in her hair, holding her so fiercely that he feared he might hurt her. But her own grip was so tight that he knew he needn't have worried.

"I'm home, Rosemary. I'm home."

And for the first time since setting foot on American soil, he knew it was true.

• • •

June 10, 1945
Echo Beach, Virginia, U.S.A.

"Here you are, sir."

The staff car slid to a stop in front of a tiny beach house, and the sergeant who'd been John's driver looked one last time at the scrap of paper John had given him, then at the numbers painted on the side of the house.

"Thanks, Sergeant."

John opened his door and slid out. For a moment, he gazed at the squat, weathered building, wondering why he felt curiously detached from the home in front of him. He had thought that once he'd arrived he…well, that he would feel like he was a part of this place. But he felt nothing but curiosity.

Taking his bag from the back, he offered a final wave as the soldier put the car into gear and rolled away. Then he began to slowly approach the front door.

As he mounted the steps, John felt a flutter of nerves deep in his gut. He hadn't written or cabled Glory Bee to let her know he was arriving—primarily because he hadn't known when the Army would be done with him. Since he wasn't a citizen of the U.S.—and his marriage to Glory Bee had been completed without all the necessary documents—he'd feared that he wouldn't be able to get into the country for months. But a few words from some high-placed generals, several military transports, and a full two days of debriefing at the Pentagon, and he was finally free to see his own family.

Clearing his throat, he set his bag on the porch and wiped his hands down his trousers. Dear God, he'd faced the Japanese without half the nerves he felt now in realizing that he was moments away from seeing his wife and little girl.

Knowing that he couldn't wait another minute, John punched the doorbell. He heard the tinny *ding-dong* and waited. But there was no answer.

His nerves compounded. In all the scenarios he'd envisioned when thinking of reuniting with Glory Bee, it had never occurred to him that she wouldn't be home.

Damn.

Pulling the screen open, he rang the bell again, then rapped his knuckles on the door. But there was still no answer.

Allowing the screen to slam shut, he shoved his hands into his pockets and looked up and down the row of identical buildings. But there was no sight of Glory Bee. The shadows were growing longer and most of those who had gone to the beach for the day were beginning to trudge home trailing beach towels and picnic baskets.

The beach.

He hadn't tried the beach.

Looking in either direction, John finally noticed a trail leading around the house. He smiled, noticing that a tricycle had been upended midway and a doll had been dropped into the grass.

A doll.

A familiar stuffed lamb.

His heart wedged in his throat as he received his first real confirmation that Glory Bee and Hope were near and his pace quickened. He circled to a back yard, taking in the clothesline that flapped with sheets and pillowcases and little feminine dresses and lace edged socks. Good lord, had Hope really grown that much?

He pushed his way through flapping laundry that smelled of sun and surf and the faint scent of roses. And there, on the other side, he came to a sudden halt.

A few yards off, a familiar red-haired beauty sat on a blanket, a book beside her, completely forgotten. She wore a simple dress, but the way the wind flattened the fabric against her body brought such a sudden crash of desire that John nearly fell to his knees.

That woman, that stunning, desirable woman…was his wife.

A peal of laughter cut through the sound of the surf, and his gaze skipped a few yards farther to where a little girl played in the lapping water. She wore a swimming suit with ruffles on her bottom and her cheeks were sun-kissed and freckled. She ran up to the water, allowing it to splash over her feet, then squealed at the still chilly temperatures of early summer.

"Don't go too far," Glory Bee warned. She glanced at her watch. "Just a few more minutes. Then it will be time to go inside and make some supper."

John could have called out to them. But he wanted to take in the sight, to burn it into his brain so that he would never forget this instant when they were finally together again.

"I don't want dinner," Hope retorted. "I only want dessert."

"That's too bad, because only little girls who have eaten their dinner—complete with vegetables—are able to have dessert. And I've made your favorite. Strawberries and cream."

"Fine. I'll eat the sandwich, but not the—"

In that instant, Hope turned and her gaze fell on John. Lifting a hand to shield her eyes from the sun, she frowned in concentration, then grinned. She looked so much like Glory Bee when she smiled that John could barely breathe.

"Daddy?" she called questioningly.

"I'm home."

Glory Bee whirled to face him, then scrambled to her feet. But even as quickly as she raced toward him, Hope arrived first, so he swung the little girl into his arms, resting her on his hip as he pulled her mother close.

Glory Bee threw her arms around him, kissing him over and over again, cheek, lips, anywhere she could reach and Hope giggled, then grew still.

"Mommy, are you crying? Aren't you happy that Daddy's home?"

At that, Glory Bee looked up at him with such blatant love, that it was John's eyes that grew wet.

"Yes, Hope. I'm so, so happy Daddy is home."

Hope kissed John on the cheek, then wriggled free, running toward the house.

"Then we'd better eat dessert first, don't you think? After all, it's a special day."

Glory Bee framed John's face in her hands, searching, ensuring herself that he was safe. He was real.

Then her smile was slow and sweet. "That's right, Hope. It's a special day." She lifted on tiptoe, her lips hovering near John's, her arms encircling his neck. "Because we're finally all together where we belong."

As he bent to kiss her, a surge of happiness and reverence flooded through John's body.

This was what it meant to come home.

It wasn't merely arriving at a certain place on a map.

It is stepping into the warmth of another person's love and knowing, beyond all doubt, that this is where you belong.

Acknowledgments

I want to give a special "shout out" to all those who have helped *After the Fall* become a reality. First of all, I want to thank my family, who allowed me to disappear from the realities of being a wife and mother long enough to capture the words that seemed to spill from my brain, unchecked, once I'd begun writing the book. To the gang at Browne and Miller Multimedia, especially Danielle, Joanna, and Abby. You've been there to back me up time and time again with read-throughs, phone calls, and negotiations. To the team at Diversion, Hannah, Sarah, Brielle. And to my editor at Diversion, Randall, whose insights have helped me hone my craft, and whose letters have lifted my spirits when I've needed it most. I'll refrain from sending any more stuffed animals your way.

I would also like to thank all those who have served our country, past and present. I am humbled by your sacrifice. And to those who fought in the Pacific, I hope that I have been able to capture a portion of your service and your stories. If mistakes have been made, please forgive me.

Also By Lisa Bingham

From national bestselling author Lisa Bingham comes a story of London in its darkest hours. As a city holds its breath, two women discover within themselves the bravery to persevere, the grace to rise above the war, and the unstoppable power that love can bring.

RueAnn Boggs meets Charles Tolliver, a handsome Brit with a secret job, and in the course of twenty-four hours, RueAnn is swept off her feet—seduced, wed, and then left by dashing Charlie, who hastily departs for an assignment in England. When weeks go by and she hears nothing from her new husband, RueAnn becomes determined to find out if she's a wife in name only, and she travels to London for answers. But what she finds there is not at all what she expects…

Susan Blunt has spent her life staying put, retreating into her books while her vivacious twin sister, Sara, lives life to the fullest. The start of the war hasn't stopped vibrant Sara from collecting a throng of beaus in uniform, including Paul Overdone, an RAF pilot heading for the front. When Sara pressures Susan into switching places and going to a dance with Paul, Susan reluctantly agrees. Little does Susan know that a single night is more than enough time to fall deeply in love with Paul—who returns her ardor, even though he thinks she is someone else…

When the Blitz begins and bombs start raining down on London, both RueAnn and Susan must find the strength and courage they never knew they had in order to survive. They form a friendship out of the city's ashes, one that helps them weather the storm as they wait for news from the front—from the men they love, have lost, and hope desperately to find once more.

Set against the backdrop of a remarkable era, *Into the Storm* brilliantly explores relationships in wartime, when the passion shared in just one day could sustain love for a lifetime and the love borne of one night's deception could become the truth that saves a life

The Bengal Rubies

A young woman makes a desperate attempt to find freedom, only to fall prisoner once again—to love.

Condemned to be auctioned off to the highest bidder by her own father, Aloise Crawford makes a desperate attempt to escape. When the ship she is imprisoned on docks, she jumps overboard. When she finally swims ashore, she finds herself at the feet of a dark stranger with a face as angry as it is alluring.

For years, Slater McKendrick has lived in hiding, awaiting his chance to seek vengeance against the man who stole his family's precious jewels, the Bengal Rubies. So when Aloise arrives on his lonely beach hideaway, it seems as if the opportunity has at last been delivered to him. But while he holds her captive on his estate, he recognizes the same broken spirit in her that sees in himself.

As the flame of passion ignites, Aloise knows that Slater remains the force standing between her and freedom. But while she cannot trust him, will she have the strength to resist her newest captor?

Distant Thunder

A chaste beauty, a hardened lawman, and a love impeded by the shadows of the past.

A haunting truth too terrible to share drives beautiful Susan to live as a nun, hiding the reality of her past even from her lifelong friend, Daniel. Growing up, Daniel was her protector and savior, yet when he returns to town, her orderly life is abruptly thrown into disarray. No longer is he the boy from her childhood, but a striking lawman, both dangerous and desirable.

Determined to make Susan his wife, Daniel arouses her deepest passions and unlocks her darkest secrets. But before they can embrace the promise of the future, Susan must confront the past she worked so hard to keep hidden.

Eden Creek

From the seeds of haunting secrets grows passion and love

After a devastating betrayal leaves Ginny Parker broken and alone, she hastily agrees to marry a man she's never met and start a new life in Eden Creek, Utah. Orrin Ghant only wants a woman to help raise his three daughters, and a companion with whom to share life in the Utah wilderness. But upon the arrival of Ginny, he soon finds his new wife has brought with her more than he could have hoped.

As they slowly settle into their new lives together, Orrin never expects to fall so deeply for Ginny's sweet smile and gentle charm, nor does Ginny expect to find such comfort in Orin's strong embrace and the tranquility of Eden Creek. But while their marriage of convenience blossoms into true love, secrets from the past loom over them, testing the bounds of their fragile new beginning.

Silken Dreams

A wanted man seeks refuge with the girl who wants him most.

Lettie Grey is in love with a man who exists only in her thoughts. The highwayman, dark and dangerous, dwells in her most wanton fantasies where he stirs her deepest desires. But when Ethan McGuire, a bank robber and fugitive, arrives in her small town, Lettie realizes the sensual stranger of her imagination is more than just a dream.

On the run from the law and a ruthless band of vigilantes, Ethan seeks shelter in the safety of Lettie's small attic bedroom, and in the heat of her embrace. But can a man who trusts no one give away his heart in the midst of a fight for his life?

Silken Promises

In games that are as perilous as they are passionate, everyone plays for keeps.

When Fiona McFee first meets the straight-laced deputy Jacob Grey, he is naked and bound in a field of foxtails. A con man's daughter through and through, Fiona leaves him there as he swears to never forget her. True to his word, Jacob tracks Fiona to Chicago years later, and he has an offer for her that she can't refuse: A full pardon for her and her father in exchange for her help in catching a counterfeiter. All she must do is pose as a wealthy British widow and play poker on a tourist train heading West.

With her freedom at stake, as well as another chance to outwit Jacob, Fiona must perfect her poker face as she gambles for the fate of her future. But neither she, nor Jacob, can ignore the undeniable attraction between them, and as the stakes of their deadly game soar to new heights, the thin line between inevitable danger and unyielding desire begins to blur.

Now both Fiona and Jacob have more to lose than either of them bargained for—their hearts.

Temptation's Kiss

To tame the beast in a man, one woman must unleash her own animal nature.

Chelsea Wickersham seeks a new start. The conservative English governess agrees to tutor the long-lost heir of the mysterious Cane estate. But when she arrives expecting to find a boy to teach, she is instead introduced to a strange and terrifying sight: Sullivan Cane, a feral, uncivilized man.

But Cane is craftier than any beast. Taken from his island hideaway, forced to return to his family estate in Scotland, he strives to outwit his calculating brethren. He plays the role of wild man that they all believe him to be, but even as he grows exhausted of his savage pretense, he also discovers an unexpected pleasure in watching the walls of Chelsea's façade crumble.

As passion sparks between teacher and student, a sinister enemy lurks in their midst, threating their love and their lives. To survive, and to be together, this untamable man must learn to act his part, and this upright woman must learn to unleash the animal inside of her.

CPSIA information can be obtained at www.ICGtesting.com
Printed in the USA
BVOW03s1352260715

410339BV00002B/6/P